THE VERMILION RIBBON

THE VERMILION SAGA
BOOK 1

HAYLEY PRICE

A catalogue record for this book is available from the National Library of Australia.

The Vermilion Ribbon was previously published by Australian Self Publishing Group. This (second) edition has been revised, updated, and includes a brand new cover.

National Library of Australia Cataloguing-in-Publication entry

Author: Hayley Price

Title: **The Vermilion Ribbon**

ISBN: 978-0-9756238-0-0 (Print)

ISBN: 978-0-9756238-5-5 (ePub)

ISBN: 978-0-9756238-4-8 (PDF eBook)

❦ Created with Vellum

This book is dedicated to my partner, Ailsa.

Without a doubt, she is the greatest thing to have happened to me, and the best person I know.

At times this book will change point-of-view. Please note that each new scene does not necessarily follow the same timeline as the last.

A note for my American readers. This book is written in UK/Australian English. Many of the words will be spelled differently from what you're used to - realised, colour, centre , grey etc. We pronounce the "h" at the start of "herb", so we preface it with "a" rather than "an."

In addition, we do not share your fondness for the letter 'Z'. I realise you may find this difficult and offer my humble apologies. We make up for this by using a plethora of "L's where you would make do with one. Marvellous

All the writing and artwork in this book was created by a real person. No AI was used at any time.

Dur
Northern Ocean
Northlands
Chanoban
Forest of Dar
Dur City
Taro's Farm
Ort
Eastor
Yerrsun
Solgarr
Delean
Ortlands
Mount Belram
Eastlands
Wantu Mountains
River Ate
Vjore
Wantu River
Freelands
Asemouth
Eastport
Torne
Torr Sea

"When one lies down with monsters, one must eventually become a monster."

OLD DUR EXPRESSION

ONE
THE MEAL PREPARED

Like all young girls of Dur, Corelle dreamt of love. In her dreams, she arrived at a ball in a luxurious carriage drawn by four spirited white horses. She took dainty steps down from the carriage as though she floated on the very air itself, arrayed in a spectacular gown created by her father in his garment shop. She waved to the assembled revellers, who gasped and swooned with envy as her lover descended from the carriage and swept her onto the dance floor. Corelle and her lover danced all night before they returned to their home and made love until the sunrise.

Unlike most young girls of Dur, the voice that moaned in the hot, passionate nights of Corelle's dreams belonged to a woman. Her lover, tall and exquisite, had a voluptuous figure and long blonde hair that spilled around Corelle's face like sunlight as they lay together in the sumptuous bed in their enormous house.

Corelle's sighs of contentment filled the bedroom and mingled with the fragrance of the exotic flowers that stood on every flat surface.

Over time, the dreams became nightmares. Her lover whispered, "I love you," and blood pumped from a gash across her throat. As Corelle opened her mouth to scream, her lover's blood poured into it and congealed. No sound could escape through the dense blood, and Corelle woke wet with sweat and tears. Those three words had betrayed her and killed the woman she adored. *"You must never love,"* she told herself. She could not allow love to rob her of the woman of her dreams.

From her earliest years, Corelle worked in her father's shop, learned fast, and became skilled at making: the work with needle, thread, and scissors that created the garments the wealthy citizens of Ryl desired. Corelle's most notable talent, however, lay in the design of elaborate dresses for the rich women of the city. Ryl might have the smallest population of the Five Cities, but it boasted more than its fair share of well-off residents, and those fortunate enough to possess vast quantities of coin were more than content to spend large sums of it on appearances. Corelle's designs soon became well known around the city.

Midway through her teenyears, the Portreeve himself visited Corelle's father's shop. In any town or city, the Portreeve, appointed by the Duke's Bailiff himself, symbolised success. Rich and powerful, he controlled the commercial and legal heart of the city, but Corelle had no interest in Portreeves. Men in Dur did not wear dresses, and whenever Corelle created wescoats or elaborate tunics for men, she did so with reluctance and none of the artistry she poured into her gowns. She found no joy in the male body, and always envisaged the woman from her dreams dressed in every gown she created.

The Portreeve brought his wife, who wished to try on an intricate dress Corelle had completed two days earlier. Corelle's father took the Portreeve into the office at the rear of the shop while Corelle and her mother busied themselves with the Portreeve's wife and the dress, which required few adjustments to fit the woman.

The Portreeve's wife gazed at herself in the reflecting glass. The dress, with painstaking, detailed lacework on the bodice, had a modest hoop skirt that stopped a span short of her ankles. Although Corelle feared the Portreeve's wife might think the length of the dress improper, the woman's adoration for it shone from her eyes. She cooed at Corelle's mother as she spun before the glass and leered in envy at the woman reflected at her. "Such a marvellous dress. The making is wonderful. Your talent is unsurpassed in Ryl."

Corelle's mother flashed a proud smile at her daughter as she replied. "My thanks. I did not make the dress, however. It is my daughter, Corelle's, making."

The woman turned to Corelle, disbelief on her face. "Can it be? You are still in the spring of your life. To possess such skill so young is remarkable."

The heat of embarrassment burned in Corelle's cheeks. She could not explain why she felt uncomfortable with the compliment and wished she could vanish. Anxiety brought her to the brink of fainting. Eyes downcast, she whispered, "My thanks."

The Portreeve's wife tossed her head, a woman used to a life of privilege. "I must have it. Have it delivered to my residence as soon as you can. I shall wear it to the next Portreeve's Ball. Your little shop will be the talk of Ryl."

Corelle's mother gushed over the Portreeve's wife's appearance in the dress and thanked her for her business, but it rankled Corelle when the woman offered no payment for the dress, nor said "please" or "my thanks." Resentment gnawed at the young woman that the Portreeve's wife had spoken of their shop with such condescension. *"Little shop,"* she growled in her mind. *"Not so little you do not recognise the finest making in the city."* Corelle choked on her disappointment that the woman had helped herself to the dress as she swept away insistent visions of the Portreeve's wife as one of the covetous attendees who fawned at the feet of Corelle and her tall blonde lover at the ball in her dreams.

The woman's sense of entitlement ate at Corelle all day, and at dinner she complained to her father. He, however, believed the Portreeve's wife in her new gown would attract the most powerful and influential people in the city to his shop.

Corelle's bitterness threatened to turn to anger, and she lashed out at the Portreeve and his ungrateful wife. "Why did they even come here?"

Her father looked like a cat that had been thrown a delectable fish. "He invited me to contribute to the levies."

Nothing about the levies or the politics of Dur interested Corelle, and her father's reply did not quash her resentment about the woman's self-important attitude in the shop. She stifled a bored yawn. "I do not care about the stupid levies."

Her mother smiled at her; the patient smile of a parent required to teach a stubborn child the error of its ways. "You must learn to care. One day, when we are too old, you must take over the shop."

The final insult, and Corelle could not contain her derisive laughter at the slender chance a woman might be permitted to own a business in Dur. She knew only one woman who did; Saboti, the old woman who owned a general shop across the road. Saboti had kept the shop after her husband, the original owner, had died several years before.

Her father seemed to misjudge Corelle's contempt as entitlement. "There is no certainty some handsome fellow will whisk you off and keep you in grand style."

"Good." The face of the woman from her dreams swam into Corelle's mind. "I do not desire such a thing and never will."

Her mother gave her a sad smile, and her father stared, open-mouthed. Corelle had gone too far—dreams such as hers found no acceptance in Dur, and few people would dare to mention them. She and her lover danced only in her dreams, and Corelle did not believe she would ever enjoy such pleasures in her life. Anger had prompted her admission, and she changed the subject. "And what is the purpose of these levies?"

Her father seemed surprised by the question. "The Portreeve uses the funds to maintain the city. Any balances are remitted to the Duke's Bailiff, and those balances serve to retain the city charter, without which, Ryl would be nothing more than a town."

Did her father expect her to know these mundanities? "What pompous nonsense." Corelle struggled to contain her contempt for her father's fascination with such a dull subject. "I am content to design and create my gowns and will leave such high affairs to you, Father." She excused herself from the table, went to her room, lay on her bed, and cursed the fates that had been written for her. Bad enough to be born a woman in Dur, but to be born a woman who wished for the intimate company of other women guaranteed a life of dissatisfaction and frustration. Corelle would be unlikely to meet another woman who felt as she did, and for the remainder of her days, she must bury her desires deep within herself where society could not see them. Involuntary, bitter tears filled her eyes, and she pressed her face into her pillow to muffle her anguished wails at the unfairness of her fate.

Before Corelle fell asleep, she thought about a girl who sometimes came to the shop with her mother, and whom Corelle had felt some attraction toward, although the girl never showed any interest in her. Tonight, when Corelle closed her eyes, she saw the girl again, and her hand drifted between her legs. Before she reached satisfaction, the girl had been replaced by the woman of her dreams.

When Corelle's first moon cycle began, it surprised her. Her mother, who had not warned her about the cycle, took her to a local shop owned by a woman named Orgel, and Corelle recalled the conversation with her father after the Portreeve's visit. She now knew of two women who owned their own businesses—a development that did nothing to sweeten the bitter taste of exasperation and frustration.

Orgel sold a sweet, spicy drink that helped relieve the cramps of a cycle Corelle deemed an injustice. *"Why must women be so cursed?"* Every twenty-six days, eleven times a year as the moon crossed Dur, it came on her, and she could not imagine why she deserved such an unfair life, or why it became more unfavourable at every turn. By chance, she enjoyed the taste of Orgel's drink and visited the shop often thereafter, even outside her moon cycle.

To her disappointment, Corelle's father had been correct about the impact on their business of their new-found popularity with the Portreeve and his wife's wealthy friends. One cold, grey day when Corelle was seventeen years, she decided to visit Orgel's shop and take a cup of the spicy drink as relief from a complex design, a commission from a friend of the Portreeve's wife. The fussy, pretentious making irritated her, and she struggled to remain focused on the work; uncharacteristic for her.

Corelle pulled her cloak about her, told her parents she would return later, and set off toward the shop. She pushed the door open and came to an abrupt halt, open-mouthed. A blonde woman sat alone at one of the tables, and the woman's bright blue eyes pierced Corelle to her core and brought a flutter to her heart. Long blonde hair hung in curls beyond the woman's shoulders.

Corelle had never seen the woman before, but fate had brought her the woman from her dreams. The woman bore such a remarkable resemblance to her dream lover, Corelle had to steady herself on the door frame as light-headedness threatened to overcome her, and her stomach tied itself in knots. They stared at one another, and Corelle longed to dive into the deep pools of those blue eyes, reckless, content never to surface again.

Corelle ordered a cup of Orgel's drink and gazed in feigned disinterest around the shop at the six other women there, seated in two groups of three at separate tables. They had all looked up when she entered, but their interest had returned to their own conversations soon enough. The lone blonde woman still watched Corelle, and the way her blue eyes drank in Corelle's body tantalised the young garment maker. Corelle's stomach spasmed as a need sprang to life inside her far beyond anything she had felt for the girl she had been attracted to at her father's shop.

Orgel handed her the drink. Corelle left a groat on the counter and headed to the woman's table. "May I join you?"

"Please." The woman pointed to the vacant chair opposite her, her eyes locked on Corelle's own.

Instead, Corelle chose to sit on a chair to the woman's left. "My name is Corelle." The brazenness of her own actions excited her, and her sex tingled more than she had experienced before.

"Arella." The woman's smile held more than a mere introduction; there could be little doubt of it.

Arella looked older than Corelle, although the citizens of Dur did not celebrate the day of their birth and did not reckon their ages with any accuracy. She had full, moist lips and flawless skin, but above all else, her eyes captivated Corelle and took her breath away.

Corelle's body shook with excitement, her throat turned as dry as sand while her palms ran wet with sweat, and as she gazed into Arella's eyes, she felt positive she saw an invitation to a journey she had never taken but now longed for with every beat of her heart. They sipped their drinks in silence for a few moments until, as her heart raced so fast she feared it might burst, Corelle found the courage to ask, "Do you have rooms nearby?" Her voice trembled as she spoke, and she could not decide whether fear or desire lay behind her tremor.

"That I do." Arella had a clear, gentle voice, like a soft cloth that wiped a fevered brow.

Corelle laid a hand on Arella's arm and stared, unblinking, into her eyes. She had become breathless with excitement, and she struggled to coax any words from her throat. "I would very much like to see them."

The shameless invitation appeared to take Arella by surprise, and she glanced around until she seemed satisfied none of the other women took any notice of them. Her voice lowered to the softest of whispers, intended for Corelle's ears and no others. "That might seem inappropriate to many."

"That it might, although not to me." Corelle gave a gentle squeeze of the woman's arm, the final confirmation of her availability. "Nor to you, I hope."

Arella did not reply as she appeared to consider the proposition, but her eyes betrayed her. They gleamed with desire, narrowed—Corelle had not missed her guess. At last, Arella stood and leaned forward, her response once more so quiet, none but Corelle could hear. "Please join me at my lodgings, where there are things we might…discuss that would be pleasurable to us both." Corelle let out an involuntary moan.

Arella turned and left the shop without a backward glance. Corelle waited five frantic heartbeats, impatient to fall into Arella's arms and bring her dreams to fruition, then drained her cup. She rose to follow the blonde, who strolled to a nearby house. At no time did Arella look behind her as she dawdled along the street, though Corelle longed for her to walk faster so they could tear at each other's clothes sooner. Arella stopped at a door and bent down to speak to a cat that sunned itself on the step outside the house.

Corelle's voice startled the cat, and it scampered off along the street. "What delightful lodgings." Corelle followed the blonde-haired woman up the stairs, afraid to speak in case her voice chased the illusion away. As she watched Arella's supple body move ahead of her, Corelle ached with desire, and the stairs seemed endless.

Arella satisfied Corelle countless times over the next two hours. Her tongue flicked at Corelle and drove the younger woman to heights of ecstasy she had only dreamt of before now but were realised at last. Corelle responded with soft cries, her hands entwined in Arella's blonde hair as pleasures she had not imagined could exist tore through her body and left her sated yet desperate for more at the same moment. By the time Arella had satisfied Corelle's urgent needs, rivulets of sweat ran across her body, trickled between her breasts, and pooled in her navel. Corelle had never guessed she could so abandon herself to the touch of another and be taken to such frenzied levels of excitement. She pulled Arella up the bed, lay next to her, and traced the curve of the older woman's back. Her hand dived between the blonde woman's legs, and Corelle thrust her fingers into the older woman over and over until Arella's passion reached fever pitch, and she shook at the pleasure that surged through her.

They lay, silent and content, in each other's arms for some time, Corelle breathless, happier than she had ever been. If this had been a dream, then she hoped never to wake from it. Arella kissed her forehead and ran her fingers around Corelle's nipple, which stood proud under her touch. Soon, Arella's hungry fingers once again teased at her, and Corelle buried her face in the mass of blonde curls as she tried to stifle the moans and cries that might otherwise draw unwanted attention from other rooms in the house.

Arella smiled at Corelle as they lay winded and spent on the bed. "Where in the Five Cities did you come from?"

Corelle took the question at face value. "Here in Ryl."

Arella laughed, and Corelle laughed with her. "I did not mean my question in so literal a fashion You appeared from nowhere and gathered me up like some object of your desire on a market stall."

Corelle smiled. "You were the object of my desire from the

moment I opened the door of the shop. Can you tell me you did not feel the same?"

"How did you know?"

"I knew as soon as I saw you. You knew also. I saw it in your eyes."

Arella seemed to grapple with the subtleties of this revelation for a moment. "I do not think I have ever known, as you claim. But if you do know, then by the fates, I am grateful for it."

Corelle had lost track of how long they had been in the room together, but in the darkness beyond the room's small window, the lights of the night sky twinkled as though they shared Corelle's ecstasy. She longed to never rise from the bed again, to spend the remainder of her days here, their bodies entwined, the smell of their passion in the air. Arella kissed her long and hard, mayhap in hopes of further pleasures, but Corelle's parents would worry about her if she stayed away too late. "I should go home." She rose and gathered her clothes together. "I could call again, if that would please you."

Arella gushed her response. "That it would."

"Then I shall come to the shop in two days, at three hours after the midday. If you are there..." Corelle did not finish the sentence, but a suggestive smile danced on her lips. Arella's sensual pout confirmed Corelle's meaning had not been lost on her.

They met at the shop two days later and many times afterward, and the amount of time they spent together increased. Although Corelle found Arella easy company, the older woman became guarded whenever they shared tales of their past and spoke of little but her life as a street urchin in Zhanghar. Corelle's own life appeared dull and repetitive in comparison, and while she shared occasional stories of her father's shop and her own making, she preferred to hear tales of the vibrant city where Arella had been born.

No matter how hard Corelle pressed, Arella would not reveal

the reason for her journey to Ryl. As she had travelled west by ship from Zhanghar to Ryl a year before she met Corelle, Arella had fetched up over the rail countless times. As a consequence, she dreaded the return journey, convinced the swells of the Northern Ocean would distress her stomach again. Arella's insistence she would return to Zhanghar at some undetermined point brought a heaviness to Corelle's heart every time the prospect they might be parted came up.

The winter had been long and wet, but spring arrived at last. A large spring market took place in the city square each year, and Corelle and Arella wandered around it together. They came across a side stall that rewarded participants with sweet treats as a prize for a feat of skill. A wooden board with a small circle drawn on it hung at the rear of the stall. The game required the player to throw a knife at the board, and if the knife became embedded in the board within the circle, the player won a handful of treats. The two women stopped to watch a man who tried to win some treats for his female companion. The man's throw missed both the circle and the board, and the knife sailed past it to land on the ground. The man and woman laughed and moved on.

Corelle bridled at the unjustness of the game. "That circle is so small, it must be all but impossible to hit. The game cheated that man of his entry fee."

Arella studied the board. "It looks simple enough to my eye."

Corelle clapped her hands together, thrilled by Arella's bold claim. "You say so? Then prove yourself."

For a heartbeat, Arella seemed consumed by irritation, but a smile sprang to her lips in its place. "That is unnecessary. If you desire sweet treats, I will buy you some. Name your flavour."

"You seek to deflect me." Corelle wagged a reproachful finger at Arella, determined to hold the blonde woman accountable for her boast. "You have claimed it, and now you must prove it." She leaned close to whisper in Arella's ear, consumed by an abrupt rush of desire that thrilled her. "If you want me tonight, then prove it."

Arella stared deep into Corelle's green eyes as she hesitated and appeared to be caught between doubt and uncertainty, as the old phrase went. At last, she spoke, a determined glint in her eye. "Very well, I accept the challenge." With the faintest touch on Corelle's wrist, she leaned forward to whisper, and Arella's hot breath on her ear aroused Corelle. "If I make the throw, I will want you for more than tonight. I will want you for the rest of my life."

Arella's words stunned Corelle, who stared into those deep blue eyes for any hint of mockery. She found none and took a deep breath as she weighed the unexpected response. Her dreams had been laid bare before her, the dream made flesh. She had the opportunity to spend the rest of her life with Arella, and she must not spurn this one chance. The frivolous moment had become charged with tension, promise, and a sense of danger. Arella excited Corelle, while the mysteries in her past, and now this offer to became one for the rest of their lives, enthralled her. Her breath caught in her throat as her heart pounded so hard, she felt it must burst out of her chest. In a raspy voice, difficult even for her to hear, she announced her portentous decision. "Then make the throw, I beg you. Make me yours."

Arella stepped up to the stall, but the man who ran it ignored her and called to the crowd for another player to take a chance at the game. Arella moved to stand in front of the man so he could not continue to overlook her, and her confident voice rose above the hubbub of the fair. "I will play." He flicked his gaze to her, dressed in a silk dress with a simple boned bodice, and he drank her in like a fine wine. He seemed to think her words had been a jest, and he did not move to take the groat she proffered as her entry fee. A resolute tone in her voice, Arella emphasised each word. "I will play."

He hesitated, then sneered. "Very well." He snatched the groat from her outstretched hand, gestured at the crowd with great drama, and shouted to those who watched, "The lady will play." Ironic cheers greeted his announcement, and Corelle again clapped her hands in excitement, anxious for Arella to make the throw, impressed by her determination.

Arella took the knife from the stall operator, studied it. Corelle knew nothing about knives, but this one seemed a crude thing with some frayed string wrapped around one end as a makeshift handle. Its point had bent back on itself, and Corelle doubted it would stick in the board even if the circle could be hit. Her initial assessment that players were cheated out of their entry fee seemed accurate. Arella stared at the board, the knife held by the tip, her hand at her shoulder. She took a long, deep breath, half-closed her eyes, and threw the knife. It flew true and straight, turned end over end in the air like an insect struck by the back of a hand, and thumped into the board in the exact centre of the small circle. It quivered as it stuck in the board for one, then two heartbeats, then fell out. Those assembled let out a collective gasp; they must have been shocked to see a woman throw a knife with such competence. Corelle stared at Arella, speechless, and she covered her mouth with a hand, astonished by the accuracy of the throw.

The stall operator seemed taken aback as much any of those who watched, and he glanced at Arella as he struggled to recover his composure before he cried aloud, "Unlucky the lady." He clapped his hands in what Corelle took to be sympathy.

Arella did not seem content with his pity. "I made the throw." Her tone had become flat, devoid of emotion.

The man managed a brave smile, but nervous blinks betrayed him. "The knife did not stick."

Arella glowered at him. "The tip is so bent, it is a wonder the knife pierced the board at all. I made the throw."

He seemed to wilt under her fierce gaze and took a half step backward. An uncertain smile flitted around his lips, and his voice lacked conviction. "The knife did not stick." Some members of the crowd murmured as they debated the rights of the matter among themselves.

Arella appeared furious that the man cheated at a loaded parlour game with no more than a few sweet treats at stake. Her stern face flushed in striking contrast to the pretty blonde curls that framed it, and when she folded her arms across her breasts, her fingers slid into her bodice as though she reached for something hidden there. Arella seemed bent on menace, violence even, and Corelle sensed she should intervene, so she laid a hand on Arella's arm and forced a jovial tone to her voice as she shouted to the crowd gathered around. "The knife did not stick, though by the fates it would be difficult to imagine a finer effort." Some of the crowd cheered and applauded Corelle's apparent sense of fairness. Corelle pulled at Arella's arm and stared at her with wide eyes that implied Arella should abandon the argument, then added, "Let us leave, for I desire a cold beverage."

Arella tore her murderous gaze from the stall operator. "Then you shall have one." She smiled at Corelle and seemed to regain her self-control. With a final fierce glance at the shaken stall operator, she walked away, Corelle a step behind her.

Once they were a safe distance from the stall, Corelle stretched out a hand to tug on Arella's arm. "I would defy anybody to make that throw as well as you did. The odds were against you, yet you made it. You may claim your prize."

Arella looked deep into Corelle's green eyes and heaved a long sigh. "By the fates, I love you."

Corelle's heart leapt in her breast and a lump formed in her throat that threatened to choke her. Her dreams had suggested tragedy would strike whenever she heard those three words, but the dream remained what it had always been: a dream, no more. Blood did not pour from Arella's throat, and Corelle could not keep a smile of relief from her face. "As I love you. Now, please explain how you made that throw, then take me to your room and show me what you reached for in your bodice."

They returned to Arella's room, where Corelle unbuttoned Arella's bodice but found nothing but Arella's breasts beneath it, to her confusion. "What did you reach for, then?" Arella ignored the question, pushed Corelle onto the bed, and made frantic love to her, their groans of joy mingled as their hands and tongues excited one another.

Afterward, Corelle could not shake the incident at the market from her head, and she pressed Arella to explain. Arella sighed and looked away for a heartbeat, then sat up on the bed next to Corelle. "What I have to say will be difficult for you to hear. It may even lead you to wish you had not met me, but these things can no longer lie unsaid between us if we are to make a life together. I offer you the chance now to know my secrets or not—you must decide. If you do not wish to hear it, I will understand, but you might still learn these things at some later date and resent the fact you did not know sooner."

Corelle lay still and considered Arella's words. Despite the implied danger in them, she wished to understand what had turned at the market. "I will hear you."

Arella took a sharp breath before she began. "I reached for a weapon, a stiletto I sometimes conceal in my bodice, but I did not find it there. I prefer not to carry it when I am with you, and in my anger, I had forgotten I had left it behind." She paused, mayhap to gather her thoughts. "I kill for coin. Most people do not believe there is any serious or violent crime in Dur. There is, and much of it exists in a clandestine organisation. Not all of it, of course. An intoxicated brawl gone wrong, a crime of passion; these things happen at times. This organisation calls itself the Guild, and I am a member of it. Our customers pay a fee, and we take a life."

Corelle wanted to ask who the customers were, but as she drew a breath to speak, Arella held up a hand for silence. "Hear me out, then ask questions, please. When I am commissioned to end some-body's days, I do not concern myself with the 'why' of it. Instead, I kill them and receive my coin as reward. I can make throws such as the one you saw thanks to the training I received from the Guild."

Corelle tried to concentrate on the tale as it unfolded rather than become mired in how she felt about it. Some explanation for Arel-la's involvement in this organisation must arrive at some point. Her lover continued the story, a sadness in her eyes. "I had been intro-duced to the Guild as a young woman, no older than I reckon you to be now. I grew up a street urchin, and on a particular day I marked a man as a target whose pouch I intended to pilfer so I might spend his coin. He read my intent and had a dagger at my ear before I could succeed. He had a foul temper that day, and my attempt to pick his pocket worsened it. 'Away with you, vagabond,' he said, and he knocked me into the gutter." She paused.

Corelle concentrated on Arella's words, anxious to hear the tale to its conclusion so she could ask the countless questions that accu-mulated in her mind. "Go on."

"His name is Wilash, and he is a good man at heart. I believe his goodness ate at him as soon as he struck me. He apologised, helped me to my feet, and invited me to take a drink with him at a nearby tavern. I misread his intentions and had no interest in that which I believed he sought, so I refused. He put away his dagger, begged me not to judge him too harshly, and insisted I allow him to buy me a drink. Ale"—she pulled a face of disgust—"is horrible. I took one sip of it and pushed it from me. We shared tales of our lives." Arella looked wistful for a heartbeat. "Life had been cruel to both of us. He had been recruited to the Guild after his parents died from the fevers. Wilash is a blacksmith who became mired in debt as he tried to keep his late father's smithy in business. He told me Styrrach, the leader of the Guild in Zhanghar, saved him from the Debtors' Gaol, and he joined the Guild."

Corelle interrupted. "There is a Debtors' Gaol?"

"It seems so, although I confess, I do not know where it can be found. Styrrach had not mentioned the Guild's true nature, and as young as Wilash was, the offer of a job seemed preferable to the Debtor's Gaol. Although he soon learned the true purpose of the Guild, he never killed anybody. They used him as a courier or to gather intelligence most of the time, and the day I encountered him he had been ordered to take a position in the Portreeve's Office. That had frustrated him and turned his mood black. He thought he had fallen from favour, that Styrrach no longer wished him around the Guild building.

"The tale entranced me. By the end of the night, he had become so inebriated, he offered me a chance to join the Guild, which may have been a jest. He now regrets he did so, I think, as do I. The fates were written, however, and I joined. You doubtless ask why I would take such a loathsome occupation. I have asked myself that question down the years. I lived a street urchin's life and saw no future for myself, despised by almost everybody I ever met. Nobody had ever respected me until that day. Well, one person..." Arella seemed to drift off somewhere in her memories until she snapped her head up and returned to the tale. "Wilash showed me respect and convinced me others would respect me also. Other Guild members, anybody who learned I served the Guild. It intoxicated me more than ale could ever have done."

Arella gave a snort of derision and shook her head, as though she had proffered excuses to herself rather than to Corelle. "I told myself I would not have to kill often. 'There is almost no violence in Dur,' I assured myself." Her eyes closed as she hesitated, and a tear ran down her cheek. When she spoke again, her voice had become so quiet, Corelle had to lean forward so she did not miss her words. "I lied to myself. There is violence." Her train of thought seemed to drift off again, and Corelle waited for her to return to the tale that had captivated her throughout. "There you have it. You thought you loved a sweet, blue-eyed woman. You love a monster." Arella fell silent.

An important element had been missed, and Corelle could not let it pass. "This took place in Zhanghar, you say, but that does not explain how you come to be in Ryl."

"A favour between Styrrach and the Guildmeister here. Guild-meister is what Styrrach calls himself, as does the man here, Krage. One of the Ryl members had been hanged by the Portreeve, so Styrrach loaned me out to Krage. I am a commodity, traded like a courtesan, it turns."

Corelle lay on her back for long moments as she digested all Arella had told her. She recalled a murderer had been hanged, a year ago and more, after the death of a local man. Some of the customers in her father's shop had gossiped about it, outraged, as she remembered it. Rumour had it marital infidelity had been involved—a crime of passion. A question troubled her, and she asked it. "Would you take my life if somebody paid the fee?"

Arella did not hesitate. "By the fates, I would not. I would rather take my own. I could neither hurt you nor see you hurt. Not ever."

Corelle imagined Arella had expected her to be horrified by the tale, but it had not surprised her, in truth. There had always been an air of menace about Arella, and now she understood. The woman in her dreams would not hesitate to kill to protect Corelle's honour or her life, and she imagined the deaths Arella spoke of must be little different. She felt none of the revulsion Arella had seemed to expect when she began the tale. Arella's confession had not changed her feelings for this woman who had brought more purpose to her life in a few passes than she had enjoyed in all the years before they had met. In truth, it excited her to think Arella might kill to save her from some danger.

The woman of Corelle's dreams had come to life and loved her, and she persuaded herself the blood in the dreams had been the blood of others, spilled by Arella. Love might not betray her as she had once believed. She turned onto her stomach, raised herself up on her elbows, gazed into Arella's eyes, and found no hint of danger to herself despite all that had been disclosed. She brushed her lips against Arella's. "The prize is as we bargained."

Tears pooled again in Arella's eyes. "Then we should seal the negotiation." She reached for Corelle and pulled her mouth to her own.

Six more passes went by, and Arella reckoned she had been in Ryl close to two years. They spent most nights together but did not often discuss Arella's deadly work. Corelle spent her days at her father's shop but did not often sleep in her room above the shop. From time to time, Arella suggested Corelle should spend the evening with her parents, and Corelle imagined Guild business occupied her lover for the night. Corelle remained distant from Arella's lethal work and closed her mind to the consequences of Arella's actions on those nights.

As the wet season set in, long-dreaded news arrived at last. Arella lay on her bed and spoke the moment Corelle entered the room. "Letters came from Zhanghar today. Styrrach calls me back. I must take ship tomorrow."

Corelle slumped to the floor, devastated. Arella's words ripped her heart from her breast and crushed it. "Why? Why must you go? Can you not resign your position and stay here?"

Arella spoke through her tears. "My love. If only it could be so simple. I cannot leave the Guild, now or ever. My life would be forfeit. I might suffer Guild justice, and that I do not wish, for it would be terrible."

"Guild justice?" Corelle could not comprehend the term.

"Nobody can leave the Guild. We all know too much of how it operates. We know where the Guild is based in Ryl, Zhanghar, Alcmouth, and Torric. We know the names of some members from other cities. The Guild does not permit this knowledge to spread outside its control. Guild justice awaits any who try to leave, and

Guild justice means a slow, painful death. I do not wish it." She shuddered as though she imagined herself the victim of this so-called justice.

Corelle sat on the floor, disconsolate. The woman she loved, had thought she would be with for the rest of her life, would leave for Zhanghar the next day, and the news left her hollow, her insides ripped from her body with brute force. Heartbeats passed, then moments and more moments, and no words came to either of them. At last, Corelle could see no other solution, and she gazed up at Arella. "I shall come with you."

Arella gave a defiant shake of her head. "Your parents are here. Your friends are here. Your life is here. You cannot come with me."

Corelle stood and took Arella's chin in one hand to tilt her head upward as she spoke. "You are my life, and you will be in Zhanghar. In truth, my life is not here. What time will you leave tomorrow?"

"I will take the first ship that sails to Zhanghar. By the fates, to ride that wretched wooden beast again, even with my memories full of the time we have spent together, will be beyond me. I would rather die."

The prospect horrified Corelle. "Do not say that."

Arella smiled. "I am sorry. I maunder. Ignore me. I shall lose my insides to the deep waters of the ocean and dream of you."

"Wherever your insides go, I go also. I will come with you. My mind is made up. There need be no further debate."

"What of your parents? How will they manage without you in the shop?"

Lies came with ease to lips unused to them, but Corelle would not lose this love, not now. "I do little enough these days. They are far more skilled than I am. I will tell them I must leave. They need know nothing of why."

"Your friends?"

Corelle gave a short, bitter laugh. "I have no friends. You are all I need."

Arella appeared dazed. "I cannot ask this."

"You do not ask it. I offer it." Corelle looked around the room. "I have grown fond of these lodgings this last year and a bit."

Arella snickered. "'And a bit?' What does that mean?"

Corelle laughed. "You are not Rylfolk, that is clear. It means 'a little part.' You will never be accepted here if you do not learn to speak as we do."

Arella shook her head. "I wish I had more time to learn the strange expressions you westerners use, but Zhanghar calls, and I must away." A bashful smile flirted with her lips. "We must away."

Her words lifted the despondency from Corelle. "That we must. But there is time for us to enjoy these lodgings once more, as we have this last year."

Arella grinned as she pulled Corelle onto the bed. "And a bit."

TWO
FROM GIRL TO WOMAN

DEINEIKE LAY AWAKE ON HER COT, THE LIGHT OF THE MOON THROUGH A small window the sole respite from the dark of the night.

Across the room, her mother and the man who lay with her cast noisy shadows on the wall of the room. Her mother almost never brought the same man home more than once, and the young girl did not recognise this one. The pair also sounded different from previous nights. The man's voice became a growl filled with malice, a menace that sent a shiver of fear through Deineike's young body. The little girl pulled her threadbare blanket up to her chin, ready to dive beneath it to hide if necessary, and her mother sobbed. The man's voice grew louder, angrier. "You think to cheat me?" His shadowy arm rose and fell, and Deineike winced at the crack of his hand as it struck her mother. Moonlight glinted on metal, and her mother gave a short cry, then fell silent.

The man crossed the room, and the young girl shrank back on her cot as he stood over her, his face twisted in the ugliness of fury. Her heart raced as he raised a knife over her, and something dripped from it, warm on her cheek. She opened her mouth to scream, but fear trapped her voice in her throat as her young body convulsed with terror. The man glared at her, then lowered the knife and ran from the room. Tears stung her eyes as she ran to her mother, found her chest soaked in warm, sticky liquid. She buried her face in her mother's neck and sobbed. "Mother, mother." Her mother would not answer, refused to hold her and tell her not to be afraid.

The Portreeve's men came later. Deineike did not know who summoned them and did not care. The men told her that her mother would not be back, and they would find someone to look after her. They never did, and she found herself on the street, coinless and with nobody to care for her. She learned how to fend for herself, and she lasted a year, then another, her nights spent in whatever shelter she could find. As she grew older, she never forgot the man who had killed her mother, and she vowed to find and kill him, to run him through with a giant sword and slice off his hands.

In her teenyears, Deineike met Arella. Some of the street urchins passed the cold winter nights in an abandoned smithy, the blacksmith long dead, and the building gone to ruin. Arella was older than Deineike, a smart girl with her street skills honed to perfection. She could charm the hatchlings from the nest, as the old expression went, with her angelic face framed by adorable blonde curls that hung beyond her shoulders.

Deineike found herself drawn to Arella from the first time they met, and to her delight the older girl took her under her wing. Arella encouraged the younger girl to bathe when she could and to tidy her hair. Arella often lent Deineike the worn comb she carried with her and persuaded her to care for the long dark hair that had been ignored for years. Deineike's greatest satisfaction came on the nights when Arella combed her hair for her and sang a gentle melody that transported her away from the brutal life of a street urchin for a time.

As she lay with her head on Arella's lap one night, lost in the latest version of the song that threaded through Arella's life, Deineike decided she loved the blonde-haired woman. It felt scandalous to love another woman. Forbidden fruit; unacceptable and unfathomable to most of the citizens of Dur.

On a whim, Deineike raised her head and kissed Arella on the lips. Arella placed a hand on the back of Deineike's head and held it in a firm grip as her tongue pushed its way into Deineike's mouth. Deineike had never experienced the levels of ecstasy Arella coaxed from her body that night, and her own endeavours in response felt clumsy and inadequate. That soon changed, however, and as winter turned to spring, then a summer that brought a new year, they found fulfilment with each other most days. Memories of her mother still pained Deineike, but at the worst moments in the darkest nights she could reach for Arella and find solace.

As summer faded and the nights grew colder, the wet season that prefaced each winter set in. Arella's superior street skills provided for them both, and Deineike almost never stole food or picked a pocket, content to live on the bounty the older girl provided.

The first night Arella did not return to the smithy terrified Deineike, as the man with the knife had done when she had been so much younger. She could not understand why Arella had abandoned her. Dark thoughts crowded in on her, and fear and anxiety drove her to irrational conclusions. Had Arella been caught as she picked a pocket or stole bread from a stall? Could she have been thrown into the River Alc, her blonde curls spread around her head like a cloud? Almost no violent crime took place in Dur, but Deineike could not shake the horrible image from her thoughts. She cried and wished Arella would return to her, but she did not come the next day nor the day after. The young woman grew more despondent, unable to understand why she had been cast adrift again, certain she could not survive alone a second time.

Arella may have been locked in the stocks, located in a small plaza off the main square. Deineike had spent more than one night in the stocks herself before she had met Arella, punishment for the theft of food or coin. She ran to the stocks to check but found only a boy clamped between the heavy beams. His face seemed familiar to her, but he had gone the next day. With no sign of Arella either day, Deineike wandered back to the smithy more disconsolate than before.

Outside, people on the street wandered past the building's broken windows beneath a bright moon. Inside, they became shadow figures who flitted across the rear wall of the smithy as Deineike lay on her cot, her soft cries the only sound in the still night. Arella had failed to return for a fourth night, and Deineike feared she would never again see those soft, blonde curls fall around Arella's blue eyes. She had no explanation for the mysterious rift between them that had left her alone and bereft and blamed herself for whatever drove Arella away.

Arella's voice startled her as it whispered her name in the loneliness of the night, and Deineike leapt from the cot, ran to her lover, and wrapped her in her arms. She nuzzled into the blonde hair and showered kisses on the face she had missed so much, she had believed she would die. Arella prised Deineike's arms from around her even as the younger woman slid a hand down Arella's back to thrust it between her legs.

Arella spoke in a soft, sad voice. "Deineike, I am here to say goodbye."

Deineike froze, uncertain. Her heart turned to stone in her breast. "Goodbye? What do you mean?"

"I must leave you. I am sorry."

Arella's succinct words stunned Deineike. "You must leave?

Why? Have I upset you? Tell me what I have done wrong, and I will set it right. Arella, I swear it. I love you."

Tears pooled in Arella's eyes. "You have done nothing wrong. I must go. I..." Arella seemed to struggle for words to explain the emotional flames that burned Deineike to ash and scattered her remains across a city that had turned as bleak as the harshest winter. She kissed Deineike's lips. "Goodbye, Deineike. Find joy." She turned, walked away, and did not look back.

Deineike collapsed to her knees, hands on the back of her head, and her hysterical sobs rose into the inhospitable night as the woman she loved walked away from her without a backward glance. The younger woman's hoarse whisper scratched the desolate dark of the smithy. "Arella. I love you."

Deineike lost track of how long she knelt there in tears, tears that came without end and splashed down her cheeks onto her crude tunic. At some point, she crawled onto the cot and held her knees close to her chest with her arms. She lay there until the dawn drove the contemptuous darkness away, her mind filled with images of Arella and the night the man had killed her mother.

Deineike never saw Arella again, but as she left her teenyears behind her, she grew tall and worked on physical exercises that lent her a muscular physique. As she grew into womanhood she took charge of her life, moved into a small room over the stable of an inn, and hoarded any spare coin she could come by. The innkeep gave her frequent work in the tavernroom or the stable. He taught her to read, and she developed an aptitude for numbers that helped her obtain some work in the tally houses at the docks, where she learned to tally the chits for the items that came and went on the ships that visited Zhanghar.

As another summer waned, Deineike despaired at how little she had achieved or had tried to achieve. She never found the man who had murdered her mother, and she never bought the sword to kill him with either. Her life had amounted to nothing to this point, and the time had come to correct that failure. One evening as she bedded the guests' horses down in the stable, she decided to leave Zhanghar. The next morning, she dressed in a plain tunic and soft leather trousers, then retrieved the pouch of coin she had hidden beneath her mattress. She knew of a stable that sold horses, and she set off toward it. As she crossed a market square that led to the stable, she lingered there, wandered from stall to stall, distracted, and her resolve wavered.

As Deineike picked over some trinkets on a stall, a coldness came over her, as though somebody watched her, but when she looked round, she saw nothing unusual. Her resolve returned, so she continued onward to the stable where she exchanged a sum of coin for a grey gelding and some tack. Though she had no experience as a rider, the stable owner assured her the grey would be docile and easy to ride, and so it proved. She pointed the grey toward the nearest city gate, out into the lands beyond, the first time she had ever left the city, and headed toward the small inland town of Delcan in search of a new life.

To her disappointment, Deineike found Delcan sleepy and characterless, and as the wet season arrived, nothing had changed within her. She could not shake off her memories of the night her mother had died, and although she now believed she would never see Arella again, she longed for her touch, her voice, her smell, her kisses. She determined to leave for the port town of Ort once the cold season arrived. Rumour spoke of Ort as a large, vibrant town with abundant work. It stood on the Alc, and Deineike missed the smell of the river and the bustle of the docks. The wet season this year proved stubborn, however, and Deineike grew frustrated at its reluctance to release its grip on the land. The roads became impassable by cart as they turned into ribbons of mud, and to travel by horse would be difficult, but Deineike had run out of patience. She set out again, hopeful the rains would stop before she and her horse sank into the mud, never to be seen again.

Deineike and her horse trudged through the dreadful conditions for day after miserable day. The grey struggled through mud that threatened to catch its legs with every step and trap them there until the rain drowned them. Each night, if she could find no inn, she begged farmers for shelter in barns, desperate to avoid the incessant rain. Seven laborious days out from Delcan, she spotted a light ahead in the twilight and reined the grey to a halt. "With luck, we can spend another night in the luxury of a barn." The horse pricked up its ears at the sound of her soft voice. Her impulsive decision to journey around Dur, aimless, had been exposed as folly, and once she reached Ort, she might sell the horse and settle there, or take ship back to Zhanghar, if she could raise sufficient coin.

Deineike kicked her heels into the grey's flank, urged it forward, and turned into a lane that led down to a small house. She made out the silhouette shape of a barn across the yard, dismounted, and led the grey to the door of the house. She did not knock—an air of unease had settled on her for reasons she could not explain. The horse snickered as though it urged her to knock and find them some shelter for the night, but Deineike stood motionless in the rain while her horse snorted and pawed the ground. A moment later the door swung open and a tall, thickset man stood there, a lantern in his hand.

THREE
BODIES IN THE NIGHT

Arella and Corelle boarded a ship in Ryl, and Arella asked Corelle to wait nearby while she talked to the ship's master, who led them to a simple cabin. When Corelle asked Arella how she could afford to pay for travel on a ship, the older woman told her Guild members carried a token that guaranteed them access to any ship in Dur.

The swell had no effect on Corelle as they sailed to Zhanghar, although Arella declared the return journey even worse than the outward trip, the seas heavier and the journey longer as the wind battled them all the way. The effect of the waves on the ship wreaked devastation on Arella's stomach, and she spent a great deal of time on deck as she fetched up over the rail. More than once, she begged Corelle to end her misery with her own stiletto. Corelle did all she could to make Arella comfortable and balanced her concern for her lover's sorry condition against her own amusement at it.

Arella lived in a simple room above a Zhanghar inn called The Ship's Yard. Nothing but a bed, a chair, a trunk for clothes and other important belongings, a chamber pot, and a vanity bowl occupied the room. Arella claimed nothing had been disturbed, although everything in it wore a grey mantle of dust. Corelle moved into the room with the older woman, excited by this new phase of her life.

Corelle had paid a hasty visit to her parents on the morning she and Arella had left Ryl. She had been vague, and said she must leave but would explain more later. Her mother had cried, and her father had been disappointed, but Corelle had cried as she kissed them both, then hurried to the docks to meet Arella. In Zhanghar, she scribed a letter to them with her new address. She had no idea how her parents would react, but she told them she loved a woman. She felt content in her life with Arella, and they were happy together despite the spectre of Arella's unsavoury work.

The Guild used the term "gest" as a description of their work, and Arella carried out five or six gests in their first six passes in Zhanghar. Arella did not return to their bed on any night she carried out Guild business. She claimed she felt unclean after she killed, and did not want to bring her disgust at herself home to Corelle. Instead, she slept on a cot at the Guild building, though she did not tell Corelle the location of that building.

Arella received a gest to kill the owner of one of the smaller tally houses at the docks. The Guild used a courier named Pilos to perform some early reconnaissance for the gest, and since the target often worked alone late at night in his tally house, Arella judged it the safest place to take him.

For three nights, Arella watched the tally house. Once she completed the gest, she would spend the night at the Guild building and be home the next morning. On the first two nights, she returned to their room late at night. No opportunity had presented itself, and she abandoned the gest for the night. On the third night, the perfect opportunity appeared. The large doors at the front of the tally house stood open, and the man worked alone in his office, nobody else in the building.

As Arella strode into the building, confident, her mark came out of his office, and she guessed he had finished his work for the day as he had extinguished the lantern. Arella had intended to take him in the office, further back in the building where it seemed doubtful anybody who strolled by would see the deed done. As he moved toward her, Arella hesitated, unsure whether to continue or mumble an apology as though inebriated and delay until another day.

Before she could decide, he spoke to her. "You are…Arella, correct?"

She wondered how he came to know her name, but she did not care. Arella told her marks her name if they asked, against the advice of other Guild members. It did not seem dangerous to her; she never failed. She answered his question without hesitation as she walked further into the building. "That I am." Somehow, he had recognised her, and there could be no element of surprise if she came for him another night. She must take him now.

"I met you at The Boat Haven tavern two passes ago. You were with a friend of mine." Arella could recall the night in question but did not recognise his face. "Somebody killed him that night, a few nights after he had argued about his share." He mumbled, and it seemed as though he addressed his words to himself. "Now, I argue with them, and you…" He paused and held up his hands. "Spare me." He took a step backward, eyes wide with terror as Arella thrust her stiletto into his neck, and he fell to his hands and knees at her feet as his life blood pumped out of him.

Arella turned, strolled from the building, and risked a backward glance. He had collapsed onto his face in a pool of blood that spread around him. She held her blade pressed against her thigh as she walked away from the tally house. Arella recalled the gest the man had mentioned. Her mark that night had owned another tally house further along the dock. On the night, she had thought the gest had been successful, and she had not foreseen this night's complication. Her training had taught her it served no purpose to dwell on a gest, but despite that, she brooded on it and struggled to pry a bothersome thought from the depths of her mind as she wended her way back to the Guild building.

The two men's friendship may have been fortuitous, but the comment about the arguments tied them together in a more sinister way, and she wondered how many more of her victims might be connected to one another, not random folk who had angered a competitor or been discovered in a dalliance with a powerful man's wife. Everybody Arella had killed at Styrrach's behest had been the owner of a prominent business, often among the largest and most successful in its field. What had her mark meant when he said his friend had been killed after he had argued about "his share?" She pushed the thought away from her mind. What did it matter, after all else? The Guild had her trapped, and she must kill or be killed. The dead posed no threat to her, but those who ordered her to kill them did, and they would not hesitate to take her life if she questioned them.

Back at the Guild building, she reported her success to Styrrach, cleaned her blade with a piece of cloth until it gleamed, then climbed the stairs and lay on a cot, her mind a whirl of thoughts. She woke often and rose from the cot in the morning tired and with no answers to any of her questions. Although the sun had not long risen, she returned to The Ship's Yard, tumbled into their bed, and used Corelle's body to drive the tangled thoughts from her mind.

Corelle woke in surprise when Arella entered the room and slid into their bed at such an early hour, but her lover's fingers soon dispelled any complaints. She moaned as familiar sensations of bliss surged through her body, but when they lay together afterward, Arella appeared distracted. Corelle pressed her until Arella said her target had recognised her from a previous gest. Corelle pursed her lips. "You will always be at risk of this. There are more men. Are there no other women?"

"None but me."

Corelle propped herself up on an elbow. "Then you would be easier to remember. You are the only woman, and a beautiful one, difficult to forget." Corelle stroked Arella's hair, but the older woman said nothing, stared at the ceiling, and chewed at the inside of her cheek. Corelle nuzzled at Arella's neck. "My love, this coincidence bothers you?"

Arella turned her head to stare at Corelle. "That it does. It exposes me to risk. What if my mark had drawn his conclusion days or passes earlier, and at the moment he saw me, he knew my purpose? I might be the one killed, not him."

"You must raise this with that Stirrup fellow."

Arella's laughter clashed with the sombre mood between them. "It is Styrrach." Corelle aimed a playful slap at her but missed, and Arella continued. "I cannot raise it. He would see it as criticism."

She closed her eyes, and her body shook for a moment. "I cannot take that risk."

"Then—"

Arella raised a finger to Corelle's lips. "Let us speak no more of it today. We should go for a walk. The fresh air may clear my head."

Over the following days, Corelle could not shake the exchange from her thoughts, afraid Arella would be placed in danger because there were no other women in the Guild. She could not recall whether Arella had ever mentioned how many members the Guild had overall, but more women members would reduce the risk of recognition in future gests. Most women, however, would not wish to undertake such terrible work.

Her father had often said, *"If you will not lead, others will not follow."* He used it as an excuse whenever her mother urged him to work less and leave more of the making to her and Corelle. If Corelle wished for more women to join the Guild, then in accordance with her father's words, she herself must join, rather than leave it to others. She could not do so, of course. Her mind strove to imagine what it must be like to stab a knife into a person and see them fall dead at her feet. Corelle could not kill.

That thought irritated her more and more over the next days. In truth, women could do it, and more. Every pass, women bled and lived through days of discomfort and pain. Corelle thought of childbirth and shuddered in horror. She knew the size of both her own and Arella's intimate regions and could not imagine how a baby could come from such a small place without almost unbearable agony. After all else, how many women would not kill to protect their baby if danger threatened it after all they had endured to birth it?

She pondered the idea for days, strove to convince herself she could take another's life. Each time she rejected the notion, her father's words returned to remind her of her weakness. Her own thoughts also plagued her. *"If Arella can do it, why can you not? Are you different because you were raised by a family, and she became a street urchin? Have you not already become a killer, after all else? You tolerate Arella's work without complaint. You are complicit in some way in all the ruin Arella has wrought."*

Arella's safety mattered to Corelle more than anything else. She could not imagine life without Arella, and if a gest went awry and Arella died, Corelle would be lost. She visualised a scenario where Arella slid from the shadows, and a knife slid into her heart. Corelle clenched her teeth together and balled her hands into fists. She would kill anybody who harmed Arella. At that thought, she turned to a reflecting glass in shock and realised she had admitted she would kill to avenge Arella.

"That would be a crime of passion," she told herself. It would be different to kill in cold blood for nothing more than coin. The arguments went on in her mind. Her father's words, her guilt that she approved of others who killed but would not do so herself, her anxiety for Arella's safety; these matters strove against her conviction that she could not kill.

After days of consideration, she had come close to madness from the inner turmoil, and she needed to arrive at a conclusion, must decide. Only one decision could bring her relief without the destruction of her sense of self-worth. As she sewed a new tunic by the small window in their room, she blurted out, "I will join the Guild."

From the bed, Arella replied with a derisive laugh. "That you will not. You are a garment maker, and that is how you should earn your fortune."

"Fortune? Is that what they pay you? I have yet to see my share of this fortune." Corelle gestured around at their humble surroundings and returned her attention to her work.

"You will not join." Arella's tone grew stern, and she sat up. "I will not hear this talk again. Bad enough I do this awful thing. You need not be drawn into it as well."

Corelle insisted. "It would be safer for you. The more women there are, the less each would stand out in people's memories. Even a woman as beautiful as you."

A smile played on Arella's lips, but she seemed reluctant to allow it to develop. "That is nonsense. Even if you join, there would be no more than the two of us. The risk would not be reduced by any substantial amount."

"It would be reduced, however. How many members are there in total?"

Arella frowned. "I do not know how many altogether across Dur. There are four other members here in Zhanghar, plus me, Styrrach, and Porl."

"I have not heard you mention this Porl."

"He is Styrrach's Senior Aide." Arella shrugged as if the diversion into the explanation about Porl irritated her. "Do not change the subject. You will not join."

"Four men and one woman. With four men and two women, you would be safer. You know I have the right of it."

"That I do not. Cease this. I will not talk of it further." Arella stood with her hands on her hips for emphasis; the conversation had ended.

The conversation had not ended. Corelle continued to pick at it over the following days. Her parents had often told her that she had a stubborn streak as wide as the River Alc, and that stubborn streak showed itself as she harped about her suggestion day after day. Arella tried to dissuade her and spoke of the danger, of the rigours of the gests, of how Corelle would find no release from the grip of the Guild once they had her in their talons. She talked of the brutal initiation rite, and her own heartbreak to think of Corelle subjected to it. Above all else, she talked of the horror of the moment when a life ended before her eyes and at her hand, all the guilt and self-hatred she felt each time she witnessed somebody's last breath. Corelle rejected all her objections. She had decided, and her stubborn streak left no room for a change of mind.

Corelle's conviction that there could be no better solution grew, and her persistence wore Arella down over a tenday until at last she agreed to speak to Styrrach about the proposal, though she maintained she did so against her better judgement. They both agreed Arella should cast Corelle as a friend. Styrrach might not approve of their relationship, and Arella had no desire to test the theory.

Even after she had agreed, Arella procrastinated for four more days, and seemed to find a new excuse every day to delay further. In the end, her resistance crumbled in the face of Corelle's insistence, and Corelle met with Styrrach and Porl in the Guild building. They appeared impressed by her and pressed her about the motivations behind her desire to join them. She stood by her story that her friend's safety concerned her, a story so close to the truth, she did not believe she would be caught in a lie. They made a strange pair; Styrrach thin and wiry with an air of menace that unsettled her, Porl gaunt, with a demeanour that led Corelle to distrust him from the outset. They did not dress their words in deception as they laid out their expectations of any who joined them, but they did not respond to her question about who their customers were.

That evening, Corelle asked Arella her opinion on whether Styrrach and Porl would allow her to join. Arella nodded, a glum expression on her face. "You have met them and know the location of the Guild building. You face one of two outcomes now—you join, or you die. You have set in motion matters that cannot now be arrested. I tried to warn you."

Corelle poked out a tongue at her, then laughed to show she felt no fear. "Sorehead. It will be fine. Trust me." She hoped she had the right of it.

Three days later, a man came to the door and summoned them both to the Guild building where Porl told them he and Styrrach had agreed to induct Corelle into the Guild. She would receive training from another member, and Porl forbade Arella to interfere in her training—any failure must not be overlooked for the sake of friendship. His stern, testy demeanour seemed to intimidate Arella, to Corelle's surprise. She had never seen Arella seem so nervous, nor as anxious to leave anywhere as that day.

Porl told Corelle the initiation to the Guild involved severe violence. She could ask for it to stop at any point, and she would be free to leave but must never tell anybody about the Guild. Once back in their room, Arella begged her not to believe him. The ritual could not be stopped without ruinous consequences.

Corelle pressed her to explain, and with a tight-lipped sigh, Arella told her she had endured the same initiation when she had first joined the Guild. She could imagine no punishment more violent, and though she had considered a plea for it to end, she had persevered. Around a tenday later, before she had been assigned a gest, Pilos summoned her to the Guild building where she learned she would take part in the initiation ritual of another applicant.

Arella grimaced as she spoke of her disgust at the blows she had rained down on the naked man. They had been nothing compared to the violence the other men had meted out on the applicant, and he had broken. He had cried out for it to stop, and Styrrach had snapped his fingers in the air. The man had cried, and Styrrach told him to put his clothes on, sympathetic, or so it seemed, then pressed a dagger into Arella's hand as he whispered in her ear, "Kill him." When she protested that the man had been promised he could end the ritual without consequence, Styrrach had screamed at her. "Kill him."

Arella paused and rubbed at her face. "I can still feel his spit on my face." She spoke in a quiet voice, cowed by Styrrach's menace even though he could not hear her. "The man stared at me aghast, pleaded with me. 'You said I could leave.' Styrrach answered, even though the fellow had spoken to me. 'That you can.' His voice,

Corelle. So cold. It frightened me more than it did that poor man, I am certain. They dragged him out to the street and insisted I kill him. I stabbed him over and over until he lay dead at my feet." Tears trickled down her face.

Corelle took her hand and stroked the back of it. "Do not blame yourself. I guess they would have killed you both had you not followed their instructions."

Arella sobbed and shook her head. "Do not ask them to stop, I beg you. I do not know how I will bring myself to strike you, but they will insist, I am certain of it."

Corelle jested in an effort to lighten the mood. "If you hurt me, you will not touch me in our bed for a pass." She feared the ritual but would not admit it. At first, she had believed Arella over-exaggerated it in her attempts to dissuade Corelle, but Porl had confirmed it, and it frightened her. Such violence might kill her, but she hoped it would not go that far. Her short, frail body had been unused to violence of any kind. In the days that led up to the ritual, she tried to anticipate the pain and humiliation in the hope she might be better prepared for the ordeal to come.

She had not been prepared, not by some margin. Despite the efforts of Arella, she endured a brutal assault. Styrrach ordered no blows be delivered to her face. Doubtless he recognised the value of a pretty face. What man would not invite death into his home when it came in a package as attractive as either Corelle or Arella? Six men and Arella watched as Corelle removed her clothes, and the men leered at her and whispered to one another. When Porl ordered them to begin, one of the men punched her in the stomach without warning. Her breath whooshed out of her, and she almost fetched up. Styrrach and Porl did not beat her, but they watched on expressionless while their members punched, kicked, and bit her as each blow piled agony upon agony until she could stand it no longer. Arella's words burned in her mind. The ritual could not be stopped without ruinous consequences.

Corelle gritted her teeth and endured, although her body screamed at her that it could take no more. Tears ran from her eyes, and she collapsed to the floor, but they showed her no mercy. The blows continued to rain down on her.

Styrrach cried aloud at last. "Enough." The blows ceased. Corelle lay on the floor, destroyed in mind and body. Though her face remained untouched, her arms bled, and she feared to look at any other part of her body. Somebody had tugged at her bush without mercy, and another had punched her in her sex. They had broken her, and she lay on the floor and sobbed, tragic and pathetic. "Step back." Styrrach knelt before her, scorn on his face. He leaned close to her ear, and his whispered words chilled the blood in her veins. "Guild justice would be worse. You belong now. You will always belong."

Two men picked Corelle up and dumped her into a chair. Arella helped her dress again, though one of her arms hurt so much she could not move it. Tears ran from Arella's eyes as she sat on the floor and looked at Corelle's battered body. "You fool."

When Corelle felt able to move, they struggled back to their room. Although her face had not been marked, the initiation had left Corelle's body bruised and battered, and she could not leave the bed for some days afterward. Every breath brought her agony, and she suspected the violence might have broken a rib or two. Her arms, legs, and entire body were covered by cuts and dark, grotesque bruises. Arella fussed over her without cease and gave her herbs to ease the pain.

After some days, Corelle pulled herself out of the bed and hobbled to a chair. She groaned with every step. "By the fates, I ache."

Arella's sad eyes empathised. "I am aware of how much you ache, believe me. I warned you, but you are stubborn."

"That I am. Curse me for it. But I endure it for you. I hope you will be safer now. With luck, there will be no repeats of incidents such as the one you described to me." Arella's eyes turned blank, and she seemed to stare at something far beyond the walls of their room. Concerned, Corelle asked, "What is it? What is wrong?"

Arella pursed her lips and exhaled. "That time—the one you mention. He said his friend had been killed after an argument over his share. It puzzled me then, and now it comes back to me. What did he mean?"

Corelle thought for a moment. "Share of what?"

"What indeed? The man implied he had become involved in a similar argument, then I think he realised I had come to kill him, as I killed his friend."

"Is it the share of the levy they must pay?" Corelle could think of no explanation. Her body screamed with agony, and if it were not for Arella's anxiety about the matter, she would have been content to drop the subject.

"Nobody would refuse to pay the levy, would they?"

"Rylfolk would not refuse. I cannot speak for Zhanghar. Would they be killed if they refused to pay the levy, after all else?"

Corelle shifted in the chair, winced as pain shot through her, and Arella knelt at her feet as she spoke, her voice soft. "You are in agony, you poor fool. You should return to bed." Arella's concerned expression soon gave way to one of concentration. "To suggest that somebody would refuse to pay the levy seems..." A suitable word seemed to elude her. "After all else, the levy is paid to the Portreeve. Our gests come from business rivals or jealous husbands or..." She paused and stared into Corelle's eyes. "Do they not?" Arella frowned.

Corelle had no suitable answer. "I have yet to be assigned a gest. I cannot say where they come from." She took Arella's hand. "Put these thoughts away. I have been in bed for days, but now I wish to return there, though not alone." She pulled Arella toward her and kissed her. "Help me to the bed. I ache for you in ways that have nothing to do with my injuries."

Corelle's recovery progressed, aided by herbs and occasional visits from a healer Styrrach arranged for her. After a further seven-day, she felt well enough to begin her training. Before she began, they rented a smaller second room at the tavern. Arella, desperate to keep their relationship secret from Styrrach, thought it would attract less attention if the Guild believed they lived in separate rooms. Now they would both earn coin for their dreadful work, they felt they could afford the additional cost of the small room. The innkeep charged a pittance for the rooms and appeared to have some sort of arrangement with the Guild, and the women were wise enough not to question it.

At first, Corelle's assigned mentor bored her with tales of how the Guild worked; how they often used couriers to gather intelligence on targets or carry letters and coin. A courier would sometimes place a weapon in a convenient location ahead of the gest if the Guild member might find it difficult to carry it on their person ahead of the kill. He emphasised that Styrrach or Porl alone assigned the gests, and they were intolerant of failure.

Stalbarn, her mentor, taught her how to follow a mark, unseen, and how to detect any who followed her. He walked her around the city for days as she tried to spot him, and she practised the techniques that would expose him when he followed her. Despite his skill in both aspects of pursuit, she soon became better than him. She developed her own improvements to the methods he taught her, and more than once he slapped her face when she confronted him after she spotted his attempts to be discreet. He did not take well to a woman whose skill exceeded his own.

He called an end to the surveillance training after she outwitted him one final time. Corelle returned to the Guild building as arranged, with Stalbarn nowhere to be seen. Styrrach and Porl stood in the parlour with grins on their faces for almost an hour as she sat in a chair until Stalbarn returned, flustered. His face turned deep crimson as he endured the mockery of the Guildmeister and his Senior Aide.

Stalbarn taught her the vulnerable areas of the body, how to make a quick kill, and how to strike with minimal risk of detection. "Walk away at a steady pace and never run. A person who runs attracts attention as decay draws flies." He taught her how to focus on a mark and remain aware of her surroundings at the same time. "Never panic. No complication is irredeemable." Stalbarn told her this over and over. She trained hard and believed his rebukes owed more to jealousy than any error on her part.

Wilash visited her and Arella from time to time. Corelle liked him, and the three of them became good friends. He passed no judgement on their love for each other even as he urged them to be careful and, above all, not to allow Styrrach to discover it. Wilash seemed a kind man, as Arella had implied in Ryl, but a bitterness dwelled in him.

Wilash told Corelle he had joined the Guild in the belief he would be tasked with the creation of weapons of superior quality but had been put to work in the transport of letters and such. At whiles, he carried out intelligence tasks, when he would watch a mark for a time and discover their habits and routines. A different member of the Guild would always be assigned the gest, and Corelle thought he must despise Styrrach, since he never said a good word about the Guildmeister.

He had been ordered into a humble job in the Portreeve's Offices where Styrrach told him to keep an eye on the Portreeve and report on who visited him, where he went, what orders he sent out and other trivial titbits. Wilash hated it, but he endured it rather than the Guild justice that would be the alternative if he argued with Styrrach.

Wilash made no secret of his disappointment when he learned Corelle had joined the Guild. "You are a sweet girl, Corelle. What moved you to undertake this hideous work? It will destroy you in the end. Such a waste of a life that could have achieved so much." His words embarrassed her, and to distract him from his unhappiness, she asked him to make a weapon for her, one of her own design. She requested a razor-sharp blade, concealed in one guard of a folded fan. When she pressed a button concealed in a rivet at the bottom of the fan, it sprang a hinge that released the blade from the guard. Because of the release mechanism, the fan would not open in any functional sense, but Corelle favoured the concept over a traditional weapon. A woman with a fan would never look out of place, as most wealthy women carried them all year round as fashion items, and many more women used them to cool themselves, more so in warmer weather.

At last, Porl called her into the Guild building by courier. The time had come to prove her worth. Stalbarn would follow her and would intervene if she failed or felt she needed assistance. Porl ordered her to conduct her own intelligence without the aid of a courier for this, her first gest. The owner of a tavern close to the docks would be her mark. She watched the tavern for four nights, and each night she changed something about her appearance so she would not attract unwelcome attention. Whenever her target came out of the tavern, her heart leapt in her breast, her throat became as dry as sand, and she shook with anxiety.

Corelle had never stared abject failure in the face before. If her making went awry in her father's shop, she could unpick it and begin again. If things went awry here, her life might end—either at the hands of the mark or the Guild. She could no longer hide from her casual belief she could kill, and it weighed on her mind. She feared for her life for the first time ever.

The mark travelled to a local house most nights. He left the tavern an hour or so after the sundown, walked through a local alleyway to the house, and entered through the front door. Corelle imagined he attended some dalliance in the house.

After five nights, the night turned cloudy with little moonlight, and she judged it the ideal night to strike. Her heart beat so fast, she felt certain he would hear it inside the tavern. She gazed into a shop window and studied the reflection of the tavern across the street until the tavern door opened, and her mark set off on his usual route. She followed him from across the street and blended into the shadows so he would not see her. Nerves frayed, her body shook with anxiety as she pursued him through the alleyway, twenty paces behind him and unseen, like a shadow that has become detached from its caster. She watched from the mouth of the alleyway as he entered the house.

She had already decided to take him on the return journey. The workers in his tavern would note his lateness, but they would think he had extended his dalliance, or so Corelle hoped as she crouched in the darkness halfway down the alleyway. She noticed Stalbarn straight away, and his lack of subtlety on such an important night irritated her. Her mentor waited at the tavern end of the alleyway, positioned to kill the mark if she failed.

Sweat beaded on her forehead despite the cool evening, and her mouth had become so dry, it felt as though her tongue had cleaved to its roof. She clutched her fan in a clammy hand and wished she had asked Wilash to ensure she could open it so she might waft cool air across her overheated skin. She waved it before her face, nonetheless, grateful for any small relief from the fire that consumed her.

After she had waited for an hour, nervous, the mark returned to the alleyway. Corelle pressed a sweaty finger on the button of the fan, and the blade sprang out with a small metallic sound. She let out a long, slow breath and strove to calm her rapid heartbeat. He may have heard the breath, because he slowed and looked behind, then carried on. The moment had come, and she stepped out in front of him. The sound of her blood as it rushed past her ears deafened her, and she felt faint. Without hesitation, she raised the fan and struck, afraid she would collapse from fright at any moment.

A slash across the throat, a fast way to end the life somebody's coin had bought. The slash would almost always sever at least one of the important vessels that carried the vital blood to and from the brain, the victim would lose consciousness within a few heartbeats, and death would follow in short order.

A gash appeared, a vermilion ribbon across the man's neck that followed her blade. A stream of blood pulsed from one side of his neck where the blade had done its lethal work, and it sprayed onto her face. The warm blood had a coppery smell that disgusted her.

The mark clutched at his throat as if he might somehow mend the damage Corelle had wrought, but he fell to the floor as his life blood pumped out of him, and his brain shut down, denied the air it craved. With no thought for the blood that now coated it, Corelle folded the blade back into the fan and set off for another alleyway across the street ahead of her. She longed to enter it and be away from inquisitive eyes that might wonder at the blood that covered her. Halfway down the other alleyway, she stopped to wipe at her face with the sleeve of her tunic.

The full impact of what she had done shocked her. Her nerves, the revulsion that had come upon her as his life ended, the blood that had pumped out of him; it all overwhelmed her. She fetched up, and tears streamed down her face. Her first gest had been completed, and it appalled her. What had she done? Why had she agreed to this dread life?

Stalbarn appeared from the shadows. "It is done." He handed her a small cloth. "Attend to yourself. You must not draw attention to yourself as you return. Carry such a cloth with you in the future."

Corelle hated him for the contempt she heard in his voice, but to strike him would bring her ruin. "My thanks." She imagined she sounded meek in the face of her shame and the threat of Guild justice as she wiped at her face with the cloth.

"You made a clean kill. You performed well." Corelle had not expected his praise, and she felt the heat in her cheeks as he turned and left. She leaned back against the wall and waited for her rapid breaths to slow and her heart to cease its relentless attempt to burst from her breast. She fetched up once more, then pulled herself together and tried to remain calm as she walked back to the Guild building to report her success to Styrrach.

The volume of blood that had come out of the man shocked her, and she scrubbed at her fan with a wet cloth for around half of an hour until she had cleaned it to her satisfaction, then climbed the stairs to spend the night on a mattress at the Guild building as arranged with Arella. She struggled to sleep and wondered how Arella had coped with this life for so long. Corelle must not discuss that with Arella, lest it shatter the last vestige of her confidence she could kill again. If she refused to do so, her own life would be forfeit.

Two of the other members climbed the stairs during the night to sleep in cots next to her. The stairs creaked as each of them climbed the rickety staircase, a loud, wretched sound, and Corelle wondered how any of them had been able to tolerate it over the years. The next morning, crushed by guilt and shame, she decided to repair the staircase rather than return to the inn and face Arella.

Corelle could find no tools in the house, so she resorted to her boot heel in the absence of a hammer. She had no skills in this type of work, and she grunted and perspired as she pounded at a nail that protruded from the first tread of the stairs. Porl ran from Styrrach's office at the sound, his face as black as a burnt log. He yelled at her. "What in the Five Cities are you about?"

"I fix this stair—" His hand lashed out, slapped her cheek, and her head shot to one side under the blow.

He stared at her with venomous eyes that burned into her own. "Leave it, you fool. How else do we hear feet in the night if our enemies come for us as we sleep?"

Corelle blinked several times, and her throat constricted as she fought off tears. What enemies could these men have? The Portreeve, perchance. Nobody else would dare attack these violent, vicious men. "My apologies." She could not meet his eyes, dejected and ashamed.

As she trudged back to the inn, she wondered where he had come from. He might have arrived early or slept in Styrrach's office. He had not been in the cots; she knew that for certain. Both men had slumbered on as she had risen.

Arella rose from a chair as Corelle entered the room above The Ship's Yard. With a look of compassion, she ran to the younger woman and swept her into her arms. Arella held her tight as all Corelle's shame, anguish, and fear poured from her in salty tears that soaked into Arella's tunic.

Over time, Corelle grew detached from the marks and the death. Her targets became nothing but lives to snatch away. She did not wonder why they needed to die; she stole their tomorrows in exchange for the coin Styrrach paid her and gave it no further thought. If any shadow of doubt or shame tried to enter her mind, she pushed it away. She refused to dwell on how she did what she did; no answers would serve, and she told herself if she ever hesitated, she would die. Although the other members seemed not to warm to her, she believed Styrrach and Porl held her in high regard. Popularity did not concern her; she had little enough time for the other members, in truth. A change had come over her. The innocent, carefree girl who had first propositioned Arella had disappeared, and a woman cold, merciless, and detached had replaced her. Despite her efforts to maintain a lighter mood with Arella, much had changed between them since she had joined the Guild, and little of it for the good.

FOUR
WRETCHED CHOICES

Styrrach ran the Guild across Dur with a fist of iron. Any who did not follow his orders did not live long enough to disobey him a second time. The Guild operated in four cities, each city managed by a Guildmeister and a Senior Aide, all answerable to Styrrach. Seven men plus Styrrach, and none but those seven belonged to his inner sanctum. They benefitted financially from his patronage, but they were dispensable, commodities that could be traded and replaced as necessary.

Of the three other Guildmeisters, Styrrach only respected Krage, who had been with him from the first day. By rights, he ought to be Senior Aide in Zhanghar, or Guildmeister in Alcmouth, the largest city by far, and the capital, but Krage had been born in Ryl. He loved the little city for reasons Styrrach could not understand, and he preferred to remain as Guildmeister there with two or three members. Although his operation had begun in Ryl, Styrrach despised the place, full of arrogant rich people and low-born Durfolk who had no ambition and less intelligence.

He had not seen Krage for many years but had sent letters that ordered him to come to Zhanghar. Styrrach wished to discuss some issues with his oldest servant, but he also desired to see the man and reminisce about things they alone knew of; the days when they had started the Guild, the large ambitions they had both believed in and had developed together until the reality now exceeded even their expectations. Porl had been loyal and dependable, but he had not been there in those first days.

When Krage arrived, Styrrach greeted him like a long-lost brother. They sat in the office and talked for hours. Styrrach had always been a focused man, and they discussed the business matters that had brought Krage to Zhanghar first, the expansionist plans Styrrach had for Ort, the town on the Alc he now cast his jealous eyes toward.

They talked about the old days and laughed as they reminded each other of gests from those early times, and about women they had used and abused. Krage wore a lecherous look on his face. "On the subject of women, thank you for the loan of Arella. In truth, it disappointed me that you recalled her when you did, for I intended to make her mine."

"You were enamoured of her, then?"

"I still am, in truth. I would be delighted to cure her of her deviance." His salacious laughter rang through the office.

Styrrach leaned forward, his smile gone. "Deviance?"

"She is a deviant. She lies with women. Do you not know this?"

Styrrach did not, and he spat his contempt out in terse words. "I would have fed her piece by piece to somebody's dog, had I known. Such behaviour disgusts me."

Krage's smile and laughter had been chased away by Styrrach's reaction. "I intended to cure her deviancy, but you recalled her before I could do so."

Styrrach's revulsion twisted his stomach. "How do you know this about her?"

"I saw them with my own eyes. I noticed them one evening as they walked together, Arella and some other, short, with long brown hair, and I followed them. Their hands touched often, and they entered a house together. I saw them kiss before they closed the shutters."

Styrrach could not believe his ears. "Short, brown hair? Arella introduced such a woman to the Guild. We took her in around ten passes ago."

"Kill her then. Do not hesitate."

"She is excellent. Corelle, the other. She is my best killer." It infuriated Styrrach that Arella and Corelle had misled him, despite Corelle's unquestionable ability. Friends, Arella had said. Friends, indeed. Arella must be taught a lesson, one she would never forget, and Styrrach never wasted time once he had made up his mind. He called for Porl and ordered him to send for Arella without delay.

Krage seemed disappointed. "You will kill her? What of the other?"

Styrrach had a different plan for the deceitful jade who had brought deviancy into his Guild. "I will not kill Arella, not today. You desire her, and you will have her."

Krage licked his lips, and they waited close to an hour before Arella entered the office. She froze as she did so, her eyes fixed on Krage.

Styrrach waved a hand toward Krage. "You know one another?"

Arella's voice remained calm. "That I do. You sent me to Ryl to work for him."

"He sent back high praise for your work." She smiled, but Styrrach intended to wipe the smile from her face. "Now, he brings more details from your time in Ryl." Arella's smile froze in place.

The Guildmeister had to admire her stoicism. "Corelle, your friend."

"What of her?"

Styrrach dispensed with further niceties. Words could torment, but he wanted to debase Arella for her deception and her deviancy. "Krage will take you now, here on the floor, and you will know what it is like to be mounted by a man."

Arella gave a nervous laugh. "You jest."

"Lie down, or Corelle will die." Styrrach's simple reply contained so much nuance, and he thought it delightful to be alive at that moment. She did not move, but her face dissolved into abject terror. He screamed at her. "Lie down."

She flinched as he roared the command. "Do not hurt Corelle. Please."

Styrrach waved a dismissive hand at her. "I am sure you imagine you love her, but you are deviants. Krage will teach you the intended ways of sex."

Krage had already unbuttoned his trousers, and Styrrach regretted that he glanced at his old friend, whose manhood stood stiff and proud, ready to skewer the deviant.

Arella whispered as she sat on the floor. "Do not hurt her, I beg you. I will do this if you promise not to hurt her."

Styrrach laughed. "You will do this because I tell you to. I will kill her if you do not. I make no further promises, but you should do all you can to please my friend." Arella slid her trousers down her legs, kicked one foot out of them, and Krage fell on her with glee. Arella stared at the ceiling, motionless and silent as Krage's rear end humped up and down for a short time. He cried out in release and pulled out of Arella, a triumphant expression on his face.

Krage's performance disappointed Styrrach. It had been too short. He would have called all the members in from the parlour, but that might destroy the harmony between the women and the men, which could damage his business. His business came first, even over revenge. He snapped a command at Arella. "Leave us." Tears streamed down her cheeks as she pulled her trousers on and left the office, her dignity in shreds.

Krage returned to Ryl, and Styrrach assigned any gests that arose to the men as he stewed on the women's deception for the next two passes. He came to a decision at last when a rumour came to his ears that fascinated him. He called Porl into his office. "Shroud Corelle." Styrrach turned his attention back to his journals.

A year had passed since Corelle had joined the Guild, and it had so changed her, she could no longer find peace. She glanced around non-stop and could no longer walk the streets without some evasive manoeuvre designed to reveal any who might follow her. Above all else, she feared the Portreeve's men. Not long after her first gest, the Portreeve had caught Stalbarn and hanged him in the square. Nobody knew how he had been apprehended, and when she asked Porl, he snarled at her to be about her business.

A new member had been recruited, and Corelle and Arella were ordered to participate in his induction ritual. Corelle remained detached from his cries of pain and treated it as nothing more than another gest. The feverish blows of some of the other members shocked her, but the man endured it.

As another summer brought its welcome warmth to Zhanghar, there had been no gests for either Corelle or Arella for at least two passes, and they enjoyed simple walks around the city and basked in the warmth of the sun before the wet season arrived with its grey skies and incessant rain. Arella had become despondent during those two passes but would not say why, no matter how often Corelle asked. They found a stall at a nearby market that sold delicious, sweet buns with a creamy centre. They liked to break their fast with one or two of the buns, and they wandered the marketplace as they ate them. On such a day, Corelle noticed a tall, dark-haired woman who picked, disinterested, over some trinkets on a stall. A lostness radiated from the woman, a hopelessness that resonated with Corelle. She felt some affinity with the stranger she could not explain and almost longed to approach the woman and ask what gave her such an air of dejection.

Corelle turned to point out the woman to Arella, but her lover already stared at the stranger, the half-eaten bun forgotten at her side. Corelle placed a gentle hand on Arella's arm. "What is wrong?"

Arella shook her head as though to dispel whatever thought had pestered her. "Nothing. That woman is like us, that is all. It is unusual to see another."

Corelle looked at the woman again but saw nothing remarkable about her. "How do you know she is like us?"

Arella smiled. "I just know, little one, I just know."

Corelle frowned. "'Little one?' That is a horrible phrase. I despise it. Do not call me that."

A curious expression flashed across Arella's face, but she smiled it away. "It is a term of affection, nothing more, but if it offends you, I shall say it no more."

Corelle studied the other again. "How do you know she is like us?" She longed to discover the tale behind Arella's words. "Do not say again that you just know, or I will leave you forever. You claimed you did not 'just know' when we first met, and that story will not suffice today."

Arella turned to face her, and the look returned to her face. Sadness, doubtless, but more. Loss, or grief? She smiled it away once more. "Because I have lain with her."

Corelle had never considered that Arella might have lain with others before her. Her practiced touch on that first night ought to have suggested there had been others before Corelle, but it had never occurred to her until now. She could not decide how she felt about it and searched for something non-committal to say. "Oh? How does she perform in bed?"

Arella gave an immodest laugh. "She is good. Her tongue—ah, such a tongue that one has."

"As good as my tongue?"

"Better." Arella repeated the suggestive laugh.

Some women might feel jealousy at the comment, but Corelle did not believe Arella had intended to taunt her, so she laughed at the jest. She turned and sought out the tall woman, who snapped upright and stared around as if she somehow sensed they watched her, then strode away, purposeful. Corelle watched the dark-haired stranger approach the stables beyond the market. "What is her name?"

Arella remained silent with her arms folded as she watched the woman vanish from their sight. Then, her eyes still focused on the spot where the woman had disappeared, she answered. "Deineike."

As they lay in bed that night, Corelle could not shake the incident from her mind, and she badgered Arella to tell her all she could recall of the woman they had seen in the market. Arella told Corelle a tragic story; how Deineike's mother had been murdered and the vow of vengeance she had sworn, how they had been lovers at the time Arella had joined the Guild, how she had abandoned Deineike to protect her from its terrible nature. Arella sniffed back tears as she bemoaned the fact she had been powerless to protect Corelle from that same taint.

Deineike's story touched Corelle even though her time in the Guild had all but eroded her compassion. To have a mother taken from her as Deineike had would be unthinkable, and doubtless that loss had deepened when Arella shunned her in favour of the Guild.

Little wonder the woman had seemed so broken as they gazed on her in the market. It shamed Corelle to have turned into the monster she had become. "Did you love her?"

Arella remained silent for ten heartbeats or more. "That I did, after a fashion. She was young and a burden, with little motivation to care for herself, and she needed me. She loved me and said so constantly, though I never said it to her, despite how much I liked her. She needed me..." Arella's voice trailed off, her face unreadable. "What I did to her cannot be forgiven." A tear ran down one cheek.

Corelle wrapped Arella in her arms. "Do not blame yourself for fates that cannot be unwritten. She has survived all these years." Arella cried, and Corelle held her until the older woman fell asleep. Corelle lay awake for a long time and listened to Arella's soft, rhythmical breaths. She thought again of the happy, untroubled girl she had been when she first met Arella, and she regretted her decision to join the Guild. There had been mistakes in her life, but until now, none would have cost her life to undo.

Corelle had grown tired of the gests and locked deep within herself any desire to question why those she killed deserved to die. To dwell on it would have driven her to madness. She had forever changed the love that existed between her and Arella, a thought that clawed at her insides and threatened to tear her to shreds. She cried for all she had lost in her young life, and sleep eluded her until deep into the night.

In the morning, Corelle woke unsettled and irritable but could not determine why. She decided to go to the second of their rooms close to the midday and rest, as she guessed her disrupted sleep the night before might be the reason for her mood. Less than an hour later, Arella entered the room and shook her awake.

Drowsy from sleep, Corelle looked up at Arella. "What is it?"

"Pilos is downstairs."

Corelle tried to understand Pilos's visit through the fog of tiredness. "Is there a gest?"

"That there is, for me, and an urgent one. Pilos has intelligence that it must be done tonight, so I shall be gone until morning. He waits for me in the tavernroom."

Corelle's still drowsy mind struggled with the apparent urgency of the gest. She preferred to carry out her own intelligence, unlike all the other members, Arella included, but any member given a gest would take a day or two at the least to study the intelligence, add some of their own. It seemed unusual that this gest must be completed tonight, and Corelle had come to distrust anything she could not control. Something more played on her mind. "He named the gest himself?"

Arella chewed her lip, nervous "That he did. It is unusual, is it not?"

"That it is." Corelle could not connect the threads that wove in her mind. Styrrach or Porl often assigned gests whenever a member called into the Guild building, but if a gest suited a specific member who had not been seen for a day or two, a courier would be sent to summon them to the Guild building. The courier would not know why the member had been summoned, so it seemed irregular for Pilos to know this urgent gest had been assigned to Arella.

Gests were planned in meticulous detail, and urgency had never been a factor in any gest Corelle knew of before now. It alarmed her, but she could not determine why. "Take care, my love." She clung to Arella for some time before the older woman pulled away, shrugged, and left.

Styrrach listened with grim satisfaction as Porl confirmed the arrangements that would see Corelle shrouded. "All is in hand. It will be tonight. Pilos has been dispatched to summon Arella. We learned the mark has requested his normal courtesan tonight. A few coins and some hard words bought all the information we sought. Arella will present herself in the courtesan's stead. Pilos will take her to pick a suitable dress on the way here. They should arrive within the hour."

Styrrach hated procrastination. Once he had decided on a course of action, time lost to trivial delays infuriated him. "Curse that buffoon Tarjkay. He has delayed us. This should have been arranged days ago."

Porl snickered. "Nothing happens fast enough for you. He acts at his own pace and has been slow to action in the past. If he no longer suits…" The Senior Aide raised his eyebrows.

Styrrach waved a hand. "That is a conversation for another day. The others?"

"All summoned. There will be no mishaps."

Styrrach nodded again. The night had been well planned, and there should be no mistakes. He sat on the only chair in his office and waited for Arella. Porl stood silent in the room as time passed. At last, the street door opened, and fingers rapped on the office door. Styrrach had always made his office, no more than a room three paces square, the nerve centre of his business and of his menace. Styrrach never invited any who knocked on his door to enter. It gave him great pleasure to send unwelcome visitors away with vicious barbs.

The door opened, and Arella entered, arrayed in a red dress that shimmered in the lantern light. Her face had been painted and her hair arranged to fall in curls around her pretty face. Styrrach could understand Krage's attraction to her. The tight, fitted dress high-lighted the flare of her hips, and the rounded tops of her breasts protruded above the bodice, suggestive and provocative. She would pass as a courtesan, and a high priced one.

Porl gave her the details of the gest, along with a fanciful story about its urgency. Styrrach forgot the tale as soon as it ended. Arella could not meet the gaze of either of them, and Styrrach smiled. It seemed obvious she hated him but feared him too much to act on her hatred, and that pleased him a great deal. In his opinion, nothing inspired loyalty more than fear of the consequences of disloyalty.

Once she left, Styrrach sent Porl into the parlour to pass the time with the members so the Guildmeister could finish some paper-work. It would be two hours or more before Arella reported back, but he had no doubt the mark would be dead before the night ended. Arella had never failed. She could be reckless, but she never failed. Corelle took a different approach. A meticulous planner who would not trust any intelligence but her own, she balanced all her actions to the highest probability of a successful outcome. If she had been a card player, he would not have wagered against her.

Two hours later, the street door opened. He finished the letters he worked on; Arella would not begin her report until he entered the parlour, and she waited on him, not the other way around. He pushed his chair back from the small desk and strode into the parlour. Arella stood with her head down as the others talked or gamed. Some blood had spattered onto the dress, but other than that, nobody would take her to be anything more than her appear-ance suggested. Styrrach placed a finger under her chin and lifted her head until she met his gaze. "Begin."

The mark had been killed, along with a servant who saw her face. Styrrach saw compassion cross her face as she mentioned the servant. He disliked it, but she had killed the man, so he let it pass. He had always made his orders clear; the mark died, but innocents were not harmed. He did not care whether these worthless people lived or died, but he had no desire for his business to attract unwelcome attention because of a murderous spree in the middle of the night. Witnesses were a complication, however, and one best dealt with without delay; they had cost him several members down the years. Painstaking, planned gests should involve no witnesses, but this gest had been something of a convenience, and he reasoned the death of the servant had been unavoidable.

He complimented her, but the street door slammed open and interrupted him. The members all reached for daggers, but relaxed when Wilash entered the parlour, his bright red face doubtless due to exertion rather than heat at this time of night. His breaths were rapid and heavy, and he bent forward from the waist with his hands on his thighs. With obvious difficulty, he gasped out portentous words. "My Guildmeister, the Portreeve mobilises." Styrrach flashed Porl a querulous stare and received a shrug in response as Wilash continued to blurt out his news. "His men leave to take Corelle into custody." A murmur rose from the members, the anger in the room at this news palpable. "She has been betrayed, sold for coin. We must act. She must be taken from the inn and brought somewhere safe, or…" He fell silent, mayhap unable to give voice to the alternative. Cries of assent went up around the room, and the members looked to Styrrach for a decision. All the members except one, the Guildmeister noticed. Arella had already left.

Corelle had not slept since Arella departed. She could not shake off the unusual circumstances of the gest that had been assigned, but try as she might, she could not unpick the doubts that lay on her mind. When darkness came, she climbed into bed, but sleep eluded her. The hour grew late, and someone came through a back door into the silent, darkened inn below. Corelle wondered if Arella had returned for some reason. Had the gest not proceeded, after all else? The visitor crossed the floor without haste, then paused at the foot of the stairs.

Whoever had entered the inn climbed the stairs and stopped again. The lightness of the person's steps suggested a woman, but Corelle did not take chances. Naked, she slipped out of bed, reached under the mattress for her fan, sprang its blade, and crouched in the darkest corner of the room with her eyes fixed on the door. If the person tried to enter the room, they would have little time to identify themselves before she could strike if they posed a threat.

The person moved to the door of the room but did not touch the latch. Instead, they knocked twice, then a pause and twice again, a pre-arranged knock between Corelle and Arella. The door opened, and a figure entered and stepped to one side of the door frame, little more than shadowy movement in the dark room.

"It is Arella."

As the familiar voice relaxed Corelle, she straightened and let out a soft breath. "You did not intend to return tonight. Has it gone awry?"

"Not that. The gest is completed, but there is little time." Arella's shadowy form moved toward Corelle. "The Portreeve's men come. Someone sold you to them tonight. I do not know who, but you are sold, and they come for you."

Corelle found the flint and lit the lantern, bewildered. "Sold how?"

"Betrayed. They are on their way here now."

Corelle's mind tried to unravel the implications of Arella's words. "How do you know this?"

"Wilash brought the news to the Guild soon after I had returned to the Guild building." A momentary sob interrupted Arella's tale. "If the Portreeve's men do not take you, the Guild will. They will not risk your capture now you are known to the Portreeve. You must leave now and head south or west—anywhere but here." She paused before she continued in a softer tone. "My love, I was with Styrrach when Wilash brought this news. He will know I warned you." Corelle froze, as motionless as the night air as Arella went on. "I do not wish Guild justice. You must make it quick."

Corelle tried to ignore the suggestion in Arella's words. "Come with me. We can leave together."

"That we cannot. There would be too much danger if two travelled together. One can hide where two may not. They will seek us both now, for I have betrayed them. I have warned you, and I would not change that. I love you." Her voice dripped sadness into the still of the room. "Corelle, there is no time for debate. You must leave now. We both know what must be done. Farewell."

Arella had implied Corelle should kill her, but the brown-haired woman did not believe she could do so even as Arella pulled her blond curls back from her face and tipped her head backward. Corelle's voice rasped in her throat as her misery grew. "Come with me. Please."

"I cannot. Strike now and be gone."

Long moments passed as Corelle debated her options within herself. Arella had the right of it. The Portreeve and the Guild would both hunt them now, and winter would arrive soon enough. Two women on the road together in winter would doubtless attract attention. The Guild might not have pursued her had she fled alone, but without question they would seek them both now Arella had betrayed them. Desperate, Corelle reached for an alternative. "We could separate and meet up later at some pre-determined place."

Arella's sobs gave her voice a stop-start timbre. "There is...no time to plan...such a venture. If we leave together, we...will be found. If we separate, we may...never meet again. If we are found..."

Corelle wiped at tears, desperate to find an alternative solution. "You must kill me and flee. I cannot do this." She would prefer to die herself rather than kill Arella.

"You know I cannot do that. You asked me in Ryl, and I gave you my answer then. It has not changed. I cannot flee with..." A pause. "My death here will buy you scant time as it is, and you might still not escape. Do not fall into their hands. Do not let me fall into their hands, I beg you." She raised a hand to Corelle's face. "Corelle, they come. Act now, or we shall both die." Arella's hands ran down Corelle's arm until they came to a rest against the open fan. Despite Corelle's resistance, Arella pulled the hand up toward her throat and pressed the blade against her skin. She breathed terrible words, soft as a feather that drifts past a face with the merest of touches. "Do it now."

Corelle had become trapped in a web of thoughts from which there could be no way out. Desperate, she searched for a solution that might free her from what Arella wished her to do, but they had so little time. The longer they waited, the higher the chance they would both die. Neither would have a quick death if the Guild arrived before the Portreeve's men. If the Portreeve's men took them into captivity, they would both be tortured for information, then hanged.

In truth, they could not both live, and Arella would not kill her. Worse, Corelle could not strike, could not kill the woman she loved. Arella must have seen the doubt in Corelle's eyes. She pressed against the back of the blade, and Corelle did not react in time to prevent her.

As the keen edge sliced through Arella's flesh and bit into her throat, Arella released the blade, cried out in agony, and Corelle pulled her fan back, horrified. She breathed Arella's name in desperation as blood poured from the deep wound. Tears fell from Arella's eyes, and she slumped back against the wall. The fan had not found an artery or vein but had carved a terrible gash across the front of Arella's neck, and dark, venal blood flowed from it, soaked into her tunic. Despondent, Corelle whispered Arella's name over and over as she pressed the palm of her free hand against the gash in a vain attempt to stem the flow of Arella's blood.

Such a wound could not be repaired without a chirurgeon, and time was not on their side. Arella's life ebbed away before Corelle's eyes, and her options appeared to be limited—she could stay with Arella as she died and risk capture by the Guild, she could leave Arella behind to die cold and alone as her precious blood gushed from her body, or she could give her a quick end, then flee. All three reeked of cowardice, but Arella's agonised face and eyes pleaded for release. To kill the woman she loved would be an unpardonable crime, but Arella could not live now; she would bleed to death, or the Guild would arrive to find her at death's door and would not hesitate to end her life. The agony of the situation seared through Corelle's mind—she had no choice, after all else. With a strangled cry, she cut into Arella's throat where the vital arteries hid from sight, and lighter, vermilion blood pumped from the new wound to splash, warm, on Corelle's naked body. The fan had found its mark. Arella's eyes glazed over, and she slid down the wall.

Corelle's life no longer had any purpose. She despised herself for what she had done. When she had decided to join the Guild, she told herself she would kill any who harmed her lover. Arella had been killed, and her killer must be brought to justice. She raised the blade to her own throat, then hesitated. While she despised the hideous thing she had become, her fury and hatred did not end at her own doorstep. Other blood must be spilled in payment for Arella's life. Vengeance must be visited on those whose hands had meddled with Arella's fates. Only then could she end her own life.

She vowed to slit her own throat once those who had brought about Arella's ruin had paid the price of their betrayal.

Corelle dressed hurriedly and reached under the mattress to retrieve their coin pouch. As blood pooled around Arella's head, Corelle's feet padded down the stairs toward the back door, out of the inn, and into the night.

FIVE
A SHIP SAILS SOUTH

STYRRACH APPEARED UNCONCERNED BY THE NEWS WILASH BROUGHT before the Guild. "Corelle will hang. That is the risk we all take."

Such a simplistic approach would not suffice, and Wilash said as much. "She will do more than hang." He had noticed Arella slip from the building as he delivered his news. "She will give us all up to the Portreeve. We will all hang ere morning breaks." The others muttered in agreement. Styrrach's face turned from unconcerned to furious, and it seemed to Wilash the fury might be directed at him. Wilash pressed him. "We must act."

Wilash despised himself even as he urged the Guild to kill Corelle, but she could be stubborn and might sell them all to the Portreeve if offered a deal, more so if Arella had told her everything. A sevenday ago, Arella had confided to Wilash all that had turned at the hands of Styrrach and Krage. She had insisted he must not tell Corelle, but she might have poured the story out to her now the women faced such dangers. "We must act. She must be taken before the Portreeve's men arrive." It hurt him to say the words that condemned Corelle, but as much as he liked Arella's lover, he did not wish to be hanged.

A short, wiry man next to Wilash agreed with him. "That she must. She must have Guild justice."

Wilash wheeled on the man. "Corelle has done nothing to warrant Guild justice. She served this Guild well, and that loyalty has earned her a quick, clean death. She must not fall into the Portreeve's hands, or all our necks could be stretched, but if Corelle must die, it should be a painless journey wherever it is she travels to afterward."

Someone shouted, "Wilash speaks the truth," and a chorus of agreement rippled around the room.

Another look of intense annoyance crossed Styrrach's face, and Wilash could not understand why the Guildmeister seemed so angry. His voice bore resentment more than resignation. "So be it. Wilash will lead us to their rooms." He pointed to two others. "You two will come, and Porl. The five of us should suffice." Wilash thought five might not be enough against both Corelle and Arella, and he had no desire to fight them or die under the blade he had crafted for Corelle, but he would not argue with Styrrach.

As Wilash led them toward The Ship's Yard, he fought to hide his disappointment at how things had turned. He introduced Arella to the Guild, and now he guessed she would warn Corelle that the Portreeve moved to capture and hang her. Arella would be marked for Guild justice for that betrayal, though it had been driven by love. He felt responsible for much of the horror of the night. He had been fond of them both, but it seemed certain they would both be dead before the sun rose over the River Alc.

"There will be payment. Corelle must die, but at my hands alone." Styrrach looked down on Arella's corpse, careful to hide his emotions, his hands loose at his side. He raged inside but would not reveal his anger at how the night had turned so awry. "I will reward any who bring me news of her, more so if they bring her to me. But let it be also known that any who slay her in my stead will suffer Guild justice." Styrrach motioned for Wilash and the other two members to wait where they stood while he and Porl stepped out of the room. He lowered his voice so none but his Senior Aide heard him. "This is a sorry turn."

"That it is. We must tread with care here lest all be lost. This night is now gone awry. Wilash's intervention has cast it in shadow."

"He acted as he should. If there is to be blame, it is that the thing has been ill planned."

"You tread too light with him. You always have."

Styrrach shook his head in rejection of Porl's words as he replied. "I cannot blame him for what I brought about. I saved him from his debts because I coveted his smithy skills. He had no potential for our work, and as I grew to distrust the schemes of that sad excuse for a man who holds the office of Portreeve, I saw a use for Wilash. It has served us well to have eyes and ears in the Offices, and we have learned much that has been advantageous to us down the years. Tonight, he did no more than I asked him to. I do not tolerate failure, but I will not hold him to account for this. Rather, I would ask why he was not in the room when you assured me all had been summoned." Styrrach glared at Porl, who could not return his stare.

Porl sighed. "I overlooked Wilash, I confess. I see so little of him..." He paused. "After all else, we must not be caught here. We must save what little remains to be saved."

Styrrach nodded, a grim frown on his face. His Senior Aide had the right of it. It would be an embarrassment to be caught here if the Portreeve's men arrived, and disastrous if they killed any of them. He returned to the room. "The Portreeve's men will not be far behind. Let them not find this." Two men moved forward without a word, bore up Arella's body, and carried it from the room. "We must leave." Styrrach strode from the room, furious. As they passed through the inn's rear door and into the street, Porl gave a quiet cough, and Styrrach turned to Wilash. "Who betrayed her to the Portreeve?" He had almost forgotten to ask the question; he needed to calm himself. Anger brought poor decisions, in his experience.

Wilash's contempt twisted his face into a scowl. "Pilos, the courier. Gold lured his knowledge from him, I fear, and this turn results."

The Guildmeister nodded. "Indeed, it is as you say." His eyes burned into Wilash's own as he continued. "It is an honour gest." Wilash nodded his head in confirmation. Honour gests were rare and could only be issued by the Guildmeister. No coin would be involved, but no other gest carried the prestige of an honour gest, and every Guild member would strive to be the one who completed it. Pilos had but a few hours left to live. Styrrach shook his head, sad beyond words.

Wilash raised his voice, doubtless so the two who carried Arella's body could hear. "The honour gest must be issued when all members are assembled. To do otherwise might give one or another an advantage. They might reach the traitor before others learn of the gest. Pilos has betrayed us. All will want the honour of his ruin."

As the Guild slipped away into the shadows, they heard the Portreeve's men draw near. They were clumsy and noisy, and

Styrrach laughed to himself, for he knew Corelle to be a talented killer who would have heard the Portreeve's men long before they reached her. They might not have taken her at all. The night and all the work involved in its conception had been for naught, and while the honour gest should ensure everything Pilos knew would die with him before the dawn, Styrrach still had other problems to solve.

The Guild members vanished like early morning mist beneath the sun, unseen by the noisy Portreeve's men, but seen by the hidden figure who watched from a vantage point that allowed her to hear some of the conversation. The name Pilos had been mentioned, and there could be little doubt of the context. Corelle moved through the streets like a shadow. She ought to have been on a ship or a horse out of Zhanghar by now. Instead, she had lingered and concealed herself, determined to learn all she could about the events of the night, events that had destroyed her life.

Pilos's involvement confused her. The courier had summoned Arella to the unexpected, urgent gest that night. Had that been part of some deception or a mere coincidence? Answers would be needed before she cut him down.

All Guild members knew where he lived. Nobody could hide secrets from the murderous, clandestine organisation to which Pilos provided his services. Doubtless, he would not be there—he would be hidden, she reasoned, but somebody at the house might know where he cowered, and she fancied they might tell her if she placed them under her blade.

With great caution, Corelle approached the house in which Pilos kept his room. She hid herself across the street from the house to watch for any sign of danger. Wilash had told Styrrach the honour gest must be offered to all Guild members, but Corelle could not fathom how Pilos's wretched act warranted anything less than the Guild justice Arella had been so desperate to avoid. It baffled her.

It also baffled her when she noticed Pilos stroll down the street, to all appearances unconcerned, as though he returned from a night at a tavern. She left her concealment and moved forward through the shadows to step out before him. As she walked, she pressed the button on her fan, and the blade glinted in the moonlight as it sprang out.

He stared at her as though she might be an apparition. "You should be dead. How are you here?"

"I am not dead, but you will be soon enough. You die tonight, by my hand or by that of another Guild member. An honour gest has been called on you. You do not deserve it—"

He interrupted, his eyes wide in alarm. "This is not true. It cannot be. An honour gest? There has been a mistake." He ran the fingers of one hand back and forth across his forehead. "Am I to be killed for what I did, then? Has Styrrach betrayed me?" He appeared confused, and the colour drained from his face.

Corelle could make little sense of his words. "Did Arella's gest form part of your scheme?"

He spluttered. "What? Arella? My scheme? There should have been no confusion. She would not be a part of this and could not be taken. Only you were to be taken. Yet you were not, and instead you stand before me." He gulped. "Are you my ruin?" Corelle's fan gave him his answer.

Corelle turned and walked away before Pilos's body reached the ground, headed for the docks. She had intended to take her own life once she killed Pilos, but his strange words mystified her. Could there be more to the tale than Pilos's simple betrayal? She needed time to reflect, so she fled the scene and took a circuitous route, senses heightened for any sign of pursuit by the Portreeve or the Guild. She saw nothing untoward and crept down to the docks in search of a ship that might be ready to leave. For two hours or more she hid in the shadows on the docks and watched mariners bustle about the ships as they made ready to cast off. The sky had not yet lightened as dawn approached, but the winds and tide were favourable, the ships loaded and ready to depart.

The last mariner walked up the ramp to board the nearest ship, and the dockhand below prepared to pull the ramp clear so the master could direct his vessel out into the water and away. Corelle judged her dash and ran past the surprised dockhand even as the mariner above him pushed the ramp away from the ship. She grunted as she jumped from the ramp at the moment the dockhand below pulled it clear, and she reached the deck. She cleared the rail by the narrowest margin, and she sprawled on the deck, but she had made it aboard.

The ship moved out into the deeper water and picked up pace as the sails filled with the cool wind that blew down the river from the Northern Ocean, and the tide pushed the wooden vessel out into the River Alc.

The mariners on the deck had been stunned when the slight woman had first leapt aboard, but they recovered their composure and surrounded her. One of them snarled, "What do you think you are about?"

Corelle ignored his question. "Where are you bound?"

"Ort, for what business that is of yours, then on to Alcmouth."

"That will suit." It did not matter where the ship took her. She needed a safe place to consider her next move, and Ort would serve as well as any other town or city.

"It will not suit us to carry you there." The master had appeared, doubtless curious about the disturbance on the deck of his vessel.

Corelle turned to face him. "I think it will." She held out a balled fist. When she opened it, the small token lay in the palm of her hand, and the master blanched at the sight of it. Corelle had never used her token before, and the reaction it invoked from the man intrigued her.

He spluttered and seemed unsure of himself but muttered a reply. "We will ready you a cabin."

"My thanks, but that will not be necessary. I will sleep wherever I find myself if sleep comes at all. I have no belongings, and my needs are simple. I need transportation and some refreshment along the way. Beyond that, you need extend me no further hospitality." He nodded once before he turned and walked away.

Corelle needed to sit before she collapsed. The full horror of all that had turned in the small room above The Ship's Yard had not yet sunk in, but despite her best attempts to push it away, the terrible deed filled her mind. She slumped to the deck and leaned back against the rail of the ship as Zhanghar slipped away behind them.

Grief and exhaustion took their toll on her, and she slept where she sat. None of the crew woke her through all the hours she sat there. Whenever she did wake, guilt and revulsion from the previous night consumed her. Tears streamed from her, and she could not shake from her mind the vision of the two men as they bore Arella's body away. Arella had died at Corelle's hand, and the terrible self-inflicted wound that led to her death provided no excuse; Corelle's fan had delivered the final, fatal blow. Would they give Arella a Pyre and a Sending? Doubtful, she guessed. It had been Corelle's responsibility to arrange both, and instead she had killed the woman she loved, abandoned her body, and broken her vow to kill anyone who harmed Arella. She disgusted herself.

Three days later, she left the ship in Ort. She had used the token and felt sure word of her passage would come to the Guild, but she had a start on them and some time to plan her next move. As she walked from the docks, she looked back and noticed the little two-masted ship bore the name "The Jorinda."

She had some coin—twenty regals, more or less—but she and Arella had not saved as much as they had planned. Her hurried departure left her without so much as a change of clothing, and she did not want to waste her precious coin too soon, so she would need work if she stayed in Ort for any length of time. She feared to seek work as a garment maker, since Wilash knew of those skills, and that meant the Guild knew. The risks would be too great if the Guild learned of the recent arrival of a high-quality seamstress in Ort, more so once word of her voyage aboard The Jorinda came to Styrrach.

Could she obtain work in a tavern? She believed the work would be simple enough and an excellent opportunity for anonymity, since she imagined tavernroom staff came and went like the tides. She walked into the first large tavern she saw, introduced herself, and asked the innkeep if he had need of new workers.

He looked her up and down, doubt in his eyes. "What is your name?"

"Jorinda." She abandoned her real name now she had become a fugitive from both the Guild and the Portreeve, and the ship's name would suit. She did not know whether Portreeves in different towns and cities communicated with one another, but it seemed safer to err on the side of caution rather than tempt the fates.

The innkeep studied her with narrowed eyes. Jorinda stood a full two spans below him in height, and her slight build might make her seem unsuited to tavernroom work. Patrons filled the tavernroom, however, and only one other worker bustled about the room while a great many empty tankards stood on the tables. If he needed an extra pair of hands, he might take her on. Her guess proved correct, and he offered her a two-day trial. He would not agree to pay her during the trial but would allow her to sleep in a small room over the stable and eat two meals per day of the food provided by the tavern for its customers. She accepted the employment and settled into the small room that night.

The next day, Jorinda began the trial. To her surprise, she did not suit the work, which she found far more physical than she had expected. She did not enjoy the small talk with the tavern's patrons, men for the most part, and as they became inebriated, she disliked them more and more. She imagined she would kill at least one of them before her trial ended, and by the evening she had already turned her thoughts to her next move when a tall, thickset man with an untidy mop of long dark hair ordered a tankard of ale from her and took a seat at a table. He sat alone and looked out of place in the tavern. None of the other patrons spoke to him as he sat and stared at the table.

Jorinda took his tankard over to his table, and he looked up at her. "My thanks." He had a strange accent, a raspy, singsong brogue she had not heard among the other patrons, and she decided he must not be from Ort. He nursed his tankard all night and ordered no more even when Jorinda wandered over to ask if he wished another. As the night wore on, many of the other drinkers left, but he stayed at his table. He stared at her several times, and she worried he might be a courier from the Guild, that they had discovered her already, and this man watched her in case she left. She feared Styrrach, Porl, or Wilash might enter the tavernroom at any moment.

Three patrons remained, and she longed for them to leave so she could retire upstairs and sleep. The work had exhausted her, she had snatched no more than one brief rest throughout the day, and her back burned with agony. She went to the strange man's table again, determined to shoo him out of the tavernroom by one means or another. "Are you finished, sir?" She gave him a weary smile.

"I am Taro." That seemed like no kind of an answer, but he said no more.

The silence became too much for her to bear. "Jorinda."

"You are very pretty." He seemed to think that an acceptable thing to say to a woman he did not know, but it irritated Jorinda.

The silence stretched out until it reached another unbearable point. "My thanks." She sighed in frustration.

"You have a pretty face. Can I come in again tomorrow? Will you serve me?"

Jorinda bit her lip and checked that no Guild members had entered the tavernroom while she traded pointless chatter with this man. Doubtless, men would find her attractive, but they would be disappointed to learn she felt no mutual attraction, and his blatant attempt to lie with her shocked her. "This is a tavern, and I imagine you can come and go as you please, if you pay for your ale and do not start a ruckus."

He blinked at her. "Ruckus?"

Curse it. She must avoid language that announced her as Rylfolk. "A fight."

"I had a fight with my cousin once. He broke my fishpole and would not apologise." Jorinda stayed silent, uncertain of how to respond. "I beat him."

Did he possess all his faculties? His conversation roamed from point to point without any purpose, but he used few words. He infuriated her, but the silence had become uncomfortable again. Devoid of anything more to say, she offered a weak response. "Well done you." When she glanced around, the other patrons had all left. "I am sorry, sir—"

"Taro."

With a quiet tut, she continued. "I am sorry, Taro, but we are about to close for the night. Why not come back tomorrow, and tell me more about your fight?"

"That I will." Jorinda cursed herself again. Doubtless he had heard an invitation in her words. He slid two groats across the table at her. "One for the ale, one for you. Goodnight, Jorinda. 'Rinda."

She almost screamed with frustration at the unwelcome familiar name he had given her without her permission. "Goodnight, Taro. Sleep well." At last, he rose and left the inn. When she turned, the innkeep watched from his counter and laughed as though she had taken part in the most hilarious festival performance ever created. She fought down her anger and contented herself with a contemptuous grimace.

Dreadful nightmares assailed her throughout the night, dreams filled with visions of Arella, her throat slit wide but her voice as clear as a crisp winter morning. She said, "I love you," while her baleful, reproachful eyes stared at Jorinda, who stood before her with a bloodstained blade in her hand.

Some two hours after the midday the next day, Taro returned. He spent the rest of the day alone at a table with a tankard of ale. Early in the evening, he asked Corelle for some food and a second tankard of ale. When she took a platter of bread and cheese to his table along with the tankard, he tore a piece of bread off the loaf, placed a small amount of the cheese onto it, and ate them both together. Jorinda had never seen bread and cheese eaten in such a manner, but he interrupted her amusement with a question. "Are you from Ort?"

How to reply? She did not wish to tell him any version of the truth but feared to trip herself if she claimed she came from Ort, then could not answer any questions he had about the town. "That I am not, and I will not stay here long." She returned to her work, anxious to avoid further difficult questions.

The next time she passed his table, he spoke to her again. "I travel to my farm tomorrow morning. Would you like to come with me?"

What answer could she give? He had done little more than watch her as she busied herself with her inept service skills, had exchanged a few tortured words with her, but had felt bold enough to ask such a brazen question. She passed him by, irritated by his oddness.

As the evening wore on, she thought more on his proposition, and an idea formed in her mind. She believed farms would be remote, although she had never seen one, in truth. He had called her "'Rinda" all day, not Jorinda, and while 'Rinda seemed unattractive and harsh to her, it might be a safer option than Jorinda. A ship with that name plied the Alc, and while one might share a name with somebody or something else, parents invented names for their children based on their own whims, and they were not often duplicated.

If she travelled to his farm for a few days, it might give her more time to gather her thoughts in safety. It would be dangerous to linger in Ort; the Guild would seek her here, and the Portreeve in the town might also track her down. After all else, her back would be shattered within a few days if she continued to work in the tavern.

She returned to his table. "Where is your farm?"

"On the road between Delcan and Ort. North-west of here."

She glanced around, still wary. "Why are you in Ort, then?"

"I needed a new horse, and I bought one at the market today. You can ride it back if you like." She noted the use of "can." He appeared to have made up his uncomplicated mind she would return with him.

"If I ride the horse, how will you get back?"

"I will walk."

Curse it. His farm must be close if he would walk. "How far is this farm from here?"

"Four days' walk." She stared at him anew, certain the reply must be a jest, though he did not smile.

"You walked for four days to buy a horse, and now you are prepared to walk for four days back again?"

"That I am, for I must walk if you come with me. If not, I will ride the horse. It may be strong enough to bear us both at times, in truth." He paused. "I did not walk here. I rode with a neighbour in his cart. He has a farm half a day from mine."

Jorinda lacked the will to ask why his neighbour came to Ort or why Taro would not travel back with him. She looked around at the patrons of the dreary tavern, most of whom stared without purpose into tankards of dreams that would vanish in the morning light like so many clouds on a windy day. "Meet me here tomorrow at the midday."

"For what purpose?"

Had the whole idea been a mistake? She longed to reply, *"So I can slit your throat and push your body into the Alc, you oaf,"* but settled instead for, "You asked me to travel to your farm with you, did you not?"

"So, you will come with me?"

She gazed down at him for some time. The silence became uncomfortable, but she said nothing as she turned over the advantages and disadvantages of the decision. His farm should be safe, and he seemed harmless enough despite his peculiarities. At last, she decided. "That I will." Jorinda turned and went back to her tavernroom work for the last time.

SIX

THE END OF THE BEGINNING

THE RAIN POUNDED THE ROOF OF TARO'S FARMHOUSE. A FIRE crackled in the hearth of the tiny parlour, and a lantern sat on a wooden cabinet close by. Jorinda sat on a stool at the table and concentrated on the repair of a tunic Taro had torn earlier that day. The sleeve had almost torn away from the body of the tunic, and he had told Jorinda he would throw it away. It seemed he would have done so before she arrived, but such waste irritated her. She had tutted and said she would mend it, so he had taken it off and now sat in the parlour bare chested despite the cold, wet evening. Jorinda had grown sick of the weather, but Taro seemed to take it in his stride, unaffected by the chill in the air.

The repair finished, she handed the tunic back to Taro, and he pulled it on, his voice muffled as he battled with it. "My thanks." Frustrated by his clumsiness, she climbed the narrow stairway to the bedroom to replace the needle and thread in the small making kit he kept in his trunk.

He had told her his mother owned the making kit before her death, and he kept it from some nostalgic inability to discard it. That seemed like nonsense, since she guessed he had never used its contents and had been prepared to throw the old tunic away rather than mend it. He claimed his parents had both died young, and she could believe it. Life on the farm appeared brutal, and she doubted any in the Ortlands lived to see old bones.

Jorinda had bought herself a tunic and a dress in Ort before Taro had arrived with his new horse, and they set out for his isolated farm. He carried a sleeveless tunic with him he said he had bought as a present on the way to meet her. He could not have spent a great deal of coin on such poor quality making, and it had been far too big for her in truth, so she never wore it. She stored her few belongings in a second trunk on the floor next to his.

She lit the lantern in the bedroom and put the needle and thread away. It had grown late, and the foul weather seemed to have set in for the night. She could climb straight into bed and leave him downstairs until he realised she had not returned. With any luck, she would be asleep by then and could avoid his clumsy attentions for tonight, at the least.

Her stay at the farm had gone on far longer than she had intended. Nobody had visited the farm since their arrival, and she had decided the isolation offered a safe refuge until she faded from the memories of those who wished her dead, and they abandoned their search. At first, Taro appeared patient, but as time went by he pressed her for intimacy. Jorinda had never lain with a man in her young life thus far and had no desire to do so, although it worried her he might find it strange. Revelations about her preferences were undesirable, but sex with him might be more unpleasant.

Jorinda resisted for more than a pass, but one night as he pestered her again, she recalled a phrase from Ryl, *"The need may be greater than the desire."* She could have killed him, but how could she assuage her guilt that she had taken advantage of his hospitality to hide from her enemies, then killed him because he found her desirable? If she continued to resist, he might throw her out of his house, and she had no idea where she could go on foot in the wet season nor how far away the nearest village would be. Although she begrudged the concession, she went upstairs, lay on her back on the bed, and opened her legs. He seemed inexperienced, and he did not satisfy her. It hurt but, to her relief, had not lasted more than a few moments. She cried herself to sleep that night as she longed for Arella's touch and cursed herself that her own hand had deprived her of it for the rest of her life.

Jorinda suffered his attentions as little as possible as five more passes went by. Taro must never have encountered moon cycles and had been horrified the first time Jorinda leapt from the bed in search of a cloth as blood ran down the inside of her thighs. She now used it to her own advantage and exaggerated the length of her cycle every pass without shame.

She froze, still as death. The soft whinny of a horse drifted through the rainy night, but no knock came at the door, and the horse snorted and pawed at the ground. Below her, Taro rose from his chair, and she guessed he had also heard the horse. Not long after she had arrived at the farm, Jorinda had hidden her fan under the straw mattress of the bed, and Taro had not found it—he did no housework, content to leave it to Jorinda. She knelt, scrabbled around beneath the mattress, and pulled it free. She held it pressed it to her side and moved to one side of the window where she could look out into the darkened yard below. A cloaked figure stood beside a light-coloured horse, but no detail of the shadowy visitor could be seen until Taro opened the door and the lantern light tumbled out. Jorinda pressed her free hand to her mouth to stifle a gasp of shock. Below her stood Deineike, Arella's former lover.

Taro paused when his lantern light fell across her, then stepped forward to peer at Deineike and her horse, side by side in the downpour. He glanced up and hunched his shoulders as if that would keep him dry. "Who are you? What do you want?" The rain on his hair formed rats' tails about his forehead.

"My name is Deineike." The woman's quiet, velvety voice proved harder to hear than Taro's gruff Ortlands brogue. "I wondered if I might pass the night in your barn, in the hope I might see out the worst of this rain."

Jorinda's heart and mind raced as anxiety consumed her. Had the Guild found her? Did this woman seek to confirm that Jorinda hid at the farm, then summon her ruin into the house from the darkness beyond the pool of light that spilled out from Taro's lantern? Jorinda shook her head from side to side. That would be impossible, yet her fingers worried at the button on her fan, ready to spring its blade and dispatch Deineike wherever she travelled to afterward.

Arella had insisted she had not mentioned the Guild to Deineike on the day she abandoned the younger woman. Jorinda doubted Deineike could have been a member of the Guild before she joined; Arella's surprise when they saw Deineike in the market suggested Arella had not seen her former lover since the day she broke Deineike's heart. It also seemed ridiculous to think Deineike had somehow been recruited since that dreadful night to hunt Jorinda down and bring her to Guild justice. Jorinda disliked coincidences but accepted they sometimes occurred, and this must be no more than a coincidence.

An unexpected thought sprang to mind. When they had seen Deineike in the market, Jorinda had asked Arella, *"How do you know she is like us?"* After six passes of Taro's attention, the woman brought the prospect of some true satisfaction. Jorinda shook her head, determined to put her desires aside and focus on the threat the arrival of Deineike might signify. She needed to be closer to the door if the encounter went awry, so she held the fan against her side and ran down the stairs.

As Jorinda reached the bottom of the stairs, Taro asked Deineike why she wanted to sleep in the barn, and Deineike flicked her eyes upward and held both hands palm up to the rain. The movement shook water from the reins of her horse in droplets that showered the woman and Taro. "I have already explained why. The rain is heavy, and I seek a dry shelter for the night. I will be on my way in the morning, and you will have my thanks." Her eyes flitted to Jorinda as she spoke.

Taro hesitated before he continued. "Rains can last days here. Weeks." Jorinda thought he had spoken out of habit; that he pondered her request, and his words had no part in the outcome of his deliberations. At last, he replied, a gruff refusal. "I think not. It seems wrong, somehow, a woman who wanders around on her own. How come you wander around on your own?"

Deineike sighed. "I am not on my own. I have my horse." Jorinda smiled at the jest.

"I see that, but why do you travel around the countryside, just you and your horse?" Taro sounded irritated, and Jorinda judged he had either not spotted, or had not understood, the woman's jest.

Deineike paused for a heartbeat before she spoke again. "I mean no disrespect, sir, but that concerns me, and me alone. All I ask is that you allow me to pass one rainy night in the shelter of your barn."

Taro sucked air through his teeth as he appeared to wrestle with thoughts that competed in his mind before he answered. "I think not. Strangers, you understand…" His voice trailed off.

His decision disappointed Jorinda. Despite her concerns, it seemed callous to deny the woman shelter from such weather. "It is a foul night, Taro. Let her sleep in the barn. What harm could there be?"

He glanced back at her, and a look of anger flashed across his eyes until he swept it away with a series of rapid blinks. He took an unexpected step toward Deineike, who stood her ground as her horse flicked its head up and showered them with more water. He shot a question into her face. "Can you work?" She drew in a short, sharp breath, and her eyes flitted from side to side. Jorinda wondered whether Deineike checked whether he had addressed his question to some other who stood to one side of her, and she bent forward to see more of the yard, the fan still pressed to her side, concealed by the fabric of her dress that folded around her hand.

"I..." Deineike paused. "What sort of work?"

"Barn needs a good tidy up, clean out the muck. You can stay if you attend to it tomorrow."

Taro often used strange speech; not his accent alone, but the way in which he used words. Jorinda had listened to him for six passes but did not recognise the word "muck" and imagined he referred to the repellent mess strewn about the inside of the barn. Jorinda did not enter the barn if she could avoid it. Soiled hay and items Taro had cast from himself covered its floor—broken straps, tools, other things that did not interest her.

A faint smile played on Deineike's lips. "My thanks." She turned from the house and walked toward the barn. The tall woman pushed the door open, pulled the horse inside, then closed the door again without a backward glance.

Taro turned and gestured to Jorinda to make room. She took a pace backward, and he returned to the house. Water pooled at his feet and trickled out beneath the door like some prodigal that returned to the fold.

Deineike took three steps forward into a barn as dark as her mood. The barn stank, and Deineike's stomach roiled as the odour threatened to overpower her. Somewhere ahead of her a horse whinnied, and her own horse snorted in reply.

The man's reticence and rudeness had angered her, and she had struggled to control her temper. She had not wished to ride on in case she did not find any other shelter, but his unhelpful attitude had frustrated her so much, she had thought she might leave, after all else. As she waited for her eyes to adjust to the darkness of the barn after the bright lantern light, the door opened behind her, and when she turned, Taro stood there with a lantern in his hand. She squinted at the light as her eyes struggled to adjust once more.

His strange, gruff accent sounded awkward in Deineike's ears. "Brought you a lantern." He held it out toward her.

"My thanks." The lantern must have been the woman's idea. The man, Taro, did not seem the sort to be concerned with her welfare; he had wanted her to ride on until the woman had intervened, after all else. Nonetheless, the light would be welcome, and she favoured him with a smile as he turned to leave.

In the lantern light, Deineike saw why the barn smelled so awful, with animal droppings and hay scattered around the floor. A broken bridle and other equipment lay discarded in the centre of the floor, and a pitchfork lay on the floor nearby. A rusted axe head lay embedded in one of the support posts, the splinters that protruded from its shoulder the only indication it ever had a handle.

A small pile of clean hay had been heaped against one wall, and she placed the lantern on a crate that stood there before she stripped the pack and saddle from her horse and dropped them next to the hay. She led the grey to the small stall at the rear of the barn where a scrawny dun watched them, nervous, its ears flat and its eyes wide, then draped her saturated blanket over the rail of the stall so it could dry overnight. Once she had pushed her own horse into the stall with the dun, she snatched up a handful of the clean hay, wiped down the grey, and threw some hay to the two horses. Both animals lowered their heads and ate.

Deineike took off her cloak and spread it over the rail next to the blanket. The tunic she wore when she left Zhanghar had become saturated and smelled so bad, she threw it away the previous morning, and she now wore every item of clothing she possessed. The soft leather trousers were comfortable to ride in but difficult to dry. Once she reached Ort, she would buy herself some new clothes. Until then, these must suffice.

Despite the cold night, she did not wish to sleep in wet clothes, so she tugged at the crude buttons of her tunic, then hesitated and cast a wary glance around, concerned the man might linger outside the barn to catch a glimpse of her without her clothes on. She walked to the door, pulled it open, but could see no sign of anyone outside. The upper window of the house had been shuttered, and light shone through the cracks. She closed the door, went back to the hay, and removed the tunic and trousers. Naked, she shivered as she searched in vain for a dry blanket and tutted with annoyance as she dried herself with some hay, then burrowed into the pile on the floor and fashioned a crude bed.

Before she turned down the lantern's wick and blew out the flame, she dug around in her pack and found a small knife with a bone handle. She placed the knife in the hay near her, said goodnight to her horse, and fell into a weary sleep.

Jorinda urged Taro to take a lantern over to Deineike to allow her time to replace the fan beneath the mattress and a moment to gather her thoughts, to decide what the arrival of the woman at the farm implied. More than compassion had driven her to urge Taro to permit Deineike to sleep in the barn. Although it excited her to think of Deineike's body so close at hand, she reminded herself she might be in great danger and must tread with care. It seemed foolish to believe Deineike's arrival could be linked to Jorinda's fugitive status, but she would be on her guard while the other woman remained at the farm.

While the surly farmer crossed the yard, Jorinda hid the fan, slipped her dress off, and slid under the blanket. When Taro returned to the house, he took off his wet clothes downstairs and came up to the bedroom naked. He used a cloth that hung near the vanity bowl to dry himself before he climbed into the bed next to Jorinda. He must have believed her already asleep and put out the lantern. Within moments, he snored loud enough to wake the dead.

The next morning, Jorinda rose before Taro, lit the fire, and prepared some oatmeal in a pot hung over the flames. When it bubbled, she shouted up the stairs for him to come down, ladled some of it into a bowl, and set it before him. He said nothing, as usual, even though good manners required no coin, as her father had often said. It fell to Jorinda to suggest they treat their guest with some kindness. "I think we should invite our guest over to break her fast."

"Why?" He paused between spoonfuls of the oatmeal, his face a blank.

His lack of manners annoyed her again, and she strove to ignore his inherent rudeness. "If she is to clean the barn, she will need some food first. It will be strenuous work."

He did not reply as he returned his attention to his food, so Jorinda took it upon herself to walk across the yard to the barn. She did not see Deineike as she pushed the door open and wondered whether she had ridden off early until movement at the rear of the barn caught her eye. Deineike must have spent the night buried within a pile of hay. Jorinda stepped forward and smiled at the tall woman. "I hope you slept well."

Deineike sat upright, and the hay fell away from her. The older woman had no clothes on, and Jorinda looked away, but she could not keep her gaze from Deineike for long, as she yearned to feel those muscular arms around her and nuzzle those small breasts. Deineike appeared unabashed to sit naked before a stranger, so Jorinda gave a polite cough before she continued. "You are welcome to come into the house and take some breakfast with us if you wish. You may wash afterward also."

"My thanks." Deineike had deep blue eyes, not unlike Arella's. "You have not yet told me your name." Deineike reached for her tunic.

"Jorinda. Taro calls me 'Rinda." Jorinda turned and left Deineike to dress and follow her.

Taro still sat at the table with the empty bowl before him when Deineike entered. Jorinda stood at the fireplace and stirred the pot of oatmeal as Taro greeted Deineike with a nod of his head and kicked a stool out from beneath the table. "Sit down. 'Rinda, fetch food for our guest." Jorinda did not miss the edge to his voice as he copied the word "guest" from her, and she tensed at his tone, delayed for a heartbeat so she could retain her composure.

Deineike made some attempt at conversation. "The barn will take some time. It has not seen a pitchfork for several seasons." She smiled, mayhap to take the curse off her comment and turn it into a jest. "At the least, the rain has stopped." Jorinda placed a bowl of oatmeal and a small wooden spoon on the table in front of Deineike, who smiled up at her in thanks. Steam rose from the oatmeal and flew away across the room in time with Deineike's breaths.

Taro stood. "Take as long as you need. Stay another night if you must." He stalked out into the yard, his body as tense as his words.

Taro might have felt unhappy at how Deineike's arrival had

unfolded. He might have told himself Deineike's appearance at the farm disturbed the idyllic life he believed he shared with Jorinda. As he had said, it did seem unusual for a woman to travel alone in the winter, but Jorinda did not want to dwell on supposition. She would find answers if she could and decide on a plan of action when she had all the facts in her possession. With an apologetic smile for his surliness, Jorinda sat in the chair Taro had vacated; his chair, the only one in the parlour. She offered the best explanation she could come up with. "He is not good with people. We get few visitors." None at all, if Jorinda had been truthful.

Deineike dipped the spoon into the hot food before she spoke again. "How long have you been married?"

Questions might tease out truths Jorinda did not wish to reveal, and she picked at an imaginary splinter in the table as she answered. "We are not married." As Deineike blew at the spoonful of the oatmeal to cool it, Jorinda looked up and studied the other woman across the table. Long black hair straggled around a face that looked old before its time thanks to wrinkles around her blue eyes and at the corners of her mouth. The lines around Deineike's face were to be expected after all that had turned in her life, and, mayhap because of them, Jorinda believed her guest was older than her.

Jorinda thought it safer to exaggerate the time she had spent at the farm, lest this woman did have some link to the Guild. "I am from the north, in truth. I came down here a year and a bit ago." A soft smile sprang to Deineike's lips, her eyes sparkled, and Jorinda felt the heat of her face as it turned red with embarrassment. Unsure what Deineike found funny, Jorinda asked, "Do I amuse you?"

"I have not heard this expression, 'and a bit,' before, that is all. I am sorry if I appear rude."

Jorinda looked down at her imaginary splinter and recalled how Arella had been amused by the same expression, and she fought back tears. Deineike must not learn anything about her relationship with Arella, and Jorinda strove to keep her emotions under control. It would be wise to avoid any further Ryl expressions, so she ignored Deineike's amusement at the phrase and continued with her tale. "I met Taro in a tavern in Ort. He had travelled to the market to buy the dun after his own horse had died from some illness. I had fallen on hard times and had obtained a job in the tavern in return for room and board, and he took a shine to me."

"Took a shine to you?"

Another Ryl expression. Clumsy. "*Concentrate,*" she told herself, though she wearied of the frequent interruptions. "That he did. He liked me and offered me the chance to come here with him, which seemed better than tavern work at the time." She stopped to pick at the imaginary splinter again and noticed Deineike had finished the oatmeal. "Would you like some more food, or to wash before you return to the barn?"

"My thanks. I have had sufficient food, but I will wash if I may." Jorinda showed her guest to a room at the back of the house where she kept a small vanity bowl filled with water on a table. Jorinda left Deineike a clean cloth with which to dry herself, then went upstairs to smooth out the bedsheets and allow her some privacy.

Below Jorinda, Deineike's footsteps crossed the parlour, and the door opened and closed. Jorinda watched from the bedroom window as Deineike crossed the yard and stopped for a moment to study the two small pens that stood to one side of it. There were two milk cows in one and some hogs in the other. Deineike might have spoken to the animals, but Jorinda could not be certain, then Deineike pulled open the barn door and went inside.

Jorinda spent the morning in the parlour and contemplated the situation in which she found herself. She understood how Arella had become involved with a woman as attractive as Deineike. It would be pleasant to exchange Taro's clumsy advances for a night of pleasure with Deineike, but how could she bring about such a dalliance? She must endure her frustration.

As the midday came and went, Jorinda decided she should offer Deineike some food. Taro might also return for lunch at any time, so she gathered up some bread and cheese and laid them on a large platter on the table, then crossed the yard and opened the barn door. She stopped the moment she entered the barn, stared around in astonishment, and could not believe her eyes. The barn had been a terrible mess, but now all the clean hay lay piled in one place, and the soiled hay and animal droppings lay in another large pile near the door. The horse stall had also been cleared. Deineike leaned on the pitchfork, her tunic plastered to her by sweat. Jorinda smiled at the tall woman as she tried to keep her eyes from the nipples outlined against the wet material. "You have worked hard. You must be hungry."

Deineike's breathy reply indicated how hard she had worked. "That I am."

"I have put together some food for us."

"That is welcome news." Deineike wiped her hands on her tunic as she dropped the fork to the floor.

Jorinda stared at Deineike's clothing, horrified. "Your clothes are in a terrible mess. I will wash them for you later. Do you have others you can change into?"

Deineike shook her head. "That I do not."

Why would a woman travel during these rains without so much as a change of clothing? The revelation worried Jorinda, but she hid her concerns as she proposed an alternative. "You could borrow something of mine for the rest of today." Deineike shrugged as though she doubted any of Jorinda's clothes would fit her, since Deineike stood, at the least, a span taller than Jorinda with a more muscular physique. Jorinda gave an embarrassed laugh. "You could wear something of Taro's." Deineike joined in the laughter.

Her eyes lit up when she laughed, and Jorinda liked the sound of another woman's merriment at the farm.

Jorinda invited her to come to the house when she felt ready, then headed back across the yard. Deineike followed her into the house soon afterward and sat on the same stool she had used at breakfast. She tore off a chunk of bread and a piece from the cheese. Jorinda helped herself to some food and placed the cheese on the bread before she ate it. Deineike smiled at her. The bread and cheese stalled between Jorinda's mouth and the table, and for the second time that day, Jorinda asked Deineike what had amused her.

Deineike's eyes twinkled as she replied. "I have never seen anyone eat bread and cheese together like that."

"Taro." Jorinda waved the food toward the door. She had not realised she had begun to copy Taro in the way she ate bread and cheese, which she decided must be an Ortlands affectation.

"Where is Taro?"

Jorinda lowered her gaze to the table. She did not know the answer but guessed he avoided Deineike, still sullen about the intrusion into his daydream life with Jorinda. "Some fence repair delays him, my guess."

"I can be on my way later." Deineike's tone suggested she felt uncomfortable at her intrusion into their life.

"That will not be necessary." The reply had been too eager, and Jorinda cursed herself for it, sought a way to recover her dignity. "You must stay tonight. I must wash your clothes. It is only fair."

"You have already fed me twice and given me shelter for the night. That is fair enough, and more than we bargained."

Jorinda looked down at the table again and fiddled with a piece of hair that had fallen out of the bun she had piled it into. "I insist." She looked up and saw no emotion in Deineike's eyes, so she repeated the words. "I insist." Would the woman stay? The thrill of the exchange reminded Jorinda of the first time she had met Arella. Dangerous, full of excitement and promise.

Deineike shrugged. "Very well." They ate in silence for a few moments.

After a time, Jorinda stood. "I will find you some clothes unless you prefer to choose yourself. I do not have many clothes, but you are welcome to any I have."

"I would be happy to choose."

Jorinda nodded and led the way from the parlour up the creaky, narrow stairs to the bedroom, furnished with nothing but a bed, the two trunks, and a small table on which a lantern and a vanity bowl stood. The crude bed looked as though Taro, or his father before him, had built it. One exhausted blanket covered it, Taro's only blanket. Jorinda pulled her trunk open, knelt before it, and dug around inside for a heartbeat before she pulled out the sleeveless tunic Taro had bought for her in Ort.

She held it in the air above the trunk. "This is too big for me. Taro bought it as a present before we returned here, but I never wear it." Deineike unbuttoned her tunic and let it slide from her shoulders. Jorinda paid closer attention to Deineike's body—the small, firm breasts, the flat stomach, and the well-muscled arms.

Deineike took the tunic and tried it on. It would have been a better fit if it had been bigger, but Jorinda it would suffice while she washed the other. Deineike buttoned the tunic up and made a face that implied acceptance, eyebrows arched, lips together. "It fits well enough." Jorinda returned her attention to the chest and Deineike knelt beside her. The dark-haired woman smelled musky—no surprise after her labours that morning. Jorinda preferred the smell of her to the odour of Taro, nonetheless. Three dresses, all of Jorinda's making, and a tunic much too small for Deineike remained in the chest. Deineike pushed them around with little enthusiasm.

Jorinda apologised for the lack of choice. "I have no trousers. Taro does not like them on a woman. He can be quite stubborn about some things." She hoped Deineike did not sense her resentment. It had been ironic that he bought her a tunic as a present, then complained about how much he disliked trousers on a woman once they arrived at the farm. Such attitudes annoyed Jorinda, and she wondered again whether she should move on.

"Your…Taro's clothes may be better suited to my needs."

Jorinda pointed at the other trunk with a soft laugh meant to tease Deineike. "Do my simple dresses not appeal to your refined tastes?" Deineike scrambled across to the second chest and lifted the lid. Inside were several tunics and three pairs of trousers, all plain but clean, some with neat mending where they had torn in the past. Jorinda would not let Taro cast away any clothing she could repair.

Deineike took out a pair of trousers and held them up. They looked too big for her, but with no alternative, she stood and slipped off her own trousers. Jorinda continued to laugh and found gentle amusement in an otherwise mundane incident, but she watched unabashed as Deineike pulled Taro's trousers on. The sight of Deineike's bush aroused Jorinda, and she longed to bury her head between the older woman's thighs. The trousers were an ill fit, and even when buttoned they slipped low on Deineike's hips and threatened to fall down if she moved.

Jorinda laughed louder, and Deineike joined in even though she could only guess at how ridiculous she looked. Deineike looked up, the lines around her blue eyes exaggerated by her laughter. "Do you have a belt?"

Jorinda shook her head. "We do not own such a luxury, but we could find some rope with which we could fashion such an accessory." Though she tried, she could not contain her laughter. "You are a sorry sight."

Deineike bent down to roll up the legs of the trousers that lay on the floor beyond her feet and threatened to trip her. She mumbled, "Taro is tall," and held the trousers in place with one hand as she straightened.

"You are funny." Jorinda gasped for breath between tearful

laughter. "It has been a long time since anyone has amused me this much." Guilt washed over her. How could she laugh at all after the things she had done in the last three years?

"What in the Five Cities are you about up there?" Taro's voice from downstairs cut off their laughter, and Jorinda turned to the door.

She placed a finger to her lips in a gesture of silence toward Deineike as she called out, "Nothing." She ran down the stairs and explained to Taro that Deineike had done a wonderful job in the barn, but her clothes were filthy and must be washed.

He did not hide his irritation that she needed to wear his trousers. "Women have no place in trousers."

"My dresses will not fit her. She is much bigger than me." Taro would have no idea what size a woman might be. Jorinda sighed, a vision of Deineike in the trousers, and without them, in her head. She looked better in them than he did, in truth. He said nothing, so she gestured at his chair. "I prepared some lunch. Why not sit and eat while we finish up with the clothes?"

He sat and set about the bread and cheese while Jorinda hunted down a piece of twine from a small shed at one side of the house. She ran upstairs with it in her hand. Deineike stood where Jorinda had left her. Anger simmered in Deineike's eyes, but Jorinda could not tell whether she directed it at her or Taro.

As she handed the twine to Deineike, Jorinda gave a terse explanation. "He has returned for lunch." Deineike took the twine from her, silent, sullen. "I will wash your clothes now." Jorinda stooped to pick them up from the floor. As she straightened, their eyes met, and their faces almost touched. Neither spoke, but something passed between them in that instant that required no words. Though she may have been the slighter of the two, Jorinda's breasts were larger than Deineike's, and they rose and fell as her breath came in rapid gasps, her face flushed and hot as blood coloured her cheeks.

Deineike lifted a hand and touched Jorinda's cheek. The soft, smooth, warm feel of the hand sent shivers of desire through Jorinda, and she tilted her head into the touch. Deineike dropped her hand to Jorinda's shoulder, and Jorinda reached upward to take Deineike's fingers in her own. Her body trembled with lust as Deineike pulled Jorinda's hand toward her, then lowered her head to kiss Jorinda's slender fingers. She looked up again, and Jorinda stared into the seductive blue pools of Deineike's eyes.

A chair scraped below, and Jorinda glanced toward the door at the top of the stairs, pulled her hand away from Deineike's at the same time. Jorinda cleared her throat, afraid her voice might not be trusted to speak. "I will wash your clothes, then." She turned and left the room.

Deineike remained in the bedroom for a time. Jorinda ached to run back up the stairs and throw her arms around her, kiss her, and push her onto the bed. The moment had passed, and Deineike came down with the twine tied around the waist of Taro's trousers. Jorinda stared at Deineike as she went out of the door, but Deineike did not glance at either of them.

The moment Deineike entered the barn, she spotted the dun back in the stall, so she walked toward it and spat at its head, then regretted both the impulse and the crude reaction to her own anger. The dun flinched backward, and her own horse pricked up its ears with a snort, as though it sensed her fury.

Deineike snatched up the pitchfork and threw herself into to her work. Visions of Jorinda danced before her as she piled the soiled hay from the barn some way from the building. Twilight had turned the farm to grey shadows around her by the time she felt she had done as good a job as Taro could expect, so she returned to the barn, dropped the pitchfork where it had lain when she had first arrived, and took some hay into the stall.

Hot and sweaty, she rubbed her horse with the hay and whispered to it. "Should we leave now?"

"You have done a good job." Taro's voice surprised her, but she did not flinch as she turned to look at him. "I see my trousers do not fit you too well."

"They will serve. My thanks to you both for your generosity. I will leave as soon as my clothes are dry enough."

He glanced down and kicked at the barn's doorframe, a cloth-wrapped bundle in his hand. "You are welcome to stay another night. I fear it could rain again ere the night has passed anyway." An awkward hush descended between them.

The tense silence became intolerable, one Deineike felt compelled to break. "My thanks." To her relief, he nodded, placed the bundle on a shelf near the door, and left without another word. She rubbed her horse with the hay, her thoughts filled with Jorinda: her smell, her laugh, her eyes. She could not decide what had captivated her, but she had been enthralled by the younger woman. Jorinda's unavailability might have made her more desirable. Jorinda lived with Taro, and although the moment in the bedroom had been charged with carnal excitement, it could not be repeated without great risk that Taro would discover them. The consequences were unthinkable.

Questions gnawed at her, demanded answers. Why did Jorinda live here with this sullen man? Why had Jorinda left her home to come to this farm in the desolate depths of nowhere, by all accounts on a whim? Why had she chattered away and laid out her tale of love found in some tavern in Ort, but shown no interest in what brought Deineike to the farm? Taro had said he found her travels suspicious, but Jorinda appeared unconcerned, disinterested.

Deineike shook the thought from her head. Jorinda did not concern herself with others' affairs, nothing more. Why seek complications where none might be found? Deineike preferred to keep her tongue still and let others wag theirs, and Jorinda doubtless did the same. Deineike retrieved the bundle, ate the food she found wrapped in the cloth, then lay down in the hay as the incident in the bedroom replayed itself over and over in her head until sleep took her.

SEVEN
A DEATH IN THE FAMILY

STYRRACH SENT LETTERS TO THE OTHER THREE GUILDMEISTERS, described the renegade, Corelle, and ordered a thorough search of Zhanghar. He left no stone unturned in his pursuit of her. Word of her voyage to Ort aboard The Jorinda came to him, but when he sent two Guild members there to learn more, they could unearth no further information. She had taken work in a tavern near the docks, but beyond that, she seemed to have disappeared like a dream that can no longer be recalled.

Styrrach's frustration had never been greater. The deaths of Arella and Pilos right beneath his nose rankled him. He would not rest until he had Corelle in his clutches, and she would pay a terrible price for the inconvenience and aggravation she had brought to him.

He should never have permitted the two women to join the

Guild. Porl had persuaded him there would be advantages to killers with pretty faces, but now one had died at the hands of the other. Corelle had made him look foolish, and not to the members of the Guild alone. Tarjkay, the Portreeve, had the temerity to ask questions about a night that should have seen him hang Corelle from a tree but had turned into a fiasco.

The Portreeve should know better than to doubt Styrrach. Arrogance of that sort carried potential consequences far worse than the stupid man could realise. Portreeves came and went, and at the snap of Styrrach's fingers, Tarjkay would go to bed one night and never wake, pieces of his body scattered across Dur. He enriched himself at Styrrach's pleasure, but the Guildmeister would allow nothing to come between him and his coin, not the jade Corelle, not his Guild members, and without question not the idiot who served as Portreeve only as long as he enjoyed Styrrach's patronage.

Corelle. The name alone set Styrrach's teeth on edge. He would find her, and for such time as she lived when she came into his hands, she would regret she had ever met him.

Jorinda had washed Deineike's clothes and sat, sullen, across from Taro. One dreadful night in Zhanghar had turned her life into an endless bout of self-recrimination, and frequent dark moods had settled on her. She hovered on the edge of life every day as she sank deeper into despair at her actions in the room above The Ship's Yard, and she berated herself at how easy she had found it to become complicit in Arella's suggestion. Arella had died not for love but out of her lover's self-interest, and Jorinda could never forgive herself for so heinous an act. At times, she wished Styrrach and Wilash would burst through the door and put an end to her torment.

Tonight, her mind had another thread to worry at. Deineike seemed to pose no threat after all else, and now Jorinda ached for some respite from Taro. The object of her desire worked across the yard in Taro's barn and appeared to crave the same fire that burned within Jorinda. If she pursued satisfaction in the barn, however, she could be in danger, and from more than the risk that Taro might find them together. If some casual word alerted Deineike to what she had done, Jorinda might as easily find a knife in her ribs as a tongue in parts of her body that yearned for satisfaction. Jorinda had killed—bad enough in itself. Worse, she had killed the woman Deineike once loved, and that could not be forgiven.

Two hours passed, and Taro did not seem ready to return to the fields or whatever task he had been about that morning. When she questioned him about it, he said he thought it might rain again at any hour, and he would do no more today. If he intended to loiter around the house for the rest of the day, how could Jorinda spend time with Deineike? She cursed her life and her luck. Every turn she took brought her nothing but despair.

Taro stood and looked out of the window. "The woman might have finished the work."

Jorinda's lips drew back into the hint of a snarl behind Taro's back. "Deineike." Men like Taro used phrases such as "the woman" without a second thought, and she loathed them for it. A day might come when the stupid farmer would learn of the danger that lay in such casual disregard for women. At once, she hung her head, ashamed she had sunk low enough to consider she might kill someone over a perceived slight.

He gave a dismissive grunt and pulled the door open. Jorinda called him back, wrapped some bread and meats in a cloth, handed them to him, and he walked out into the yard. To Jorinda's surprise, darkness had begun to steal the light from the day outside. How many hours had she moped here, her thoughts occupied by her desire for the long black hair across the yard to cascade around her as they took pleasure from one another?

Some members of the Guild used herbs in their gests, both as poisons and as drinks to subdue the victim and simplify the task. Could she concoct such a brew and keep Taro in a sleep deep enough to allow her an hour or two with Deineike? One of the Zhanghar Guild members had used valerian more than once, and it grew wild near the road.

What excuse could Jorinda come up with that would allow her to walk up to the road alone in the last breaths of daylight? *I shall not be long, Taro. I wish to pick a herb, use it to put you to sleep, and lie with Deineike in the barn.* Jorinda gave a sardonic laugh as the thought ran through her head, but it spurred her to action. Without hesitation, she ran from the house and up the lane. The thrill intoxicated her, and she felt invigorated beyond anything she had felt since she arrived at the farm. In the meagre light of day's end, she picked a few flowers from those nearest the house.

With little time to linger, she jerked the plants and their roots from the wet earth, then turned and ran as fast as she could back to the yard. She tripped on unseen stones, but the fates did not throw her to the ground. Breathless from the exertion, she hesitated when she saw the farmhouse door closed. She thought she had left it open, so Taro must have returned from the barn while she ran up the lane. That would be an inconvenience, and require awkward explanations, but when she peeped into the parlour, he did not appear to be in the house.

"The fates have smiled on me," she thought with a sigh of relief. He must have lingered in the barn, full of talk about things that must be as dull to Deineike as they were to Jorinda. He shattered the illusion a moment later when he came through the rear door and stared at her, aghast. She guessed he had been in the privy.

Confusion on his face, he asked her, "What have you been about?"

Her boots and the hem of her dress were caked in mud, her breaths were short and heavy, and the bun atop her head must be a bird's nest, with strands of hair that hung loose as she raised a muddied hand to her head. One wild lock of hair hung down her face and across her mouth, and she blew at it as if she might somehow blow it back into place. It flipped up, then fell over her mouth again. "Herbs. I needed cloves for the broth." It had been the first thing to enter her mind.

He stared at her as though she had lost her senses. "Broth?"

"A broth. I shall make us a broth. For supper." She reached into the small pantry and assembled ingredients to throw into a pot and create a broth.

"You have no cloves. That is valerian."

Jorinda stared at the valerian in her hand. "Oh." She paused, then gave a small laugh and dropped the valerian on a shelf in the little pantry. "It is dark out." She favoured him with a stupid smile as she prepared the items she had pulled from the pantry.

"Your clothes are ruined. There is mud on them."

"I shall clean them tomorrow. Do not fret. The mud will wash out once it is dry."

Taro stared at her. His mouth opened and closed twice, then he shrugged and sat down with a sigh. Relieved he had abandoned his questions, Jorinda busied herself with the creation of the broth. She waited until Taro's eyes closed for a moment, then hurried to tear the roots from the valerian plants and add them to the broth. The pot bubbled away on the fireplace for some time as Taro dozed on. Jorinda sat on the same stool Deineike had occupied that morning and waited, impatient for him to wake up. If the broth sent him into a deep enough sleep, she hoped to slip over to the barn and satisfy herself. Only tonight, and only sufficient to remind herself of what love could feel like—enough to drive the distasteful nights with Taro out of her mind for an hour or two.

He awoke with a start and coughed and spluttered for some moments, his face red. He coughed so hard, Jorinda thought he might be about to die, and she became concerned about his health, Deineike forgotten for now. She asked him if he needed help, but he waved her offer away. After some moments, the coughs subsided, and he croaked out an explanation. "I swallowed my tongue."

The idea puzzled Jorinda, who could see his tongue as he talked —he had not swallowed it at all. Indeed, she doubted it would be possible to swallow one's own tongue, and she pulled several faces that she imagined were most unattractive as she attempted the feat to prove to herself it could not be done. Taro did not appear to notice as his coughs continued, and his eyes teared up.

At last, the coughing passed, and he spoke, his voice even gruffer than usual. "This has afflicted me before. I urge you, do not allow me to sleep in this chair in the future."

"That I will not." Jorinda remained nonplussed, but her worry had diminished. "Would you like some broth? It may aid your recovery." He grunted, and she guessed he meant the sound as confirmation he would take some food. She ladled some of the broth into a bowl and placed it on the table before him. "Some bread?"

He gave a dismissive wave, another habit that irritated her. He sipped at the broth for some time, then gave her a look of curiosity. "Do you not eat?"

"I ate while you slept." He seemed content to accept the lie, and she fell silent. He ate all the broth, pushed the bowl toward her, and she picked it up and swilled it clean. With luck, the herb would send him into an immediate slumber, although he remained seated in his chair and seemed in no hurry to retire.

He broke the lengthy silence. "The broth had a pleasant flavour. I suggest you do not use cloves in the future."

Jorinda stifled a grin. "Very well." She had never used them in any meal she had ever cooked, since she disliked their spicy taste, and although she had eaten meals that contained them, she would not cook with them herself. "How is it possible you swallowed your tongue?" The question had not left her mind since the strange explanation.

"It is no more than a phrase. You do not use this phrase in Ryl?"

"That we do not." They both fell into an awkward silence again.

Despite Jorinda's impatience, some time passed before, at long last, his eyes closed, and she gave him a gentle shake. "Wake, Taro. You told me not to allow you to sleep in your chair." He started and looked at her, bleary-eyed. She leaned close and whispered, her voice seductive. "Away to your bed. I shall tidy things here and soon join you." She hoped the prospect of sex would send him to bed. Unsteady, he rose from the chair, headed up the stairs, and a familiar creak from above confirmed he had climbed into their bed.

Before long, his snores drifted down the stairs, and she ran up to the bedroom and shook him again, harder this time. He did not wake, so she slipped off the muddy dress, stepped out of her boots, and skipped downstairs naked. With Taro's cloak wrapped about her shoulders, she opened the door, took a deep breath to calm her nerves, and headed for the barn.

The barn door creaked as she pushed it open, like everything on this wretched farm. Jorinda hoped it would wake Deineike but not Taro. The moon struggled to pierce the cloud that used its malice to hide any light from the land below, but a soft glow came through the open door. Jorinda ran to the shadowy mound at the rear of the barn and knelt beside it while her heart pounded hard enough to break her ribs. "Deineike, wake up." She fought to keep her voice quiet, anxious about Taro despite the valerian.

Deineike moved in the hay but did not rise. "Why are you here? What of Taro?"

"He is sound asleep." Jorinda rested a hand on Deineike's

shoulder, and Deineike reached up to free the dishevelled brown hair from Jorinda's bun. The explanation seemed inadequate, and Jorinda added, "We will not be disturbed."

Jorinda shrugged the cloak from her shoulders, gratified by the intake of breath as Deineike realised she wore no clothes beneath it. Deineike whispered, "By the fates, you are beautiful."

Jorinda blushed and hoped Deineike did not notice in the low light of the barn. "That I am not, but I burn for you, and no words of flattery are needed." She found Deineike's lips with her own, and their tongues entwined in Deineike's mouth. Jorinda lay on her back in the hay, breathed, "Take me," and Deineike did.

As the night turned to the first hours of morning, they gave each other complete satisfaction. Afterward, they lay silent in each other's arms for some time and held one another while their fevered emotions subsided.

As their breaths slowed, Deineike brushed Jorinda's forehead with her lips. "Why are you here with Taro when..." She left the question unfinished.

Jorinda did not reply straight away, but she clung to Deineike as she considered what satisfactory answer she could give. At length, she spoke. "I have my reasons, but I cannot tell you. You might say I found it convenient."

Deineike seemed to ponder this for a moment. "Do you and he, well, does he...?"

"That we do." Jorinda hoped her tone would tell Deineike how she felt about Taro's attentions. No doubt it must seem bizarre to the older woman that Jorinda suffered the advances of a man while she ached to lie with a woman, but Deineike must not learn the truth behind that riddle. Jorinda stroked the long dark hair, still damp with sweat, and wished Deineike did not have to leave so soon. "I am sad you must leave today."

"I have no reason to stay. The barn is tidied, and that is the limit of our agreement. Taro might get suspicious if I do not leave."

"He does not know. He sleeps." Jorinda had replied too soon again, and she cursed herself once more. Conflict tore her emotions apart. The hours in Deineike's arms had awoken sensations in her that had lain dormant for six passes. To unlock those sensations again might pose a great risk to her life, however. The shadow of Arella's memory tried to take form in her mind, but she pushed it from her the same way she had pushed away any guilt over the numerous men she had killed for the Guild.

Deineike remained silent for some moments, then spoke again. "As you say. He does not know tonight, but he might come to know if I remain." Jorinda sighed, and Deineike gave her a tender kiss. "Jorinda, Jorinda, do not sigh. There will be others."

"I want no others. I mean, I do not crave others." For a heartbeat, Jorinda had given in to the thought that this moment might last for days, passes, years, but such a situation would require caution with any woman. With the past that lay between them, unspoken by her and unknown by Deineike, the dangers were beyond count. The thought left her disconsolate. "I must return now. He may wake and find me gone. There could be problems."

Deineike barked a dark laugh. "There would be substantial problems were he to find us together like this, my guess." Jorinda knelt in the hay and felt around for the cloak. Once found, she draped it around her shoulders as Deineike laughed and picked some strands of hay from her hair. "We cannot permit him to know you have rolled in the hay."

"That we cannot." Jorinda bent down and kissed Deineike one final time before she jumped up and ran from the barn without a word. The door creaked shut, and she left Deineike behind her.

The night had almost birthed a new dawn as Jorinda ran across the yard. The heavy, musky aroma of imminent rain suffused the air as the stubborn wet season clung to the land rather than relinquish it to the cold season that should follow it. Like the barn door, the stairs defied any attempt at stealth. There were no more than two or three in the crude house that did not creak, and Jorinda climbed without haste, sure Taro would sleep for some time yet.

Jorinda already pondered how she could find a way to enjoy Deineike's body again. The tall woman should leave later that day, but it would be simple enough to give Taro more broth tonight so Jorinda could lie in the barn with her once more. She smiled at the memory of the night of passion. Arella had been right about the tall, dark haired woman's skill in the art of love. Deineike had awoken Jorinda in ways Arella had not, but Jorinda drove the thought from her. She would not—could not—bring herself to betray Arella in still more ways. She would not think it.

Jorinda reached the bedroom and cast the cloak from her. Taro did not snore, and she feared he had awoken, but realisation dawned, and she closed her eyes, balled her fists as horror swept through her. She found the flint and lit the lantern, even as the sun peeped over the horizon outside the shuttered windows. Taro lay still, stiff and unnatural, and she knelt beside him on the bed to feel for a pulsing, the telltale sign of life at the side of his neck. Her fingers searched for the same vital arteries her blade sought when it stole life from another. No pulsing could be found, and his cold skin felt eerie to touch. Jorinda had never touched a body that had been lifeless for anything longer than a moment, but there could be no doubt. Taro had died.

She sat back on her ankles, her mind a blur of anxiety and confusion. How had he died? She had wanted him to sleep for a few hours, nothing more. Because she had not known how much valerian to use to induce sleep, she had used the roots of three of the plants, but had not believed it could be fatal, even in such quantities. Did the earlier episode, when he had coughed so hard, have some connection to his death? Angry, she slapped a hand against her thigh. Her guilt would not escape through some flimsy door created by her mind. She knew how he had died; she had killed him.

Jorinda had killed many men, and none but Pilos had earned it for any wrong they had ever done to her. More than any, Taro did not deserve this fate, and she raised her hands to her face and cried. Her tears fell for Taro, but for herself also, and for what she had become.

Nobody might come to the farm for passes, or ever. Taro had a cousin, she thought. In Ort, he had told her some tale of a fight with a cousin, though he had never spoken of the man again. She snapped her head up as another concern jostled for attention in a mind already crowded with anxieties. The Portreeve's men might come from Ort, four days' walk away, but less on horseback. News of Taro's unexpected death might come to the Portreeve's ear if it were reported to local busybodies, then reached the port town. She could not be here if the Portreeve's men came, or the jig would be up. They would hang her as a murderer here in the Ortlands, then doubtless hang her again for her crimes in Zhanghar.

Her mind made up, she rose from the bed and dug under the mattress for her fan, then ran downstairs naked, out to the privy. High up in the roof space of the crude structure, a small sack lay hidden. She pulled it down and took out a pouch of coins and a pair of trousers, the coins hidden away almost as soon as she arrived at the farm and the trousers some days later when Jorinda tired of Taro's complaints that he did not like to see her in them. He had believed her when she told him she had thrown them away.

She ran back into the house, up the stairs again, pulled the trousers on, and grabbed her tunic from the chest. Sadness washed over her as she realised she again wore the tunic she had worn after she killed Arella. The dark tint of bloodstains on the inside had never quite washed out, and the sight of it saddened her even more.

What could she tell Deineike? The older woman might be in a deep sleep after their hours of passion and may not even wake. Jorinda wondered whether Deineike might travel with her but dismissed the thought straight away. Jorinda must take to the road, and she could not place an innocent woman in harm's way for no reason other than to enjoy further satisfaction with her.

Deineike had no reason to stay at the farm, and she would be gone before anybody discovered Taro's body. None knew she had been here except Jorinda. Deineike would be unscathed by this turn. Jorinda pulled her boots on, slipped the fan into one of them, and ran across the yard.

Deineike sat up as soon as the barn door creaked open. Jorinda headed straight for the dun, grabbed Taro's saddle and tack, and threw it onto the horse.

Deineike stood, hay falling from her magnificent, naked body. "Jorinda?"

"I must leave." Jorinda cinched the saddle's girth under the dun's belly as she had seen Taro do.

"What? Why? What has turned?" Jorinda did not reply, her focus on her preparations of the horse. "Jorinda?" Deineike sounded insistent.

Jorinda stopped and rested a miserable forehead on the shoulder of the dun. "He is dead."

"Dead? Who is dead?"

"Taro."

"Dead?" Deineike now sounded perplexed. "How?"

Jorinda sighed. "He slept because I gave him some herbs in a broth. I must have given him too much, or it affected him in some other way. It matters not. He is dead, and I must leave. As must you."

Deineike seemed unprepared to accept Jorinda's words at face value. "Why must you leave? You did not intend his death."

Jorinda spun to face her, and her arms flailed about her as she spat out frustrated words. "I killed him. I cannot be here when his death is discovered. You need know no more." She slumped back against the dun, her arms dropped to her side, and she shook from anxiety. "Deineike, forgive me. I spoke out of frustration. No blame attaches to you for this moment. I alone must bear the responsibility, and I should not have raised my voice to you."

The dun skittered, and Jorinda feared she might fall, but Deineike took a step forward, pulled Jorinda close to her, and folded her arms about her. "You owe me no apology. I would guess you have never killed anybody before, and your reaction is to be expected in such circumstances." She kissed Jorinda's lips.

Jorinda whispered a response, guilty at the fabric of deceit she spun. "You have the right of it. My thanks for your tolerance." Deineike could not know Jorinda had killed so many times she had lost count.

Deineike seemed to turn the events of the last few moments over in her mind. "Come. I will ride with you. I planned to leave today after all else, and you have need of somebody to look over you for a time while you come to yourself."

"You cannot come with me." Jorinda's anxiety increased by the heartbeat even as Deineike appeared as calm as the surface of a lake at the break of a windless day.

"Jorinda—"

Jorinda interrupted her. "You cannot come. I must go alone." Tears trickled from her eyes.

The mystery that played out before her must have confused Deineike, but she gave no indication of it. "I will come, nonetheless."

Frustrated at Deineike's stubbornness, Jorinda weighed her options. Her fan could end the argument, but she dismissed that thought without further consideration. She could stand here and argue with Deineike until the Portreeve's men came; she also dismissed that thought. One course of action remained open to her, and she conceded rather than waste further time. "Very well. Saddle your horse and let us be gone."

"That I will. While I do so, please run back to the house and bring my clothes out, for I cannot travel in those ridiculous trousers. Bring your blankets also, along with some food."

"Blanket."

"What?"

"We—I only have one blanket."

Deineike looked upward as though to suppress a sudden impatience. "Then bring it. Now, go. I will bring the horses out soon." Jorinda hurried from the barn toward the house and left Deineike to prepare the horses.

Taro's body had become tangled in the threadbare blanket, and Jorinda struggled to pull it out from beneath him. She threw some bread and cheese into a small sack and grabbed Deineike's clothes. Hooves echoed across the yard, so Jorinda turned and ran from the house. She dropped the blanket as she came out of the door and muttered to herself as she retrieved it from the floor. "It took longer to collect the blanket than I expected. Taro had become rolled in it as he slept. He is heavy."

Deineike muttered a dark response, mayhap aware of how morbid her words sounded. "He is heavy no more." She took the blanket from Jorinda, rolled it, and together they fastened it behind the dun's saddle. Jorinda pushed the sack of food into the pack on her horse. Deineike pulled on her trousers in the yard and climbed up onto the grey. "Let us be on our way."

"Indeed." Jorinda raised a foot to a stirrup. She struggled to mount the dun, and had it been any taller, she doubted she could have climbed up into the saddle. She fought to bring the horse under her command while Deineike looked on in apparent consternation. Once Jorinda had the beast under some semblance of control, she urged it toward the lane and shouted over her shoulder, "Let us leave."

Before Jorinda reached the road, she pulled the dun to a reluctant halt. She turned to look back at Deineike close behind her. "Where are we headed?"

Deineike laughed, and even Jorinda could not keep a smile from her lips. "Fine murderers we are. We cannot even escape because we do not know where we will travel. We can head for Ort. In truth, I intended to journey there, and now you and I will travel there together."

Jorinda had no wish to return to Ort. Despite the lengthy stay at the farm, the Guild might still seek her in the town. She needed an excuse again. "I do not wish to go to Ort. It is too close to the farm, and I fear I may be recognised. Some may recall me from when I left with Taro." Her story sounded weak, but it must suffice.

Deineike sighed. "That seems unlikely, but very well. I have heard of another town, to the south-west, though it is much further to travel. It lies in the foothills of the Wantu Mountains and is called Vjort. We could ride there."

Jorinda hesitated. "I would prefer to keep away from large towns and cities. They could be dangerous. A village would suit me more."

Deineike frowned at her. "Towns are as safe as villages. Crowds might make it easier to hide. If we are to travel together for a time, I am sure it would be best for us to reach a large town where we can come to a decision about where each of us goes." She frowned. "Why a village?"

"There is no Portreeve." Jorinda had no desire to reveal too much.

Deineike appeared curious. "Villages have no Portreeves?"

"You do not know this?"

Deineike wore a foolish grin. "That I do not."

The confession astonished Jorinda. "How can you not know this? If the Duke's Bailiff appoints a Portreeve, then a village becomes a town and pays levies to the Duke." She could picture her father on the day he had explained the politics of Dur to a young Corelle. It had bored her at the time, but she had managed to retain some of his words.

Deineike frowned. "What difference does a Portreeve make to you?"

Jorinda sighed as she fought to keep her lies aligned. "I have killed Taro. In a small village, there may be no local law enforcer, and if there is, he is less likely to hunt me down than a man dressed in the shiny buttons and grand tunic of a Portreeve's man."

Deineike pursed her lips. "I see. What then of cities?"

"What?"

"How does a town become a city?"

Deineike had been a street urchin and had no parents to educate her in these matters, but still… "The Duke grants city status to towns whose Portreeves pay him levies substantial enough to earn the privilege. Although in truth, Ort is at the least equal in size to Ryl, yet Ryl is a city and Ort is not, so…" Her thoughts skipped ahead of her words, and she lost her grip on the point that had occurred to her.

"Does the Portreeve of Ryl spend his own coin to supplement the levy? Mayhap he sends the Duke a cask of his finest wine as a bribe." Deineike laughed at her own jest.

Jorinda smiled. "You know much of fine wine, then, who knows nothing of villages and towns?"

"That I do not, but last night in Taro's barn, I drank wine as fine as any I have tasted."

Jorinda blushed and looked down as she recalled the pleasures of the previous evening. "We should leave." She longed to escape the praise she had always found so intolerable.

They kicked the horses forward, turned left at the end of the lane, and rode with care along the muddy road toward Ort. Jorinda knew a turn existed that would take them south because Taro had pointed it out to her as they rode from Ort to his farm, and Jorinda recalled his concise explanation. "Road to Vjort."

Deineike trotted up alongside Jorinda. "Why must we leave in such a hurry? It seems unlikely anybody will travel these muddy roads to this remote farm in the depths of winter."

Jorinda could not reveal the truth behind her desire for such a sudden departure. "Someone will come in the next day or so." Deineike hesitated, and Jorinda sensed her doubt. She raised her voice as she battled to control her anxiety. "It is his sister, or his cousin. What does it matter? We must leave without delay."

"I…"

Deineike's voice trailed off and Jorinda gave a terse nod. "I must leave. You may come or stay, but I cannot be here when his body is discovered, be that today or a year from now." Deineike shook her head, a strange look on her face. Fear? Jorinda softened her tone. "You are frightened."

"That I am not. Confused, but not frightened."

"Does nothing frighten you, then?" Jorinda saw a potential opportunity to change the subject and avoid further questions about her motives for such a hasty departure.

Deineike sighed and did not answer for a dozen heartbeats. "There have been things that have frightened me, but I would rather we did not discuss them."

She looked so unhappy, Jorinda resolved not to pursue the matter. "Come then, let us leave poor Taro and your fears back at the farm." She smiled, and Deineike managed a weak smile in return.

They battled the state of the road, which at times became a sea of mud. They did not press the horses hard in the poor conditions, and they saw nobody as they rode along side by side.

The grey skies matched Jorinda's mood. They rode in silence for around an hour before Jorinda spoke again. "I am glad you decided to come with me. You did not have to do so."

"I cannot think of one good reason why I did. I have proved myself as guilty as you."

Jorinda had not anticipated such a gloomy response and barbed her own reply with bitterness. "Do not worry. It is unlikely we will be caught, but if we are, I will say you knew nothing of Taro's death. I will say I killed him and asked you to travel with me. Rest assured; no blame will attach to you."

"They will hang me nonetheless when they learn I lay with you."

A raindrop's dull thud on the sleeve of Jorinda's tunic heralded the arrival of further bad weather. "We should stop and rest beneath a tree until we see how heavy this rain becomes." She abandoned the discussion of Deineike's part in the death of Taro.

Deineike looked thoughtful. "Later. For now, we should distance ourselves from the farm, I think." Jorinda shivered but lacked the resolve to argue, and they rode on in silence once more.

The bleak Ortlands were, for the most part, agricultural land interspersed with large areas of rugged rocky terrain where even hardy muttons struggled to survive. Far to the west, a circle of craggy peaks thrust their heads into the grey of the sky. Jorinda did not know what name they went by but guessed they might be the Wantu Mountains Deineike had mentioned earlier. The road might be well-travelled in the warmth of spring or summer, but they did not encounter anybody as their horses trudged through the mud. Jorinda believed it unwise to keep to the roads, but Deineike thought they might become lost or bogged in the mud if they took to the fields.

If they did meet somebody, two women who rode together in such atrocious weather would provoke more interest than Jorinda wished to leave to chance, and she thought it best to mention it. "We should put our minds to an explanation of why we travel together with no men in our company, in case we are questioned on that issue." The grey morning had given way to a miserable, wet day after the midday, but they still did not rest. Deineike nodded her agreement but said nothing.

In the silence of the ride south, Jorinda grieved over Taro's death, but despite her remorse that she had hastened his demise, Deineike concerned her more. It seemed like madness to travel with this dark-haired woman when their pasts were so entwined. Jorinda could not abide the thought she might bring danger to Deineike or, worse, that Deineike would somehow learn all Jorinda hid from her. She welcomed the company for now, nonetheless, and there would be time enough for decisions later.

As they passed an outcrop of rock near the road, they spotted an overhang big enough to shelter the horses. Deineike wheeled her horse and pointed at the rocks. "Let us stop for a while there. The horses can rest, we can eat, and we can dry off a little."

They ate some of the food Jorinda had brought, unsure how long it must last. As she sat and stared at the rain, a thought occurred to Jorinda, and she balled her hands into fists and stared back the way they had come. "The dog."

"Dog? What dog?"

"Taro's dog. We have left it behind with no thought for its survival."

"You seemed bent on your...our survival. Besides, I saw no dog."

"He kept it over where he ran his muttons, what few of them still lived. He kept it to guard them, although it could not have been worse at the task." Jorinda knew little of dogs and believed them wild, vicious animals, untrammelled creatures that thrived best when left to pursue their own nature, not shackled to the whims of people.

"I am sure it will be fine."

If Deineike's words had been intended as reassurance, they failed. Jorinda frowned in contempt. "I did not like it, in truth. A wretched animal. Still..."

"Worry not on it. We cannot go back. It must fend for itself now."

They sat under the rock, reluctant to restart their journey in the heavy rain, and Jorinda's mind wandered from thought to thought like a child that leaps from rock to rock across a stream. Distracted, she hummed, then sang under her breath.

"Two rivers flow to the sea, they flow too fast for you and me."

Deineike had heard. She leaned forward to listen, her head tilted to one side. "What is that song?"

Jorinda abandoned the song, worried. "It is nothing. It is a song I sing from time to time, nothing more." The tale had been a lie—Arella had often sung the tune. It had come unbidden to Jorinda's mind, and she had not appreciated she had sung it aloud, in truth.

"Such a beautiful melody. Please, sing it again."

Jorinda felt embarrassed to take praise for something she had not created, and she must not explain the origin of the song to Deineike. She could not discount the possibility Arella might have sung it during her time with Deineike, and she wished with all her heart she had not sung any word of it. She mumbled another disconsolate lie. "It is nothing. It goes no further than that in my memory. It is a tune my father sang to me as a little girl."

Deineike appeared thoughtful for a moment, then sang the song herself. She had a clear, high voice, and she remembered the words and melody Jorinda had sung; so well, in truth, Jorinda imagined Deineike must indeed have heard Arella sing it. Jorinda listened, filled with apprehension that a terrible truth would be revealed by a song she should never have begun.

"Two rivers flow to the sea, they flow too fast for you and me.
Two highways, make your choice, two songs to sing but only one voice."

Jorinda did not recognise the line about the highways. Either Arella had never sung those words to her, or Deineike had invented them. In truth, she found the mention of highways strange, for only one highway existed in Dur—the Duke's Highway, which ran from the main square in Alcmouth through magnificent gardens to the Ducal Highhome, so the stories told. If the rumours were true, the Highhome's size defied belief, with a window glass for every light in the night sky.

Despite her admiration for Deineike's voice, Jorinda felt great discomfort that they sang Arella's song, and she searched for a way to change the subject. "Two highways? You have created a second?"

Deineike gave her an innocent smile. "That I have. I name it Jorinda's Highway. It passes through the great Ortwood trees of Dur Forest to your home in a shady grove deep within the forest. I shall walk it every day and come to you in your bed..." She stopped, her cheeks bright red with embarrassment.

"You have quite the imagination." Jorinda stared in wonder at the dark-haired woman, then added, "And a beautiful voice." She stroked Deineike's arm in affection.

After a lengthy silence, Deineike sighed and cast an unhappy glance at the sky. "We should be away. We should get as far as possible from the farm before Taro's sister, or cousin, or whomever turns up." They mounted the bedraggled horses, walked them away from the outcrop back to the road, and turned south-west once more.

EIGHT
THE ROAD TO VJORT

Jorinda shivered in the cold morning air. Two wet blankets provided inadequate warmth, even with Deineike pressed tight against her. Their fire had burned out, a misjudgement on their part. Unable to find a farm where they could beg for a night in a barn, they had been compelled to spend their first night beneath the lights of the night sky. Jorinda had passed an uncomfortable night, her sleep broken and restless. It had been perilous to sleep outside, but no travellers or animals had disturbed them. Had they decided to press on further in search of a barn through the darkness of the night, they could have become lost or separated, or one of them could have fallen. By the time they found a farm, the hour might have grown so late, they would have been unwelcome guests, and the farmer might well have refused their request for the shelter of the barn.

Jorinda slid from beneath the blankets and piled some twigs on the remnants of their fire, then struck Deineike's flint until a small blaze sprang up to challenge the bitter cold of the morning. She rubbed her hands close to the flames, grateful for any warmth. They had eaten all their food, and Deineike had spent most of her coin to obtain more. Farmers had let them sleep in their barns on the first two nights of the journey. There had been curious looks, and they had felt obliged to concoct an explanation as to why two women travelled without a man. Jorinda came up with a story that they were carnival performers who travelled to Vjort, then onward by ship to Torric to perform at a major festival. It had sounded weak to them, but it had served, and they were grateful curiosity did not get the better of folk. After all else, few in these parts would know whether any such festival took place in Torric. Most people of Dur never left the immediate area in which they were born, and all they knew of other parts of the land were fanciful tales from travellers who passed by.

Deineike stirred, stretched, then pulled the blanket tighter around herself. "It is cold. Come back to bed." Sleep slurred her voice.

Jorinda gave her a sarcastic laugh. "Bed is it, two saturated blankets, your cloak for a mattress? Not much of a bed, if you ask me." Deineike blew her a kiss but did not open her eyes, so Jorinda prodded her with a stick. "Rouse yourself, if you will. More travel awaits."

Deineike rose without haste, still dressed since the nights were too cold to dispense with clothes. The horses grazed close by, tethered by a rope from Deineike's pack. Jorinda had brought none— she had fled twice in six passes and had been unprepared on both occasions. She seemed unsuited to the fugitive's life.

Nightmares had plagued Jorinda since she had left Zhanghar and had grown more intense since they left the farm. Taro's lifeless body now appeared in them. Her mood worsened as they rode south. Taro's death, whilst unintended, compounded her guilt over Arella's, and as they plodded through the mud, the rain, and the cold, she found little to cheer her. From time to time, she wondered whether Deineike might welcome further pleasure as they lay huddled together for warmth, but the nights were bitter cold, and such thoughts did not linger for long.

She often wondered why Deineike decided to come with her. The night in the barn had been wonderful, but death seemed too high a price to pay for a few short-lived hours of pleasure. Deineike herself had acknowledged her neck would be stretched alongside Jorinda's if they were apprehended for Taro's death.

As the cold, wet, miserable days passed, they often paused to eat a light snack around the midday as near as they could guess before they moved on again. From time to time, they dismounted to give the horses some rest from the bit, walked side by side, and chattered about insignificant things. Jorinda's spirits would lift a little, and they even managed some laughter as they trudged across the countryside. The moments were brief, and as the weight of all that lay behind her returned to Jorinda's thoughts, her mood would darken again.

As they lay covered in hay in a barn one night, Deineike said the next day might be the last they need spend on the road for a time.

Hope sprang up inside Jorinda. "Will we reach Vjort tomorrow, then?"

"I believe so. There is a building in Delcan that holds artefacts and items from all over Dur, and they had a book of maps. It fascinated me, and I am confident the village we passed at twilight lies close to Vjort."

"Good. I long for a bath and a decent bed." Jorinda wiped at her nose with a sleeve.

Deineike let out a long sigh. "And a warm meal."

Jorinda fell silent for a time and thought back on the recent days. She wondered again why Deineike stayed with her despite the potential danger. Jorinda brooded on all that had turned in her life and recognised she must be poor company. Despite the things she did not dare reveal to Deineike, Jorinda had grown fond of this woman who had refused to abandon her on the journey despite the risks. She kissed Deineike on the lips and moved closer to her.

Deineike could not have expected the kiss, but she grasped Jorinda to her as their lips touched. The cold could no longer hold back the excitement that surged through Jorinda at the closeness of Deineike's body. Deineike's small breasts pressed against her own, and desire burned within her. Jorinda reached down and slid her hands into Deineike's trousers. Deineike parted her legs, and they forgot the cold as they gave one another comfort despite their uncomfortable situation.

As they lay in each other's arms afterward, Jorinda broke the peaceful silence that settled on them as their passion subsided. "I look forward to a night of pleasure in the decent bed I mentioned earlier."

"As do I. I weary of hay as a bed."

"That will change once we reach Vjort. I long for a decent meal. Then I will become senseless with wine, drag you to bed and torment you until you scream."

Deineike teased her. "While you are senseless from wine?"

The mischievous conversation served to dispel some of the coldness of the night, and Jorinda chuckled. "Very well, then. I will not drink too much wine if you intend to be such a killjoy."

Deineike also laughed, a quiet laugh that warmed the cold night. "Killjoy?"

Jorinda wriggled closer and kissed Deineike's neck. "My thanks that you have stayed with me."

Deineike looked into Jorinda's eyes. "Do you promise to make me scream?"

Tired from the lovemaking, Jorinda's sleepy brain struggled to remain focused on the conversation. "You will scream."

"Nobody has ever coaxed a scream from me before."

"I will. Lots of screams."

Deineike pulled her even closer, and a smile formed on her lips. "Lots of screams." Sleep would not be denied, and the whispered words were the last Jorinda heard that night.

They were soon on their way the next day, as they both wished to reach Vjort before nightfall. They rode faster, and the mountains loomed vast on their right. They skirted around another small village that Deineike felt certain stood not far outside the large town, and so it proved. They topped a slight rise and saw a large cluster of buildings in the distance with a river that ran past to the north. It must be Vjort. They had reached their destination at last, and their spirits rose.

Hedgerows and trees gave way to houses and shops. The condition of the road improved, and the horses trotted faster despite their weariness, as though they could sense a proper rest close at hand. They met riders and cart drivers, all wrapped up against the cold, but they avoided conversation, content with a half-hearted wave at any who bade them good day. Late in the day, they came across an inn with a faded sign over the door that announced it as The Waysmeet. Only one road ran past the inn, and they were baffled as to how it came by its name. They stopped and gazed at the smoke that billowed from a chimney, and the sounds of conversation and laughter called to them to enter the warmth and conviviality of the tavernroom.

Jorinda sucked in a breath of cool air. "Come. Let us avail ourselves of the meal and the room we talked about last night. This cold wears me down, and a comfortable bed would be more than welcome." She had kept her coin hidden from Deineike even as Deineike had spent her own on food, but this seemed an excellent time to spend some of Jorinda's coin on some comfort for their bone-weary bodies.

Deineike appeared reluctant. "Why must we seek a room at the first inn we happen across when we could have more choice if we ride but a little further?"

Jorinda gave her a wicked grin as her mood improved. "We discussed more than food last night. I seem to recall some talk of screams."

Deineike smiled but shook her head. "You forget the most important issue of all. We have almost no coin. We spent it all on food."

Jorinda's grin grew wickeder. "That is incorrect." She stood in her stirrups and reached into her pack. She pulled the small pouch out in triumph, waved it at Deineike as if to taunt her, then yelled, "Coin." The dun moved forward at her shout and almost unhorsed her. She almost dropped the pouch as she struggled to regain control of her mount.

Deineike gasped, her jaw set in anger. "What in the Five Cities? You have had coin all this time? Why did you say nothing of this earlier?"

"I wanted to surprise you. I wanted to save it for an inn where I could repay you for your company on the road." Jorinda smiled and jingled the pouch.

Deineike stared at her for some moments before she replied. "If I do not scream tonight, then tomorrow I leave alone, and I will take your coin with me." The sparkle in her eyes belied the stern words.

"Done." Jorinda dismounted and tugged the dun toward the small rail outside the inn. They entered the inn and sought out the innkeep, who served drinks to a small but boisterous crowd in the tavernroom. Some of the patrons wagered on the throw of dice while others watched on in amusement.

They waited while the innkeep served another patron, then turned to them, a curious smile on his face. "Good day, ladies. What can I do for you?" His tone suggested women did not often frequent his tavernroom unaccompanied and that he had already determined their purpose.

Deineike leaned forward and lowered her voice so none of the other patrons would hear, and Jorinda stepped closer so she could hear Deineike's words. "We wish to bathe, we wish to eat, and we wish to sleep. In that order." His smile faded.

Jorinda joined the conversation. "My friend forgot to mention wine. We wish to drink some wine."

Deineike waved an arm at the crowd in the room. "These do not interest us."

The innkeep spluttered as he attempted to recover his composure. "Oh? Then tell me, what does interest you?"

Deineike sighed and looked upward in undisguised consternation. "Food, wine, a bath, and a bed."

Something in his demeanour changed. Coin softens the hardest heart, as the expression went. "Very well. I will show you to your room. Your baggage will be quite safe there, for I run a respectable house here. Afterward, you may come down for a plate, and I will have my daughter prepare you a hot bath, which none could deny you need." Jorinda favoured him with a sardonic smile. "The cost will be five groats each. That covers the room, food, and bath. Wine will be extra." He held out a hand in anticipation of payment in advance.

Jorinda imagined he had inflated the price. She laughed, leaned forward, and he swayed backward. "I think you meant four groats each, innkeep."

He seemed annoyed for a heartbeat, then he shrugged. "I am not busy tonight, and it is not the travel season."

Jorinda handed over a regal, worth ten groats. "That should cover the room and some wine with our meal." She smiled, and the innkeep huffed as he took the coin and slipped it into his apron. He led them up a narrow stairway and showed them into a small room with a low cot and no window, not even a table for a vanity bowl.

Deineike raised something Jorinda had overlooked. "May we stable our horses?"

"That you may." The innkeep sighed and rolled his eyes. "I imagine you do not wish to pay for that either."

Jorinda stifled a laugh. "Not for the stable, but we will pay a fair price for oats and hay."

"My thanks." His voice dripped with sarcasm. "Come down to the tavernroom whenever you are ready. I will have a meal prepared for you." He turned and left, and laughter overtook them both at the same moment.

Jorinda lowered her voice to mimic that of the innkeep. "That will be five groats each."

"I think you mean four, innkeep." Deineike effected a high, squeaky voice.

Jorinda's eyes widened in horror as though hurt. "I do not talk like that." They both laughed again, and Jorinda slid her arms around Deineike's waist. "We have reached Vjort, but I do not think we need to part yet. More pleasure awaits us, I think."

Deineike kissed her. "Until we are caught."

Jorinda looked away as bitter memories battered at the happiness of the moment. "We will not be caught. I will not allow us to be caught."

Deineike frowned. "You speak in riddles. What does that mean?"

Jorinda had spoken without thought as her memories had sickened her for a moment. Deineike did not deserve the same fate Jorinda must face. She longed to recreate the relaxed mood her sombre words threatened to dispel, so she gave Deineike's nose a playful flick. "I will not allow my fun to be spoiled, and you are the most fun I have had for many passes." They kissed again; a long, slow kiss, full of the promise of what could be later.

They went back down the stairs and took a seat at a small table in one corner of the tavernroom. The innkeep brought them each a bowl of thick broth, along with still-warm fresh bread and cold meats. Steam rose from the tasty, wholesome broth, and they ate with relish after their austere provisions on the road. They washed it down with three goblets of sweet, heady wine, and their mood brightened further. Some of the other patrons turned interested glances their way, but none approached their table or spoke to them. The wine eased the stresses of the journey from them, and they became light-headed.

Their hunger sated, Jorinda approached the innkeep to say they were ready to bathe. A few moments later, a young girl appeared, introduced herself as Helie, and led them to a room at the rear of the inn where a tub of hot water stood, a cake of soap and a pair of cloths to dry themselves beside it.

As Helie made to leave, Jorinda stopped her. "We have a problem I hope you can help us with."

Helie gave them a bright smile. "Anything I can do to be of service."

"Our clothes are dirty from the road, but we have no others."

The girl nodded and appeared unperturbed by two women who shared a tub and had no spare clothes. "I will take your clothes and have them clean and ready for you in the morning. I will find some clothes you can wear back to your room, although I doubt you will find them suitable for the tavernroom."

Jorinda smiled her appreciation. "My thanks." Helie left with their clothes, and Jorinda threw herself into the tub.

Only one of them could fit into the tub at a time, so Deineike sat on the floor next to her. "That girl could teach her father about good manners."

Jorinda revelled in the warmth of the water and splashed some of it over the side of the tub. "That she could. We should give her a groat for her troubles." She sloshed a substantial amount of water over Deineike.

Deineike laughed and swayed backward. "Leave some for me."

"Groats or water?"

"Both." Deineike leaned forward and kissed Jorinda. A polite cough from the door interrupted them, and Helie stood there with clothes in her arms.

"These should suffice." The young girl placed the clothes on the floor, then left.

Deineike looked crestfallen, red-faced. "Caught in the act." Jorinda pulled her forward and kissed her again.

The tub refreshed them in mind and body, though they were still light-headed from the wine. They donned the clothes, which were nothing more than outdoor cloaks, doubtless left behind by inebriated patrons. They pulled the cloaks about them and ran up the stairs to their room.

In the seclusion of the room, they threw off the cloaks and lay on the bed. Jorinda lay with her back to Deineike as she wrestled with a dilemma. She could not deny that physical intimacy with this sensuous woman whose hands and mouth could set her body afire entranced her, but she remained anxious about a relationship with a woman bound to her own fate in such a complicated manner.

Deineike's soft voice interrupted her thoughts. "Jorinda?"

A hand rested on her hip, gentle pressure that compelled her to turn and face Deineike's blue eyes and honest, compassionate face. She lay on her back as Deineike's eyes burned into hers, filled with lust.

Jorinda breathed Deineike's name, unable to resist any longer, and she pulled the taller woman on top of her and kissed her, hungry with desire. Deineike moaned and pressed her pelvis against Jorinda's. For more than an hour they drew cries of abandonment from each other and lifted one another to ever higher crests of satisfaction until they reached a final peak, their spent bodies covered in sweat and their hair plastered about their faces.

Some time passed before Deineike spoke again. "I did not scream."

Jorinda reflected on the past hour before she replied. "I heard parts of you scream that none outside the door would hear. Your body screamed."

Deineike's face wrinkled in concentration, and Jorinda pulled her hair in jest. The tall woman conceded Jorinda's point. "You are correct. Never has my body screamed so much."

"Nor mine. Nor mine." Jorinda had whispered another comparison between Deineike and Arella. Deineike possessed exceptional sexual skill, and every nerve and sinew in Jorinda's body trembled in response to her hands and tongue, but she could not understand why she felt as though she betrayed Arella when she lay with Deineike. She dismissed the unhelpful thought.

They fell asleep wrapped in each other's arms. Fatigue took them, and Jorinda enjoyed her most peaceful night in many passes. For the first night since Taro's farm, no nightmares plagued her.

A knock on the door early in the morning woke them, and the young girl's voice came through the door. "It is Helie. I have brought your clothes."

"You may enter." Sleepy still, Jorinda gave no thought to the fact they both lay naked on the cot. Helie opened the door, but if what she saw surprised her, she gave no sign.

"I could scarce get the leather trousers dry."

Deineike reassured her. "Do not be concerned."

Jorinda reached down to her pouch. "Here, take this. You have been most helpful." She held out a groat.

Helie stared at it open-mouthed but did not move to take it, and Jorinda waved the coin at her in an invitation to accept it. "Father does not like me to take coin from the guests. We run a respectable house and give such service as we can with no need for extra payment."

Jorinda smiled. "Nevertheless, I want you to take it as a gift from a friend, if nothing more."

Hesitant, Helie reached out and took the coin, then said, "My thanks." Eyes bright with excitement, she dropped the clothes on the bed and ran from the room.

Deineike stood, stretched, and picked up her trousers. "These trousers were a mistake." She spoke half to herself, it seemed. "I left in a hurry and gave no thought to practical clothing."

Jorinda knelt on the bed and kissed the dark-haired woman's nose. "Poor Deineike, overdressed and under-coined."

"I have no need of coin, for I have obtained a wealthy lover."

Jorinda laughed and teased her. "You must tell me about her."

"Someday, someday." Deineike's smile lit up the room, brighter than any lantern.

They went down to the tavernroom. The hour was early, and the innkeep swirled tankards in a bowl of soapy water. "Good morning." He sounded friendlier than the previous night. "I trust you slept well?"

Deineike nodded. "Well enough, my thanks."

"I can fetch you some oatmeal if you wish to break your fast."

Deineike affirmed their hunger. "That we do." They took seats at a table before she added, "My thanks." Jorinda smiled at the small courtesy. They ate in silence, rested but still weary in their bones after the journey south. After the meal, they gathered their packs and settled for the horses' feed before they rode off toward the centre of the town.

Despite Jorinda's words the previous night, her heart told her she should end this dangerous liaison. Resolve abandoned her at the last as she thought back over the journey. Deineike seemed a tender, affectionate woman, soft spoken and considerate, and a skilled, energetic lover who had sated every need in Jorinda each time they had lain together.

Nonetheless, a darkness hung between them, and although Deineike could not see through that ominous veil, Jorinda could. She feared the consequences of a tear in the veil, but now it came to it, she cared for Deineike and could not bring herself to turn from her. Rylfolk often said, *"Time salves the deepest burn."* Time might lessen the risks, but if Deineike learned the truth—

Deineike's voice interrupted Jorinda's thoughts. "I have no plan to speak of now we are here, but I thought we might either move south in a day or two or rest here until spring." Deineike reined the grey to a halt. "We will need more coin, if we are to stay."

"We could sell ourselves." Deineike did not laugh at Jorinda's jest and touched her heels to the grey. "You could clean out a barn or two." Jorinda persisted with her jests, but Deineike seemed in no mood for them, so Jorinda gave up and followed her in silence. Deineike would need little persuasion to stay with Jorinda until she learned the gruesome truth, if she ever did. For now, Jorinda would stay with the dark-haired woman and await whatever fates were written. She lacked the conviction to part ways even as common sense told her it would be a safer choice.

Vjort sprawled around a central square comprised of wooden buildings, some more grandiose than others, all dedicated to commerce. There were inns, shops of many kinds, and at the northern end the Portreeve's Offices' ornate carved Ortwood doors watched activities in the square like two stern, authoritative eyes.

The change from the compressed dirt of the street to the worn cobblestones of the square amplified the steady clop of the horses' hooves, which echoed around the almost deserted square. They gave the Portreeve's Offices a wide berth and rode past the few stallholders who set out their wares in the centre of the square and the occasional person who crossed the cobbled expanse to some destination or other. The women rode toward the dock area where the river flowed past the town, mayhap on its journey from the mountains in the north.

Despite the early hour, the docks were busier than the square as ship's crews bustled about the decks of the three vessels moored there. Workers loaded goods onto a two-masted ship, which might depart that day, and large crates of what Jorinda took to be fish were unloaded from two smaller vessels further down the dock.

Many buildings surrounded the docks: taverns, shops, and offices, as well as numerous tally houses for the goods that passed through the dock. The women gazed at the scene as they walked their horses along the dockside, unhurried and in search of inspiration. The scene reminded Jorinda of a smaller version of the docks of Zhanghar, and she reasoned the river might lead south to Torric.

Deineike made a half-hearted suggestion. "We could take passage on that ship."

"We do not have the coin for such a voyage. Ship travel is the domain of the wealthy." Jorinda doubted she could use her token without awkward questions from Deineike. "In truth, I am not sure we should journey south. I like it here." She guessed she had sounded unconvinced by her own arguments, but she did not wish to head for Torric. A Guild operated in that city, and she had no desire to walk into their open arms. She would try this town for now, and for a time she would share it with Deineike.

"Then we must find work and somewhere to stay." Deineike wheeled the grey back toward the square. At that moment, a man dressed in a distinctive red tunic that marked him as one of the Portreeve's men stepped from behind a building. He fumbled at his trousers and did not see them, and Deineike's horse bumped him— gentle, but hard enough to send him feet over breakfast, and he landed on his behind on the ground.

Deineike gasped, and Jorinda leapt from her horse, stood over him, and gushed an apology. "We are so sorry. We did not see you. Are you hurt?"

"Never panic. No complication is irredeemable." The mantra she had heard so many times throughout her training. She checked their surroundings. Some dock workers nearby had turned to watch as the unfortunate man had landed on his embarrassment, and despite her instincts, it would be difficult to slit his throat and

tip his body into the river unseen. She must bluff her way out of the encounter.

The man looked up at her, his pride the worst bruised part of him. Jorinda gave him a sweet smile and offered him a hand. He spurned it and struggled to his feet while he clutched at his dignity the best he could. "My thanks for your concern. I am not hurt, and I trust neither of you is."

"That we are not, my thanks." Jorinda adopted a deferential tone, head bowed.

His glance flicked from one to the other. "It is early for you to be about these parts." He studied their clothing and horses. "It can be unsavoury down here at times, in parts at the least." He gestured further down the dock.

Deineike said nothing. It would fall to Jorinda to extract them from the situation. "Not this early, I suspect. In truth, our brother is due in on a ship this morning and we are excited to see him." She gave an embarrassed laugh and lowered her voice to a conspiratorial whisper. "We are early, I confess."

He nodded. "May I suggest you check at the Master's Office? They may be able to tell you where his ship will dock. It is some forty paces in that direction." He pointed further down the dock.

"My thanks." Without hesitation, Jorinda led her horse in the direction he had indicated. The grey's hoofbeats clip-clopped behind her as Deineike followed in silence.

His voice stopped them in their tracks. "What is the name of your brother's ship?"

Without hesitation, Jorinda turned and beamed a cheerful smile at him. "The Jorinda."

He shook his head. "I cannot say I have heard of it." In the corner of Jorinda eye, Deineike's head slumped forward. "I do not often patrol here, in truth. I hate the smell of the fish. Good day to you."

"And to you." Jorinda favoured him with a small wave before

she turned and walked along the dock without a backward glance. They found the Master's Office, and Jorinda glanced back, surreptitious. The man had wandered further down the dock and did not look back at them. She mounted the dun, and they rode off toward the square.

"The Jorinda?" Deineike seemed ready to burst, unable to contain herself any longer, her face red, a wildness in her eyes.

Jorinda reminded herself to be cautious. She could not reveal that what appeared to be a moment of inspiration had in fact been the first name for a ship that came to mind. "I thought it a reasonable name for a ship. You did not leap to my rescue with a suggestion of your own."

Deineike sighed. "That I did not. I feared we would be found out, and I could think of nothing to say. You did well in the circumstances." She snorted and shook her head. "The Jorinda."

Jorinda worked to calm herself after the shock of the incident. Such a harmless encounter, yet fraught with so much danger. "Vjort is a small place to hide, after all else, but I know of no other towns hereabouts. I have not seen your map book." She managed a smile, but Deineike did not return it, so Jorinda followed the path of her thoughts. "Another long ride does not appeal, I confess. If we rested here for a few days, we might find some odd job to do and earn a little coin."

Deineike snapped her fingers in the air. "I have thought of the perfect thing." A grin spread across her face.

NINE
A DANCE WITH FATE

THEY RODE BACK TO THE SQUARE, FOUND AN INN, RESERVED A ROOM, and stabled their horses. Deineike explained she had experience at tally work and might find employment in one of the smaller tally houses at the docks. Jorinda dithered, worried that if Deineike worked at the docks every day, she might come across the man she had knocked down. The work would bring in useful coin for a short period, however, so she set her fears aside, and they returned to the docks.

They found several small tally houses, and Deineike's theory proved correct. Rewherran, the owner of one of the smaller houses, offered her a position that incorporated tally work and assistance with the movement of goods on and off the dock. He had been impressed by her physique, but he had bargained a wage Jorinda believed too low for the work. She reasoned he might have paid a man more, but they would have an income, at the least. Deineike laughed as she told Jorinda she would start the next day and recounted his final words. "Do not be late. I despise tardiness."

Rewherran pointed Deineike to a friend, Moren, whose husband had died not long before and who had a room available to rent, and Moren took them in, grateful for the extra coin. To allay suspicion, they told her they were sisters come to town to make some coin and happy to share a bed, and she seemed content to accept the tale. She might guess the truth and report it to Rewherran, a risk the two women could not discount, but they rolled the dice and told themselves they only intended to stay in Vjort for a short time.

Jorinda's nightmares had not abandoned her for long, and Pilos intruded into her life more now he no longer lived than he ever had while he had been alive. Her troubled sleep often featured Arella dead at her feet and Taro seated nearby, his eyes filled with accusations. Pilos, his throat a hideous vermilion gash, would appear before her. "Am I to be killed for what I did, then? Has Styrrach betrayed me?"

Arella's voice would rise from the floor in response. "I love you." Jorinda would awaken in a cold sweat. Deineike sometimes woke with her and attempted to calm her before they could drift back to sleep.

Their fortunes improved further when Jorinda found work in a local garment shop that made good quality clothes for the wealthier residents of Vjort who could afford such items of finery. If word of her making in Vjort somehow reached Zhanghar, Styrrach or the Portreeve might decide to investigate, but the extra coin would help them to plan for the future, and they relaxed as the days passed without event. Their short stay in Vjort extended to a pass, then more; they were content together, and life appeared calm. All three women wore fine clothes thanks to Jorinda's work in Moren's parlour in the evenings.

Jorinda's fan created a ripple on those calm waters not long after they arrived in Vjort. She carried it with her in her boot wherever she went, and one evening it fell out as Deineike picked up the boots in their bedroom to move them. Jorinda rushed to scoop it up before Deineike could do so, but Deineike asked to see it as Jorinda clung to it and shook her head, unable to find any rational excuse for why she would not let Deineike hold it.

Deineike smiled away her confusion after a heartbeat. "It matters not. It is dear to you, as you are to me. I understand."

Jorinda mumbled a sad explanation. "I apologise. I carry it as a lucky token in truth, nothing more. Nobody has ever touched it but me, and I fear that if someone else held it…"

"Jorinda, I understand. We will not chance our luck, for that might take us from one another. Put it somewhere safe and I shall never touch it again."

Although Deineike claimed to understand Jorinda's hesitant excuses about the fan, she could not have done so, and Jorinda felt ashamed of everything the fan represented. Shame for the deaths its blade had wrought and for the deception she perpetuated against Deineike. Above all, she felt a bitter shame that Arella had perished under its dreadful caress. From that moment forward, she would keep it from Deineike's eyesight in her boot or beneath the mattress.

One night, after they had made love for long hours, a slow journey around each other's bodies as each took countless moments of fulfilment from the other that left them spent and satisfied, they lay on the bed, exhausted, wet with sweat.

Jorinda had feared love would arrive sooner or later and dreaded it, with good cause. Her nightmares had come true, after all else. Arella said the words and paid a terrible price. Deineike fixed Jorinda with a stare from her expressive eyes, eyes that revealed all before she even spoke. No more than a look, but Jorinda 's heart raced as Deineike spoke. "You are incredible in every way. I am…" She paused. "I lo—"

Before Deineike could finish the sentence, Jorinda raised a finger to her lips to silence her. Although she cared for Deineike, she did not wish her to speak the three words that had damned Arella, could not bear the guilt of another life lost because of them. The past stalked her, and while it insisted Deineike must learn the truth one day, that truth might destroy the dark-haired woman. Jorinda could not leave Deineike, but neither could she be honest with her, not yet. Their fates were written, and she could do no more than hope that, when the moment arose, it would not shatter them both so completely, all the pieces could never be recovered. "Do not say it. Please, do not say it."

"Why? Does it pain you to hear it?"

Jorinda could find no words to explain herself other than to repeat her plea. "Do not say it."

Deineike's face radiated compassion. "You are a mystery, Jorinda. Some anguish I do not understand gnaws at you and will not cease, an agony you choose not to reveal to me. At whiles, I think the"—she seemed to struggle for the correct word—"menace of you should worry me, but I cannot bear to be apart from you for a heartbeat. You are all I think of in the day and all I dream of at night. If I do not say it, it will not change the truth, Jorinda. I love you." Deineike wiped tears from Jorinda's cheeks and placed a tender kiss on her lips.

Jorinda looked at her for long moments then gave a small, tearful laugh. "You said it. I asked you not to, yet you said it."

"That I did." Deineike's smile seemed as warm as the midday sun.

"Then it is said, and we go on as we will. The fates are written."

"That they are. You look tired. Sleep, little one."

Jorinda grimaced. "I cannot abide to be called that."

With a warm smile, Deineike brushed Jorinda's brown hair back from her forehead. "It is an expression, nothing more. I meant no harm by it." She put out the lantern and soon fell asleep, but

Jorinda lay awake beside her and wished her life had turned in a different direction. For so many years in her dreams, a woman would whisper of love, but now those words set a chill in her heart. Sleep eluded her for close to an hour, then brought the nightmares again.

Each spring, a festival took place known as Springfest. Most local businesses locked up for the day, there were street parties, and the residents decked their houses with homemade streamers. A vast market took place in the square with a great many performers and minstrels to entertain the large crowds. Vjortfolk and visitors alike flocked to the market ready to spend the coin they had hoarded for many passes on the items they found on stalls scattered around the square, or on delicacies such as spit-roasted meats, exotic fruits, and spiced wines.

Jorinda and Deineike had been busy in the pass that led up to Springfest. Many ships arrived laden with goods and travellers, which kept Deineike occupied at the tally house, and the wealthy citizens of Vjort pressed Jorinda's employer to make them fine garments to show off in, which compelled Jorinda to spend long days at work to fulfil all the orders. As a boon, they had both been granted a day's absence from work for Springfest, and as the day approached, their tiredness gave way to excitement as they became caught up in the air of anticipation that pervaded the town.

On the day of the festival, they rose early and walked to the square, which lay five streets from Moren's house. Moren walked with them for a time but soon left them to seek out her friends and family. Deineike and Jorinda were in high spirits, and they paused at most of the stalls, entranced by the goods brought in by far-off merchants for the occasion. They ate lunch at the inn where they had stayed for a few days before they had moved in with Moren and where their horses were still stabled. The women shared a pitcher of wine and visited the horses to check on them.

Afterward, they returned to the celebrations, which were in full swing. People danced to music from the many minstrels who performed around the square, the large crowds wandered from stall to stall, and everyone made merry beneath the impressive facade of the Portreeve's Offices. Even the Portreeve himself attended, in a roped off enclosure, to entertain the local businesspeople who paid the highest levies. He provided a massive feast and large quantities of the finest local ales and wines as recognition of their contributions. Jorinda's employer had told her of the Portreeve's Springfest tradition, although he had not received an invitation.

Deineike and Jorinda stood near an energetic band of minstrels, clapped along as they watched the festival-goers dance, and declined several requests for dances from men who approached them. A hand-drawn sign near the minstrels announced them: "Khittie And Her Travelling Ensemble." The musicians strummed, plucked, and beat their instruments while an older woman whom they took to be Khittie sang. She had a voice that captivated them and could bring a tear to the eyes or a laugh to the lips in accordance with the mood of the song. Jorinda turned to smile at Deineike but found the tall woman's attention occupied by a short man with cold grey eyes and a paucity of white hair that made him look old before his time.

The man shouted at Deineike over the hubbub. "May I?" Before Jorinda could tell him to move along and find another dance partner, Deineike smiled at him. At that, to Jorinda's surprise, the man took the taller woman in his arms and whisked her around in an erratic circle. He appeared to be the worse for drink, and once or twice they almost fell.

Jorinda had no idea who he might be, but she could not force the pair apart without the risk of unwelcome attention. It shocked her how much she resented this man's intrusion into their day. In truth, neither Arella nor Deineike had ever given her a reason to be jealous, but to her surprise her blood boiled with envy as the man's hands moved around Deineike's back as though she were a sheet on a bed he smoothed for a night's sleep. She watched them cavort, Deineike gripped in the man's arms as he shouted something into her ear.

Their dance took them away from Jorinda, so she followed them as the man continued to speak to Deineike, words Jorinda could not hear but could guess at well enough. Angry, she pulled her fan from her boot and held it at her side.

Without warning, Deineike stumbled and slumped in his arms. Tears came to her eyes, she rubbed at an ankle, and he relaxed his grip. She sank to the cobbled ground and continued to rub at the ankle while he fussed over her.

Jorinda took the opportunity to step forward. "Sister, are you hurt?" She pushed between Deineike and the man.

Deineike made a weak reply. "My ankle."

The man tugged at Jorinda's sleeve. "I am about to escort your sister home."

Jorinda fixed Deineike with a pointed stare and shouted backward at him. "My thanks, but that will not be necessary. I shall take her home myself."

"Come now, you are but a woman, and she is bigger than—"

Jorinda wheeled and cut him off in mid-sentence. She glared at him and raised her fan to her waist as she fought her impulse to spring its keen blade, and he glanced down to it, then looked back to her as she spat out, "Do you suggest I am unable to help my own sister?" He spluttered, uncertain.

Deineike's miserable voice rose from the ground. "We will manage, Rewherran. Please go back to the festivities. I am sure I will be fine in the morning."

He hesitated as he appeared cowed by Jorinda's fury, then glanced down at Deineike. "Very well. Do not be late tomorrow. I detest tardiness." He spun before she could reply, disappeared into the throng, and Jorinda glowered after him until he became lost in the crowd.

"Jorinda, your intervention could have been dangerous. He is my employer."

Venom spilled from Jorinda's every word. "My intervention? You dance with him, but I am the one who places us in danger?"

Deineike looked taken aback and spread her arms, palms to the sky. "He is my employer. What could I do?"

Jorinda paused while she tried to gather herself together. "Are you hurt?" She could not drive the anger from her voice.

"That I am not. I did not stumble. I pretended, in an attempt to end the dance sooner. A mistake, as he insisted that he take me home. A sorry turn." Deineike hesitated. "You have your fan in your hand. Did you think to cool his passion with it, then?" Deineike smiled, but the jest did not amuse Jorinda, and the older woman waved a pathetic arm in the air. "You must help me to my feet lest Rewherran watches us from somewhere nearby. The deception must be maintained." Jorinda slipped the fan back into her boot and offered Deineike an arm. Deineike's face became a portrait of misery as she mumbled, "I am sorry, I did not know he would be such a nuisance. Forgive me. Please."

The unhappy apology shamed Jorinda, and she coerced a smile to her lips. "Lean on my arm and limp. He may see us as we leave." Deineike did as requested, and they moved away from the square. "By the fates, you are heavy. Do not act so well, or I cannot support you. I should try to find Rewherran and ask for his help, after all else." Deineike laughed, doubtless pleased the moment had passed, and they continued toward the house.

Jorinda struggled to dampen her fury and bring her temper under control. There had been no reason for her to act as she did. As far as she knew, the man did no more than dance with Deineike. Jorinda had done far worse with Taro to maintain a façade as she hid herself away. It staggered her, the pace at which jealousy had consumed her, a jealousy that awoke the killer she believed she had kept hidden away.

She had wondered whether she could kill the Portreeve's man on the docks when Deineike's horse had knocked him down. After all else, it seemed her time in the Guild had created a beast she could not tame. A grim thought came to her. *"When one lies down with monsters..."*

Rewherran appeared to have put the affair behind him. The next day, Deineike said he had enquired about her ankle and seemed satisfied with her reply that it had not been as serious as she had first thought. Six days later, however, Deineike looked troubled when she came home and urged Jorinda to follow her to their room. Breathless and anxious, she spoke as soon as the door closed. "Rewherran called me into his office today. He asked me about you, curious I had never mentioned you before."

The development troubled Jorinda. "What answer did you give him?"

"I attempted to distract him. I asked him whether he had brothers or sisters and told him he and I know all but nothing about one another's lives."

Jorinda nodded her approval. "A wise response. Did he accept it?"

Deineike bit her lower lip and shook her head once. "I am unsure. Mayhap." She fell silent.

"You think he suspects we are not sisters?"

"I do not know, though that is my guess. We should be careful. I wonder if he has spoken to Moren."

"Would she tell him anything about us, if he has?"

Deineike shrugged. "I would not expect her to lie to him on our behalf. Do not forget Springfest."

Jorinda sighed and pulled Deineike close. Deineike's words brought troublesome news, but the women could do nothing about it for now, so Jorinda abandoned her anxiety. "Let us think no more of it tonight. I have a better idea." They kissed, and their passion for each other overtook their concern. They tore at each other's clothes and made frenzied love.

The next morning, Deineike went downstairs early and left Jorinda in bed. As Deineike reached the scullery, which lay beneath their room, voices carried up to the bedroom.

Deineike's voice drifted through the ceiling. "Good morning, Rewherran. Have you come to escort me to work this morning, or am I tardy?" The floor between them muffled Deineike's already quiet voice, but her words were clear enough.

Rewherran's deep voice answered Deineike. "Moren tells me you and your sister are close. So close, it sounds at times as though you are—" He hesitated, and Jorinda slid from the bed above him. "Curse it, you lie together."

After a pause, Deineike spoke again. "We are frivolous at times, I agree. But do I lie with my own sister? Really, I think—"

"Do not play games with me, Deineike. This Jorinda is no sister of yours. The two of you are..." He seemed unable to find the word he searched for but would not allow that to deter him in the delivery of his rant. "Two women together. It is obscene." He spat out the word "obscene" as if it were a piece of rotten fruit, bitten into by mistake. Moren gave a startled gasp, and Jorinda reached under the mattress for her fan, then ran down the stairs.

Deineike did not answer straight away, as though she weighed the course her words would follow. "Jorinda is my lover, as you have guessed. That is not a matter for you to concern yourself over, and what you make of it, I do not much care. I would rather you kept your opinions to yourself, more so while you are in this house, which is our home." Jorinda had reached the scullery doorway. Deineike had her back toward the door, and Rewherran stood beyond her. Moren sat on a chair at the table to Deineike's right, a hand over her face as though she might hide from all that took place in her home.

Rewherran's face contorted with rage. "This house belongs to Moren."

Jorinda intervened, and Deineike turned her head at the sound of her voice, surprise on her face. "That it does, yet it is still our home."

Rewherran spat his anger at Jorinda. "Ah, so speaks the partner in this deviant charade."

An ominous silence fell in the scullery. Jorinda fumed that this vile little man might destroy all the happiness she and Deineike had found since they had arrived in Vjort. He would rush from the house to tell his friends, who would tell their own as soon as they could. Two women who lay together—such a juicy, scandalous story. The tale would spread until it came to Zhanghar, where Styrrach would learn of it. The Guildmeister would dispatch Guild members, and she and Deineike, and quite likely Moren, would go to bed one night but never rise in the morning. Jorinda exaggerated the danger, but she preferred to prepare for the worst and not be taken by some surprise she had not anticipated.

Moren's sharp words broke the palpable tension in the room. "Please leave, Rewherran. I wish you had not come. They harm nobody, and you have told me Deineike is a good worker. Nothing but ill can result if you pursue the matter further."

He shot her a dark glare but turned to leave. "You need not come to work today or any day, Deineike. You will not find work in Vjort in the future unless you can find someone as deviant as yourselves to pay you." Dust motes swirled and cavorted in the beam of sunlight that shone through the scullery window as he swept, furious, from the house and slammed the door behind him.

Moren loosed a sad sigh. "Oh dear, now see what I have done. He has pressed me so on the matter, ever since Springfest. I should have kept quiet. I am sorry."

Deineike crossed the room and put an arm about the old

woman's shoulder. "You did nothing wrong, Moren. He would have learned at some point or other. I will find work, despite his bluster."

Through the window, Jorinda stared at Rewherran's back as he stomped away. She held her fan against her chest, and as she stared after him her fingers flitted over the button that sprang the blade, consumed by her fury.

Moren sat at the table and sniffed back tears. Deineike sidled over to Jorinda and placed a hand on her arm. Jorinda inclined her head upward as she spat out curt words. "Let us go upstairs and talk." She turned and climbed the stairs to their room. Deineike closed the door behind them, and Jorinda stood with her back to Deineike as she gazed down from the small window and contemplated their options. "We must leave. Today. Now."

"What?" Deineike sounded stunned. "Why?"

Jorinda wheeled on her. "He will talk. People will know about us."

"Let them gossip. I do not care. I love you, and I am not ashamed of that." A pause, then a soft repetition of the words. "I love you." Tears pooled in her eyes.

Jorinda looked up at the ceiling in exasperation. "Have you forgotten I am a murderer?"

"How could I forget such a thing?" Anger flared in Deineike's voice. "I fail to see how the fact we are in…that I am in love with you would lead anyone to take you for a killer."

"I would prefer they did not have the opportunity." Jorinda folded her arms in an act of defiance, a challenge to Deineike to gainsay her. Deineike did not understand; the Guild might hear of them, and Jorinda could not point it out to her. To do so would unmask her. Jorinda doubted she could retain her sanity if this pretence must be continued any longer, but she could not reveal the truth. She could not lay that at Deineike's door.

Deineike looked away and wrinkled her forehead. "Might Springfest have made him suspicious?"

"It is of no consequence. The cat is out of the sack, and how it came by its freedom is not important. What is important is that we leave now, before tongues wag and awkward questions are asked."

Deineike sighed but seemed unprepared to pursue the argument any further. "Very well. I think you are over-cautious, but we planned to head south after a short rest here, as I recall. I had begun to like it here, nonetheless."

Jorinda feigned excitement. "As had I, but a fresh challenge awaits us. The road calls to us; the fun we anticipated, and the next part of our journey." Deineike must not know that doubts circled Jorinda, closer than ever, or that her apparent easy demeanour concealed fears that ripped her insides apart.

Deineike sighed again. "I wish I could share your enthusiasm. Let us gather our things, then break the news to Moren. She will miss the coin."

Jorinda felt some guilt over Moren's financial situation but held the old woman in no small part to blame for the morning's outcome. She did not, however, want to delay their departure with an argument about a few coins. "We can leave her some. We have hoarded a good bit over the winter."

Deineike laughed despite the tears that still pooled in her blue eyes. "A good bit? Sometimes you speak in the strangest way." Jorinda poked her tongue out at her, and Deineike teased her. "Very stylish." Jorinda ran her tongue around her lips with a suggestive pout. Deineike's face flushed, and her nostrils flared as though she imagined Jorinda's tongue as it licked the juices of desire from her. "We do not need to leave right away, do we?" Deineike slid her arms around the slender waist of her tormentor.

"That we do." Jorinda wished to leave Vjort as soon as possible now Rewherran had discovered their relationship. She pulled Deineike's arms away, gentle but meaningful.

Deineike sighed, then turned to the preparations, and they went down the stairs to tell Moren they must leave.

The news saddened the old woman. "All because of me."

Deineike reassured her. "No blame can be attached to you, Moren." She kissed the old woman on the temple. "We always intended to move on, and Rewherran has provided the impetus for us to do so."

Jorinda did not hold Moren blameless, but she kept her opinion to herself, placed two regals on the table, and smiled at Moren as she spoke in a cheerful voice. "We will leave you this coin, since you have been a good friend to us. We hope you will soon find a new lodger to take our place."

Moren picked up the coins and more tears sprang to her eyes. "You have no need to leave me this, dears. After all else, I confirmed Rewherran's suspicions. My thanks, nonetheless, and my best wishes for the rest of your journey. Where will that journey take you next?"

Jorinda did not hesitate. "Dur City." Moren nodded.

Deineike picked up her pack, and they left without another word. The warm sun climbed the sky of a bright spring morning as they strolled toward the inn, where the grey and the dun seemed excited to see them. Both horses looked overweight from lack of exercise, but Deineike hoped the journey would soon have them fitter.

The women paid the innkeep what they owed, saddled the horses, then walked beside them toward the southern outskirts of the town, where they paused as though Vjort whispered to them to remain. Jorinda hoped the journey they embarked on would be easier than their winter slog from Taro's farm.

Deineike spoke aloud, almost as if to herself. "Vjort has been kind to us." She shrugged her shoulders. "Until today, that is."

Jorinda glanced at her; a woman who had set off from Zhanghar alone, arrived in Vjort in the company of a virtual stranger, and now left it with the woman she loved. So were the fates written, she imagined, and what is scribed, must be. As she whispered, "Farewell, Vjort," she mounted the dun and pressed it forward toward Torric.

TEN
A MEETING IN PARMEN

Styrrach summoned Wilash to the Guild building. When Wilash arrived, he found Styrrach and Porl in the parlour outside Styrrach's office.

The moment Wilash entered the parlour, Styrrach turned to him. "Word has come from Vjort. Two women arrived there four passes ago or so. They lay together, it seems." Wilash said nothing, and Styrrach continued, a cold glint in his eyes. "A tally master there mentioned it to one we know, and the news found its way back here. Women who lie together. It disgusts me." His face twisted with revulsion as he spoke of the women. "Nonetheless, it seems one of them carried a fan. Does that seem familiar to you?"

Wilash kept his reply non-committal, careful. "Many women carry fans, more so as the weather warms."

Styrrach pondered this. "That they do. It may be nothing. Did you know Corelle lay with women?" He fixed an accusatory gaze on Wilash.

Lies would not serve Wilash here. He paused, but no acceptable version of the truth came to mind, and Styrrach would not wait overlong for an answer. "She lay with Arella, I believe."

"You knew this, yet you said nothing to us?"

Wilash met Styrrach's stare and did not look away. "Are relationships between Guild members forbidden, then?"

Styrrach laughed, but his cold laughter and mirth were strangers. "Relationships between Guild members were not forbidden because they would not have taken place before you brought a woman into the Guild." He paused. "It seems you introduced deviancy into our ranks."

Wilash dug his fingernails into his palm. He must control his temper. Corelle and Arella had enjoyed a warm bond, full of love. Their connection did not resemble any he had known during his casual dalliances with women he met, but he dared not rebuke Styrrach. He said nothing.

Styrrach pressed onward. "It is no surprise, but she now appears not to travel as Corelle, though the name she now uses has not reached us." Wilash suppressed a smile as he detected a note of frustration in Styrrach's voice at the incomplete information he had received. "We understand they have left Vjort and may be headed for Dur City. We have few dependable eyes in Ort and none in Dur City. Better intelligence should come soon. I have dispatched a courier to Vjort, and we will see what new information they return with, if any."

Wilash could not fathom why Styrrach had summoned him from the Portreeve's Offices to tell him this mundane story. "Is there something you wish me to do?"

Styrrach looked at Porl, who shook his head. "That there is not. I wished to know whether you knew of this deviancy, nothing more. As it turns, we already knew it, and it serves us she is this way. It is unusual and unnatural, and it disgusts me, but it will help us, I feel. It will make it more difficult for her to hide."

He turned and walked into his office without another word. Porl inclined his head toward the door to the street and Wilash left, his heart heavier than it had been when he arrived. He had been cast in a poor light, since he had not revealed the women's relationship to Styrrach. He already knew Styrrach had learned of Arella and Corelle's relationship and had wondered how long it would be before the Guildmeister mentioned it. Although he had hoped Corelle would escape, never to be heard of again, for some reason he could not guess, she had shown somebody the fan and announced herself. The unknown woman with her had been drawn into a dangerous situation she must know little of. He did not envy the fate that awaited her if the Guild caught up with her and Corelle. He plodded back to the Portreeve's Offices and cursed the day Styrrach had come to his father's smithy.

Jorinda and Deineike rode south for three hours as the sun climbed over them and began its descent toward the western horizon. The southern road remained in remarkable condition despite the lengthy rains of the recent winter, and they allowed the horses to walk at a relaxed pace. Both mounts stopped and nibbled at clumps of grass from time to time, motivated by laziness rather than hunger. Soon after the midday, Deineike suggested they stop for a rest and some food. They dismounted, took the packs from the horses, and allowed them to graze beside the road while the women took out some of the bread and cheese they had bought at the inn.

Jorinda looked around before she spoke through a mouthful of food. "This road seems well-travelled. I imagine we will find inns to spend the night in."

Deineike agreed. "You are right, my guess. Such accommodations will prove a hefty drain on our coin, however, and while the weather remains agreeable, we may prefer to sleep beneath the lights of the night sky."

Jorinda shuddered. "I do not prefer it. I loathe it. It is bad for my back." Back pain had troubled her ever since the tavern work in Ort, and she did not wish to make it worse with uncomfortable nights on the hard ground.

With a quiet laugh, Deineike shook her head. "You expect all the comforts of home even when we have no home."

Jorinda pouted. "That I do not. I pointed out that to sleep outdoors—"

"—is bad for your back. I know. We will see, little one, we will see."

The sound of distant hoofs came to Jorinda, and she sat upright, concerned. Worry hardened Deineike's eyes. "What is it?"

"Riders approach from Vjort. Several riders." Jorinda stood up and gazed north. She believed she could see a dust cloud some way behind them. Had they been followed? Had Rewherran sold them to the Portreeve so soon?

Deineike also stood and stared along the road. "I see nothing, nor hear any riders. Are you sure?"

"I am sure." Jorinda scanned the road, uncertain now, but loath to admit it.

Deineike seemed unconvinced. "It means nothing, some merchant, bent on trade with a village hereabouts." She cocked her head to one side and frowned in concentration. "I still do not hear them. You are certain?"

"Of course. Do you doubt me?" It aggravated Jorinda that Deineike questioned her while their lives might be in danger.

"That I do not. I just..." Deineike's words trailed off as Jorinda stood quite still and continued to stare northward. "What should we do?"

"There." Jorinda pointed north to a smudge on the horizon.

Deineike squinted forward, and Jorinda glanced at her, annoyed she could not see the dust. Deineike appeared to admit defeat. "Your ears and eyes are superb indeed, it seems."

The sand fell, and decisions must be made. What Jorinda thought she saw might be nothing more than a tree or a cloud on the horizon. "We should move on." Jorinda picked up her pack, approached the dun, and tried to sound calmer than she felt. "You are right, and there is nothing to fear. We should not take chances though, I think." She fastened her pack to the horse while Deineike busied herself with her own.

Deineike paused from her preparations. "Are you too worried? It has been a few passes now since Taro died, and none have looked for us as far as we know."

Jorinda mounted the dun, concerned the Portreeve might have heard of them from Rewherran or one of his friends. If Rewherran had revealed all to the Portreeve, and if he knew the Portreeve in Zhanghar sought a woman of her sexual preferences for heinous crimes, he might dispatch riders to find them. Deineike would find that improbable, and so she should if the death of Taro at Jorinda's hand were the sole matter of interest before the Portreeve. Jorinda must invent something to lend a greater sense of urgency to her desire to evade capture. She looked down at Deineike and strove to keep any emotion from her eyes. "Taro is not the only complication."

"What? What more could there be?" Deineike looked up and shaded her eyes with a hand as the dun skittered and placed Jorinda between her and the sun.

Jorinda bit her lip, and stared north as she strove to create a plausible story to appease Deineike. After all else, she could no longer see whatever had caught her attention. She sighed and looked down on Deineike once more as the spark of an idea came to her. "I have a debt—a substantial debt."

Deineike favoured Jorinda with a doubtful look, then shook her head in bewilderment. "With you, nothing is simple. I do not understand why this is, but nothing is ever as it seems, that much is clear." She pulled herself into the saddle of the grey and wheeled it around to the south. "You can explain more as we ride." She kicked her heels into the grey's side.

They rode at an even pace for two hours while the sun dipped ever lower in the skies, the shadows lengthened, and the horses settled into the exertion after their long rest. Jorinda spoke little, preoccupied with the creation of the story of the sham debt she had invented on an impulse. She judged it prudent to confirm she still saw nothing. "Hold." They both reined in and turned in their saddles to look north.

Jorinda squinted northward for some time. Deineike seemed impatient and made it obvious she saw nothing out of the ordinary. Jorinda accepted she no longer saw the cloud of dust she had been certain she had seen earlier. "Nobody follows, after all else." Deineike wore a surprised look. "Doubtless you were correct. I saw nothing more than a merchant who has camped early so he can feed his face."

Deineike shook her head, a wry smile on her lips. "Somebody follows us, then nobody follows us. How can you tell with such certainty, when I see nothing different now from when you first claimed you saw something?"

Jorinda smiled. "I have good eyes and ears, as you said."

"Better than good, it appears. If you are satisfied now, can we continue? I hope we can find a barn before darkness falls. Then you can tell me all about your debt."

They rode on, and they saw a light ahead as the twilight deepened. They were in luck, and the light shone from the window of a farmhouse. By the time the farmer had agreed to allow them to spend the night in his barn, and they had bedded their horses down for the night, darkness had fallen, and they were both tired from their first day on horseback in some time.

They ate a small meal, and to avoid awkward conversation, Jorinda busied herself with the creation of a bed in a hay pile. She hoped Deineike would not press her further on the debt story, but to her disappointment, her lover urged her to tell the tale as soon as they lay on the makeshift bed.

The tale began with a lie about when she arrived in Zhanghar. "About three years ago now, I was in Zhanghar—"

Deineike interrupted. "I thought you came from Ryl."

"That I do, but I had travelled to Zhanghar three years ago, and there I incurred a rather large debt."

"How did you incur this debt?"

"Do not interrupt." Jorinda aimed a playful push at Deineike's upper arm. "I do not think you realise how often you interrupt." Deineike held up her hands as if to say she would allow Jorinda to continue without further intervention. Jorinda scratched at the back of a hand in a bid to gain more time to pull a story together that would convince Deineike. "As you know, my father owns a garment shop in Ryl, and I arrived in Zhanghar determined to set up my own shop. I had little coin, however, so I struck a deal with a coinlender to obtain funds sufficient to rent and equip a shop. The shop did well at first, and I met the repayments with ease, but over time, custom declined, and I fell into arrears. Coinlenders do not favour those who do not meet their obligations, and I fled in fear of reprisals. I still owe the man a substantial sum." She came to an abrupt halt, concerned further embellishment might appear suspicious.

Deineike looked thoughtful. "How did one so new in Zhanghar know the whereabouts of this coinlender?"

"The coin trade operates from the docks in Ryl as well as Zhanghar. One city is much as another." Jorinda had not anticipated the question, and her reply sounded weak in her own ears.

"Whereabouts in Zhanghar might I have found this shop of yours?"

Jorinda replied without hesitation, the better to sell the story. "The poor quarter." Deineike came from Zhanghar, and Jorinda feared to elaborate on the location of her imaginary shop, lest Deineike be familiar with the area and catch her in the lie.

Deineike's mouth turned down in unmistakable disapproval. "That story is the least plausible of the many you have told me since first we met."

"You think I lie to you?" Jorinda strove to wear a picture of pained surprise on her face.

Deineike's soft reply hinted at no recrimination, no disappointment. "My love, I wear your making. The Portreeve himself would be fortunate to wear a wescoat of your making. The square of any city should be built around your shop. Nobody in the poor quarter could afford for you to even hem their dress. Those who could afford your making would not travel to the poor quarter to buy it. It is not true."

They lay in silence for a while as Jorinda brooded on how to extract herself from the falsehood. The injustice of it threatened to break her spirit. They had been happy in Vjort. The nightmares still plagued Jorinda, but her simple life with Deineike had stilled some of the torturous thoughts that crushed her after the death of Arella. She still despised all she had become, but she no longer yearned to fulfil her previous vow to end her own life while she could spend more time with the woman who now lay beside her. Rewherran had ruined it, curse him; ruined it all. Twice he had drawn her ire. The recent inability to control her temper worried her, and the incident in Moren's house, in particular, might prove dangerous to them. *"Boiling water scalds, and boiling blood scalds the more,"* as the old expression went.

Jorinda could see no alternative other than to apologise and hope to avoid any further explanation. "Deineike, I am sorry. I lied to you. Do not be angry with me. Forgive me."

Deineike sighed. "Whatever your lie conceals must be some horror you are unable or reluctant to share. That may change one day. It is me who should apologise. Some terror drives you, and I pushed you to reveal it when I ought to have attempted to help you. I am the one who is sorry."

Jorinda pulled Deineike toward her. Jorinda had been caught in a lie, but Deineike had not stamped her feet and screeched about dishonesty and betrayal. Instead, she had praised Jorinda's making, found virtue even as she knew Jorinda had lied, and apologised as though it had all been her fault.

Jorinda kissed Deineike, soft and tender, then buried her head in the taller woman's neck and nuzzled her skin as she breathed in her smell. Deineike had played no part in the creation of the pain that crushed Jorinda beneath its weight, and Jorinda could not bear to punish the woman who loved her when it should be Deineike who punished Jorinda for all she had done. She whispered, "You are special."

Deineike turned and kissed Jorinda's forehead. "Let us resolve this argument." She pulled Jorinda closer and fumbled at her clothes.

They woke early, wrapped in each other's arms in the hay. Jorinda stretched with a moan. "Hay is no more comfortable than the ground." Her back screamed in agony, and her neck ached when she attempted to move her head.

Deineike gave her a sympathetic look. "Tonight, we will sleep in an inn if we can find one. We cannot afford to do so every night. It will take us several more days to reach Torric." She reached for her pack, and they improvised a hurried meal. Before long they were on the road again, and the warm spring morning drove the previous night's unpleasantness from their minds.

They rode throughout the morning and encountered one other traveller, who acknowledged them with a slight wave and a curious stare, but they did not stop or speak. They passed several farms and isolated cottages as the road wound south into the Freelands.

Jorinda continued to wrestle with her anxiety as they rode toward Torric. Guild members had described Torric as a larger city than Zhanghar. The Guild must have been told to watch for her, but in such a large city where nobody knew her, she hoped to be difficult to find. The presence of the Guild brought increased risk, nonetheless, and concern gnawed at her that it might be unwise for them to remain in Torric. If the tale of her departure from Vjort reached Styrrach's ears, he might conclude she travelled south and send orders to the Torric Guild to track her down. Caught between doubt and uncertainty, Jorinda could think of no place where they might be safe from the Guild in Dur, and frustration sat heavy on her heart.

As the night drew in around them, they spotted a village some way ahead of them and quickened their pace, anxious to reach the warmth and comfort of the inn they had promised themselves for the night. Despite the warmer temperatures of spring, the nights remained cool, and a fire would be a welcome luxury.

A faded wooden sign announced their arrival in Parmen, and lanterns gleamed from behind the unshuttered windows of the single-storey wooden buildings that lined the street as they rode in search of an inn. Halfway down the street they located The Parmen Inn, rode through the high arch into the courtyard, and handed the reins of the horses to a tall thin youth who appeared from a building to their left.

They entered a neat, tidy inn with, they hoped, a fastidious innkeep, good food, and a clean and comfortable bed. A rotund man, a leather apron tied tight about his ample waist, stood behind the bar and wiped tankards with a cloth. He looked up as they approached but showed no surprise at the arrival of his new patrons.

"Good evening, ladies. Welcome to The Parmen Inn. What can I do for you?"

Deineike smiled at him. "We are in need of a bath, a meal, and a room, if you please."

Jorinda chuckled, and added, "In that order." The innkeep raised his eyebrows at her words.

Deineike hurried to explain. "My friend jests about a less hospitable welcome in an inn some way to the north."

"Ah." The innkeep nodded his head as if all had now become clear. He put a tankard down beneath the counter. "I will prepare a bath for you while you store your belongings in your room." He turned, walked to a door behind the counter, and called out, "Kellen, take these guests to the room please." A small wiry lad, his hair a thick mop of brown curls, appeared after a few moments and raised his eyebrows to indicate they should follow him. He led them through the tavernroom to an area at the rear of the inn and into a corridor. With a large metal key, he opened one of the doors that led off the corridor, then passed the key to Jorinda. They entered behind him and looked around as he turned to leave.

The small room had two small cots rather than one bed, and Jorinda fumed inside. She wanted a bed in which they could enjoy each other that night, but did not wish to reveal it, lest their preferences come to ears they should not. Once Kellen had left, she grumbled to Deineike. "The beds are too small." She pointed a finger at the offensive items.

"Too small for what?" Deineike sounded puzzled.

"You know what for." Jorinda slid her arms around Deineike's neck and pouted, her eyes narrowed.

Deineike pulled Jorinda's arms away. "They will be fine for sleep. The other can wait." Her eyes twinkled with mischief. "I am sure we can survive."

Jorinda brought her saddest look to her face. "But I wish to make love with you in comfort, while we have the chance. Who knows when we will be able to sleep in a bed again?"

Deineike laughed and seemed unconvinced. "Since your back appears unsuited to anything but the finest mattresses in the land, I am sure we will sleep in comfort again tomorrow night. I need a bath, and afterward I am hungry for food other than bread and cheese. Later, we will sleep in the beds and live with our frustrations." With that, she dropped her pack on the floor and walked from the room toward the tavernroom. Jorinda hung back and hoped she had been teased, but Deineike did not return, so she locked the door behind her as she followed Deineike toward the tavernroom, frustrated.

The innkeep said a bath had been prepared and showed them to a small room with one tub and no windows. Water filled the tub, and steam rose from it. Some plain soap and two cloths lay nearby, and a small fire burned in one corner with a pitcher of water suspended over it that could be used to refresh the tub as the water cooled. They each spent a short time in the tub and allowed the warm water to sooth them and slough the fatigue of the road from their bodies. Jorinda nuzzled Deineike's neck as she dried the older woman's back. The hardness of Deineike's muscular physique under her hands aroused her, and her frustration over the beds increased.

Dressed again, they headed back to the tavernroom and sat at a small table to the rear. The entourage of a plump man in the fine robes of a merchant occupied a table in one corner. Four other men sat with him, one in well-cut clothes—a tally clerk or some such. The other three wore rougher clothing and looked like either bodyguards or dogsbodies. None of them carried any visible weapons, for most inns in Dur forbade arms in tavernrooms. The companionship of sharp blades and large quantities of alcohol could turn volatile in a heartbeat. As Jorinda and Deineike sat, one of the men looked over at them and spoke to a companion, and they both laughed, then favoured the women with lewd smiles that were not returned.

Kellen appeared with two bowls and placed them before the women. "I will bring some meats and roasted tubers soon. Would you like anything to drink?"

Deineike picked up a spoon and took a mouthful of broth from her bowl before she answered. "A goblet of red wine for each of us, I think, Kellen."

He left, and Jorinda gave a suggestive chuckle. "Wine makes me amorous."

Deineike whispered an exhortation for Jorinda to control herself. She inclined her head toward the five men, and Jorinda glanced at them. The man who had spoken to his companion when they entered still stared at them as Deineike replied. "If you find your desire uncontrollable, there is always that fellow." Deineike wore a malicious grin.

Jorinda groaned. "That lout? I would rather sleep with a dog." The man smiled, and Jorinda realised with a sigh that he may well be flattered they discussed him and might cast it in his favour.

They ate in silence for a time until Kellen reappeared with two goblets, each filled with a dark red wine. "I trust this will be acceptable. Your meat is ready if you would like me to bring it to you."

"Our thanks, Kellen." Jorinda smiled her gratitude at him, and he blushed and returned the smile, hesitant. As he turned to leave, the man at the corner table shouted and beckoned him to attend their table where he spoke to the lad in hushed tones for a moment. Kellen shook his head and muttered some reply, but the man grabbed his arm and snarled up at him. Kellen turned ashen as Jorinda watched from the corner of an eye and gave no indication she had noticed the lad pull his arm free and scuttle off to the scullery.

Kellen returned with another tray laden with two plates piled high with tubers and meats. Both women were delighted by their wise, if fortuitous, choice. After he placed the tray on the table, Kellen hovered over them.

Jorinda looked up at him. "Something is awry?"

Kellen cast an anxious glance at the merchant's table, where all five men watched with amused smiles. He stuttered as he explained. "One of those…gentlemen wishes to buy you a pitcher of wine and asks to share it with you."

In the corner of Jorinda's eye, Deineike scowled at the men, two of whom sniggered, but Jorinda focused on Kellen. "Please tell him we are travellers, not courtesans, and we require no more wine." She returned her attention to her food, and Kellen shuffled over to the other table and said something to the man who had called him over. Raucous laughter erupted at the table, and many of the other patrons turned to look at the men in curiosity. Kellen scurried from the tavernroom. Deineike and Jorinda did not discuss the development as they hurried through the meal.

They had almost finished their food when the man who had spoken to Kellen loomed before them, tall and muscular. He pulled a stool out from under their table with his foot and sat opposite Jorinda. He slammed his tankard onto their table with such force, the dark liquid within leapt upward, and some splashed over the brim of the tankard onto the table and into Jorinda's food. The impact toppled Deineike's goblet, and wine ran along a groove in the wooden table like the vermilion ribbon of Jorinda's terrible work. Both women turned their attention from the food to the man.

He had long, untidy dark hair, and his pinched face sported a small beard. His eyes appeared unfocused, and Jorinda imagined he had consumed more than one tankard of ale, that the ale emboldened him, although his demeanour suggested he had little need of liquid encouragement to seek out trouble. He wore a thick, worn leather belt cinched at his waist. His rough-spun clothes were torn in places, and he gave off enough stale odour, it could be smelled above the reek of ale that arrived with him.

"The lad tells me my company is not welcome." He cast a sly look at his companions, who all appeared to take great pleasure from his show. "I am sure he tells me wrong." He leaned forward and placed his elbows on the table.

Jorinda said nothing, and Deineike filled the awkward silence. "He tells you what we said. We are weary from travel and wish to retire."

"Retire? The night is yet young. Join me and my companions." He swept his arm about and embraced most of those in the bar in the gesture, the majority of whom had by now turned their attentions to the dance he choreographed. "I am Hiw, by the way." He slapped his chest as he shared his name.

Deineike half rose as if to leave the table. "Your offer is generous, but we are tired."

Jorinda remained silent and reached down to pull her fan from her boot. Most of the men she had killed had given her no reason to snatch their lives away, but Hiw seemed determined to give her adequate cause to rob him of all the breaths of his future. All eyes in the crowded tavernroom had turned toward them. She must be cautious in such a delicate situation, calculate all the probable outcomes, and choose the one that offered the most favourable result. Hiw seemed to seize on her silence as a sign of potential interest in his advances. "You seem less keen to leave than your friend." He gave her a bawdy smile. "Mayhap you will join us."

Deineike fell silent and sat down again as Jorinda returned Hiw's smile with a cold, passionless one that froze his in place. His size and belligerent manner would quell most potential opponents into submission, and he would not expect any violence in response to his brutish attempts to bully them. He had not frightened Jorinda, however, and she focused on her breaths to slow her heart rate, then leaned toward him, and he toward her in response as she raised the fan in her right hand. She had been ready to spring her blade, but both women risked death if she did so, either at the end of a hangman's noose or beneath the hidden blades she guessed Hiw's companions carried.

A different plan came to her. She would use intimidation rather than death, and she switched the fan to her left hand and whispered, so quiet, he turned his head as if to hear her better. "Hiw, if you do not leave us alone, I will take out your eyes with this fork and eat them as a dessert." She picked up her discarded fork and held it close to his face. Beside her, Deineike gasped, and Hiw appeared stunned before he leaned back and roared with laughter. Jorinda remained motionless as he laughed, and every man in the tavernroom joined in, though they could not know what he laughed at.

At once, his laughter stopped, and his eyes narrowed. "If you tried, you would die from a broken neck." His lips twisted into an ugly snarl, and he held both hands close to her throat as though to prove himself capable of such a deed. Jorinda did not flinch, but she moved the fork until it all but touched one of his eyeballs, her hand as steady as a rock. He strove to keep his eyes focused on hers and off the fork. The room fell silent as curious looks replaced grins. Hiw and Jorinda glared at one another, relentless wills that strove one against the other, and Deineike let out a long breath.

"Now then, what is all this fuss about?" The innkeep had appeared behind Hiw, and Kellen fidgeted at his side and licked at his lips, nervous. "In my tavernroom, no man brawls with ladies."

Jorinda's eyes never left Hiw's as she spoke. "There will be no brawl, innkeep. We retire now, and Hiw wishes to spend the remainder of the evening with his companions." Slow and deliberate, she stood, her eyes still fixed on Hiw's. "Come, sister, let us go to our room." She stabbed the fork down so it stuck into the table, and as she moved alongside Hiw, she traced a finger through the spilled wine, inserted the finger deep inside her mouth, and sucked the wine from it as she pulled it out.

Hiw scowled at her, and half rose, but the merchant's voice stopped him. "Hiw. That will be enough, I think. Come, join us again. The ladies do not wish company tonight." Hiw sat down and gave Jorinda a hateful stare, but the women left Hiw and the hushed tavernroom behind as they made for the stairs.

Satisfied to have escaped Hiw's attentions, they hurried to their room and closed the door behind them. Deineike sat on one of the beds and shook her head in shock. "What a foul man. I thought the threat to gouge his eyes out a little risky, nonetheless." She tipped her head to one side and gave Jorinda a look of accusation.

"I could have done it."

"Anybody could have done it, had he kept still for long enough, but I doubt he would have been cooperative."

"He would have had little say in the matter." Deineike stared at her, and Jorinda realised what she had said. She had been so focused on the intimidation of Hiw, she had forgotten she spoke to Deineike, who knew nothing of her Guild history. She summoned a smile as she recovered her composure. "Besides, you would have saved me with your big muscles." Jorinda knelt before Deineike, ran her hands up the older woman's arms, and pushed beneath her tunic toward the powerful shoulders. The taut muscles beneath Deineike's soft skin again aroused her. The huskiness in her own voice surprised her. "How did you obtain such muscles?"

"I developed exercises to build them up, and the physical work at Rewherran's tally house helped. I have neglected those exercises since I met you. Other exercise has occupied me." Deineike wrapped her arms around Jorinda's neck.

Jorinda nuzzled upward into Deineike's own neck. "You should start your exercises again. I like it."

Deineike looked down into Jorinda's eyes. "I love you." She kissed Jorinda's forehead.

"I am very loveable." Jorinda stretched up and kissed Deineike. Deineike returned the kiss, one hand entwined in Jorinda's hair as they lay back on the bed, Jorinda above Deineike. They took their time as they removed each other's clothing and savoured each other's bodies. Deineike slid a hand between Jorinda's legs, and Jorinda cried out as fingers teased her wet sex.

Jorinda lost count of how many times Deineike's fingers tore her body apart as they cajoled satisfaction from her and refused to stop even when Jorinda herself felt certain she could endure no more. At last, Deineike stopped and held her exhausted lover in her arms as Jorinda's frantic gasps calmed. She brushed sweat-soaked hair from Jorinda's forehead, a contented smile on her lips.

With a smile, Deineike whispered in Jorinda's ear. "You see. These beds are fine after all."

Jorinda moaned in pleasure and gave Deineike a gentle kiss. "The bed served well enough, as did you."

Deineike slapped Jorinda playfully on the behind. "Well enough? I believe you meant exceptional."

"That I did. Exceptional is the word I intended." Jorinda buried her head in Deineike's neck again. "Though I did not scream." They lay still for some time and held, kissed, and stroked one another, gentle touches that spoke of comfort and intimacy.

Deineike broke a silence so different from the one between Jorinda and Hiw earlier. "We should rise early in the morning and leave at the sunrise. I do not wish any further contact with that ugly lout."

Although Jorinda ached to the bone from travel and felt ready to sleep for a day, she saw the sense of the idea. The incident with Hiw had been perilous, and she would rather not be compelled to use her skills in so public a place. "We will depart before he wakes and leave him with naught but the headache the ale will bring him."

Weariness, tension, and sexual satisfaction had left Jorinda ready for sleep. She had been taken aback by the pace at which desire had overwhelmed her, and she had been wet before Deineike stirred her need. Could the confrontation with Hiw have excited her? It would be shameful to admit the prospect of his ruin had aroused her, and she had never felt any hint of such a reaction before, although other than Pilos, those she had killed had been paid gests and not personal to her. She chased the thought from her head, not ready to sink to such depths of depravity, she could find the same excitement when she killed she found when she lay with Deineike.

Jorinda sniffed and rubbed at her temple where a mild headache had developed behind her eyes, and it took considerable time for her to drift off to sleep wrapped in Deineike's arms, but those arms did not keep the nightmares away. In her dream, Hiw stood in the corner of a room, and Deineike knelt before him. Blood poured from his empty eye sockets. He took a fan from his boot, sprang a blade from it, then slashed it across Deineike's throat. Jorinda tried to cry out, but her mouth refused to open, and she could make no sound. Deineike turned toward Jorinda as blood pumped out of her throat into Jorinda's face. Deineike croaked, "I love you."

Hiw joined her, and they both repeated it over and over. "I love you."

When Jorinda woke, she felt dreadful. Her throat burned, last night's headache had become intense and painful, and her blocked nose had filled with mucus.

Deineike greeted Jorinda as she opened her eyes. "Good morning, sleepyhead." Even as she spoke, she seemed concerned. "Are you all right?"

"That I am not." The words croaked from Jorinda's throat and were agony to speak, as though they had claws that scraped great gouges in her throat as they left her.

"What is wrong?" Deineike sat up in the bed and held a hand to Jorinda's forehead. "You are ablaze." She sounded alarmed.

It cost Jorinda dear to talk. "That wretched hog of a man has given me an ailment."

"He may have. I will fetch you some water. Are you capable of travel?"

Jorinda shook her head—she had no energy to leave the cot. The thought of the dun wearied her more, and she closed her eyes and felt Deineike rise from the cot before a blanket fell across her. There was a pause, then the door opened and closed, and she fell asleep again.

The door woke her, and she squinted as Deineike and Kellen entered the room. Kellen hovered above her, anxious. "Oh my. You look terrible."

Jorinda groaned. "My thanks."

Kellen gave a soft laugh. "I will bring water, and some honey to mix with it."

Deineike thanked him as Jorinda pushed at the blanket Deineike had thrown over her. Deineike's urgent whisper stopped her. "Jorinda, Kellen is still in the room."

"I burn." Jorinda winced with pain as she spoke. She pushed the blanket further down her legs.

Kellen gave a small cough. "I will bring the water. One other thing. I am sorry to bring this to you."

Deineike sounded worried. "What is it?" Jorinda's ears were blocked and sore, and she struggled to concentrate on their words.

"Hiw asked me to bring you a message. He asks you to forgive his inebriated advances and to join him at breakfast."

Before Jorinda could find her voice, Deineike answered him. "That is not possible with my friend in this condition."

Kellen hesitated. "What shall I tell him?"

Jorinda managed to wheeze her response first this time. "Tell him to fall dead where he sits."

Deineike tutted. "Tell him we are unable to accept his kindness as Jorinda has taken ill."

"Very well." The door opened and closed again, and Jorinda groaned. The cot moved and Deineike felt at Jorinda's forehead again. Jorinda pushed the blanket away from her, hot and sweaty.

Deineike's soft, gentle voice created hammers that pounded at Jorinda's skull. "When Kellen brings the water and honey, you must drink some." Jorinda nodded. She had no strength for an argument. "I will stay in the room until Kellen tells me Hiw and his cursed friends are gone, then I will leave you to sleep."

A knock at the door seemed so loud, Jorinda grimaced, and Deineike pulled the blanket over her, but Jorinda pushed it away again, unable to bear the heat. Deineike tutted and went to the door. She held a whispered conversation with whomever had come to the room, then sat on the cot once more. "Take a drink." With Deineike's hand behind her head, Jorinda raised herself somewhat to take a sip of the sweet drink, but the effort exhausted her, and she fell back to the cot with her eyes closed.

When she woke, Deineike had left the room. A chair had been pulled close to the bed and a cup placed on it. Jorinda reached for it and smelled the honey drink. She took a sip, placed it back on the chair, and lay back in the cot. Sleep carried her away again.

Hiw could not recall the name of the tavern boy. "Which of them is ill?"

The lad shuffled his feet with embarrassment. "The shorter. The one with the fork."

Hiw picked up some of the salted hog and chewed on it, thoughtful. "That will be all." Hiw thought the lad repressed a smirk, and he waved a dismissive hand at the youngster, who scampered off.

Feak's grin mocked Hiw, as did his words. "You are out of luck." The plump merchant could not be touched—Sisnop would not permit his envoy to be harmed. They had been gone from Torric for days as Hiw and his men escorted the merchant and his whiny servant to Vjort and back. Sisnop had told Hiw important Guild business must be attended to in Vjort, and no more than that. The bulbous pack Feak had carried to Vjort no longer dangled from the merchant's saddle on the return journey. Hiw guessed it had held coin for some purpose he had not been privy to, but it still made no sense for him and his men to babywatch the merchant for days on end. With so little crime in Dur other than that committed by the Guild, there could be little danger anybody would have stolen the coin.

The Guild never told him much, but they looked to him often for such mundane work. He wished he had never met them but doubted he could escape their clutches alive now they had ensnared him. Sisnop, the Guildmeister in Torric, could be a vicious, cruel man, but Styrrach ran the Guild, in truth. He operated in Zhanghar these days, and the rumours held him to be the evilest man in Dur, worse even than when he had been Guildmeister in Torric.

Hiw had been excited when he saw the two women enter the tavernroom. He had not lain with a woman for days and found the tall one attractive. The shorter one had a hint of unspoken danger about her, but he preferred the taller woman, in truth. It had turned awry, and in his anger, he had been ready to kill them both before the innkeep interfered.

Now it seemed an illness would rob him of his pleasure. He had slept his anger away and had intended to make one more attempt at a dalliance before they rode on, but it seemed he must make do with his hand again. He pushed his plate away, stood, and headed back to the room to gather his belongings for the onward journey.

At first, he brooded on the insult from the short woman. She had humiliated him before his men and Feak, and he wanted her to pay for that in the worst way. As they rode south, she faded from his memory as he anticipated a dalliance with one of his regular women in Torric. They rode into the city some days after they had left Parmen and went to the Guild building where Sisnop awaited them. Hiw waited in the parlour while Feak reported whatever he had achieved in Vjort. With luck, Sisnop would soon let them leave for the day.

Instead, Sisnop emerged and ushered Hiw into the office and, to his discomfort, ordered him to tell the entire story of the women in the inn. No doubt Feak had mentioned it, some jest at Hiw's expense. The mention of the fan excited Sisnop more than any other aspect of the tale. The Guildmeister picked up a parch and waved it at Hiw, who could not read. Sisnop knew that, and Hiw imagined Sisnop sought nothing more than to humiliate him further, then realised the Guildmeister waved the parch in glee.

The Guild, it seemed, longed to capture the short one alive, and Sisnop instructed Hiw to ride north again and intercept the women as soon as possible. The Guild had no interest in the tall one, and he and his men could do whatever they wished with her. The short woman must be taken alive, however, and delivered unharmed to Sisnop. Some more sinister fate awaited her in Zhanghar, it seemed.

He left the Guild building, brim-full of excitement and anticipation. He told his two men to be ready to leave for their next job the following day. He spent the night with a courtesan he met at the docks, but as he lay with her, another face occupied his mind. He saw the short woman, and this time she submitted to him before he ran her through with his sword. He would not be allowed to kill her, of course, but he would make her watch as her companion paid a terrible price for the incident with the fork.

ELEVEN
A DEADLY ENCOUNTER

Styrrach came out his office and beckoned to Wilash, whose employment at the Portreeve's Office seemed little more than a sham; he came and went as he pleased. Although he attended the Guild building as little as possible, he had been summoned by Styrrach, and few dared question orders from the Guildmeister. For more than an hour, Wilash had sat in silence in the parlour while he waited on Styrrach, and his patience had long deserted him.

When he entered the office, Styrrach stood alone near his table, his back to the door. Wilash wondered at Porl's absence, then realised he did not care. He disliked the Senior Aide almost as much as he did Styrrach. Without a word, Styrrach pointed to letters on the table, so Wilash picked them up and skimmed through them. They came from the Torric Guild, nothing more than an account of the activities of the Guild in that city, scribed in the usual cryptic language.

Wilash looked to Styrrach for some clue as to what the Guild-meister wished him to see in the letters, but the Guildmeister still had his stern back toward him. Uncertain of what Styrrach wanted him to see, Wilash had no choice but to ask, "What do the letters portend?" Yet more of the unnecessary intimidatory behaviour Styrrach seemed to derive such pleasure from and that Wilash had tired of long ago.

"You will find reference to a man named 'Hiw'. Read the report and tell me what you think."

Wilash scanned the letters for the name. He found it and read the report. His heart sank as he read a tale he had overlooked the first time. He read it again. The Guild scribed its correspondence in cryptic language lest it fall into the wrong hands, but some Guild members had been taught to decode the obscure language, Wilash among them. Hiw worked as a courier for the Torric Guild and had encountered two women in a village north of Torric, one of whom had threatened the courier with a weapon. The report mentioned a fork, but forks were not weapons, so Wilash guessed it must be an ambiguous and unfamiliar Torric code. Fork began with the same letter as fan, which might explain the word and unmask the woman who wielded the weapon.

Styrrach spoke again as Wilash dropped the parch to the desk. "I know this Hiw. He worked for me in Torric, many years ago." The Guildmeister still did not turn, and Wilash's frustration intensified. "He is a vile insect of a man, and I do not doubt he attempted to press his lechery upon them, and they spurned him."

Wilash feigned ignorance, though he knew who had threatened the courier. "The woman with the weapon. You suspect it is Corelle?"

"It is her. Parmen is south of Vjort. She makes for Torric. I have no idea who the other is, and I care less. It may well be the same deviant she lay with in Vjort." Styrrach chuckled, a malicious sound that turned the air around Wilash cold. "I confess I would have enjoyed it had she sent him wherever he travels to afterward with a fork. That would have amused me."

"You believe the fork is literal, then?" Unlike Styrrach, Wilash did care about the other woman and how much she knew of the ruin she embroiled herself in while she travelled with Corelle.

Styrrach gave a cold, unpleasant chuckle. "Corelle, Corelle. So dramatic. She would not dare to use that…thing you created for her in a place as public as a tavernroom. She knows we would learn of it, so she improvised. It is her."

"You thought her bound for Dur City when last we spoke."

"I said it. I did not think it. We were told Corelle had said it, but had she wished to travel there, she could have done so after she arrived in Ort, many passes earlier. I reasoned she journeyed to Torric, and it appears I had the right of it."

Wilash glared at his back. "You misled me?"

Styrrach ignored the question. "What do you propose we do?"

Wilash pondered both Styrrach's words and the consequences behind them. He must take care, so he bartered for time. "Can this Hiw be trusted to bring her to us?"

At last, Styrrach turned and fixed Wilash with a malevolent glare. "I did not ask you to seek my opinion, Wilash. I asked what you propose we do." He emitted such menace as he spoke, Wilash took an involuntary step backward, and the very air itself seemed afraid to touch the Guildmeister lest it become tainted by his malice.

If his father had lived, the young Wilash might have evaded Styrrach's clutches as he had struggled to keep the smithy in operation in the face of his debtors. No time to ponder that; Styrrach would not wait long for a reply. "Send letters. Let the Torric Guild track her down and ship her here to face your justice." With luck,

Corelle would either not be found or would dispose of those dispatched to apprehend her.

Styrrach's stare did not falter. "It is well you answered so, for it confirms you remain loyal to us, and not Corelle." Wilash opened his mouth to protest, but Styrrach held up a hand to silence him. "You have your detractors, and I confess, I had my doubts. The matter is in hand already. We informed the Torric Guild we sought her long before Hiw met them at the inn, a stroke of luck, in truth. To his shame, Hiw appears not to have realised who he met at the inn, but I am certain that by now they search high and low for her. Corelle may already be under their daggers, and within days I anticipate I will have her here. I shall enjoy that work." He sat at the table and turned his attention to other letters that lay there. Wilash hesitated, unsure whether the conversation had ended. "You are still here." Styrrach did not look up at Wilash.

Wilash turned and headed back to the Portreeve's Office, his temper foul, and his disappointment that Corelle had been discovered immense.

For two days, Jorinda lay in bed in Parmen until she found the strength to rise. They rested for one more day, but the incident with Hiw returned to Jorinda over and over again, and although she had not recovered, she bullied Deineike into the continuation of their journey. Anxiety swirled in her mind and urged her to reach a city where they could disappear among the crowds. They arrived in a small town, one day from Torric, and agreed to stay at an inn for the night after a day of spring rain had dampened their spirits and their bones. They enjoyed a meal and a bath before they retired to bed.

Jorinda snapped awake, her senses alert, no drowsy hangover from sleep. She could not now hear the noise that had woken her, but it had been there. Deineike slept on, her breaths slow and steady, an arm draped across Jorinda's stomach. Darkness blanketed the room, the window shuttered against the moonlight outside. Jorinda's ears rang with the scream of silence as she strained her senses for something that did not belong: a footfall, an intake of breath, the scrape of a body against a wall, any tiny change in the air that would betray whoever lurked within or without the room.

Heartbeats beyond count passed, but Jorinda did not move. She slowed the tempo of her breaths to regulate the beat of her heart and strove to hear some telltale whisper of noise from a source beyond the bed, but none came. Deineike stirred, mayhap disturbed in her sleep by the fact her lover had woken, or as the result of a dream, but her movement had been overheard, and the door handle creaked, almost imperceptible. Whoever waited outside had been patient—even more patient than Jorinda. They had listened for the drowsy movement to confirm the women slept before they committed to their move. The door opened little by little, and Jorinda slowed her breaths further to control her pulsing, which sped up as tension coursed through her.

In the dark doorway, Jorinda could discern the darker shape of a man who gazed in at them, tall and well built, but agile and silent. No hiss of metal on leather whispered in the darkness as he drew a weapon. If he had one, he already held it in his hand. Jorinda lay still and quiet as she waited to learn what would turn. Deineike rolled over and lay across Jorinda's chest with her head on the slender shoulder furthest from her, and she murmured, "I love you." The man responded without hesitation, and encumbered by the weight of the heavier woman, Jorinda could not react in time.

The stiletto slid between Deineike's ribs and pierced her heart as Jorinda screamed in anguish.

"Jorinda, do not be afraid. I am here." Deineike's voice broke the dream, and Jorinda sat upright. Deineike also sat up and gazed in concern at Jorinda before she struck a flint to the lantern. "You had a nightmare." Deineike stroked the hair back from Jorinda's sweat-soaked forehead "Poor Jorinda. What did you dream of?"

Jorinda shook her head at the horror of the nightmare. "I dreamt somebody came in here and killed you as we slept." She fell forward, Deineike's arms folded around her. "A stiletto into your heart. It was awful." She paused. "A stiletto."

"Shh." Deineike kissed the top of Jorinda's head. "Nobody will kill either of us. I will make sure of that."

"Taro." Jorinda looked up, and a cold fear gripped her, churned her stomach, and squeezed her heart. "He wanted to kill me."

"Taro is dead." Deineike pulled Jorinda's head tight against her cheek.

"Then he returns from wherever he travelled to. It is true; he has returned. How else?" Jorinda's distress tore at her innards. Taro had killed Deineike with Arella's stiletto. It could not be denied; she had seen it in the nightmare.

Deineike held Jorinda at arm's length and stared fixedly into her eyes. "Nobody will kill you, not while there is breath in my body. You had a dream, nothing more. We are safe."

Deineike's firm words helped, and though Jorinda still shook with fear, it relaxed its grip on her heart. "You will protect me?" The salt sting of tears burned her eyes.

"That I will, though I die myself."

Jorinda placed a finger on Deineike's lips and whispered, afraid and anxious. "Do not say that. Never say that. Never." She could not abide the thought of Deineike's death.

Deineike pulled her close again. "I will sleep with my knife under our heads if it makes you feel safer."

Despite Deineike's soft, calm voice, Jorinda scowled as doubt whispered, "*Danger,*" in her head. "Knife? What knife?"

Deineike grimaced and blushed. "I have a knife. It is in my pack." She shrugged. "I did not want you to know about it in case it alarmed you."

"Fetch it. Let me see it." The story of the knife pushed the nightmare into the background and introduced fresh terrors.

"Now?"

"Now." Jorinda clenched her teeth, her fear replaced by anger. Deineike had a weapon she had not revealed. Why would she keep such a thing hidden?

Deineike repeated the shrug, her voice a meek, apologetic thing. "It is just a small knife."

"Fetch it."

Deineike rose, padded across the room, and scrabbled around in her pack. She came up with a bone-handled knife, then returned to the bed where Jorinda sat upright, her hand outstretched, palm upward. Deineike did not climb back into the bed as she placed a crude knife on Jorinda's hand. The younger woman studied it for long moments and ran a thumb along its blunt blade.

The blunt, short-bladed knife could not be considered a viable weapon. "You would protect me with this toy? It is blunt. It would not cut a soft cheese." Deineike carried a knife, nonetheless. Could all that had passed between them have been nothing more than an elaborate ruse to bring her to Guild justice? Jorinda did not want to believe it.

"It used to be sharp, I imagine. I have not used it for a long time."

Jorinda shook her head. "You protect my life with a dinner knife while every Portreeve in the land seeks my neck for a hangman's noose. Where is your sword?"

Deineike stared at Jorinda, open-mouthed. "Sword? What sword? Why would I have a sword?"

Jorinda paused and gathered her thoughts. She had made a mistake when she mentioned the sword Arella had told her about after they saw Deineike in the marketplace. Deineike had vowed to kill her mother's murderer with a sword, although almost nobody in Dur possessed such a weapon. They were expensive and hard to come by, and even if somebody owned a sword, they were unlikely to wield it to good effect. Jorinda had let slip that she knew the story about Deineike's mother and needed to recover the situation before Deineike became suspicious. "You must have a better weapon than this sad thing, if you are so determined to protect me."

Deineike's voice grew quiet, she hung her head in sadness, and she seemed unsure of herself or the moment. "I have no sword."

Jorinda handed her the knife, handle first. "Put it away." She had become used to the nightmares, but Taro had never come to kill her with Arella's stiletto before. It had shaken her, and she now felt embarrassed she had imagined Deineike might use the knife to kill her. The inescapable irony of her irrational reaction mocked her. Jorinda had seen a threat in the knife, driven by her concern that Deineike had concealed it from her, even as Jorinda continued to conceal the true nature of her fan from her lover. She softened her tone and held out her arms. "Come here."

"That I will not." Deineike folded her own arms, resolute. Jorinda lay back, pushed the blanket from her, and exposed herself down to her knees. Deineike did not move as Jorinda slid her hands up to her full breasts, then cupped and kneaded them. Deineike's face flushed as she seemed to battle her base desires. "Do you try to tempt me? Do you hope this will distract me from your foolishness over my knife?"

Jorinda licked at her upper lip. "That I do."

"It will not work."

"Then why are your breaths so heavy?" Deineike cleared her

throat, and Jorinda demanded satisfaction, her voice husky. "Take me."

"I can resist you." Deineike clenched her fists and swallowed hard.

Jorinda pinched one of her nipples and moaned as the hint of pain drove a surge of pleasure through her body. Deineike could not resist, after all else. An hour or more later, both women lay together on the bed, spent, legs entwined. Jorinda ran her hands through Deineike's long dark hair.

Deineike let out a wistful sigh, her eyes filled with the emotions that must have surged through her, and she whispered, nothing more than a breath filled with almost inaudible words Jorinda's ears grasped for in desperation before they could fly away, lost forever. "By the fates, I love you." Jorinda smiled and wrinkled her nose. Although Deineike never appeared disappointed when Jorinda did not return her declarations of love, it must hurt Deineike never to hear them. They lay silent for some time before Deineike pulled herself away, stood, and spoke again. "We should ready ourselves." The words carried little conviction. "Torric is close, and we will be safer when we reach it."

Jorinda shrugged, content to lie in the warm afterglow of their passion all day, if she could. "It will still be there if we are a few hours late." Deineike sat down on the bed and stared off into some imagined distance, and Jorinda reached up and stroked her cheek. "Dress yourself, then, and we will depart."

Deineike smiled and retrieved her clothes from the floor. She reached for Jorinda's pack, then stopped. "What will you wear?"

Jorinda rose from the bed, slid her hands around Deineike's waist, laid her head on Deineike's shoulder, and gave her a soft kiss. "It matters not, does it?"

"That it does not, as long as you put some clothes on, and soon." Jorinda grunted, but Deineike left no doubt she wished to leave, so Jorinda reached past her for the pack and dressed.

They left their room to collect and saddle the horses from the stable. The sun already rode high in the sky by the time they were outside the inn, ready to ride south, and Deineike declared it to be the midmorning or later. As they rode off, the innkeep ran out, waved his arms, and yelled for them to wait. Curious, they wheeled the horses to meet him. They had paid for the room in advance the previous night, and it perplexed Jorinda that he pursued them.

"I almost missed you." He panted, and his red face marked him as a man unused to exercise.

Jorinda agreed with him, sarcasm in her words. "Indeed. Almost."

He shot her an angry glance and spoke to Deineike. "A man asked for you earlier this morning." Deineike did not respond, but her eyes flicked from side to side as though she looked for the man of whom he spoke. Jorinda recalled a similar reaction at Taro's farm, some nervous affectation mayhap.

At last, Deineike replied. "What did he look like, this man?"

The innkeep scratched his temple as though he searched for the man in his memory. "Tall, dark brown hair, long and untidy. A beard. A strong build, as I remember. He said he wished to catch up with you, that he brought important news."

Anxious, Jorinda pressed him. "How do you know he sought us over any others?"

"He described you close enough and said he had seen your horses in the stable."

Deineike and Jorinda exchanged anxious glances before Jorinda asked, "What did you tell him?"

"I will not have my guests disturbed, so I told him you were abed and would not be available until later in the day."

Jorinda tutted, annoyed by the innkeep's inadequate response. "Why did you not say you had not seen us?"

Anger flared in his eyes. "I had no reason to know you wished your presence here to remain a secret. After all else, with your horses in my stable such a tale would have been difficult to believe. I am no liar."

Deineike appeared anxious to appease him, her voice soft and calm. "Of course. You did no wrong, but tell us, where is this man now?"

The innkeep shrugged his shoulders. "He said he would find you later and left."

Jorinda shot an abrupt reply and turned her horse away from the inn. "Our thanks. Come sister, let us see if we can find him."

Deineike followed Jorinda, and when she caught up with the dun, she reached out to place a hand on Jorinda's arm, breathless. "It must be Hiw."

"Hiw." Jorinda spat the name out as if it were poison she needed to expel from her mouth before it became her ruin. "Why in the Five Cities does he appear again now, when we are so close to Torric?"

Deineike shook her head. "It has been many days since he left Parmen. Why does he seek us?"

Jorinda turned to face her and smiled, anxious to reassure Deineike despite her own concerns. "No doubt he travels in the same direction by chance and asks after us in hope rather than expectation."

Deineike shook her head again. "Why ask after us at all?"

"He remembers that night with bruised pride, I imagine. I should have killed him."

Deineike stared at her, and her eyes widened. "Killed him? How? Why?"

Another slip, her second of the day. Jorinda had become too relaxed around Deineike, and it reduced her caution. She gave a wry smile; deflection, she hoped. "A jest, and a poor one. I am sorry. We must make excellent time to Torric and keep our wits about us."

"That we must." Deineike did not appear convinced, but they

rode on past the outskirts of the town and out into the open countryside.

The road from Vjort did not follow the Wantu River. Rather, it meandered across the countryside, but close to Torric it drew near to the river again to pass a range of small hills. They rode in silence for a while, each occupied with her own thoughts as the hills drew closer. As the day wore on and the road threaded through the hills, Jorinda stopped and looked about. Ahead, the road disappeared as it wound through the hills, and her disquiet increased. If she had wished to spring a trap to take Hiw by surprise, she would have been hard pressed to find a more perfect place than these hills.

Deineike stared at her, worry in her eyes. "What bothers you?"

"The way this road curves through these hills. If Hiw waits for us ahead, we could be upon him before we see him."

Deineike gazed forward. "That we could, but we do not know he awaits us."

"Nor do we know he does not." Jorinda chewed at her lip, caught between doubt and uncertainty.

Deineike sighed. "Why does he seek us? We did nothing to wrong him."

To turn from the road and seek an alternative route might take days, and none might even exist. They must roll the dice, and Jorinda muttered aloud, "The fates are written," then pressed her heels to the flank of the dun. Deineike followed and caught her as they came to the first bend in the road. Filled with apprehension, tension built in Jorinda's fingers and forearms, and she forced herself to relax her grip on the reins. They rounded the curve, but only the road lay before them. Relieved, she exhaled.

They rode on, their nerves wracked by tension as the road wound through the hills and occasional clusters of trees. Deineike rode a short distance ahead, and Jorinda scanned the trees to either side of the road, ever alert.

They rounded another corner, and Deineike turned in the saddle to speak to Jorinda. Instead, her eyes looked past her lover to something behind the dun, and she halted the grey at once. Jorinda's heart sank at the fear in Deineike's face, but before either of them could speak, a familiar voice cut the silence from ahead of them, and Deineike's head snapped around toward it.

"So, we meet again." They both started as Hiw and another man rose from the long grass to the side of the road where they must have lain hidden. Hiw held a lengthy sword, the other man a crossbow, which he levelled at them. Jorinda fixed Hiw with a hateful stare, and in the corner of her eye, Deineike turned again to look at her. They were outnumbered, since Jorinda heard the one behind her, nervous, anxious movement, the shuffle of feet on the compacted dirt of the road. Three against two. In truth, three against one since it seemed unlikely Deineike could kill any of their foes.

Hiw continued to speak as Jorinda evaluated her options. "Our last encounter passed quicker than I would have liked. I have longed to meet you again. You in particular." He pointed at Jorinda. "I recall you and I have a difference of opinion to settle." Jorinda did not reply.

Deineike's voice trembled, and Jorinda guessed the dark-haired woman might be close to panic. "What do you want of us? Let us pass."

Hiw snorted. "I wish to avail myself of your company, as I did in Parmen. I did not recognise you then, but I do now." He blew Deineike a kiss. "In Parmen, I wished for no more than a dalliance. Today, alas…"

Hysteria lent Deineike a shrill, high-pitched voice. "You have followed us from Parmen?"

He answered her, but he turned his gaze to Jorinda again. "That I have not. I had business to deliver elsewhere first. The Guild reasoned you made for Torric, sent me to find you, and here you are." He turned his attention back to Deineike and favoured her with the same lewd grin he had employed in Parmen. "Corelle is to be taken alive. You, however, are ours to do with as we please, and you will please us no end before we are done with you." Jorinda remained silent as she weighed her choices.

As Deineike spoke, her horse moved forward a pace, nervous, eyes wide. "Nothing has changed. We have no desire for your company, nor these with you."

The man with the crossbow, who seemed alarmed by the movement of the grey, shouted to Deineike and focused his weapon on her, knuckles white on the stock, nervous. "Stand." She reined in the grey and turned again to Jorinda, who had still neither moved nor spoken but allowed her eyes to flick to the older woman as Deineike asked, "Who is Corelle?" Deineike's eyes were wild with fear and confusion. Jorinda considered a plea for her to calm herself, but in her experience, the words, *"Calm yourself,"* almost always produced the opposite effect.

Hiw moved closer while the man with the crossbow stood his ground. "Come now, we are three, and we are armed while you"—he turned his gaze again to Jorinda—"do not even have a fork, unless you carry one concealed about yourself, which I doubt. I urge you not to make this more difficult for yourselves than it must be." Hiw reached for the grey's bridle, and Deineike seemed to lose the last vestige of her control. She kicked the grey hard and cried out for Jorinda to follow her.

Jorinda had remained silent as she weighed the situation. These would not be the easy marks she had practiced her art on in Zhanghar. They were thugs, and they held the higher hand, the crossbow an important factor, since it could strike either of them down long before they could reach the man who held it. She slowed her breaths, the better to control her actions when the time came, her Guild training uppermost in her mind.

Hiw carried his long sword from vanity, she reasoned. In truth, it looked poor in both making and maintenance, a token rather than a viable weapon. It would prove unwieldy at close quarters, and she must lure him close before she could act. The man with the crossbow wore a shorter sword at his belt and carried further crossbow quarrels. She did not risk a backward glance to confirm what type of weapon the one behind her bore.

The words between Hiw and Deineike had been chaff blown in the wind, useless to her until he had mentioned the Guild and called her Corelle. No Guild member would wield a clumsy sword, but a courier might, and that confirmed her fears. Hiw had not waylaid them in search of a thug's cruel sexual pleasure. The Guild still pursued her and had found them at last. Hiw believed her unarmed, which might brand him a dullard. Dullards could still be dangerous, however, and the men outnumbered her. It mattered little. Events were in motion that could no longer be stopped.

As soon as Deineike's horse sprang forward, Jorinda cried for her to stop, but too late. The crossbow sang, and the quarrel took the grey in the neck. Blood gushed from the horse, and it stumbled and fell. Deineike screamed in agony as the weight of the horse snapped her leg with a gruesome crack. The animal struggled in its death throes and tried to climb back to its feet. Deineike's foot had caught in the stirrup, and the grey fell on top of her again and thrashed about as its life gushed from it in a crimson stream.

Jorinda acted even as she shouted for Deineike to stop. She tugged her fan from her boot, sprang its blade, and leapt from the dun. Hiw had turned to watch the grey fall, which distracted him for a moment, even though the man behind Jorinda yelled his name.

Warned by the shout, Hiw tried to bring the unwieldy sword up, but Jorinda's blade slashed across his throat and took his life, a deep wound that found his vital artery. She did not pause as he dropped his sword, clutched at his throat, and crumpled to the floor. The distance to the crossbow was not great, but she needed luck to close the gap before the man drew his sword. Her fortune held—he tugged at the bowstring of the crossbow rather than pull out the sword. The crossbow seemed slow and difficult to reload, and he fumbled at the string in panic. Jorinda's blade flashed again, and again the familiar vermilion ribbon appeared, his mouth opened and closed, and his lifeblood pumped from the terrible wound.

Jorinda expected the third man to be behind her as she wheeled. Her body tensed, and it seemed she felt the vicious bite of his weapon as it ended her life, but her luck did not desert her. The man had not moved; he stood open-mouthed, doubtless unable to comprehend what he had seen unfold in so short a time. A short sword hung at his side, forgotten for now. Without hesitation, Jorinda rushed toward him as he tugged the sword free to defend himself.

Jorinda had never been a brawler, and with the element of surprise now lost, he would be difficult to kill if he had even a rudimentary idea of how to wield his sword. As she neared him, she slowed, balanced on the balls of her feet. He swung too early, and the sword hissed as it sliced the air short of her. He crouched and held the sword close to his body, its point toward Jorinda; it seemed he had some skill with the blade. She doubted she could match him in this form of combat—Jorinda killed with guile and surprise, not face to face with somebody bent on her own ruin. His short sword had a greater reach than her fan, and no doubt he imagined he held a high hand. Today, however, he pitted himself against an enemy with a shrewd mind and extensive training in the art of death, one whose actions were always weighted toward a high probability of success.

He would expect her to attack him, so Jorinda did the opposite. She stood bolt upright, dropped her hands to her side, and spoke in a fearful, plaintive voice. "Spare me. Use me if you wish, only spare my life, I beg you." He stared at her, dumbfounded, then his face tightened with concentration as he lunged at her with the sword.

Jorinda had predicted the reaction and marked the small movement as his sword arm moved backward before he struck.

As the sword point thrust toward her, she stepped to one side, winced as the sword grazed her ribs and caught in her tunic, then raised her arm and slashed at him. Jorinda had been ready to strike, and her blade whispered through the air and sliced him from collar to ear.

Blood gushed from the deep wound, and he screamed in agony. He dropped the sword, fell to one knee, and clutched at his wound as Hiw had. In a desperate situation, outnumbered and disadvantaged, Jorinda had killed three men and suffered little more than a scratch herself, but she tutted, annoyed the third man had not been taken in a clean kill. Sloppy work, by her standards.

She grabbed the man's hair and pulled his head around and up so he looked at her, terror in his eyes as he tried to speak. Jorinda felt no pity for him. He had thrown in with Hiw, and as a result Deineike lay behind her, injured or dead. Anger would come later, but for now she stared emotionless into the eyes of a dead man. "Plea—" Her blade interrupted him as she slashed his throat, a clinical end to the job she had started. She pushed him to the ground, and blood pooled around his head.

Against all odds, Jorinda's luck had held; she had killed all three men and lived to tell the tale. Deineike now needed a slice of that luck, and Jorinda ran to her. She lay motionless, the lower half of her right leg trapped beneath the horse. Her skin had turned a deathly white, and Jorinda feared she had died. A faint, irregular pulsing at Deineike's neck meant her lover had survived the fall, at the least. The stark reality of Deineike's injuries shocked Jorinda. She longed to be relieved that the older woman still lived, but at the sight of her mangled body, Jorinda's heart faltered, and she grasped for any slender strand of hope. Blood ran from an ugly wound above Deineike's ear, her broken right arm lay twisted beneath her at a grotesque angle, and a shattered bone protruded through her blood-soaked trousers three or four fingers above the knee.

Jorinda wiped the blood from her blade in the grass, then folded it back into the fan. She dropped it to the floor, grasped Deineike's leg below the knee, and pulled with all her strength, but she could not pry the leg from beneath the horse. Her head in her hands, she sat back on her haunches as she searched for her next course of action. *"Never panic. No complication is irredeemable."*

She picked up the fan, sprang the blade loose again, then cut through the saddle girth, glad Wilash could not see the crude work she now demanded of the blade he had constructed. She cut away the belt of the stirrup Deineike's foot still sat in, then manoeuvred the saddle until she could push one end of it under the grey's body near Deineike's leg.

Against the dead weight of the horse, Jorinda fought to force the saddle beneath its body. Sweat ran from her forehead into her eyes, and she panted from the exertion. Her exhausted fingers pulled in anger at the horse's grey hairs, and she grunted and kicked the saddle as hard as she could with her heels to drive it beneath the horse's corpse.

She could move the saddle no further, and she paused, short of breath, to feel for Deineike's faint, irregular pulsing again. Deineike had lain motionless and silent throughout and seemed certain to die trapped beneath the horse, but Jorinda refused to abandon her task while life flickered in Deineike's body. She tugged again at Deineike's leg, but the saddle had not raised the horse's body enough to allow Jorinda to pull the unconscious woman free, and she screamed as she beat the ground with the flat of her hands in frustration.

The dun snickered at her scream. The horse stood where it had wandered after she had leapt from the saddle, and she held out a hand, palm upward, as she took slow steps toward it. Despite the stench of blood in the air, it came to her and nuzzled her palm. She led it over to the grey and stood there perplexed, sure she could use her horse to move the grey but without any clear idea how. Anger at her own stupidity boiled the blood in her veins. She had removed the saddle earlier—she could have tied the dun's reins around the girth had she not done so, but that opportunity had vanished like steam above a cooking pot.

A new idea came to her, and she tugged the short length of picket rope from Deineike's pack, then tied one end to each of the horses' bridles. She urged the dun backward and yelled encouragement as it pulled at the weight of the dead horse. The body of the grey shifted, and Jorinda let out a small cry of triumph and struck the dun's neck to drive it backward further. At that moment, the grey's bridle broke, and the dun trotted away. Jorinda ran to Deineike, pulled at her leg once more, and winced at the crunch of bones as her attempts to free the leg pushed and pulled at it. Her face contorted with effort as she strained and heaved, grunted, and screamed, and it seemed she must fail, but at last the leg came free. Deineike's boot remained beneath the horse, and Jorinda flew backward. Fortune did not desert her, and she landed on the grass next to Deineike rather than on top of her.

Jorinda ignored the weariness that flooded deep into her bones, grasped Deineike's armpits, pulled her back, then straightened the broken leg as much as she could. She had never seen such a repulsive injury, the bone visible and the knee twisted at a deranged angle.

Jorinda caught her horse again and tethered it to a fallen branch near Deineike. With the short sword from the belt of the man who had fired the crossbow, she hacked at the wounds of all three men until she had mangled them enough that the clean cuts of her own blade could no longer be distinguished. She also thrust the point of the sword into each of them, for the benefit of the Portreeve's men who might be fooled into the belief it had been a robbery turned fatal. It occurred to her she might have found the swords useful when she hacked at the grey's tack, but in truth, their edges were dull next to her fan, and they might have been less efficient.

The men's horses must be somewhere nearby, but she decided that to look for them would waste more time than she felt she had. Somebody might come along at any moment, and there would be more deaths if they did. Although she did not want the blood of innocents on her hands for no crime other than the discovery of the gruesome scene her art had crafted, Jorinda could not permit any to live if they saw her and Deineike here.

To fashion a device to place Deineike on would take too long, and Jorinda had already pushed her luck too far, but to carry her on the dun could harm her further even if Jorinda could lift the taller, heavier woman to the saddle. With no other choice available, she dropped the sword and tore strips from her tunic and she used them to bind Deineike's legs together above and below the knee as she cursed the ill fate that had befallen them. Jorinda struggled to lift Deineike up to the dun's saddle, and the horse complicated the task as it shifted and snorted at her. Sweat ran like the river Alc from every pore, and her fingers and arms cramped from the effort. She yelled in agony but refused to give up.

It took her so long to hoist Deineike face down over the horse's back, darkness fell before she succeeded. Exhaustion had sapped her strength so much, her legs shook and threatened to give out, but now she had to lead the dun, since with Deineike across the saddle, Jorinda could not ride it, so she slid her fan into her boot and, with a weary sigh, picked up the blood-soaked sword. It could not be left at the scene. A person skilled enough to have downed the three men would not abandon the fine weapon the authorities must believe they owned. She would dispose of it along the road, and none need be any the wiser.

As she left the dreadful scene of carnage, she stopped. Deineike's dead horse might be recognised by someone who had seen them in the last few days, but she could not remedy that, and she shrugged as she led the dun away on bone-weary legs. Blood still seeped from Deineike's head wound, and her leg still gushed blood despite the cloth strips tied around the area of the break. Jorinda doubted her lover would see the morning, but she could not abandon the injured woman. Once she judged herself far enough from the scene that none would search for the sword, she spotted some dense undergrowth and tossed the sword from her. It had felt large, heavy and clumsy in her small hand, and she wondered why anybody would use such an unwieldy weapon. Swords had not served Hiw and his companions well, and had it not been for the crossbow, she and Deineike might have escaped unharmed. She heaved a miserable sigh as she contemplated the explanations Deineike would demand of her if she lived.

As she walked along beside the dun and cast anxious glances at the shadowy form of Deineike, emotion swept over her, and she wept to herself, but not for Hiw or his companions—she had felt no emotion as she had killed the three men. She wept for the fact she had become so hardened to the horrors of death, she could feel nothing as she practised her abominable art, but after all else, she wept for Deineike, who appeared unlikely to survive the night.

Death seemed a poor reward for the love and care Deineike had shown for Jorinda on the road, for the way she had stayed with her when others would have abandoned her, without question. The limitless depths of Deineike's love had somehow enabled her to endure the mysterious secrets Jorinda had refused to reveal to her, the death of Taro, and the arduous journey south. Jorinda had lived with death for years and had now, in all likelihood, dealt death to Deineike, as though Jorinda's own blade had sliced open her throat. Jorinda looked up at the unconscious figure draped over the dun and blinked back tears. She had never said it at any time when Deineike could hear it, but now she whispered, "Do not die, Deineike. I love you."

TWELVE

PATIENCE AND THE PATIENT

Jorinda led the dun through the dark night for two hours at the least, afraid to stop, although her entire body screamed at her to rest. She pressed on despite the dangers. One missed step in the darkness could bring them undone if she—or worse, the horse—fell. They passed through the hills, and lights in the distance suggested they were close to the outskirts of Torric.

A light flickered ahead of her, and she moved forward with care, so tired that when the light became clearer it did not enter her mind how late it was for a lantern to be lit, relieved to have found somewhere to seek help for Deineike before the last remnants of life ebbed away from her. Her concern for Deineike overrode any doubts she had about contact with other people, and she headed for the light without hesitation.

She approached the building, little more than a small hut, crude and shabby. Lantern light shone from the hut's one window, and Jorinda knocked on the door, heedless of the hour and the reception she might receive. A small barn, little more than a shed, stood beside the hut, and she decided to sleep there for a few hours if the occupants did not answer, then move on and find help for Deineike in the morning, if Deineike still lived.

A bang came from within, as though somebody had knocked something over, followed by angry words she could not make out, before the door opened and light streamed out. Jorinda blinked and shaded her eyes with her hand. A bent old man in tattered clothes stood in the doorway, his long white hair dishevelled both from sleep and long ages of neglect, his beard matted.

He snapped out a terse question. "Who is there?"

Jorinda's reserves of strength were all but depleted, and she fought to find breath to reply. "My name is Jorinda. My friend has fallen from her horse, sustained terrible injuries, and I fear she will die. Will you help us please?"

The man sniffed at the air. "The smell of death is with you. Is she already dead?"

Jorinda shook her head in vigorous denial. "That she is not, not yet at the least, but I doubt she will last the night unless she receives some care, and I can do nothing for her in the dark. By all the fates, please help me." She choked back a tear, and the man cocked his head to one side.

When he spoke again, compassion crept into his voice. "Bring your friend in, though I fear there is little I can do for her."

"My thanks." Jorinda turned to the dun. "Could you aid me? My friend is heavier than me." When she looked over her shoulder, the man had gone back inside the hut. Jorinda struggled to lift Deineike down from the horse onto her shoulder and carry her inside, and she panted from the exertion. She hoped the dun would not stray far from the hut, inside which she found scraps of food scattered about the floor and almost no furniture. It seemed the old man lived alone and did not waste energy on domestic chores.

He fussed with the fire, where a pail of water already rested in the heart of the flames. "Place her on my cot." He spoke in a sharp tone, an order, almost, but Jorinda did as instructed and took stock of Deineike's sickly pallor and gruesome injuries until the man knelt beside her. "Fetch the water, please. Let me have a look at your friend." Jorinda ran to the fire and lifted the pail, but when she turned, his hands wandered over Deineike's body.

Fury lent her new strength, and she snarled, outraged. "What do you think you are about?"

He did not pause, but he chuckled. "I look at her as I said I would. She is pretty, but she has suffered terrible hurt, and I can do next to nothing. Her injuries are most severe."

"Any fool can see that. Take your hands off her unless you intend to help her."

The old man chuckled again. "'Any fool can see that,' she says, but she orders me not to look." He continued to chuckle.

"You speak in riddles." Jorinda put down the pail and reached for her fan.

"My words are plain enough, but you hear in riddles. My hands are my eyes. I am blind." Jorinda blushed and let the fan slide back into her boot, grateful the man could not see her embarrassment. "Do not be embarrassed. You could not have been expected to know." His face became sombre as Jorinda's became redder. "Your friend needs better help than I can give, but I will do what I can for her while you sleep. Tomorrow, you must take her to Torric, where better help may be found. Now, where is the water? Guide me." He held his hand toward Jorinda, and she placed it on the edge of the pail. He tore a piece from his robe and dipped it into the water. "First, I must clean these wounds. But sleep, little one. You must sleep."

Jorinda tutted, annoyed by the term "little one," as she had always been. He had the right of it, nonetheless; she needed sleep, but she could not permit herself the luxury even though she struggled to stand. She slumped into the only chair in the hut, determined to stay awake and watch over Deineike despite her tiredness. The old man wiped at Deineike's face as Jorinda's eyes closed, and when she opened them again, daylight had replaced the darkness, and the lantern still burned in the window.

The old man bent over Deineike as he held a cup of water to her mouth. Jorinda sat up and yawned. "How is she?"

He did not turn to look at her as he answered. "Bad, but she lives, and that is something, for at times in the night I felt sure I had lost her."

His answer stunned Jorinda. "You have tended her all night?"

"Had I not, she might have died. I have tended her wounds as best I could, but she has lost much blood and has withdrawn deep inside herself. Where she has gone, none but the best healers can call her back, if anybody can at all."

"They must." Jorinda had no other words. "They must."

The old man continued to pour water into Deineike's mouth. "She spoke once in the night, as I believed she slipped beyond me to the place we all travel to afterward. I fought to bring her back, but I could not, and I called to you to wake you, so you could be with her when she died. The sound of your name seemed to bring her back to us and she spoke. She said, 'Jorinda. I love you.'"

Tears sprang unbidden to Jorinda's eyes, and she could not fight them off. The old man ignored her as he tended to Deineike and left Jorinda with her pain. At length, Jorinda found her resolve again. "She must not die."

The old man turned to her. "Then you must go to Torric at once and seek the best healers. Do you have coin?"

"Some. How far am I from these healers?"

"Not far, little one, not far."

He stood, and to Jorinda's surprise, she found she could bear to be called "little one" for now. Her displeasure at the phrase seemed insignificant while Deineike's life hung in the balance. He left the hut, and she crossed to the cot, knelt, and took Deineike's hand, grateful he had left them alone for a while.

"Deineike, it is Jorinda. Do not die. I will find help for you. Hold on a little while longer, my love." She laid her head on Deineike's breast and longed to feel a familiar hand run through her hair as it so often had, but nothing indicated Deineike still lived other than the faint rise and fall of her stomach.

The old man returned, and Jorinda turned to face him as he spoke. "I have recovered your horse and fastened it to my cart. She cannot travel on the horse, or she will die."

"How do you accomplish so much when you cannot see?"

"I do see, but not as you see. My ears tell me much and my hands the rest. When they are allowed to."

He chuckled again, and Jorinda decided she liked his laugh. Grateful, she gushed her thanks. "I will bring your cart back as soon as I can. My thanks. Our thanks, for all time."

He waved away her gratitude. "Take her now. Make her well, and you can both bring back the cart. How would that be?"

Jorinda blinked away tears. "That would be pleasant. Deineike will like you, I know it."

"Deineike, is it? A pretty name, well suited to her. Go. Do not tarry. Every hour could cost her life. And take this." He handed her a small pouch, which jingled with the telltale sound of coin.

"I cannot take this." Jorinda pushed his hand away, but he pressed it on her.

"Healers cost much coin, and she has dreadful injuries. Would you rather she died, after all my hard work? You may pay me back at some later time."

Jorinda looked away, even though he could not see the tears that ran down her face. She took the pouch, so choked by her emotions, she could not trust her voice to thank him. With the old man's help, she draped Deineike across her shoulder and carried her out to the small cart. Jorinda's pack occupied much of one corner, but the cart would serve Deineike better than the manner in which she had arrived at the hut. Since the old man appeared to have put Taro's saddle aside somewhere, Jorinda led the dun again. Doubtless it would find the cart hard enough to pull without her extra weight. The old man had rigged up a makeshift rope harness—she imagined he had nothing better to hand.

As she started back toward the road, she turned to him. "What is your name?"

He waved a hand at her. "Go. Save her. Time enough for names later." She smiled, and he returned the smile as though he had sensed it.

Jorinda led the dun to the road and turned toward Torric, spread out before her. Although she encountered many people on the road and attracted a great many curious stares, she ignored them, and they in turn disregarded the dishevelled woman covered in blood who walked alongside a cart that bore a second woman, also bloodstained. She hoped she would not encounter any of the Portreeve's men, but none came her way, and she reached the outskirts of the city soon after the midday.

Try as she might, she could not avoid all the ruts and bumps in the road as the cart rattled along the road. How much rougher its surface seemed now Jorinda's lover lay at death's door in a cart that found every excuse to throw Deineike's body around. Jorinda apologised often, even though she doubted Deineike could hear her. Tears would not stay far from Jorinda's eyes, and she wiped at her eyes time and again with a bloody sleeve while she wished she could wipe away Deineike's horrific injuries with similar ease. How had she brought this gentle woman to this fate? Of all the evils she had done, Jorinda could forgive herself the least for this latest outrage, perpetrated against one who did not deserve it, not by any measure.

Among the five cities of Dur, Torric ranked second in size only to Alcmouth, and its wide streets teemed with life. Although spring still lay on the land, the temperature felt warmer than she guessed Zhanghar would have been at this time of year, and sweat beaded her forehead, stung her eyes as it trickled into them, and mingled with her tears.

Jorinda had lived in cities all her life until she came to Taro's farm, but the vastness of Torric took her breath away. She had no idea how to seek out a healer. When she questioned some of those she met, they seemed unable or reluctant to aid her, and she decided this remote quarter of the city might not be the best place to find help. They moved onward toward what she hoped would be better quarters, and the rock in her chest where her heart should have been threatened to expand and steal her breath.

The dun pulled the cart, stoic and steadfast. It had pulled a cart, a plough, or a fallen bough at whiles on Taro's farm, and Taro had told her it had been a farm horse before he had bought it. The hard streets of Torric, compressed by the passage of countless feet, hooves, and wheels, must be easier on it than Taro's fields. The streets in any city were, nonetheless, as prone to become an ocean of mud in the wet season as any of the roads by which Jorinda and Deineike had journeyed south. Ruts tracked the streets, and the wheels of carts tended to sit within them, since those ruts had been formed by innumerable wheels before them.

The further they travelled, the more the streets became cleaner, the people better dressed, and the larger houses and shops suggested greater prosperity. She stopped a man in fine clothes who gave her some vague directions to a healer he had once used, but she soon became lost, and the day wore on. Frustration boiled within her. Deineike had become as pale as a washed-out cloth as her life slipped away, and she lay motionless on the cart beyond Jorinda's help.

A young girl, short and willowy with a parcel of ledgers held under her arm ran along the street, skidded to a halt, and stared at Deineike in curiosity. Jorinda beckoned her closer. The girl took two steps forward and pointed to Deineike. "She looks really hurt."

Jorinda choked back more tears. "She will die unless I can get help soon. Please, can you aid us? I must find a healer without delay."

The girl looked thoughtful for a moment. "Well, my father is a chirurgeon. I have seen a lot of people who were hurt. I notice them, like I noticed her. I intend to become a chirurgeon as well, but I am only twelve years at present—"

"Please." The girl gave every indication she would talk for ever if allowed to. "Where might I find your father?"

"My father charges a great deal of coin. He is the best around, you know." She could not keep the pride from her voice.

"I have coin in abundance." Aware how shabby her clothes must look to this girl, Jorinda would, nonetheless, spin any tale necessary to get help for Deineike.

The girl looked hard at her and at the rope harness attached to the cart, then shrugged. "Follow me. I shall see what I can do for you." Jorinda disliked the girl but felt obliged to follow her as she set off down the street. The girl chattered non-stop as they walked, and Jorinda hoped her father would be a real chirurgeon, not some fanciful notion invented by the girl to gain attention.

They came to a large house with many windows and an impressive double front door set into an arched entryway. A wooden fence and numerous tall trees formed a barrier between the house and the street, with a verdant, colourful garden spread out either side of a lengthy cobbled path that led to the doorway. Jorinda followed the girl through the heavy wooden gates and up the path to the house. The girl did not close the door behind her as she entered, and Jorinda stopped, unsure whether to follow or wait outside. She lingered outside the door, tapped her feet in impatience, and cast frequent anxious glances down the path to the cart until a tall, slender man with short, tidy hair appeared at last. The girl stood behind him in the hallway of the house.

"My daughter tells me you are in need of help." Jorinda turned and pointed to Deineike. "By the fates." He rushed down the path to the cart. "How in the Five Cities did she get into this state?" He felt for a pulsing at her neck as he appraised her injuries.

Jorinda clenched her fists and struggled to control the tears that welled up in her eyes as she replied. "She fell from a barn on our farm." To allay suspicion, she had invented the lie on their way into the city. "Our brother is away on business, and I had no choice but to walk for most of the day to bring her here." The man hesitated and looked from Deineike to Jorinda as though uncertain about something, and Jorinda hurried to reassure him she had coin.

"Indeed. Let us get her inside. Her pulsing is weak, and she needs immediate assistance." He scooped her up in his arms. The old man had bandaged all her wounds with strips of clothing and had even fashioned a crude splint for her leg with what looked like a walking cane broken in two. Jorinda followed the man as he carried Deineike up the path and into a large room furnished with a large table covered with a white cloth. Various tools of his profession had been organised in rows on a smaller side table. He laid Deineike on the larger table and removed the blood-soaked bandages from her head. "How long ago did this fall happen?" He continued to work while he asked the question.

"Yesterday, in the early evening."

"Where is this farm of yours, that it took you so long to get here?"

Jorinda feared to tell too many lies—she knew the ease with which they could trip her—but could not refuse to answer. "I bandaged her, then waited until daylight made it safer to travel."

He did not press her, but he turned to his daughter. "Rhea, run. Fetch hot water, plenty of it, and see if your sister is about." The girl ran from the room and beamed with joy at her role in the drama. "I regret I have no nurse available, since I work by appointment in ordinary circumstances, but these injuries..." He left the sentence unfinished, and Jorinda needed no further embellishment to understand the seriousness of Deineike's situation. He tore the remnants of the bandages from her arm and leg and picked up some scissors from the side table. He cut away the remains of Deineike's trousers and pulled her tunic away from her to reveal the full extent of Deineike's dreadful wounds. Deineike wore trousers Jorinda had made for her, not the leather pair she wore when they first met, and the linen trousers proved easy to remove.

Deineike's head wound had turned blue as bruises formed, and her forearm had become red and bloated near the elbow. Her leg had suffered terrible injury, and where the bone protruded through the skin, her angry red flesh had swollen. Blood and brown pus ran from the wound, and a vile smell came from both it and the brown-stained bandages the chirurgeon cast away from him.

The rapid deterioration to her injuries in less than a day horrified Jorinda. "Can you save her?"

He answered in a quiet voice that gave Jorinda no confidence. "Mayhap."

Rhea carried a large bowl of water into the room, and steam trailed behind her from the water's heat. "Mother planned to use this to cook some vegetables. She boils more for us now, and Sharee will come soon."

The man took the water, dipped some cloths into it, and cleaned the damaged areas. "The leg is my main concern at present. We must work fast and hope no infection takes hold, or she will lose her leg and, perchance, her life." He spoke without any break in his endeavours. "The knee has popped out, but that is the least of her problems. This break to the femur is quite the worst I have seen in a long time and should have been treated sooner." He glanced up at Jorinda, who returned his gaze in abject misery. "If that had been possible, of course."

He smiled at her, and Jorinda imagined he tried to encourage her in the darkness of her misery. She had not understood part of his explanation. "Femur?"

"The thigh bone. It runs from the knee to the hip." As he explained, he reached for a small box and took from it a blade the equal of Jorinda's own in its keenness, which he used to slice the flesh around the exposed bone with care and precision. "I will reset the bone, but first I must make more room for myself." As he cut at her flesh, he mumbled in apparent despair. "She has lost so much blood."

Another girl entered, around five years older than Rhea, who looked so like the young girl, she must be her elder sister. The man did not break his work as he spoke to her. "Ah, Sharee. I will need your help if you do not mind." She did not reply, but she washed her hands in the hot water. He glanced at Jorinda again. "Has she regained consciousness at any time since the fall?"

"That she has, for a short time." The words choked Jorinda. Her throat constricted, her mouth felt as dry as sand, and worry crushed her. The old man had claimed Deineike woke through the night, which Jorinda felt compelled to tell the chirurgeon in case it helped. He shook his head and returned to his work. Rhea pushed a chair closer to Jorinda, and she slumped into it, grateful, as the three of them bustled about in their efforts to save Deineike. The younger girl ran to and fro as she carried hot water in and empty bowls out while the older one assisted her father with his work on Deineike's broken body. The man's wife did not appear, but Jorinda gave it little thought in her anxiety for Deineike.

The chirurgeon manoeuvred the bone while Jorinda resisted the urge to fetch up from the horrible sight and sounds, then worked for a lengthy period to clean the area around the wound. Jorinda winced as he pushed the knee joint back into place and set splints down both sides of the leg to hold it in place. He manipulated Deineike's arm until he appeared satisfied, then splinted that also.

He cleaned and bandaged her head wound, and Jorinda guessed that all told, the man worked nonstop for close to two hours, and when he stopped and stood back from the table, all three looked exhausted.

At last, he stood before Jorinda as he washed Deineike's blood from his hands with a damp cloth. "I have done all I can. I have placed herbs on the leg wound that will draw off fluid. The wound is inflamed." Jorinda stared at him, unable to understand everything he had said. "Inflammation means it is red and warm. That is normal, a sign that her body fights infection in the injury, but it must be reduced over time, or she runs the risk of more permanent damage. The inflammation will produce fluid, which in turn will encourage more inflammation." Jorinda sighed and found only despair in his explanation. He placed a hand on her shoulder. "Do not fear. She is strong, and given the right care, she should make a good recovery.

"The arm is less of a problem since the skin is not broken, so there is less risk of infection. That is why I performed a closed reduc...did not cut the skin to manipulate it into position, in truth, since infection is our enemy here. The head is a cause for concern, not so much for the wound as for the blow itself, which may have damaged her brain. Until she regains consciousness, we have no way to assess that problem. Better to deal with what we can, as we can."

"Are there not salts that will bring her to consciousness?"

He shook his head. "Such salts do exist, but I fear they would be ineffective in this case since her sleep is so deep. Even if she woke, she would be in great pain. Unconsciousness is a boon. You will have to tend her and flush the leg wound at least twice each day. You must pour clean water into it, then mop it out. All of it. As scabs form, do not remove them. They are a sign the flesh heals itself."

"Is the wound open, then? Have you not closed and bandaged it?"

"That I have not. I have left it open to heal of its own accord, so it will be easier to flush the wound and keep infection at bay. It is vital you keep the area clean and free from infection, or we may need to cut off her leg."

Jorinda gasped at the thought that Deineike might lose her leg, but it concerned her he had not closed the wound, and she shook her head. "Not to close and cover the wound seems wrong."

She had spoken half to herself, but he had heard. "Some in my profession would agree with you. You may trust me or not—that is up to you. Because of the delay, the flesh around the wound had already begun to die, and I needed to cut it away, which left insufficient for me to draw the edges together so I could close it. An open wound is prone to infection and must be kept clean, and the easier way to do that is not to cover it. The incessant replacement of bandages can be bothersome, more so when the patient is not under the care of one trained in such tasks. It will take her body longer to heal itself, but I believe it is the best way."

Jorinda looked up at him and shrugged. "I have no choice. I will do as you say."

"Good. I will give you a supply of the herbs, which you should reapply for several days. These herbs should be applied after you have flushed the wound. You must do both: flush, then herbs, if we are to fight off the inflammation. As that is defeated, this brown fluid"—he pointed at the pus-stained bandages—"will turn clear."

Jorinda asked the hardest question of all. "Will she live?"

He paused before he replied, as though he chose his words with care. "With luck, she will. Good care from you will improve her chances. More than that, I cannot say, since she has been so badly hurt. While she is unconscious, I can make no assessment of the possible damage inside her head. Little enough is known about such injuries and their treatment, after all else. You must also ensure she drinks plenty of water as she heals."

"That will not be easy while she remains unconscious."

He nodded. "That it will not. To care for her will be difficult, I agree. But she will need plenty of water to encourage her body to reproduce the great amount of blood she has lost. Force as much down her as you can throughout the day, little and often." He gave her a smile, and she again took it to be encouragement. "Where will you stay? The journey back to your farm should be delayed for a few days to allow her the chance to recover some strength and her consciousness. We will judge whether she is ready for the return journey at that time."

Jorinda strove to betray no emotion. "I will book into an inn for a few days."

"Do you have sufficient coin?"

Jorinda did not hesitate. "That I do. I will be obliged if you tell me how much I owe you and your daughters."

He took a breath, then paused and stared into her eyes. "Ten regals will cover the work and the herbs."

Jorinda imagined his wealthy patrons might pay more than that vast sum for mundane, simple work. She could not guess how much he might charge for the complex, difficult care Deineike had required. "I think you mean fifteen regals, do you not?" She stared into his eyes with pride.

He coughed. "That I do, for I forgot to mention that you must bring her back to me for further investigation in five days when we can determine whether she can face the trip to your home." They smiled at each other as they found some small relief in a fraught situation, and she counted out fifteen regals from her pouch and handed them to him. The pouch now held too few coins for her comfort, although she still had the one the old man had given to her.

He thanked her as he took the coins, but she shook her head.

"The thanks are mine and they belong to you, sir. If she lives, we will owe you more than all the coin in the Duke's vault, although we can never repay that debt."

"I shall never try to collect." He smiled again. Between them, and with great care, they carried Deineike out to the cart, and as Jorinda led the dun away she looked back. All three stood in the doorway, and when she waved at them, she felt a sharp stab of pain in her left side and glanced down. Blood stained her clothing, not all Deineike's, and she remembered the third man's sword had nicked her. She had forgotten about the wound in her worry over Deineike. The slight pain mattered little, and she walked the dun toward the poorer quarter through which she had passed earlier. They would stay at an inn, but not one in this quarter. Darkness drew in, and she hurried, unsure of the city streets at night, her fan in her hand for protection. Nobody troubled her, and she found a clean, well-priced inn where she booked a room for several nights once she had been assured of the availability of regular supplies of hot water for her injured friend.

Deineike's brow burned with fever, and Jorinda applied cold cloths to her forehead to help keep her temperature down as she flushed the wounded leg often to drive out the infection, which she guessed to be the primary cause of the fever. Jorinda slept precious little for two days as she maintained a ceaseless vigil over Deineike, but the injured woman's temperature decreased at a steady rate, and her face regained its colour by degrees. After four days the fever had almost abated, though she still felt hot to the touch. Jorinda had become so exhausted, she had to dig deep inside herself to find strength to climb the stairs to their room with pitchers of water.

Jorinda no longer allowed herself to believe Deineike, who had not yet regained consciousness but had stirred several times, would die. Jorinda's thoughts were troubled by their lack of coin, which their stay at the inn worsened, and she wondered whether she should seek cheaper accommodation. She could not yet leave Deineike alone for any length of time, however, so she abandoned the idea for the present as she tended the injuries without fail and followed the chirurgeon's advice to the letter. On the fifth day her supplies of herbs ran out, but as the fluid that ran from the wound had turned clear and no longer smelled of decay, she decided to wait a day or two before she returned to him. Scabs had begun to form as he had said they would, and against her own belief, the wound had started to knit as the torn flesh around it healed.

After the midday, she bathed the wound, then dozed in her chair next to the bed. She woke with a start when she thought she heard Deineike's feeble voice and sprang from the chair to stand next to the sick woman, who gave no sign she had woken.

Hopeful, Jorinda whispered, her face close to Deineike's. "Deineike? Can you hear me?" Tears gushed from her eyes as she saw Deineike's lips move. No sound could be heard, and her eyes remained closed. "I am here, my love." She stroked Deineike's brow.

"Jorinda?" Deineike's voice sounded weak, but she had spoken at last, and Jorinda wanted to dance a delighted jig around the room.

She longed to hug Deineike but restrained herself, mindful of how sick her lover remained. "I am here."

Deineike's quiet voice proved difficult to hear even when Jorinda placed her ear close to Deineike's mouth. "I am thirsty." Jorinda grabbed the cup of water next to the bed and pressed it to Deineike's lips, then beamed as Deineike drank for herself for the first time in six days. The effort she expended to take the drink seemed to drain her, and she lost some of her colour.

"Sleep now, my love." Jorinda stroked the black hair that lay untidy on the pillow.

Deineike woke twice more through the night and requested a drink each time, and the second time she asked, "Where am I?"

Jorinda told her but did not know whether her reply had been heard, since Deineike's eyes did not open. The next morning, they opened at last, and she looked at Jorinda, her face creased by confusion. "Where are we?"

"In Torric. You have been hurt. You fell from your horse."

"Hiw." Deineike eyes widened, and she looked pained at the memory that must have flooded back to her. Jorinda gave her lover's left hand a tender squeeze and strove to sound calm even as panic and concern twisted her innards into knots. "Do not think on him, Deineike. He cannot trouble you here."

Deineike looked about in confusion. "Where are we?"

Jorinda fought to keep tears of both sadness and joy from her eyes. "At an inn. We are safe here, and soon I will show you around Torric. There are some people I want you to meet." The hint of a smile appeared at the corners of Deineike's mouth, and she closed her eyes again. She fell asleep straight away, and at long last Jorinda gave in and danced around the room with abandon.

That evening, Deineike said she felt hungry. Jorinda had earlier requested some broth from the innkeep, and she managed to get a few spoonfuls into Deineike's mouth before the injured woman grew tired again and managed a weak wave to indicate she could eat no more.

Jorinda mopped beads of sweat from Deineike's brow as the broth warmed the injured woman. "We may return to the chirurgeon tomorrow."

Without warning, Deineike's hand shot out and grasped Jorinda's arm, her eyes wide with terror. "Hiw."

The fear in her voice tore at Jorinda's heart, and she shushed her lover and placed her arm back on the bed. "Hiw is far from here. He cannot harm you."

"What did he mean by 'the Guild?' Who is Corelle? I do not understand."

Bitter disappointment washed over Jorinda. Deineike remembered Hiw's words, and it would be much more difficult to keep her secret now. "I know not. His words were no more than the babble of a simpleton." She hoped the explanation would suffice.

"What turned after I fell?"

"He panicked and fled, and his companions ran with him. Do not worry. I have already told you, he cannot harm you."

"Do not let him. Swear to me you will not let him." Deineike's eyes stared up at Jorinda, still wide with fear.

"I swear. He will never harm you again. Never." Jorinda kissed Deineike's forehead.

Deineike's demeanour calmed as Jorinda stroked the back of her hand, and the injured woman closed her eyes. "Tell me about Torric, then."

"It is far bigger than Zhanghar, and warmer. It is still spring, but it is already warmer here than a summer's day in Ryl or Zhanghar. There are wonderful shops and enormous houses. People here wear such finery, you will want to buy a whole trunk full of clothes to replace the poor rags I have made for you." Deineike smiled, and Jorinda bent forward to brush her dry lips with a gentle kiss. Deineike found some strength to return the kiss, and Jorinda at last felt they would survive, together.

The next day, the innkeep and his son helped Jorinda carry Deineike down to the cart and place her on it. Deineike grimaced and clenched her teeth throughout the descent of the stairs, and Jorinda asked whether they could transfer to a downstairs room on their return. The innkeep agreed and assured her the room would be ready for them once they returned. Jorinda found her way back to the chirurgeon's house with no difficulty, and Deineike looked awestruck at the splendour of the building as Jorinda walked up the path to knock on the door.

Rhea answered the door and rushed out to the cart as soon as she saw Deineike. Once she had satisfied herself Deineike had begun her recovery, the girl fetched her father, who said he had been in his rear garden. He wore faded trousers, the knees muddied, and Jorinda realised she had arrived once more without the appointment he must be used to, but he did not mention it. Between the three of them, they carried Deineike inside the house and into his room.

They laid Deineike on the table, and he inspected her. "The patient recovers well. It seems you have enjoyed some excellent care, young woman." He favoured Jorinda with a respectful smile, and the familiar warmth of embarrassment heated her cheeks. He turned his attention to the leg and seemed satisfied. He moved his finger back and forth before Deineike's face and studied her as she tried to follow it with unfocused eyes. Jorinda had no idea what the process meant but guessed it represented some important measure of Deineike's recovery. He asked the patient her name and whether she knew which city they were in before he peered into each of her ears, a candle in his hand.

After some time, he appeared content and turned to Jorinda. "She seems to be in good condition, all things considered, and although I am no expert on the brain and head, I am hopeful she has sustained no significant damage that will last throughout her life. It may be some time before she regains all her faculties, nonetheless. You have done well, and she should count herself lucky to have such a devoted sister." Jorinda looked away, embarrassed further.

On the table, Deineike croaked. "Sister?"

"Do you need me, sister?" Jorinda took one step, stood over Deineike, and glowered at her, hopeful she would understand she should say no more.

From behind Jorinda, the chirurgeon spoke again. "Where is your farm?"

"To the north, close to a day from here." Jorinda still fixed Deineike with a pointed stare, though the injured woman appeared perplexed.

"Did you pass through the hills on your way here?"

Jorinda did not hesitate. "That we did, of course. There is no other way." She turned to face him as he packed his instruments away. She hoped no other way existed, or he knew nothing of that part of the land, at the least.

"You must have almost encountered a terrible atrocity the day you came here." He sounded casual enough, but Jorinda remained on her guard. "Three men were murdered not far from where your farm must be, in the hills. A brutal incident, they tell me. Did you see any sign of this evil thing?"

Jorinda struggled to remember what she had already told him, since she had been spent in body and mind when they first met. She strove to sound innocent. "That I did not. Nothing. No doubt it took place after we passed. Are you certain you have the right day?" He did not have the right of it; it had not been the day she brought Deineike to his door, but she had no wish to confirm she knew anything about the event.

"I thought so, but it may have been the day before, or after. They were ruffians by all accounts, but whoever bested them must be as dangerous a person as can be imagined. To kill three men is no mean feat. Such violence is unheard of."

Again, Deineike croaked from the table. "Hiw."

"Hiw?" The chirurgeon raised his eyebrows.

Jorinda glared at Deineike and hoped she would say no more. "Our brother. She misses him. They are very close."

He smiled. "Of course. Well, I will detain you no longer. Take these herbs, which will help her to regain her strength. Feed her whenever and whatever she desires. The wound heals well, and there is no infection. You need not cleanse the wound as much any longer, but keep a watchful eye on it. The splints should stay on for not less than a pass. When you remove them, she can start to move her arm and leg as much as they will allow, but do not let her walk without some aid for a further pass at the least. Be guided by your eye as to how much improvement is evident." He turned and left the room.

Deineike had confusion in her eyes, on her face. "What did he mean?"

Jorinda turned to her and smiled. The more Deineike healed, the more she would press for explanations, and Jorinda knew in her heart she would have no choice but to reveal the truth at some stage. "I will tell you when you are stronger." She helped Deineike up and onto her good leg. Rhea assisted them as they shuffled out to the cart.

Rhea wore a look of admiration, and once they had Deineike settled, she whispered to Jorinda. "Did you see the bodies?"

"Bodies?" Jorinda feigned ignorance.

"The men who were killed. Did you see their bodies?"

Jorinda smiled. "That I did not, thank the fates. The incident sounds gruesome."

Rhea cocked her head to one side. "I think you know more than you allow. Your secret is safe with me. Like as not, they attacked Deineike and hurt her, and your brother died as he fought them off."

Jorinda stared at her, bewildered and open-mouthed, then winked and lowered her voice to a conspiratorial whisper. "Do not tell your father." She wheeled the dun and led it away before Rhea had the chance to ask further awkward questions.

THIRTEEN

FATES ARE WRITTEN

Deineike's strength improved over the next two days, and her curiosity about the events that followed her fall grew. Jorinda seemed determined to avoid the subject and steered their conversation to other matters, such as their limited supply of coin that dwindled as each day passed, but Deineike insisted Jorinda tell her the full story, and the younger woman relented at last. "Hiw is dead, as are the vermin who travelled with him." She fell silent.

Deineike's injuries had taken a terrible physical toll on her. The herbs had Jorinda used to ease the pain of those injuries over the last few days dulled her senses somewhat, but she had, nonetheless, tried to piece together Hiw's words and the things she overheard at the chirurgeon's house. None of it matched the frail explanations Jorinda had supplied since Deineike woke to find herself in a strange room above an inn in Torric. Hiw had died, but

Deineike had not yet heard the tale—she had heard nothing more than the title of a story still untold. Deineike thought back over words that had passed between her and Jorinda; Jorinda's anxiety to leave Taro's farm, the incident with her own knife after Jorinda's nightmare, the bizarre story about the imaginary debt, and the frequent references to death. The unavoidable conclusion left her nauseous.

Deineike looked up at Jorinda, who sat in a chair next to the bed, her green eyes cheerless pools of despair. If she pressed Jorinda now, it could unlock a door Deineike might come to wish had remained closed, but she needed the truth. Too many questions had lain unasked and unanswered between them over the passes since they had met.

There seemed to be a logical conclusion, but Deineike needed confirmation. "Did you kill them?"

Jorinda looked at the floor as she replied. "That I did."

Deineike fell silent again for some time. "How? There were three of them, as I remember it. How did you kill them? You did not even have a weapon." She paused and thought back to the day: memories, snatches of conversation, references to their previous meeting with Hiw, and she muttered, "Unless you did have a fork."

With a sad sigh, Jorinda took her fan from her boot, pressed it, and a blade sprang from one end as Deineike looked on in disbelief, afraid to believe her eyes. She whispered, "The fan is a weapon?" Jorinda nodded in misery. "Small wonder you played with it so often in duress. Why do you carry such a weapon, after all else? Why not a knife such as the one I carried?"

Jorinda heaved a long, deep sigh. "Deineike, you came close to death because of me."

"You are not to blame. Hiw…" Deineike could find no words to express her disdain for Hiw.

"Do not defend me. But for me, you would not have been in Parmen the night we first met Hiw. You almost died because of me, and I need to tell you the truth. The full truth, which I have kept from you thus far. When you have heard all this, you may wish me to leave, and I will go if you ask it."

Deineike's breath caught in her throat at the extreme suggestion. "Leave? Why would I wish this? I love you."

Jorinda's response brought a smile to Deineike's lips despite the chill, uneasy atmosphere in the room. "And I love you." Deineike liked the sound of those words on Jorinda's lips, words her lover had appeared reluctant to utter until now. "Hear me out before you decide, for the tale I must tell you is no pleasant one. First, my name is not Jorinda. It is Corelle."

Jorinda spoke in an uncharacteristic, quiet voice, as though her ruin waited to strike her down for what she must say, and Deineike lowered her own voice to match as she turned the name over in her mind. "That is the name Hiw used."

"That it is."

Deineike wrinkled her nose in distaste. "I prefer Jorinda." Her simple response disguised the abrupt realisation that what Jorinda would reveal would be sinister and unpalatable. She had never met anybody who had changed their name before as far as she knew, and she suspected Jorinda had changed hers for ominous reasons rather than mere displeasure with its sound, although Deineike disliked the name Corelle, in truth.

"As do I. Why my parents chose Cor..." Jorinda paused and drew in a long, slow breath. "The Jorinda is a ship, as I told the Portreeve's man in Vjort. I took passage on it from Zhanghar to Ort."

"To me, you will always be Jorinda, but why did you change your name?"

"Do not interrupt." Jorinda half smiled, and she moved her hand toward Deineike's mouth as though to cover it but stopped short of the injured woman's face. "I should begin this tale from the start and not halfway through." Concentration wrinkled her face as if she tried to place her thoughts in order. "I come from Ryl, where my father owned a garment shop, as you know. I had a simple childhood with little to indicate I might become what I now am. I was a quiet child with few friends, and I found boys tedious.

"It might surprise you that I knew something of your story before we met at Taro's farm. Your mother, for instance, and how she died." This development shocked Deineike, but she stayed silent despite questions without number that screamed to be asked. "That a man killed her while you were a child, and you vowed to kill that man. That later, you met Arella."

Agony grasped Deineike's heart and threatened to tear it into myriad pieces. She moaned in distress, and her mind leapt back to the bizarre incident with her knife, the strange question about the sword. "That is why you asked me about the sword that night in the inn, after the bad dream."

Jorinda nodded in agreement. "A mistake driven by anger, and it almost unmasked me. I now wish it had, for then you might have left me and not come by these horrific injuries."

Deineike chewed at the inside of her mouth and shook her head. Jorinda's story brought confused thoughts that whirled in her head, and she could not understand why Jorinda seemed so intent on their separation. "That is the second time you have suggested I cast you from me, though you know I love you. What further torment lies in this tale?"

Jorinda wiped tears from her eyes with the back of a hand. "I met Arella some years after you last saw her, and we became lovers." Deineike's eyes stung as tears pooled in them, and she half turned, placed her left hand on her ear, uncertain she wanted to hear any more of Jorinda's tale. The splints on her right arm frustrated her attempt to cover both ears, and the wretched story continued to kick and gouge and wreak havoc on her emotions. "I know you loved her, and I think she loved you in her own way. She left you because she became embroiled in something she had no wish for you to be tainted by and wanted to protect you from it. That is the reason she abandoned you. Believe me." A note of desperation crept into Jorinda's voice. "I beseech you to believe me."

Deineike turned back to Jorinda and stared into red rimmed eyes as tears streamed down the younger woman's face. Deineike's heart lay shattered in her breast, and she felt she could take no more, but she reasoned more, and worse, would come, nonetheless. She gave a feeble wave to indicate Jorinda should continue. Jorinda's voice cracked when she spoke again. "Arella had become a member of a group of hired killers, assassins if you prefer. That is the Guild Hiw spoke of when...on that day. She killed any they paid her to kill, without question. After the Portreeve in Ryl caught and hanged a Guild member there, the Guild sent her to Ryl as a favour, as I recall the story. I was seventeen years and had never lain with a woman until I met Arella in a shop there, and we became lovers. A year after we met, they recalled her to Zhanghar, and I went with her. We saw you from afar once, in a marketplace near the stables, and she still cared for you."

Jorinda smiled, but the smile did not linger long on her lips. The tale left Deineike so despondent, she felt she could draw no more breaths. She ached for the story to end, but to her distress, Jorinda continued. "Against her wishes, I also became a member of the Guild. You were young when she left you, but I thought myself an adult and took my decision against her advice. I now wish I had chosen otherwise, but I cannot erase a fate that has already been written. That is the reason I carry a weapon such as this. I am an assassin, and this is the tool of my trade."

Deineike's body shook from sobs of abject grief she could no longer contain. She turned away and raised her left arm across her eyes. Jorinda reached out, touched her, and spoke Deineike's name, her voice soft and dejected. Deineike pulled away from the touch, disgusted by it. She could tolerate no more of this tale. The woman she thought she loved had revealed herself as nothing more than a loathsome creature, a hired killer. How could Deineike trust any word from her lips ever again?

Jorinda rose from the chair and stood next to the bed, which moved as some part of the younger woman touched it. Although Deineike longed to hear no more of this frightful tale, she guessed it had not concluded. Jorinda had not explained how she came to be at the farm, and Deineike had to know why Jorinda was no longer with Arella. Between her tears, she asked Jorinda to continue.

Jorinda sat again. "Arella is dead, Deineike. I killed her."

Deineike ignored the flash of light in her eyes, the stab of pain as her head snapped around, and she stared at Jorinda with a mixture of doubt and hatred. Her ears must have betrayed her. "You killed Arella?" Her lips trembled as though they wished they did not have to form the words she spoke, and mucus ran from her nose.

Jorinda nodded, and whatever pain she suffered poured from her eyes in her tears as she threw back her head and cried out, a dreadful howl, full of the agony of all that had turned.

Deineike lost all sense of reason. The story destroyed it, and nothing seemed real anymore. She could not believe what she heard and could manage nothing but a hoarse whisper in response. "It cannot be. Why do you torture me so? This is a cruel jest."

"It is no jest. I killed her." Jorinda broke down and buried her head in her hands as she wept.

Sweat beaded on Deineike's forehead as she struggled to sit up in the bed, and she stared at the top of Jorinda's head, consumed by hatred. Why did Jorinda torment her this way? Deineike did not know where her knife had got to, but had it been to hand... Instead, she balled her left hand into a fist and held it over Jorinda's head, her mouth twisted into a vicious snarl by hatred, anger, grief, and disappointment. Every instinct cried out for her to pound her fist up and down on that head, to wreak vengeance on Jorinda for all she had done to Deineike, and for all she had done to Arella.

Deineike raised her arm and brought it down in small increments as she fought her base instincts. Her body shook with fury until her fist came to rest above the brown hair her hands had run through so many times. She could not strike, certain that with any blow some small, almost indiscernible light that still flickered within her would be snuffed out, and she would be broken beyond repair, but she glared through bitter eyes at Jorinda for heartbeats without count before she spat out her contempt. "I wish she had killed you."

"As do I." Jorinda repeated herself, softer. "As do I." They did not speak again for some time, and nothing but the sound of their sobs disturbed the miserable silence as their private pains consumed them.

Deineike lay back, spent beyond exhaustion by Jorinda's story, and fell into a fitful sleep, troubled by nightmares.

At last, Jorinda had revealed the horrible truth. She loved Deineike and had decided during the long days and nights of care she devoted to the injured woman that she must tell her the whole story, though it would devastate them both. Though she feared the consequences, the time had come for Deineike to know all the horrific truths that had lain concealed from her by Jorinda's silence to this point. At the least, Deineike deserved that much.

When Deineike fell into a sleep as troubled as either of them might ever have endured, Jorinda could not leave her side. She wept as she remembered that fateful night when she had ended Arella's life. Times without number she had revisited that night as she tried to find an excuse for her actions. How fast the night had headed down that awful path while neither of them reached for a better alternative. Would Deineike ever be able to understand? It seemed unlikely, and for the second time in her life Jorinda might lose the woman she loved, and after she had fought so hard not to lose Deineike to her injuries.

To her shame, Jorinda had begun a selfish complaint about her parents' choice of name, and she suspected the girl whose parents had given her that name would no longer recognise the woman who had abandoned it. Her own self-pity made itself more important than the pain she inflicted on Deineike. What had she become, that even as she told a tale that tore the woman she loved apart, she took pity on her own meagre afflictions?

Despite Deineike's pain, Jorinda had been unable to stop the tale once it began even as Deineike became so distraught, Jorinda wished she could stem the flow of her words. She had inflicted terrible hurt on the woman she loved, and she would never forget the emotions that passed across Deineike's face: confusion, betrayal, disbelief, and fury. Fear, too. Who would not fear the person who revealed those awful truths? Jorinda had killed Arella; might she not kill Deineike as well? Deineike must have suspected as much, yet she had not spoken one word of recrimination until she could no longer deny the truth, and she had spat out the six words that cut Jorinda to her core, though she deserved them—"*I wish she had killed you.*"

There had been times Deineike could have—should have—walked away from Jorinda, yet she had found some way to carry on alongside her when few others would have done so. Jorinda cried anew for the destruction she had wrought on so fine a heart. "*When one lies down with monsters, one must eventually become a monster.*" She had recalled the phrase once before, in Vjort, yet Deineike had lain with one and emerged unscathed.

The smile as Jorinda spoke of the day she saw Deineike in the marketplace had taken her by surprise. At first, she thought she smiled because of a recollection of Arella, but in truth she had smiled when she remembered the first moment Deineike entered her life. Jorinda had felt a sense of despair in Deineike that day, a lostness she had felt an affinity with, but now she had heaped further destruction on the heart of a woman whom life had already buried beneath the weight of tragedies too heavy for any to bear.

Jorinda had wanted to comfort her lover but to do so would have been impossible, for she had hurt Deineike more than all the dreadful injuries she sustained when the grey fell on her. Instead, she felt compelled to continue to spin the story and pile agony onto Deineike with every syllable she uttered. The further the tale went, the more devastation it wreaked on she who heard it.

As Deineike had raised a muscular arm over her, Jorinda had hoped she would strike her and drive the evil from her. She had longed for death but had made no serious effort to take her own life, despite her vow to herself that night in The Ship's Yard. It would have been appropriate if Deineike had beaten her to death, some retribution for all Jorinda had inflicted on the two women she had loved. Deineike had not struck her, though Jorinda had wished she would. Her pain must go on.

Jorinda owed a great burden of care to Deineike. The tender, dark-haired woman who slept beside her had suffered terrible injuries and would need care for some time to come. Nobody but Jorinda could provide that care, yet Deineike might wake in the morning and order Jorinda from the room. How could she refuse? The very sight of her must revolt Deineike, but she must stay and tend to her injuries for as long as Deineike could tolerate her.

That problem must wait for another day, in truth. For now, they each had pain of a different kind to attend to. In time, Jorinda also cried herself to sleep, and the morning found them both bleary-eyed from their tears, and with many words unspoken between them.

Deineike woke, and the horrors of the previous day had not diminished. Jorinda still sat in the chair beside the bed, and she sat up as Deineike woke.

Jorinda rose from the chair. "You must drink. I will fetch some fresh water."

Deineike said nothing as Jorinda carried the pitcher from the room, nor when she returned, poured a cup, and handed it to Deineike, who took it with her left hand and sipped at it.

Jorinda's soft voice shattered the agonised silence in the room. "Deineike, please know I would never harm you; not physical harm, I mean. I cannot blame you if you fear me, but I love you and would rather die than see you hurt."

Deineike remained silent, certain Jorinda would have said as much to Arella. They could both guess how little those words would mean if such circumstances as those that led to Arella's death arose again, and in truth, Deineike could not understand why Jorinda had even said it. She could come up with no response, and she struggled with too many other thoughts.

After a time, Jorinda asked, "Does your leg pain you, or your arm?"

Deineike did not look at her. "That they do, though it is nothing compared to the pain you have brought to me."

"I will fetch some herbs for your pain if that would help. I know of no herbs that will salve these other injuries I have inflicted upon you."

Deineike did not reply, and Jorinda left the room without another word. She must have gone in search of herbs as she had said. Deineike wished she could also leave the room, leave behind all the pain and grief that lay scattered around it.

Her sleep had been fitful, littered with nightmares. She had woken often, aware that Jorinda sat beside her, awake and in tears, for much of the night. Each time Deineike had awoken, words had crowded into her mind, words she longed to spit at the creature that had revealed itself to her that night. Against her desire for vengeance, she had kept them within herself in the belief she might regret them in the light of day. A cheap victory won beneath the lights of the night sky might become a costly defeat under the first rays of the sun.

The woman Deineike had loved had killed Arella. Both her mother and her lover murdered, and she had lain with one of the murderers. Deineike had Arella's blood on her hands; she might as well have killed her herself. Deineike dropped the empty cup onto the blanket and lay back, shattered. Not broken like her leg, but shattered inside. For years, she had believed her grief at her mother's murder unbearable. Then Arella left her, and Deineike realised the loss of her mother had been but a moment's tragedy. As Arella had walked away from her without so much as a backward glance, Deineike felt sure some part of her that could never be replaced had been torn from her. Instead, she met Jorinda and loved her so much, she believed that damage might repair itself in time, some gift of the fates that could not be understood. Her devastation now far exceeded the sum of those earlier losses.

How could she ever forgive Jorinda for Arella's death? In truth, should Jorinda alone bear the blame? Deineike knew from the start —something had always felt awry. There had always been violence in Jorinda. About her, at the least, if not in her. The time in Parmen when she had threatened Hiw with the fork, for instance.

Deineike had seen angry, frenzied men—the man who had killed her mother and had seemed bent on her own ruin, and others, inebriated in the street or tavernroom, or angry at one or other of the street urchins who had tried to lift their coin pouch. Jorinda displayed no such frenzy when she readied herself to strike. She became cold and passionless, as though she and her weapon were one, as Deineike had observed in the tavernroom that night with Hiw, or the time Rewherran had danced with Deineike in Vjort. Deineike had seen it and had chosen to say nothing, to do nothing to understand what lay behind the ice-cold expression that appeared on Jorinda's face.

When Deineike discovered the fan in Vjort, she had been content not to pursue its significance. Such opportunities should have been grasped, and the truth dragged out of Jorinda. Deineike must hold herself responsible for some of the agony of the previous night, for she ought to have pressed for the truth earlier. How easy it had been to ignore the signs and fabricate excuses for them. Without question, Deineike must hold herself accountable for her part in all that had unfolded.

Why had Jorinda killed Arella? Some provocation beyond Deineike's comprehension must have sparked such violence. Hiw had infuriated Jorinda in Parmen, but she had not killed him. Why then had she slain the woman she lay with?

Arella herself—another conundrum to solve. Arella had abandoned Deineike in Zhanghar to become the same despicable creature Jorinda had revealed in her tale. Arella and Jorinda may have fought, and Arella's death might have been a mistake. Much of the story had still not been explained, and she resolved to press Jorinda further when she returned. To hear it might tear her apart even more, but to not know of it would be worse.

Her mind skipped back over the time she had spent with Jorinda. Since Jorinda had burst into the barn to announce the death of Taro, they had spent more than four passes together. Jorinda possessed great warmth and passion. She had tended for Deineike every day since the fall from the horse, though it must have cost her all the strength she had. Now, however, Jorinda's words had introduced a monster to Deineike's life, a thing unrecognisable as the woman she had loved. Or had they? To her surprise, she could not deny it; she still loved Jorinda. The Jorinda she loved ate cheese on top of a piece of bread, had promised to make Deineike scream in bed, and had tended to her for days without end after the fall from the grey. She smiled, amused by the irony that, after all else, the creature Jorinda had become could not drive off Deineike's love for her. Could Deineike forgive at some point? It would be too much to ask, she believed. Or would it? Even now, the thought of Jorinda brought a flutter to her heart.

What of Arella? The older woman had known the things Deineike had refused to guess at, all that Jorinda had revealed last night. If Jorinda had told the truth, then Arella introduced her to this Guild. Regardless, would Arella have forgiven Jorinda as the woman she loved brought her ruin to her? She shook her head, unable to guess what Arella might have done. Yet she knew Arella, and she knew the kindness that dwelt in her…

The door opened and interrupted her thoughts. Jorinda smiled when Deineike looked up at her. Her smile at that moment seemed to Deineike like the first ray of sunshine through rain clouds. Deineike sat up and watched in silence as Jorinda crushed some of the herbs into a bowl of water, and their sweet smell filled the air. "*I wish she had killed you.*" Deineike had said those words last night, but the next day Jorinda attended to her needs as though she had done no more than ask for a sweet treat. Jorinda had replied, "*As do I.*" Deineike could not guess how much the things Jorinda had done must weigh on her, and the mystery of how she bore them might never be unravelled.

In the depths of her heart, she believed she should order Jorinda from the room, never to return, although she would be sure to die, alone with none to tend to her and with no coin. Did Deineike deserve that? Were pain and anguish the fates written for her? More must be said before she could understand in full the tale that had begun the previous night, and in some small corner of herself she could not bear to see Jorinda leave, and it had naught to do with her incapacitation.

Jorinda picked up the cup from the bed and poured some of the herby drink into it before she handed it to Deineike. "Drink this, my love. It will help with the pain. The physical…" She wiped more tears from her eyes. "I must look at your leg and make sure all is well." Jorinda bent over Deineike's leg as the injured woman sipped at the drink. After a time, Jorinda mumbled, "All seems well." She stood beside the bed and fidgeted with the blanket she had replaced over Deineike's legs.

"Sit." Deineike gestured at the chair. "And take this for now. I do not wish my senses befuddled, and there is more to be said. I will take some more water instead, please."

Jorinda took the cup and placed it on the floor beside the bed. She dipped another cup into the pitcher of water on the nearby table and handed it to Deineike. Then she picked up the cup of the herby brew, sat in the chair with it in her hands, and waited in silence.

Deineike did not know where to begin now she had decided the tale must be completed. "How can it be that you became this… thing? You agreed with me many times, you are a terrible murderer."

"Deflection, nothing more. I am as terrible as anybody's worst fear realised on the darkest night. In truth, I excelled at it as I have excelled at little else in my misbegotten life before or since."

Deineike tried to shepherd the jumble of thoughts in her head and form them into words to better articulate her inability to understand the dreadful things Jorinda had said. "How, after all else? You became a killer. Death for hire, sold to the highest bidder. Did you feel nothing for those whose lives you ended? What wicked things had they done, that they deserved to die at your hand?"

Jorinda did not look up. It seemed she could not face her

accuser, and she slumped down into the chair. "What you say is true, and I cannot excuse it. I denied myself permission to think of it, and that proved simple for me. I dealt out death for reasons I never understood and found myself easy to beguile, curse me."

"Arella did these things also? She shares the same blame. It is beyond my comprehension." Deineike shook her head, baffled, powerless to understand how the two women she had loved could bear to carry out such heinous acts.

"Arella told me she joined the Guild in search of respect, which she craved. I doubt she found it, but once she set her foot on that path, she could not turn from it. As for me, I joined because I believed it would protect her. There were no other women in the Guild at that time, and somebody she had been sent to kill had recognised her. I felt such situations might be avoided if there were more women in the Guild. Such a spectacular woman could not be forgotten with ease, after all else. In truth, that incident played on her mind, as others have played on mine since." A heavy silence followed.

Deineike considered the reply, found no answer that satisfied her, and felt Jorinda had allowed her answer to stray into realms unrelated to the question. She could not, however, bring herself to pursue the painful thread any further lest it tarnish her memories of Arella and she come to despise the woman whom she had loved so much, so she abandoned it. "Tell me why you killed her." Deineike could not look at Jorinda as she spoke, and she stared down into her water.

Jorinda placed the cup on the floor and cleared her throat. "I had been betrayed, and either the Guild would have killed me, or the Portreeve would have hanged me; whoever reached me first. Arella warned me of the betrayal and saved my life, but she incurred the wrath of the Guild upon herself for it. She did not wish that, for it would have meant a slow, painful death too unpleasant to contemplate.

"They call it Guild justice, and she wished to avoid it, as would any who faced it, so she asked me to kill her. I begged her to come away with me, but she would not, for she felt it would have placed us both in great danger. I tried to avoid… Ah, I will not allow myself such an easy escape from my guilt. My blade inflicted a mortal wound, and I gave her a quick death rather than leave her to die alone and in agony. That is why I changed my name and why I hid at Taro's farm. I have lived that moment every day since then. I hate myself and hate what I became." As Deineike continued to stare into the water, Jorinda repeated the words. "I hate myself."

"Did you love her?"

"Not as I love you."

"But you loved her?" Deineike needed to know whether Jorinda had loved Arella, needed to understand what Jorinda had gone through at the moment the woman she loved asked her to kill her.

"That I did."

Deineike looked up at the precise moment Jorinda looked away, but their eyes met when Jorinda turned back toward her. "Did you kill her because you loved her?"

Jorinda blinked, as though the question puzzled her. "Because I loved her? I would no more kill somebody because I loved them than I would cut off my legs. I killed her to spare her a slow, painful, awful death at another's hands."

"But you did so because you loved her?"

Jorinda paused, then, "That I did, if that is how you want to see it."

Deineike understood a little more of what Jorinda had said, in truth. Jorinda claimed to have killed Arella, but to Deineike, it seemed Arella had given her life to save Jorinda's, and she must have loved Jorinda at least as much as Deineike herself did to make such a dreadful choice. There might have been some resolution to the situation other than the death of Arella, but Deineike had not been present that night, and she would not cast any judgement on the rights and wrongs of their choices. At one point, Jorinda had been about to say more but did not continue, so the version of events the younger woman told herself and Deineike must serve. To delve deeper into the night might unleash truths Deineike could not endure.

Could Deineike have come to the same decision as Arella? She could not be sure, but she could not punish Jorinda for what the fates had written for her and for Arella, the woman they had each loved. After some moments, Deineike tried to explain the decision she had arrived at. "That is how Arella would have seen it." Jorinda seemed confused, unable to understand what Deineike meant. "You said she asked you to kill her, which suggests she gave her life for you, and I believe she would forgive you. So must I, or my resentment will be a stain on her memory." Deineike took a sip from her water and gazed into it for a moment. "Though it will not be easy." She could not decide whether she spoke those words to Jorinda or to herself.

Jorinda's eyes filled with tears again. "Last night you sang a different tune."

Deineike looked up from her water. "That I did, and I am sorry. I spoke harsh words in my pain. I am angry at your deception, though I blame myself for my own blindness to that deceit."

Jorinda's hair flew back and forth around her head like a banner in a shifting wind as she shook her head from side to side. "The fault does not lie with you. I am to blame, and I do not find my forgiveness as easy as you seem able to."

"I do not find it easy to forgive. There are two considerations here, and I cannot deny them. If I blame you, it will not change matters, for what is done is done, and the fates are written. I loved Arella, but so did you, and your pain must be far greater than mine. I always longed to be with her again, but you were with her, and the fates compelled you to do what you did because you loved her." Jorinda covered her face with her hands as though they might somehow shield her from Deineike's words. "The other reason is simpler. Despite all you said last night, despite the revulsion I feel for the thing you became ..." Her voice caught in her throat, and she could not speak again for long heartbeats as her emotions threatened to overwhelm her. "Despite this, I love you."

Jorinda lowered her hands, looked Deineike in the eyes, and whispered. "How can you? After this, how?"

"I do, and that is all I know. What you did cannot change that, for love is constant, if it is love. People change, but love does not. There are things you have said and done I despise, but as for you..." She left the sentence unfinished. Deineike still needed more detail about that awful night, so after a time, she broke the silence that had descended on them. "After you killed her, what did you do?"

Jorinda wiped a sleeve across her eyes before she replied. "I waited nearby and learned the name of the person who had sold me to the Portreeve. I killed him not long after I killed Arella." Her lips curled into a snarl as she spoke of yet another death, casual, remorseless. "Then I fled, and sailed aboard The Jorinda to Ort, where I found work in a tavern—work I am unsuited to, as it turns. I met Taro in the tavern, and he offered me far more than he knew: a perfect place to hide, and all I need do was suffer his occasional attentions." She grimaced.

"Did he die to that dreadful weapon, then?"

"That he did not. He died as I told you at the time—an accident, too much of the herbs I had used to keep him out of our way, my guess. On the night you arrived, I recognised you from the marketplace. I had become desperate after I had been pawed and pestered by Taro for so long, and I hoped to find some respite with you."

Deineike managed a faint smile despite all she had endured. "Desperate? I believed you liked me for myself, and all the while you made do with any comfort you could find."

Jorinda threw her a meek grin. "That I did. I never even found you attractive, not once."

"Not once?" The jest embarrassed Deineike. She felt they betrayed Arella in some way.

Jorinda looked down, as though she shared Deineike's shame. "Once, but no more." Her voice had become all but inaudible. Another lengthy silence ensued as Deineike reflected on all that had passed between them since the previous night.

Deineike wished different fates had been scribed for them, but such thoughts would achieve nothing. More must be explained, and she broke the silence. "The urgency to leave Taro's farm? The sister story?"

Jorinda replied, her voice as quiet as death. "Fear." A look of disdain crept across her face. "I feared any investigation into his death would betray me. I fled not only the Guild but the Portreeve's men also, and felt I had to run, to escape without delay. I have come to regret that, in my fear, I pulled you into this nightmare, but even though I worried you might expose me, I needed you. At the farm, I took you with me because I could not bear to ride in those bleak lands alone with the hideous thing I had become. After Vjort, I rode with you because I could not bear to be apart from you."

Deineike searched for some suitable response, found none, but silence weighed too much and could not be allowed to endure. Any subject would do; enough horror had already been revealed, and Deineike's body ached from her tears and her grief. "Is Corelle your real name, then, or another you have invented?"

"I am Corelle." Jorinda wrinkled her nose in distaste. "I never cared for it. Have I already said that? Forgive me."

"Corelle." Deineike tried the name on her tongue but could not warm to it. Their eyes locked. "I will never call you that. I will always call you Jorinda."

"I am glad."

"Never 'Rinda." Deineike wrinkled her nose in distaste.

Jorinda managed a weak smile. "He was a simple man, but not a bad one, never prone to violence against me. Do not be too quick to judge him. Fate placed me there with him, and because it did, I found you and all we have enjoyed. I would not lose that, despite all that has come about since then."

Deineike knew nothing of Taro, but he could not have deserved the fate that had been written for him. "I do not judge him at all. You misunderstand me."

Jorinda blinked, as though to collect her thoughts. "That I do. I apologise."

They gazed in silence into each other's eyes for some time, then Deineike took another sip of her water and held the cup out to Jorinda. "I will take the herbs now, please."

Jorinda took the water from her, handed her the herby brew, and carried the water cup to the table. "You told me you did not wish your senses befuddled while more needed to be said." She did not turn from the table, and she spoke in soft voice, difficult to hear.

Deineike hesitated before she replied as she revisited the conversation to be sure she had no further questions. One more thought came to her. "That I did. There is one final issue to be resolved."

Jorinda turned to her, concern on her face. "What is it? I swear I will tell you the truth, so ask it."

Deineike paused for a breath, then replied. "It is not a question. It is a statement. I love you."

Jorinda cried again.

FOURTEEN

THE ROAD TO RECOVERY

JORINDA WELCOMED THE OPPORTUNITY TO LEAVE THE HOUSE AND BUY herbs. She needed some fresh air and time to think after all that had turned the night before. Deineike might also benefit from some time without the despicable company Jorinda had become. When she returned to their room, the conversation took a different turn, a turn that suggested something had changed while they had been apart. Jorinda did not expect forgiveness, today or ever. Deineike still loved her, which surprised her, and she feared to believe it. She decided to settle for this fragile truce for now and see how the fates unfolded.

Jorinda could make no sense of Deineike's forgiveness, but after all else she could make no sense of the gentle nature of the dark-haired woman who refused to hate her despite all the reasons to do so that had been laid before her. She watched as Deineike took small sips of the herby drink.

Deineike took one last long sip of the drink, as though she had come to some decision. "Things are not the same—not for now, at the least."

"I understand. I will stay and tend you until you are well. Then if you wish it, I will leave you alone. I swear it." Jorinda longed to hold Deineike, for everything to be fine, even as she knew nothing was fine. The path of Jorinda's life had destroyed Arella's and now threatened to do the same to Deineike's.

Deineike nodded and replied, non-committal. "We shall see."

"I love you, Deineike. I never told you that before. It frightened me to admit it, even to myself. I almost lost you, and I could not bear the thought."

"I am very loveable."

Jorinda smiled at Deineike's soft reply as she remembered the day she said the same thing. Deineike had teased her, and Jorinda moved to the bed and gave her a tender kiss on the lips. "That you are."

Deineike looked around the room. "I am weary of this room. I want to breathe fresh air. Take me outside."

Jorinda spread her arms. "How? It is all you can do to move."

"Then I trust you will find a way, after you bring me some food."

Jorinda glowered at her, exasperated but with no malice in her heart, and she left in search of some bread and cold meats. Afterward, she managed to pull Deineike to her feet and support her as they made slow progress toward the door.

Jorinda panted as she toiled to support Deineike's weight. "It is good you can move at last. You can now bathe yourself, and there will be no further need of a bedpan, thank the fates."

Deineike managed a weak laugh at the jest, and they struggled out to the courtyard at the rear of the inn, a small area, big enough for the old man's cart, which filled one wall of the yard, and not much else. Jorinda told her the cart had been loaned to them for now, then helped Deineike to sit on the ground. She went back into the inn and grabbed a wooden chair from the tavernroom. They manoeuvred Deineike into a comfortable position on it, and Jorinda sat cross-legged on the floor in front of her, weary from the exertion.

Deineike gazed around. "How did you come by the cart?" Jorinda told her of the old man, of the help he gave them that first night after the fall, and that he had lent them some coin to help with the chirurgeon's fee, which seemed to spark another thought in Deineike's mind. "How much coin do we have left?"

Jorinda frowned. "Precious little, and I confess, I do not know how we will manage."

"Then we must leave here and find somewhere less expensive."

It seemed unlikely any other inn would be less expensive, but they might find a room they could rent. "A room in this quarter should not be too costly. I could go out later today while you rest."

Deineike protested. "All I ever do is rest."

Jorinda searched for other solutions to their financial difficulties. "I could pick up some making I could do in the room and still be on hand to tend you." Deineike nodded but did not comment.

Jorinda sensed frustration at her incapacitation and placed a tender hand on her left leg. "Do not fret. You will heal, and sooner than you might think." Deineike did not reply, but she responded with a half-hearted smile.

They returned to the room, and Deineike slept, tired by the fresh air and the exertion, so Jorinda decided to act without delay. The innkeep directed her to a street where she negotiated the rent of an inexpensive room on the ground floor of a rundown house inhabited by workers from the countryside. Jorinda imagined a great many flocked to the cities of Dur in search of wealth but found instead squalor and thankless, low-paid work. She could not find any employment, but doubtless it would take time, and the urgency would not be so great once they moved, as their coin would stretch further.

The next day, they moved into the house, which both hurt and exhausted Deineike. Some sparse furniture had already been in the rooms, and Deineike lay on the bed and made light of the pain from the bumpy cart ride. The innkeep had offered to allow them to leave the horse and cart at the inn for a day or two until they had arranged something more permanent, so Jorinda returned them once Deineike had fallen asleep, grateful for the man's indulgence. When she got back to the house, she sat with Deineike for the remainder of the day and tried to comfort her from the pain the cart ride had inflicted, then slept on the floor to allow Deineike an undisturbed night.

Next morning, her back aflame with agony, Jorinda found a stable, moved the dun and the cart, and went in search of work, again without success. The stable cost more than she expected, and the combined costs of the stable and room came close to the cost of the room at the inn. To her disappointment, the move had not much improved their fiscal position.

Jorinda returned to the house an hour after the midday and contrived a smile as she entered the room. Deineike appeared to be in a great deal of pain from the day before, and her agonised face worried Jorinda, who paused to ensure the injured woman had no urgent need of assistance, then left to buy yet more herbs. Every time she went into the street, she monitored her surroundings and used all the skills she had learned in the Guild to detect any covert pursuer. The Guild would guess it had been her who had killed Hiw, and she did not doubt they would step up their hunt for her, since she had almost been in their grip. If they knew nothing about Deineike, they might believe Jorinda had not lingered in Torric, but she used great caution whenever she went outside.

Once she had bought a small supply of herbs to ease Deineike's pain and help her to sleep, she returned to the house. Deineike became drowsy from the brew, and Jorinda chatted to her until she drifted off to sleep, then stretched her legs out before her in the worn chair and sighed, consumed with worry. Deineike's health came first, but their financial difficulties concerned her while the prospect of capture by the Guild or the Portreeve's men added extra anxiety to her already over-burdened mind. The chirurgeon had tried to place her at the scene of the crime that had come to his ears. She hoped he would soon forget about them, but they should leave Torric in search of a safer location as soon as possible.

Jorinda slept in the chair, and nightmares beset her. Arella stood before her in a grey dawn, and when Jorinda turned, Deineike stood behind her. Both women spoke, though their voices came from bright red gashes where their mouths ought to have been. "These words condemn us as they condemn you. You are touched by death."

Jorinda, confused, pressed them for more information. "What words?"

They were silent for long ages. Passes came and went, and still they did not reply while Jorinda waited in impatient silence. As she woke, the women spoke at last. "I love you."

Jorinda snapped awake, the sky outside still dark. To her relief, Deineike still slept. The nightmares drained Jorinda, as did the physical effort of Deineike's care, but the day awaited. She drew water from the pump at the back of the house, which squeaked, loud in the quiet morning air, and threatened to awaken the entire house.

Jorinda watched Deineike sleep, a woman whose steely resolve belied the lostness Jorinda had first seen in her. Jorinda could not have coped with her own revelations with the composure Deineike had displayed. Only time would tell, but she vowed to do all she could to repair the damage those revelations had done to their relationship.

Deineike woke late and complained of pain in her leg. Her moon cycle had begun overnight and compounded her discomfort and irritability. She wanted to rise and move around a little and claimed her circulation had been affected by the amount of time she had spent in bed. Even with Jorinda's help, Deineike found it difficult to move, and she grew ever more frustrated with her lack of mobility as she hopped around and leaned on Jorinda. Jorinda soon became tired as she helped the heavier Deineike move around the room, and after a few moments, they were both soaked in sweat, their breaths heavy and laboured.

Jorinda put together another herb brew and waited until Deineike dozed before she slipped out to search for work. At last, she found a garment maker in the better quarter who admired the demonstration of her skills and agreed to allow her to work in their room rather than in his shop. He offered her some simple making she could take away with her. He provided the materials, and although he did not pay well, the coin brought some relief at last. She had taken a substantial risk, since the Guild knew of her making skills, but she could not feed them both without coin. Other than garment making, she had only one other talent and no desire to ever utilise it again.

The days passed, and Stefan, the garment maker, trusted Jorinda with ever more complicated making as he saw more of her work. Deineike continued to improve and moved around whenever she could. They ventured into the street from time to time, though Deineike could not move far from the house, and Jorinda could not relax for a heartbeat until they returned to their room. A society wedding brought Stefan a large contract, and Jorinda had to work in his shop for three days on the elaborate wedding dress, the fabric too expensive, voluminous, and fragile to transport to the house. She glanced up in dread every time the bell above the door heralded the arrival of a customer or delivery person. Her tension eased once she completed the making, and she could relax as she worked in their room again.

Jorinda's work brought in more coin, so they found another house away from the poor quarter, far from palatial, but a marked improvement on the first house. They rented two rooms, which allowed Deineike to spend the day in a room other than the bedroom.

Deineike decided to learn to sketch to while away the hours. She proved hopeless at it, but it staved off boredom. She complained she could not use her right hand because of the splints but claimed she would improve once she could. Jorinda doubted this, since the artist had no eye for form or perspective, but she feigned approval whenever Deineike presented her latest dreadful work. Most of the works were so bad, Jorinda had to guess at the subject, but she used making pins to hang some of the more tolerable sketches on the bedroom wall in a bid to cheer Deineike.

They did not touch often other than the times Jorinda supported Deineike to move around, or when she needed assistance with personal hygiene. Jorinda ached to hold Deineike, the lack of intimacy the most difficult aspect of their estrangement for her to cope with. She did not force the issue, but she grew impatient for their relationship to be as it had once been. Arella's name had not come up since the inn, and Jorinda chose to stay silent rather than open old wounds.

Jorinda suggested they visit the old man who had lent them the cart and return it at the same time. A trip outside might help lift Deineike's spirits, and a change of scenery would do them both good. At once, Deineike became enthused by the idea of the visit but pointed out she could not return if they left the cart behind.

Jorinda teased her. "You have seen through my plan." Deineike's blue eyes blazed at the jest. While it embarrassed Jorinda to have teased the injured woman, it delighted her to see some life return to those eyes. She told Stefan she would be unavailable for two or three days, which he accepted with obvious reluctance. The journey out to the old man's hut would be arduous for Deineike, who agreed to quaff a large draft of the herbal brew before they set out that Jorinda hoped would soften the pain. Although her arm and leg had healed well so far, the trip would bounce her about without mercy. In truth, Jorinda regretted the suggestion the moment she gave it voice. The longer they were away from the house, the greater the risk of capture. Though Jorinda tried to dissuade her, Deineike would not abandon the trip, which captured her imagination.

They set out early in the morning of a bright, warm day and left the city behind before the midday. Jorinda spotted the hut not long afterward, the lantern still alight in the window, but the brew had sedated Deineike, and she did not seem to register the end of their journey until they stopped at the door. Jorinda wondered why the lantern still burned, since the old man could not see, either with it or without it.

He must have heard them draw near, and he stood in the doorway as they pulled up. His face beamed with pleasure as he cried out to them, "Jorinda. Deineike." He had remembered their names; an impressive feat.

Between them, they helped Deineike into the tiny hut, which remained every bit as untidy as on the fateful night she had first come upon it, then she turned to him. "How did you know who had arrived?"

The old man laughed. "I recognised the squeaks from the old cart." He ran his hands over Deineike's arm and leg. "You heal well. The morning Jorinda took you from here, I confess, I feared for your life."

Deineike smiled at him, and he smiled back as though he could sense her facial expression. "I owe you a great debt that I live at all." Jorinda wondered if he heard some tone in her voice that told him she had smiled.

He insisted he must feed them and produced stale bread and some meats, past their best. He explained he traded provisions with local farmers and undertook small jobs in return—help with sick animals or guidance with their coin and tallies. "I am not as agile as I used to be, and sick animals are all I can keep up with." They all laughed at his jest.

Deineike dozed off after the meal, no doubt fatigued by the journey, and the old man spoke to Jorinda, his voice little more than a whisper. "You have devoted yourself to her, for such a good recovery would not have been possible without excellent care and attention."

Jorinda blushed, troubled as ever by any praise. "I had no choice, since I alone bear responsibility for all that turned." Her heart pounded in her breast as she gazed at Deineike, whose black hair tumbled about her head and framed her pale face.

"Some ill has passed between you since you were last here."

Jorinda drew in a sharp breath. "Why do you say that?"

"She heals well, but she is not relaxed, and you seem troubled beyond your concern for her health."

Jorinda thought about his words for some moments, and the old man did not interrupt her reverie. Loath to reveal the full truth, she nonetheless believed she could trust him with some version of it that would serve. At length, she looked at him. "I have brought immense pain into her life, and we are estranged by it. I wish it were otherwise, but she has much to put behind her before we can be as we once were."

He frowned as he considered her words, and his head moved from side to side as though he sought something in an inflection, a word, a breath. "You killed the three men on the night you arrived here?"

Jorinda did not hesitate. "That I did." The old man deserved honesty on this matter after all the help he had rendered them. She suspected he would see through any falsehood she might attempt, in truth. He appeared to have some uncanny ability to know things he should not.

"People tell me the Portreeve's men came out from the city, which they almost never do. It created quite a stir." He chuckled. "They seek you and know you are two women, since somebody recognised Deineike's horse." Jorinda sighed, for she had feared as much, and the news that another travelled with her would also come to the Guild's ears; she did not doubt it. With an ironic laugh, the old man continued his tale. "Nobody paused to ask me, since I see nothing. They think you killed them with a sword, but they are wrong, of course. Will you show me the blade?"

Jorinda did not move, dumbfounded by his perception. As the silence stretched out, she felt obliged to give him some response. "None have ever held it but me and he who created it."

He sucked in a short, sharp breath. "Then I do not wish to, for that might curse it, and such a fine blade deserves no curse."

"How do you know I did not use a sword?"

He snorted. "You had no sword when you arrived here, and it seems unlikely anybody would carry a sword against the possibility of attack, then abandon it at the exact moment such an attack occurred. Few people own a sword, after all else." He waved a dismissive hand at her. "Even if you had possessed such a weapon, you are tiny. They were mercenary swordsmen by all accounts, men who carried their weapons for coin. You could not have bested all three of them with swordplay, since you have little enough strength to carry Deineike"—he inclined his head toward her—"over my doorstep alone. Devious is your way, cunning. Not swords. Never swords. I suspect others still seek you, nonetheless."

"You know much, who sees nothing."

"I see much—"

"I know, with your ears and hands." Jorinda laughed despite her fears.

"Beware, Jorinda. Your fate is unclear, muddied waters.

Deineike will come to you again soon, for her unease is borne of some guilt. She wants to hold you again, but she refuses to, out of grief. Her body tells me this." Jorinda knit her brow, puzzled, and he seemed to sense her scepticism. "You doubt me?"

"That I do not, but I am confused. Are you some sort of fate reader?"

He chuckled again. "You would use such a term, but I would not. I came into this life unable to see and have learned to read much into little—movement, posture, small sounds, the feel of a person, their tensions, their anxieties. I hear what many do not, for I listen with more care than most. Other than that, I have no special powers."

"I killed her former lover." Jorinda had blurted it out before she realised it.

The old man did not appear shocked, but he nodded his head, slow and steady, as he thought on the revelation for some moments. "Not from jealousy, I think. Death is a companion to you, no stranger. There is much in you I cannot read, and my heart tells me I would not wish to hear it, in truth." He paused again. "She will hold you again, I am sure of it. Be patient."

They turned to look at Deineike, and she stirred, then opened her eyes, as if she were conscious of the sudden attention. Her voice sounded heavy with sleep. "Did I say something in my sleep?"

Jorinda laughed. "That you did not. We discussed your recovery, and you woke as we did so, that is all."

"Good." Deineike smiled and turned to the old man. "I apologise. I am a poor guest, to fall asleep in your home."

"Honoured guest, you mean. And who could blame you? The journey must have been tiresome. You must both stay the night." Jorinda tried to protest, but he waved her down. "The hour is already late, and I cannot set you on the road after dark. Deineike will have my cot, and Jorinda and I will experience the comfort of my floor. I have oft woken there anyway, fallen from my cot in restless sleep." He laughed, and they joined him, his mirth infectious.

They talked well beyond dark and learned he kept the lantern lit against the arrival of guests, whom he welcomed at any hour. He had lived a long life and had many fanciful tales to tell, although it seemed he had never ventured far. Jorinda suspected many of his tales had been garnered from visitors rather than lived firsthand, but the stories entertained them, true or not. A man arrived with fresh provisions in payment for a service rendered on some prior occasion, and they dined on better fare than earlier in the day.

They both slept well, tired from the long day. He woke them early with cups of some drink he had concocted, sweet and heady. It reminded Jorinda of the drink Orgel served in the shop in Ryl where she had first met Arella. They took their leave of him midmorning and repaid the coin he had lent them. He did not insult them with any attempt to refuse it. They promised to return the cart once Deineike could ride again, but he shooed them away and said he had no need of it anymore.

They had already reached the city when Jorinda, who walked beside the cart, snapped her fingers and tutted in annoyance.

Deineike turned her attention from their surroundings. "What is wrong?"

"I forgot to ask his name. Curse my memory."

"It is Rukaal."

"How do you know this?" Jorinda could not remember the old man mention it at any time.

Deineike looked perplexed. "I do not know. I seem to remember he told me at some point. You slept and I called to you. Did I dream it?" They both stared at one another in confusion.

Jorinda could not unravel the puzzle. "The night I brought you here? You have no other recollection of his house, by all you have said. It is beyond my ability to understand." Deineike nodded her head in agreement.

Jorinda dropped Deineike at their rooms and settled her in the bed before she returned the horse and cart to the stable. Back in their rooms, she placed a chair beside Deineike and stroked the dusty black hair back from a face that bore the rigours of the trip. "Do you suffer?" Deineike nodded but said nothing. "You found the trip arduous." Jorinda's heart ached for the trials Deineike had endured to make the journey.

"A price I am happy to have paid. I am glad to have met him. He is wonderful."

Jorinda nodded in agreement. "As are you."

"How is your back after a night on the floor?"

Jorinda forced a brave smile to her face as she lied. "It is fine. My thanks for your concern."

Deineike gave her a wistful smile. "Jorinda, I know things have been…strained, but I have missed your touch, your kisses."

Jorinda waved an arm as if to trivialise the past days, afraid to trust what she heard lest it turn out to be a dream. Her heart raced, and she lowered her voice in case it shattered the fragile hope that hung in the air between them. "I have wanted you so much. I have also laid unbearable pain at your feet."

"Kiss me." When Jorinda leaned forward, Deineike's mouth opened, receptive to her tongue. They kissed, urgent and passionate, and Jorinda moaned with desire as Deineike's left arm snaked around her neck and pulled her closer.

Jorinda pulled away until she could look into Deineike's eyes. The kiss ignited a need within her that all but stole her breath, and she could only gasp, "I love you."

"You are happy?"

"I have never been happier."

Deineike's eyes twinkled with mischief. "Never?"

"Never." A slight nod of Jorinda's head reinforced her answer.

Desire turned Deineike's voice into little more than a breath. "I want you."

Jorinda sat back in her chair. "And you shall have me, once your leg has healed."

"What? Is this one of your jests?" Deineike smacked the palms of her hands on the blanket in temper.

"Not at all. I do, however, recall the chirurgeon's instructions."

Deineike looked annoyed, then smiled her anger away. "I am the practical one, not you."

"You are the injured one."

Deineike poked out her tongue, then tried to suppress a yawn. "I am the tired one. You are right, curse you. Soon, I hope."

Jorinda smiled. "Soon. I promise." Deineike closed her eyes and fell asleep within moments. Jorinda sat beside her for over an hour, listened to her steady breaths, and wondered at the change in her since their return. Rukaal's words in the hut came back to her. *"She will hold you again."*

A smile sprang unbidden to Jorinda's lips, and she spoke her thoughts aloud. "What craft have you woven Rukaal, you old fraud?" She readied herself for bed, climbed in on Deineike's left side, draped an arm across the older woman's stomach as she thought again of the old man, and smiled anew as she mumbled, "My thanks." She drifted off into a sleep untroubled by nightmares.

FIFTEEN
THE JOURNEYS TO THE DOCKS

STYRRACH HAD AGAIN SUMMONED WILASH TO THE GUILD BUILDING, his anger palpable from the moment Porl ushered Wilash into the Guildmeister's office. Styrrach paced the room and shouted louder than Wilash could recollect. "Hiw is slain. Two others with him. Sisnop holds me accountable for their deaths, since Corelle is a fugitive from our justice. Curse his arrogance. He will come to regret it. He should blame himself; he sent a courier to capture Corelle. His members might have completed the task, but to send a courier against one as dangerous as her…" He seemed to notice the tone of his words, calmed himself, then continued. "They found a dead horse, blood around it that did not come from the animal itself. The other who travelled with the jade may be injured. She may be dead, although Corelle would not spend the time to carry off the corpse of yet another woman whose death she had brought about."

Fury blazed within Wilash when Styrrach called Corelle a jade. Doubtless, the Guildmeister's anger drove the insult, the most derogatory term ever used about a woman in Dur, but the language could not be excused, and Wilash guessed it sprang from Styrrach's disgust that she lay with women. He fought to suppress an anger that raged within his breast, as he must whenever he spoke with Styrrach these days.

Styrrach, tight-lipped, spat as he spoke. "If the other is injured, and Corelle chooses to stay with her, then she cannot have gone far. They must be in Torric. All has turned awry since you told us Corelle had been betrayed. Arella and the..." He shook his head, another transition from frenzy to calm. "Arella and Pilos dead, and now the Torric couriers. I have tried to believe you had naught to do with it. I have cared for you for many years, kept you safe. I saved you from the Debtors' Gaol. If I suspect you work against us..." He did not need to complete the threat, and it lay unspoken between them.

The wild beast inside Wilash clawed and bit at his innards as it tried to escape into vicious words and blows that would see him dead. He pressed his tongue between his teeth to calm himself, then dressed a question in the clothes of a politeness he did not feel. "What would you have me do?" Styrrach had been about to say something after he had mentioned Arella's death. Did he know? How could he know? All knew better than to question the Guildmeister, however, and Wilash abandoned the thought.

"You will travel to Torric and hunt her down. Bring her to me alive. Alive, do you understand?" Wilash nodded. "The other can be handed to the Torric members after you have used her. Her fate is written by her involvement with Corelle, and she is nothing to me. Take these letters to the Guildmeister there. They tell him you are my emissary in this matter, and he is to render without question such assistance as you request. I am certain his arrogance will desert him when he reads these letters, though I care not. Do not fail me this last time, Wilash. It will go ill for you if you do." Styrrach handed Wilash letters closed by his personal seal.

Wilash took the letters, inclined his head in acknowledgment, and left the building. Rather than resign his farcical employment at the Portreeve's Office, he gathered some belongings and boarded a ship bound for Alcmouth. He did not attempt to open the letters. If he broke the seal, his life would be forfeit. Letters between Guildmeisters were sacrosanct, and none would be foolish enough to interfere with them, even if they believed the letters carried instructions that might bring their ruin. He did not relish the long journey ahead, but he relished the prospect of a confrontation with Corelle even less.

He knew Corelle, and he admired her, but to take her alive would be both difficult and deadly. She would not hesitate to kill him to save herself, and she excelled at her lethal art. Unlike most, she relied on cunning, not strength, and her blade struck true and fast—as fast as a fish will take a fly from the surface of the water. Wilash knew the keenness of her blade since he had forged it for her, and he did not wish to feel its bite. In truth, he did not deserve to die under such a fine blade, for he had played a large part in the creation of the catastrophes strewn in Corelle's wake.

He disembarked in Alcmouth after a sevenday on the river and took passage to Torric on a ship that plied the coastal route between the two cities. He arrived in Torric tired and sick from the waves, then contacted the local Guildmeister, and once Sisnop read the letters, he pledged whatever help Wilash needed. There had been no sign of Corelle, but Wilash gave Sisnop information that would help them, and the Guild members hunted for any trace of her. As expected, Wilash appeared enthusiastic, but in his heart, he hoped she fled the city straight away, if she had come there at all. She would doubtless have done so if she travelled alone, but the other might have been injured by the fall from her horse, and he did not believe Corelle would abandon her to Guild justice. Circumstances suggested she hid somewhere in Torric, and the thought brought him no joy. The search continued.

Almost a pass had elapsed since the incident with Hiw, and Jorinda surrendered at last to Deineike's constant requests for the removal of the splints from her arm. "At the first sign of complications, the splints are replaced without delay."

Deineike replied without hesitation. "I agree."

"Do you swear to be honest?" Jorinda eyed her, suspicious, certain she attempted some deception in her eagerness to rid herself of the splints.

"I swear, I swear. Please remove the wretched things, and let my life return to some normality." Jorinda removed the bandages, careful to avoid any excessive movement of the arm itself. They had not thought to replace the bandages, which were frayed and dirty. The splints reached from above the wrist to beyond the elbow. As she took them away, Jorinda watched Deineike's face for evidence of pain, but excitement shone in her eyes as Jorinda removed the restrictive items. Deineike sighed and held her arm out straight in front of her. "At last."

Jorinda tried to caution her. "Do not attempt to move it too much. I understand the bone you broke is slow to heal, and you may be disappointed at first."

Deineike beamed at her. "I am not disappointed; you may be sure." She laughed, her face a picture of concentration as she attempted to flex the elbow, which did not move. Her brow wrinkled, then her grin returned. "It will not move. Not yet, at the least. But that is to be expected, is it not?"

"That it is." Jorinda shrugged. "I imagine." She hesitated to agree to something she knew so little about.

"It has been in those wretched splints for so long. I will be patient, that is all. Movement will come."

Deineike sat on the bed, her arm stiff at her side, and Jorinda sat beside her. "Do you feel any pain?"

"That I do not." Jorinda looked at Deineike in disbelief, and the patient sighed. "Some. But it is not bad pain."

"I will make you a herbal drink if you wish it."

"My thanks, but it is not required. Hold me instead." Although they had grown more physical, they had not lain together despite the desire each of them expressed every day, and Jorinda's frustration tore at her.

Jorinda pulled Deineike close and kissed the top of her head. Deineike moved her head upward and kissed Jorinda's neck; soft kisses that tantalised her and stoked the fires of her passion. Deineike's left hand teased at Jorinda's breasts, coaxed a nipple to hardness. They had not touched one another with such intimacy for some time, and Jorinda's breath grew heavier and more rapid as Deineike's hand excited her breasts, excitement she had craved and now took greater pleasure from than ever before.

Deineike perched on the edge of the bed, her body twisted and awkward due to the splints on her leg. She shifted her position, mayhap as she tried to become more comfortable, but slid off the bed and landed on the floor with a small cry of pain.

Despite Jorinda's concern as she looked down on Deineike, who sat disgruntled on the floor, she could not help but laugh. "It appears you are not yet ready to lie with me."

Deineike laughed with her. "You are right, curse it. Help me up." She held out a pathetic arm.

Jorinda helped her back onto the bed and lifted her legs so she could sit, her back to the wall. "I long for the day when you are recovered." Jorinda fussed to make Deineike as comfortable as possible.

"As do I. I will make love to you for a whole day, I think."

Jorinda raised her eyebrows. "That should be fun. I will hold you to that promise. You have not yet screamed for me, despite your earlier enthusiasm for the idea."

"I have screamed many times." Deineike struck the bed with her left hand as though to dispel any suggestion to the contrary. They laughed and talked together until Deineike grew tired and lay down to sleep. Jorinda sat beside her, busy with her making in the lantern light, comforted by the steady breaths next to her, until she stretched and yawned, exhausted. She put down her work, blew out the lantern, slid into the bed next to Deineike, and soon fell asleep.

As the days passed, Deineike stuck fast to the plan she created. She exercised her arm more each day and appeared delighted by any perceived improvement in its mobility, and although Jorinda could often see none, she always assured Deineike she could. To Jorinda's joy, Deineike's spirits brightened as she used the arm a little at a time. She still found it an effort to bend the elbow, but she used her arm at every opportunity. At times, she would wince with pain as she went too far too fast, but she never seemed to lose patience despite the slow progress. Her discipline and tolerance amazed Jorinda, who believed she would have been driven to madness had she been in the same position. Try though she might, Jorinda saw little progress, but Deineike would not be discouraged.

As Deineike used her arm more, she persuaded Jorinda to purchase a staff so she could become more mobile without support from Jorinda. At first, she could not hold her body upright with the staff, thanks to the stiffness in her right arm, but in time she could move short distances, which allowed her to go outside the house, where she drank in the city air like the sweetest of fragrances.

Stefan confessed he could not have conceived of the making or designs Jorinda created, and Deineike urged Jorinda to set up on her own in competition to him. Jorinda feared it would be too dangerous to open her own shop and might alert the Guild to her presence. She had lied to Stefan about her name and had chosen Rhea, after the chirurgeon's daughter, hopeful the name would excite little interest if anybody came to investigate the improved quality of the dresses he now sold. Stefan had not asked her to work at the shop for some time, and Jorinda suspected he passed off her making as his own. She did not care as long as he paid her.

Jorinda returned from the shop one day with some materials for a new dress and found Deineike on the bed, her breaths heavy and her face red. "What is it?" Jorinda dropped the materials and ran to Deineike's side.

"Nothing to worry over; a little fall, no more."

"You fell? Are you hurt?" Jorinda placed the back of a hand to Deineike's forehead, which felt no hotter than normal. She scanned the already battered body for evidence of fresh damage but saw none. "Where did you fall?"

Deineike seemed embarrassed. "Outside. I had gone a touch too far and grew tired. I lost my grip on the staff. I am unhurt. Do not fret so."

Jorinda's anger roiled in her stomach like bile. "I should never have allowed you that wretched staff. You should not venture out alone yet." Tears welled in her eyes. "Curse you, Deineike. Swear to me you will be more careful in the future, or I shall break that staff over your head." She would have said more, but Deineike placed a finger on her lips to silence her. Jorinda seethed inside at the injured woman's foolishness.

"I am unhurt, but I swear it, if it makes you happy."

Jorinda fell forward with her head on Deineike's breast, her anxiety not eased. "I could not stand to lose you, not now."

"You will not. Come here, little one."

Jorinda sulked, offended by the foolish name despite her acceptance of it in Rukaal's hut. Deineike had lain at death's door on that night, and the name had seemed unimportant. Today, it rankled again, and Jorinda still could not understand why. "Do not call me that. You know I dislike it." Anger could not overcome her worry. They kissed, gentle at first, but as their excitement increased, Jorinda tore the clothes from each of them, the fall forgotten. Deineike winced as Jorinda struck her leg with an arm but would not be deterred by any physical pain that might result from their passion, and she snarled for the satisfaction she craved. She lay back on the bed and urged Jorinda to drive into her again and again, her cries feral as her body convulsed, and she thrust her hips upward toward the fingers that carried her to satisfaction.

Her left leg lay high across Jorinda's back, and still Deineike could not be sated, though the effort required to appease the heat that tore through her lover exhausted Jorinda. Deineike had never lusted for such fierce fulfilment from her, and Jorinda was wet, filled with her own need, not satisfied by the pleasure Deineike took from her. Sweat soaked Deineike's body, her eyes wild and wide, an animal passion on her face, the release of long-suppressed hunger.

Jorinda could continue no longer despite Deineike's urgent whimpers. Her hand had cramped, and her arm had grown heavy from the exertions. Deineike had given no indication she would return the satisfaction she had enjoyed, but Jorinda hid her disappointment and said nothing. She lay motionless on top of Deineike as the dark-haired woman relaxed, her breaths slowed, and her left leg slid down the back of Jorinda's legs.

At last, Jorinda stood, drenched with sweat, and looked down on her lover, who stared at the ceiling with her pupils still dilated. Jorinda smiled, happy her attentions had drained Deineike. "You screamed that time, do not attempt to deny this."

"By all the fates, never have I wanted anybody so much, and never has anybody taken me where you took me." Deineike's voice seemed little more than a breath of wind that caresses a leaf on a tree.

Jorinda blushed, fazed by the compliment as ever, and she stuttered, anxious to change the subject. "How are your leg and arm?"

Deineike grinned back at her. "I am beyond pain." Jorinda waved a hand to silence her and turned from the bed to hunt for her clothes, which lay scattered around the room, together with Deineike's. She crossed the room to the vanity bowl and splashed the cool water over the heat of her face.

Deineike did not rise from the bed as Jorinda dressed, and Jorinda's concern drove her to urge her lover to put on some clothes. "You should dress. You will become cold."

Deineike laughed and held out a hand, so Jorinda picked up her trousers and handed them to her. "Help me on with these, please." Jorinda had made the trousers and had torn them down the seam to accommodate Deineike's splinted leg. Deineike could not yet pull them on unaided, though she never asked for help with her tunic, and could pull it on alone. Her arm often pained her as she did so, but Jorinda left her to it. Once dressed, Deineike sounded tired when she spoke next. "Must you work tomorrow?"

"I have a new dress to begin. It is most elaborate."

Deineike pulled a resentful face. "I am bored with this place." She gestured about her.

Jorinda shrugged. "What would you have me do?"

"Take me somewhere on the cart. To Rukaal again. To the docks, where I can breathe in the sea air. Anywhere. Take me out of this wretched house, I beg you."

Jorinda sat in silence as she reflected on Deineike's words. The passage of time had lessened her fears, but she remained conscious of the risk if they ventured outside. She judged it unfair to keep Deineike inside like a captive, nonetheless, and doubtless the fresh air would be good for her. Resigned, she shook her head. "I imagine the dress can wait. One more day will make little enough difference."

Deineike clapped her hands, though she winced as she did so. "You are wonderful." Her eyes sparkled with excitement.

Jorinda smiled back at her. "You are beautiful when you are happy. Where do you wish to go?"

Deineike pondered this for a time. "To the docks."

Jorinda frowned. The docks might be busy, which could be both a help and a hindrance. They would be harder to spot in a crowd, but it would be harder to flee through that crowd if they were pursued. "Why the docks?"

"Why not? There is no reason not to go there. The sea air must smell wonderful at this time of year, and I grew fond of the docks while I worked in Rewherran's tally house."

Jorinda frowned but nodded her assent. She did not wish to crush Deineike's enthusiasm. "You must sleep now, for it grows late for one as old as you after such exercise."

Deineike poked her tongue out at her. "You order me to dress, then tell me to sleep. You are fickle, young woman." Despite the jest, she looked weary, and she lay back and closed her eyes. Jorinda picked up the materials she had brought from Stefan's shop and started work as she often did at this point in the day while Deineike dozed off.

The next morning, Jorinda attended to Deineike's needs, then went to bring the horse and cart round from the stables. She had invested in a proper harness, since the cart would be Deineike's sole mode of transport for some time, and appropriate equipment would be easier on the dun. Jorinda helped Deineike out of the house, sat her in the rear of the cart, then led the horse down the streets toward the docks in the south of the city.

The journey to the docks took them through three different areas of the city. Closer to the docks, they passed many taverns and shops, all anxious to take coin from the mariners who visited the city. Some of the houses appeared to be disguised pleasure lounges, where men could satisfy their lust in exchange for coin.

Not long after the midday, Jorinda stopped the dun on the quayside, and Deineike gazed around open-mouthed. The dock teemed with life, and Vjort's seemed quiet by comparison. The rush of enterprise bordered on pandemonium as workers swarmed like insects over the ships tethered at the dock and unloaded their cargoes. As in Zhanghar, some of the ships bore words neither Deineike nor Jorinda could read, and the men on their decks had darker skin or different facial features from the Durfolk, evidence those ships came from lands across the Torr Sea. Jorinda and Deineike discussed what exotic goods these foreign ships might bring to Dur and what produce they would carry with them on their return. Deineike said she had never been on a ship but had always been fascinated to watch them as they skipped along the surface of the water, held above the waves by some trickery she could not grasp.

They wandered, aimless, along the quay and laughed at the sea birds that swooped low over them in search of any morsel of food that might lie about the docks. Jorinda remained alert to any danger, but they attracted little interest, lost in the crowds that swarmed the docks. While Deineike seemed to relish the chaotic atmosphere, Jorinda found it uncomfortable, the crowd oppressive, and she grew ever more irritated as numerous passersby jostled her, even though she walked close to the horse's traces as she tried to avoid the people who barged into her.

Two hours after the midday, they were both hungry, and they stopped outside a tavern. It did not look the most salubrious of establishments, but the smell of roasted meats that wafted from the building tempted them beyond their resistance. Jorinda tethered the horse to a rail, and Deineike waited in the cart while she entered the tavern. She ignored the many calls from the assembled men inside and employed many well-placed elbows and knees as she fought her way to the counter. The noise in the tavernroom almost deafened her, and she had to shout to make herself heard as she bought two platters of meats that dripped with grease, tubers cooked in their skins and fresh bread still warm to the touch.

If her path into the tavern had been difficult, then she imagined that to carry two platters through the mob might be impossible. To her surprise, a burly man with a shaggy beard leaned down from beside her and shouted into her ear, "Hand me your food and follow close." She looked at him with some suspicion, and he roared with laughter. "Trust me, girl. I have already eaten and have no desire to steal your food. If I chose to steal it, you could do naught to prevent it, after all else." Jorinda doubted he could best her despite his size, but his stature would be an asset in her attempt to reach the door, so she sighed in resignation and handed him the platters. He hoisted them over his head and barged through the throng at such a pace, he almost left her behind. His bulk, accompanied by many loud shouts, allowed him to clear a path far better than she could have done. Soon they were outside, where he returned the platters to her.

"My thanks." Jorinda did not know what more she could say.

A twinkle in his eye, he leaned close for a jocular warning. "This does not seem the sort of place for the likes of you. Take my advice, pretty one. Eat up your food and move on, lest some less scrupulous characters latch onto you. I will carry your food, but I will not break any skulls for you, for many of this scum I reckon my friends." He waved at the tavern behind him.

"I can break my own skulls." He guffawed again, and Jorinda knew it had sounded pitiful. The man looked around, and his gaze settled on Deineike in the cart for a moment before he bid Jorinda farewell and returned to the tavern. She carried the platters over to the cart and they ate their food in silence.

The meal finished, Jorinda prepared to move off, but a huge roar erupted from the tavern and the dun skittered, nervous. Loud cheers and raucous laughter poured out of the windows and door, and Jorinda imagined a fight had broken out inside. Instead, the door burst open, and two men emerged. They engaged in a frantic dance, and many of the other patrons followed them with inebriated cheers and hoots as they cavorted. The dancers appeared intoxicated, and Jorinda could not imagine how the jig had begun. Entranced, she watched them swing each other around in manic circles, the fall that seemed inevitable always somehow averted at the last heartbeat. Her smile widened as the dance became more frenetic, and many of those who watched clapped their hands in a clumsy attempt to provide a tempo. Alcohol rather than syncopation set the erratic but enthusiastic beat of their hands.

When Jorinda turned to Deineike, the injured woman stared toward the dance, raw hatred on her face. Deineike's blue eyes had narrowed and grown as cold as steel. She balled her hands into fists, the knuckles white, and she clenched her teeth behind lips drawn back into a snarl. Jorinda could not comprehend how a dance could arouse such revulsion. "Deineike, what is wrong?"

"It is him." Deineike spat each word out with unprecedented malice.

Deineike venomous stare followed the dancers, or the crowd gathered around them, and Jorinda cast a quick glance over to the chaotic scene before she turned to her again. "Who?"

"The man who killed my mother."

Shocked, Jorinda opened her mouth but could find no words to say. She looked again at the dance, which continued with less gusto as the dancers tired. "Who?" She repeated the question and turned to Deineike once more for answers.

Deineike growled, a guttural noise unlike any Jorinda had ever heard her make. Her normal soft, velvety voice had been replaced by the feral utterances of a wild beast. "There. The dancer with the short hair."

Jorinda stared at the two, whose jig had now stopped as they leaned breathless on one another, and, in small groups, the crowd dispersed back inside the tavern. One had his hair cropped tight to his head, and Jorinda reckoned him to be the one to whom Deineike referred. He looked unremarkable to her eye, no more than another inebriated mariner dressed in baggy trousers and a soiled tunic. How could this be the man who had killed Deineike's mother? How had he come to dance here before them on this day? She could not begin to piece the puzzle together. "Are you sure? How can you be sure?" Jorinda had no idea how to deal with this development.

"I will never forget him." Deineike stared at the man, malevolent, as though she yearned to kill him with a look from her eyes.

Jorinda shrugged her shoulders as she cast another glance at the man. "It was many years ago. You may be mistaken."

Deineike spat out her response like the pips from a piece of fruit. "I am not mistaken. Do you doubt me? Do you think I lie?"

Jorinda hurried to reassure her. "By all the fates, Deineike, that I do not." The men returned to the tavern, the episode over. "What do you want to do?"

"I swore I would kill him, and kill him I must." Jorinda looked down at her feet and shook her head. She ran a hand through her hair, desperate for some words to say, but none seemed appropriate, and Deineike repeated the threat. "I will kill him."

"How will you kill him? You cannot even walk. The tavern is full of his friends. You have no weapon, and even if you did, you have never killed anyone before. How will you kill him?"

"I could use your fan." Deineike appeared distressed but rational. Jorinda dealt with no simple emotional outburst, forgotten as soon as they moved on. Deineike was serious; as serious as death itself, and if Jorinda stood by and did not intervene, that death would be Deineike's own.

"None have ever used my blade but me, and that will not change today." Jorinda's voice sounded terse, even to herself. She longed to remind Deineike again that she could not walk, but she resisted, lest Deineike became even angrier. More than anything, she needed Deineike to remain as calm as possible. "Let us leave. You may be wrong, after all else, and even if you are right—"

Deineike did not allow her to complete the sentence. "I am right. I am right, and he must be killed for what he did." She stared at Jorinda, her eyes full of hate and agony. "He killed my mother." Her miserable, plaintive voice almost brought Jorinda to tears.

"By the fates." Jorinda shook her head yet again as she searched for the right words to say, words that evaded her as never before. "How would he have come here? Your mother died in Zhanghar, did she not?"

"She did not die, he killed her." Deineike had not yet attempted to get down from the cart, but Jorinda feared she might soon do so. "He must be a mariner who could have come here aboard any of these ships. He could be found in any port in Dur, but I have found him here, and here he must die. He must pay for what he did."

Jorinda struggled to keep irritation from her voice, exasperated to the limit of her patience. "Deineike, listen to me. You cannot kill this man. To begin with, you cannot walk. You could not get near him before his friends killed you, and even if you did, you could not kill him. Though it seems simple enough, it is no easy task to kill a man. You do more than plunge a dagger into him; when you kill a man, you take his life—everything he has been, is, and will ever be. There he is before you, his blood on your hands as he begs you not to kill him, and his eyes stare into yours even as the life leaves them. It is hard; the hardest thing a person can do, if they can do it at all. You could not do it. I know you."

Deineike stared at the tavern in silence for some time while Jorinda fidgeted beside her, agitated. After countless moments, Deineike looked away, took a deep breath, then turned to Jorinda. "You have the right of it, I could not kill him. But you could."

Jorinda clapped a hand to her head, staggered by Deineike's words. "I could kill him? Have I not killed enough people already?

I have lost count of the number I have killed. I tire of death. It sickens me."

"Yet you excel at it. You told me as much. Terrible, you called yourself."

"And I tell you now, it revolts me, to the heart of me."

"You felt no such revulsion when you killed Hiw."

Jorinda stared at her in horror. Had Deineike lost her mind? The mention of Hiw at this moment sickened her. Deineike's words were so unlike her, Jorinda could not recognise the gentle, affectionate woman she had come to know. Through clenched teeth, she spat her reply as she tried to control her temper. "Hiw? Hiw threatened…By all the fates, I can scarce believe you would say such a thing." She turned her back to Deineike, furious.

"You will not do it?" Deineike kept her voice quiet, but her tone turned Jorinda's blood to ice in her veins.

"That I will not." Beyond the cries of the seabirds and the rowdy tavern noises, nothing disturbed the indignant silence between them. Jorinda turned, and Deineike stared at her, a pain in her face that cut Jorinda to her core and brought her close to tears.

Jorinda had never seen so much anguish in one face. Both her anger and her heart melted at that look, and she wanted to reach out and hold Deineike and tell her everything would be all right, but everything might never be made right. The man whom Deineike insisted had killed her mother caroused not far from them, and Deineike wanted him dead. She could not fulfil the vow she had sworn to herself all those years ago, and her look of desolation at the injustice of the situation brought Jorinda to the brink of her resistance. How simple it would be to wait for him, to catch him alone. He had become inebriated; it would be too easy. His heart could be stilled in the blink of an eye, Deineike's vengeance wreaked by her lover's blade, the next best thing to the promised sword.

If only it were that simple. Jorinda's deadly art had brought them to the brink of disaster already, and they were not yet safe. At any moment, a Guild member might step from behind a crate or within a doorway and end their lives.

What a dread legacy, to be considered among the best of her profession, and what a profession—a hired killer. What talent she had, a dealer in death. She said nothing as she took the dun's harness in her hand and led it away from the tavern. She expected Deineike to protest, but she said nothing, and her silence wounded Jorinda more than any words could.

They did not speak throughout the long journey back to the house. Jorinda helped Deineike inside, where she fell onto the bed and refused to meet Jorinda's eyes. Jorinda led the horse to the stable, removed the harness, and manoeuvred the cart against the rear wall so it would not hinder the movement of other horses in the stable. She stroked the dun's neck, distracted by Deineike's face in her thoughts—the pain in that face when she had refused to kill the man, the inconsolable grief for a mother lost, a promise pledged and held for years but not kept. Rather, a promise broken at the precise moment the opportunity to keep it had presented itself. Jorinda blamed herself for that look of pain and reflected on all the hurts she had brought to the door of the woman she loved; pain on pain, agony on agony. She had laid Arella's death at Deineike's feet, then refused to allow her any vengeance for her murdered mother. Jorinda had made the wrong decision, after all else.

Before she could change her mind, Jorinda swung herself onto the dun's back and kicked her heels into its flank as she clung to its mane. Her skills on horseback were poor, and to ride with no saddle or reins proved harder than she had expected. Jorinda could not recall what she had done with the dun's bridle and believed Taro's saddle lay in Rukaal's barn. She let the horse walk, anxious not to fall off. The trip took close to an hour. More than once, she almost turned back, loath to reach her destination. Soon enough, however, she sat outside the tavern as the gloom settled around her, and the tavern lights shone bright in the dusk. She rode the dun three streets away, tethered it outside a different tavern alongside two other horses, walked back to the original tavern, and entered without hesitation.

Death. Jorinda's domain, and her its mistress, in complete control, the hunter in search of prey, every move calculated and weighted toward the highest probability of a successful outcome. Her eyes swept the room, and she spotted Deineike's mother's killer still in the tavern. Inebriated beyond reason, he slouched in a corner surrounded by others in a similar condition, the table before them littered with empty and half-empty tankards. He had remained in the tavern, and so ended his last chance to see the morning. His one chance had been that he might already have left and disappeared for ever to his ship or whatever life he led. He had missed the opportunity, and his fate was written.

Jorinda sought out the burly man who had carried their food, relieved to find him still there. She pushed her way over to him and stood before him with a wanton smile and her breasts thrust toward him. He appeared surprised to see her but seemed to arrive at his own determination, pulled her to him, and kissed her long and hard. His breath tasted of ale, and he stank, but she suffered his attentions as she had Taro's, a necessary imposition she must tolerate to see the job done. While she flirted with him, she kept an eye on her intended victim and waited for him to depart.

Her companion tried to persuade her to leave, and his clumsy hands crawled over her body, hungry and rough. He held her pressed against him, and his manhood hardened. It sickened her, but she smiled up at him, reached for an empty tankard, and held out to him. He laughed, as did several of his friends, but he poured ale into her tankard from his own, and she sipped at it. It tasted of something she could not place, and she disliked it. She drank little —any error of judgement could be disastrous and potentially fatal, and she spat much of the ale out on the floor as the man bragged to his friends and swung her around like a toy or a trinket he had bought in the marketplace.

With some difficulty, her mark stood and teetered toward the door as his friends yelled something at him and favoured him with loud laughter and mockery. Jorinda guessed he headed outside to fetch up; he looked queasy, and his face had taken on the colour of bile.

Once the door closed behind the intoxicated mariner, Jorinda stood on tiptoe to shout into the big man's ear that she needed to relieve herself before they left. She pulled herself out of his grasp and headed for the door, aware of a fresh chorus of raucous cries from his friends as he relayed her words to them. He revolted her, and for the second time that day, the belief she could kill him whispered in her mind, but he had no further part in this gest. She needed to focus on her target alone.

The stench from a pool of vomit outside the door turned Jorinda's stomach. Her mark staggered across the road into the shadow of the building opposite as she took the fan from her boot and sprang the blade. He leaned forward, one hand against the wall of the building as he fumbled at his trousers with the other, and she came up behind him without a sound.

She had never understood the perverse pleasure Arella took when her victims knew her name. For Jorinda, satisfaction lay in a swift, clean kill. He passed water as she approached, a sound like rain as it ran from a roof, accompanied by a foul belch, and as she stood at his back, he fetched up and showered himself in vomit and urine. Though she longed to take him quick and clean, she could not resist a snarl. "I am your ruin, as you were Deineike's mother's." She reached around from behind and slashed, fast and efficient. For a heartbeat, the pair became one, joined through that dreadful steel, and familiar sensations vibrated up her arm as the coarse cartilage of his windpipe offered futile resistance to the keen edge of her blade. Jorinda dragged her hand from left to right across his throat, and another life became hers, more fuel for the Pyre of her guilt, her shame. The mariner's blood pumped out to mingle with the other bodily substances that already covered him. He slithered down the wall, and a strange guttural sound came from his gashed throat.

She crouched down to hack at his wound, to disguise it as she had done with Hiw and his cohorts, but a cry went up from behind her. When she glanced around, two of her victim's companions weaved across the road toward her. Swift as a cat, she ran up the darkened street as they reached their friend and the full horror of her deed.

She reached the dun with no sign of pursuit and rode as fast as she dared back toward the stable. As she rode, she cursed the arrival of the man's friends. Jorinda had been unable to disguise her handiwork, and she may as well have sent up a banner that read, "I am here in Torric." They must leave tomorrow, and Deineike must be ready or Torric would become their ruin. She stabled the horse and ran to the house. Deineike lay asleep in the bed, but she awoke as Jorinda washed the blood from her hands and fan.

Deineike mumbled, her voice heavy with sleep. "Where have you been?"

"It is done."

"What is done?" Deineike sat up, wide awake, questions in her eyes.

"He is dead, and we must leave tomorrow and head somewhere else."

Deineike stared at her as though unable to comprehend, then seemed to grasp the import of Jorinda's words. "You have killed him for me?"

"That I have. I have killed him for you. Now let there be an end to this, in the name of all the fates. Tomorrow, we leave for Alcmouth, and I hope I will never have to kill again. In truth, I vow it." Jorinda spoke in a firm, clear tone, determined Deineike could not misunderstand her words. "I will not kill again." She climbed into the bed and turned her back on Deineike, who lay down again, slid an arm around her, and wriggled close. Sleep would not come, but at last a troubled one filled with nightmares took Jorinda, tortured her through the night until she woke early the next morning, still tired. Outside the house it rained, while inside it, Jorinda cried.

SIXTEEN
THE LOVE THAT ENDURES

"A clean cut, you say?" The news left Wilash more agitated than he had been since his arrival in Torric.

The Torric Senior Aide nodded and seemed almost impressed. "As clean a cut as you could wish to see. It must be a remarkable blade."

Less than an hour had passed since the death, but the Guild already had the news. Wilash could not understand how the Guild had learned of the murder so soon, but he shook it from his mind. "Do we know anything about this man?"

The other shrugged. "Nothing in particular—some intoxicated mariner, it seems. His friends saw her run from the scene, and we spoke to a man with whom she had spent some time prior to the murder. Earlier in the day, two of them had been there, one on a cart."

Wilash rubbed his chin, deep in thought. So much information in so short a time. Still, he must concentrate on the task he had been sent there to complete. "Corelle is still here, and the other woman is still with her. Unbelievable luck. She must live somewhere in the city and has found some way to support them both." He knitted his brow as he searched his memories for some clue he had overlooked, then snapped his fingers in the air when it came to him. "Of course. How could I forget? She is a garment maker, and that is how she feeds them both." He turned to Sisnop, the Guildmeister. "With your permission, I would like the city's prominent garment makers visited, and the sooner the better. She must work for one of them. Start in the better quarters. Her making is too fine for the poor quarter." Sisnop nodded to the members present and they set off without delay in fulfilment of the order. In a grim mood, Wilash looked at Sisnop. "We are close. So close. We must act fast, for she will flee if she suspects we are onto her, and she will suspect." He paused and reflected that Corelle would soon be taken, or dead, then muttered, as much to himself as to Sisnop, "She will suspect."

Four hours later, news came back to Wilash as he rested in the Guild building. One of the members had found a garment maker named Stefan who, woken in the early hours and frightened half to death by the man at his door, had told them all he knew.

Wilash had not slept as he waited for the Torric members to return. "Rhea? That is not her real name, of course. I am sure it must be her, nonetheless. The description fits her too well. She has been careful not to reveal where she lives, but it matters not. Someone has seen her between the shop and her home, and that person holds our next clue. We must speak to as many people as possible without delay, for the dawn will soon be with us, and I am certain she will leave the city today, if she has not already done so."

Deineike lay on the bed as Jorinda threw clothes into a pack, chaotic and haphazard. "Why must we leave in such a hurry?"

"Because the Guild will know I killed him. I could not disguise the cut."

Deineike frowned. "Disguise the cut? I do not understand what you mean." Jorinda sighed and explained how she had been disturbed before she could disguise the clean cut to the throat of the mariner. Only a Guild member would kill with such precision, but no Guild member had performed the gest. Deineike stroked her injured leg, thoughtful. "I am not sure I can flee. Can we not find another house and hide there for a while?"

Jorinda kept her impatience in check—no need to frighten Deineike any further. "That we cannot. They will find us wherever we stay in Torric. They know we…that I am here now. We must go. Come, I am ready. I will bring the cart outside soon. Be there, ready to travel." She planted a tender kiss on Deineike's cheek and squeezed her hand in reassurance, then ran from the house with the pack in her hand. A steady rain fell from a grey sky, and she soon reached the stable and harnessed the dun to the cart.

She led the dun through the streets back to the house where she found Deineike propped against the wall, shaken and distressed. Jorinda helped her onto the cart, then jumped in beside her.

Her face pale with fear and lined by worry, Deineike turned to Jorinda. "Will it not be slower if we both ride in the cart?"

Jorinda expelled a short breath and fought back her doubts. "I trust the horse will serve us and pull the cart faster than I can walk. It will be hard on it, but I am prepared to make that sacrifice if it means we move faster."

"Then where will we head?"

Jorinda shook the reins and the dun trotted forward. "Have you forgotten what I said last night? We will head for Alcmouth. We may not be safe there, but we will see. We may need to leave Dur and sail south."

Deineike said nothing for a time. "I had never even left Zhanghar until two or three years ago. Now we might leave Dur altogether. These are strange times."

Jorinda frowned and doubted Deineike's estimate of the time that had passed since she left Zhanghar, for Jorinda had seen her there more recently. "When did you leave Zhanghar, then?"

"The day you saw me in the marketplace, my guess. I bought the grey that day." She paused. "I brought an ill fate on it."

Jorinda turned and smiled at her. Deineike must remain calm, and it fell to Jorinda to bring that about. "You did not write its fate. I did, or Hiw. That was not three years ago, nonetheless. More than a year, but less than two."

"How do you know this with such accuracy?"

Jorinda stared at her, perplexed. "I would not say I am accurate, but I do have some sense of the passes as they slip by. Do you not mark the passes at all?"

"That I do not. I do not even know how many years I am."

Jorinda's mouth fell open, and she wiped at the corner of it where some saliva threatened to run down her chin. "You do not know how many years you are? How can this be?"

Deineike's blue eyes were uncomplicated, like her view of the land, it seemed. "It does not matter to me. After that man killed my mother, I had nobody to tell me how many years I was."

Jorinda turned her attention back to the road and the dun's head that bobbed up and down ahead of them. Deineike had not allowed her bleak life to beat her down. She might have become a courtesan, or an inebriate, or turned to petty crime and ended her days young, dead in an alleyway or tossed into the Alc like some toy a child has outgrown. Instead, she had carved out the best life she could and maintained her dignity where few might. Jorinda shook her head, bewildered, and some compulsion drove her to prove she knew how many years she was. "I am twenty-two years."

Deineike did not respond for some moments. "You see? It does not matter."

Jorinda turned to her again and laughed. "You have the right of it. It does not matter." She blew Deineike a kiss.

The cart moved at a good pace, faster than Jorinda could have walked. She had rejected the theft of a second horse and believed it would not have added any speed to their escape, since she could not have ridden any faster than the dun as it pulled the cart. They could not outrun the Guild members if they were pursued, after all else. She clung to the slim hope that the death of the mariner had not yet come to the Guild's ears, that the urgency came from her own concerns. The Portreeve would also seek her, of course, but she did not fear him as much as she feared the Guild. *"Time will tell,"* she thought as she guided the dun through the streets of the city. *"Though Deineike will not mark the passage of that time."* She smiled.

Close to the midday, the Guild members had learned where the two women had their rooms, and they waited outside the house. Wilash reminded them of Styrrach's orders. "Remember. If they are here, Corelle must be taken alive, since Styrrach himself wishes her life. The other you may do with as you see fit."

Sisnop's Senior Aide replied in a cold voice. "Guild justice will not sit well with her."

Wilash shuddered, for he knew the truth of those words. He felt some compassion for Corelle's companion, who could not know what she had become involved with or the fate that awaited her. Then the Guild members were on the move, and they rushed into the women's rooms. Evidence of recent inhabitation remained, but the women did not. They had gone, and in a hurry, clothes scattered around the floor, a half-eaten loaf on a table.

Wilash turned to the Senior Aide. "Curse it, we are too late." He brooded for a time. The women would not have left by sea; that would require more coin than the rooms suggested they had. He nodded to confirm his thoughts to himself. "My guess is they will use the northern road, the one by which they came, in the belief it will throw us off their scent. I will need several men and good horses. They will be hampered by the other woman if she is indeed injured. We will soon catch their cart and run them down. I almost have her."

In his heart, Wilash felt a twinge of sadness, for he had hoped Corelle would disappear and did not relish the thought of both her and Arella dead. After all else, he served the Guild, and he owed his first loyalty to it, and his own fate. He would take her alive if it lay within his power to do so, though it saddened him that Styrrach would then kill her. Corelle's death would not be as swift as the one she had delivered to Arella, but if Wilash failed to apprehend her, Styrrach had outlined his fate in no uncertain terms, and he feared it. He shook his head and scattered his morbid thoughts. "Come. We ride without delay."

The cart rattled through the city streets, and the suburbs turned less and less populous until all houses fell away behind them as they continued northward into the countryside. They reached Rukaal's house close to the midday, but they did not stop. If the old man heard them pass, he did not appear at his door, and they continued on their way. He must live another day without a cart.

To reach Alcmouth by road from Torric, one must ride north on the Vjort to Torric road through the hills where Hiw had ambushed Jorinda and Deineike. Beyond those hills, a road turned east toward the capital. The women did not stop at the site of Hiw's ambush. Nothing now marked the bloody events that had taken place there.

They came to the Alcmouth road, and they turned right without hesitation. No cheer lay to the north, and the Alcmouth road had always been their intended route. The horse had rested overnight and showed little sign of fatigue, and the sun slid down the sky, not even a scratch left behind to trace its progress. Neither of them glanced backward. Their way lay ahead, and they rode on toward it.

After a further hour, they came to a small fork in the road where the Alcmouth road continued eastward while, to their right, a smaller road headed south, little more than a track. No sign at the junction of the two roads indicated where the smaller one led, but it looked less travelled. For all any passerby would know, it might lead to Alcmouth via quieter roads, smaller villages. It might also peter out at some remote farmhouse, but travellers who wished to avoid exposure to inquisitive eyes on the main road might be tempted by such a choice.

They swung south, and the cart bumped down the small road toward whatever fate lay at its end.

Wilash did not bother Rukaal, and he gave the old man's hut no more than a cursory glance. The sand fell, and doubt gnawed at him. Corelle would already be far ahead of him, and he did not wish to waste time. One of the members thought a blind man lived in the hut, and as no cart stood outside it, Wilash thought it unlikely the women would be hidden there. They pressed onward.

At the junction with the eastern road to Alcmouth, they paused for long moments while Wilash tried to decide what Corelle would do. She would have considered the Guild's choices and might guess they would think she headed for the capital. If so, she might seek to deceive them and travel north. Caught between doubt and uncertainty, he decided on the latter choice, and they rode on northward for a time while a whirl of thoughts nagged at him that he had made the wrong decision. He questioned whether the women would retrace their steps northward after they had already travelled south to Torric. Vjort lay to the north, a town they had already been obliged to leave once. Corelle would base every decision on the likelihood of pursuit, that the Guild would learn of the mariner's death and search for her with renewed vigour.

It seemed more reasonable they would make for Alcmouth, a city large enough for them to disappear into the throngs with ease, as a fog is burned away by the heat of the sun. He turned the Guild members south, and they rode back toward the Alcmouth junction. If the women had indeed gone north, his change of mind had handed them their freedom, and if they headed for Alcmouth, his indecision had bought them some time they could not have expected. He tutted at the conundrum, but he must follow his instincts, and after all else Corelle might not have come this way at all. His heart told him she must have come north, but he could be far from the mark, and he shook his head, uncertain of his choices.

Failure meant his own death. They rode fast, but not so fast as to expend their horses, since if they were behind Corelle, they could not fail to overhaul her while the other woman travelled with her.

Deineike grimaced, not for the first time, and Jorinda turned to her, concerned. "Are you in pain?" The cart rattled from side to side in the ruts of the road, and it shook them around like a fallen leaf in a strong wind. Unlike Jorinda, Deineike had a broken leg, and the trips the injured woman had taken thus far in the cart must have brought her agony beyond Jorinda's comprehension. She had endured them, nonetheless, and Jorinda could not fathom the reserves of strength Deineike must possess.

Deineike gritted her teeth and appeared to try for stoicism. "Somewhat. I imagine this pain is slight compared to what I can expect if we are taken by the Guild. Let us press on. I will bear it."

Jorinda cried.

Wilash and the Guild members turned left onto the road toward Alcmouth. As they rode onward, Wilash saw no sign of any other travellers ahead and questioned whether Corelle had come this way at all. He had, however, committed to a choice, and to turn back now would allow her to escape. He had no choice but to follow this road and hope that somewhere ahead, the cart plodded along.

They halted at a fork. One of the men with him believed the smaller track to the south ended at a farm and they should press on toward Alcmouth, but Wilash hesitated. He did not want to abandon the pursuit eastward, but he worried the women might hide at the farm and place themselves at his back, then retrace their tracks and elude him. After all else, Corelle could surely not know where the track led, and might not be prepared to roll the dice on a turn that might lead her nowhere. He muttered aloud. "Curse you, Corelle." He spurred his horse forward along the Alcmouth road. He questioned his choice, caught again between doubt and uncertainty, but they rode on, and a small village came into sight ahead of them.

The road led to a farm, where it ended. The nature of the countryside around the farm meant no cart could travel off the road and make easy progress in any direction. To turn around on such a narrow track and head back to the Alcmouth road would be difficult for any wheeled vehicle. Deep ditches had been cut to either side of the track, doubtless some device that kept muttons or cows in the fields and off the roads without the use of fences or rails.

The women exchanged glances but did not stop. The cart trundled onward toward the farm and whatever fate awaited them there.

An old man sat on the step of a rundown house on the outskirts of the little village, and Wilash called the Guild members to a halt, then addressed the old man. "Have two women driven a cart through this village today?"

The old man's laugh reminded Wilash of dry leaves crushed beneath strong fingers. When his laughter ceased, his gruff voice sounded as though he needed to clear his throat. "That might have brightened my day."

Wilash slapped the pommel of his saddle and startled his horse, which jumped to one side and almost unseated him. The Torric men stifled laughter as he fought to control the horse. Wilash retained his seat, if not his dignity, and turned to the Senior Aide. He had guessed wrong. "The farm track. I knew it, in my heart. Come."

The Torric man seemed unconvinced. "Might they not have travelled north, toward Vjort? We turned from that road against my advice."

Wilash's eyes flashed at the Senior Aide in anger. "That they may, and we have lost them if they have, for they are now far ahead of us and have a multitude of towns and villages in which to seek refuge. We ride back, and I hope I have not missed my guess. If I have, no blame attaches to you, and I will return to Zhanghar."

The old man shook his head and muttered to himself. "Strange fellows." He leaned back against the door to his house and closed his eyes.

The Guild members wheeled and kicked their horses back toward the fork in the road at speed. Wilash paused at the head of the track as he tried to decide whether Corelle might have headed back toward Torric while he chased shadows to the east. Even if she had, Wilash could still ride her down before they reached Torric, where her choices remained as ill as they had been before she left, so he thought it unlikely she would have doubled back from the farm lane. If she had come this way at all, of course. He suspected some of the Torric Guild members with him doubted this and wished for him to abandon the chase and return to the city.

Wilash committed to his decision. "We will search the farm. If they are not here, then I have misjudged her movements, and we will return to Torric." It hurt him to admit he could be wrong, and if he was, his return journey to Zhanghar might be his last. He smiled at the thought that, like Corelle, he might become a fugitive from the same justice he sought to administer to her. Sweet irony, and a strong possibility, given the way things looked at that moment. Wilash kicked his mount forward down the lane at a walk. He need not hurry. If she had gone to the farm, the Torric man had assured him she could go no further. If she had not, then he need not ride toward his own ruin at a gallop.

Jorinda had no time to hide the dun or the cart. Their capture could be imminent. Whatever they were to do, it must be done without delay. She scrambled from the cart and tied the dun to a rail.

Pain wreathed Deineike's face as Jorinda helped her down from the cart. Her lover's agony tore Jorinda's heart into tiny pieces and scattered them in the breeze, but it must be put aside for the moment. They were beset by more urgent need, and Deineike's suffering would be in vain if they did not do whatever it took to either escape or fight their way out of the situation. She did not know how many Guild members pursued them—she had not dared look back behind the cart from the moment they had set off, fearful of what she might see.

The dun seemed tired but in good health. They might yet have further need of it, but who knew what fate was now written for them? She had formed a loose plan last night, but the best laid plans oft go awry, and more so if the Guild caught up with them. To escape, Jorinda would consider any course of action that did not require her to kill innocents. She would prefer not to kill at all, but if she must take a Guild member to protect Deineike, she would do so. Never again would she slit the throats of those who did not deserve it. She had vowed it last night, and she vowed it again as Deineike placed her left arm around the smaller woman's shoulder for support.

Deineike grabbed for her staff, and they moved forward, cautious. Jorinda cast about, anxious and watchful. The fates were written, and everything turned on the next hour's events.

Wilash looked down on the farmhouse from the crest of the last hill in the road. A cart stood outside, the horse that drew it tethered to the rail. They had not yet had time to hide it, it seemed. Mayhap they had not had as much of a start on him as he had thought.

Again, he reminded the Torric men of Styrrach's orders. "We are to take Corelle alive. The other does not matter. If there are innocents in the house with them, they are not part of our gest. Remember your code. We do not spill blood that does not need to be spilled." He touched his heels to the flank of his borrowed horse, and they walked their mounts forward.

They stopped in the yard. A large barn stood to their left where the women might be hidden, and Wilash must be systematic. He hoped Corelle had not killed the farm's residents if they had been there when she arrived. He did not think her so cruel, although he imagined Arella might have a different view on that matter. He suggested two members should hold their position and watch the barn while the five others entered the house. The Senior Aide elected to remain in the yard. He might not kill much, Wilash reflected, and he would have little stomach for a fight with Corelle, whose blade might very well open his throat. Wilash understood his reluctance, for Corelle would prove a formidable adversary if they engaged her.

To Wilash's surprise, the door opened. Those in the farmhouse would have heard their approach, of course. Assassins could be as stealthy as a shadow on a cloudy day, but horses were not as discreet, and there had been no attempt to disguise their approach. It would end here, one way or another, and noise or the lack of it would not change that. Either the Guild members would all die, or Corelle would be taken. If they killed Corelle, Wilash might still die when he returned to Zhanghar. He shook the thought from his head. No matter how the dice fell, Corelle might kill him, and he doubted he deserved any better fate.

Corelle did not emerge from the house, but the man who did was two or three fingers taller than Wilash and with a similar, powerful, build. He had dark brown skin, and wore his hair cut short. The man seemed more curious than afraid as he looked at the Guild members. Had he been sent as an emissary? He might have come to lie to them and claim the two women were not there. Wilash might have said as much if he had been the man, with Corelle's blade at the throat of his child inside the house. He dismounted and the Guild members followed suit.

When the man spoke, Wilash did not recognise his accent. "Greetings, strangers. We see few travellers here. How can we assist you?"

Wilash admired the man's ability to remain so calm in the face of such danger to his family. A sudden thought flashed through his mind. What if he perceived no danger? What if Wilash had it wrong, and Corelle and the other were not here? The cart suggested otherwise, and Wilash took a pace forward and pointed to it. "We seek the women who arrived in that cart." He kept his voice calm, no threat perceptible.

The man frowned. "What business have you with them?"

Wilash took another step toward the house and the man threw a hesitant glance at the open door behind him. Wilash kept his voice amicable. "Is this your farm?"

"That it is. Again, I ask what business you have here." The farmer fidgeted, nervous and uncertain. The Torric men had spread out, and two of them held daggers in plain sight. The menace they conveyed rendered any further pretence at politeness futile.

Wilash abandoned his friendly tone. "Our business is with the two women who arrived on that cart. Bring them out to us and no harm will come to you or your family." Even as he threatened the man, Wilash could not maintain the menace in his voice. "Do it, man. Spare your family."

The man's jaw dropped, his mouth agape. "They are…" He appeared to struggle to form his thoughts into a coherent sentence. "My wife and daughter arrived on the cart no more than an hour since." Either he had told the truth, or he must be an exceptional liar—Wilash could not decide which. The man continued, unaware of Wilash's indecision. "Tell me what business you have with them and why you threaten us."

Wilash paused, uncertain of his next course of action. "Your wife and daughter? Arrived from where?"

"Torric. They go there every year for a night or two around the time of our daughter's bornday. My daughter shops for clothes, trinkets, any fancy that takes her eye. That is our tradition."

Wilash shook his head, perplexed. "Bornday?"

The farmer sighed and looked away for a moment. "Of course. You of Dur do not celebrate your bornday. We are not from Dur. We came here sixteen years ago, before the birth of our daughter. We are from Qanti."

Wilash had become confused beyond measure. He had no idea

who, what, or where Qanti might be. "Qanti?" Words failed him in his bewilderment.

"It lies to the south, across the Torr Sea. We heard Dur offered great opportunity." He paused, looked down at his feet, and shook his head. "Dishonesty is not the Qanti way. I apologise, stranger. I have attempted to mislead you." Wilash nodded at the grim certainty that the fugitives were now at hand. The farmer had made the wise decision to give them up.

The man's next words, however, were not what Wilash had anticipated. "We fled because our parents were opposed to our Joining. I am not Highborn, but my wife is, the truth of it. Love will out, however, so we fled to Dur and settled here. I built this house, and we scratched out little more than an existence at first. We fare better these days." He did not sound boastful but spoke with a warm satisfaction that they had succeeded though all odds may have been stacked against them. "Now, I again ask you what business you have with my wife and daughter. If you mean them harm, then I will know the reason why. I tell you now, I will strike you all down before I allow it."

He made a preposterous threat, but Wilash admired the man's courage. He showed no fear as he faced his ruin with seven trained killers arrayed before him. Wilash laughed out loud, for he had counted himself a killer, who had never once killed.

The farmer's brow creased in surprise. "What amuses you, sir?"

"Wilash is my name. I would be honoured to learn yours in return."

"So it is. I am Amharkk Tyrk, and I am of Ranharkk Tyrk."

Everything about the man mystified Wilash. His name would take as long to scribe as his life story, Wilash thought, and he laughed again. "Then Amurk"—his Dur tongue could not wrap itself around the complex name of the farmer—"I fear my journey has turned awry. We seek two women and believed they had come this way. If, as you say, we are mistaken and have pursued your wife and daughter, then we apologise and will ride on." He paused as the Torric members stared at him, astounded.

Corelle had not ridden down the track to the farm, and the cart that had convinced Wilash he would find the fugitive in the farmhouse turned out to be nothing but a coincidence. Either she had ridden north, a direction Wilash had abandoned, or they had found some other means of escape. Styrrach would not accept Wilash's best guess, however, so the house must be checked. Wilash turned to deception. "I ask a boon from you. Will you permit me to enter your home and apologise to your wife and daughter in person? We shall then be on our way."

Wilash's father had once said, "*The tale must be true that could not be invented.*" As he stood before the farmhouse, Wilash recalled the words, and they brought him nothing but sadness. He missed his father, and had his parents not succumbed to the fevers, doubtless he would not now listen to the strange speech of this man condemn him to Guild justice.

The man hesitated, then appeared to reach a decision. "Please, enter. I ask, however, that your... companions remain without if that sits well with you."

"It sits well with me." Wilash hoped he had come to the correct interpretation of yet another bizarre and unfamiliar expression.

"Very well. My wife is Jaltukk Tyrk un Amharkk." At Wilash's blank stare, he explained himself. "It is our custom to tell visitors the names of all adults in the home." For a heartbeat, Wilash hesitated. What if the man tried to warn him of potential danger and called his wife by the new name Corelle had taken? He shook the thought from his head. It made no sense, and Wilash spotted the similarities between the name of the farmer's wife and his own name.

The man gestured for Wilash to enter first. A small entrance hall led into a large parlour. Two women stood in the parlour, one older and as dark-skinned as the farmer, the other in her early teenyears, less dark but with high cheekbones and black hair that hung to her waist. Some packages and a dress were spread over the table. The women must have shown off their purchases to the farmer as Wilash rode up.

Unsure of what their traditions might be when strangers entered their house, Wilash did not approach the women. "Good day to you, ladies. I see you have parted with some of your coin. That is a quite remarkable dress."

The girl answered. "It is a present for my bornday. There is a delightful garment maker in Torric to whom I always go to. Stefan is his name, though the making on this dress is the best work I have ever seen there. I almost suspect another fashioned it, and he passes it off as his own work." She laughed, and her mother joined in.

Wilash did not laugh with them; he recognised the garment maker's name and knew the true maker of the dress, and she may have cost him his life. "The dress is well bought, though the price be heavy to pay." He aimed his words as much at himself as her. He turned from the women, consumed by a strange mixture of happiness and sadness he could not have explained to them. "My thanks for your time, and I apologise for our unpleasant intrusion into your lives today. We shall be on our way." Before he left, he turned and spoke to the girl again. "I wish you a good borndate."

She smiled. "My thanks, sir, although the correct expression is 'a joyous bornday'. I shall hold your words in my heart, nonetheless."

Wilash did not know how to respond, so he left the house and climbed onto his horse. The others sat on their mounts already and looked to him for an explanation. "I guessed wrong. They did not come this way. I imagine them long gone by now. I shall return to Zhanghar and face the consequences of my failure." He sighed, miserable that he had failed, but Wilash's disappointment would be naught next to Styrrach's. In truth, Wilash admired Corelle, who had outwitted the Guild, slain their couriers and unrelated strangers at will, heedless of the dangers, and had eluded capture once more.

Dejected, he kicked his horse forward toward Torric, and from there, a ship to Zhanghar and Guild justice. His father would not have been proud of him, and he wept to himself.

At the Torric docks, Jorinda and Deineike sat in the cart until Jorinda saw a ship she said seemed ready to depart, drove the cart as close to the ship as she could, and tied the dun to a rail. She helped Deineike hobble across the dock as the dockhands prepared to pull the ramp away, and the women boarded despite the protestations of the dockhands. Before they had left the cart, Jorinda had picked at a seam in her fan that seemed a recent repair rather than the original making. The seam opened to reveal a small pocket, within which sat a token. As the master of the ship approached them, fury on his face, Jorinda showed him the token. His face blanched, he appeared afraid, and he made a cabin available to them.

Jorinda explained she had feared the token would no longer function as it once did, but nothing appeared to have changed. The Guild still struck terror into the heart of any it dealt with. Deineike felt a cold chill in her breast and could not deny that the Guild frightened her as much as it must have frightened the master.

The ship departed Torric bound for Alcmouth. Once there, they would decide on their next course of action. Jorinda stood at the rail as the dock slid further behind them, then came down to the cabin. She had seen no potential Guild members arrive to search for them. Jorinda hoped the Guild would not expect her to use the token, that if they looked for her, they would guess she had fled northward. The Guild might not have guessed it had been her who killed the mariner, but it mattered little; they had escaped for now, though much lay ahead of them. On balance, the morning could have turned far worse.

Deineike had never sailed before. She badgered Jorinda to take her up to the deck rather than force her to remain cooped up in the cabin. Jorinda relented, and they struggled up the steps and out through the door onto the deck. The wind whipped their hair about them as the ship ploughed through the waves. Jorinda helped Deineike to the rail, and she gazed out in wonder as the ship rode the surface of the water in a manner that baffled her. It also nauseated her, and she fought to control her stomach as she clung to the rail.

The coastline receded behind them as the ship ploughed a path south through the Torr Sea before it turned east toward Alcmouth, and Deineike took Jorinda's hand. The overt display of affection did not concern her, as Jorinda said none of the crew would bother them no matter what they did, for fear of the Guild. It would not matter if the crew guessed they were lovers, for the Guild would hear of their voyage on the ship within hours of their arrival in Alcmouth regardless. The use of the token had ensured that.

Jorinda turned to her. "We have escaped, for now at the least."

"That we have, and you have avenged my mother. My thanks." She kissed Jorinda's hair, and Jorinda blushed and looked bashful. Deineike laughed. "Oh, my poor, embarrassed love. I am happy to be here with you, but my stomach holds a different opinion. It will recover a merrier demeanour when my feet stand once more on a surface that does not threaten to pitch me into the depths of the sea, do not fear."

Jorinda laughed. "The sea afflicted Arella the same way." Arella's name had not come up between them since the night Jorinda had laid bare her tale.

Deineike's mind raced back all those years, and she imagined her head in Arella's lap as that tired comb fought its way through her hair. She heard Arella sing the song she so often sang to herself. How did it go? Try as she might, it would not come to her. She smiled at Jorinda, comfortable with the way their relationship had been repaired. "Poor Arella."

A comfortable silence settled on them as they watched the waves rise and fall around them. Deineike had no thought for what they might do when they arrived in Alcmouth. When they had left Taro's farm, she made all the decisions, she seemed to recall. The ride to Vjort had been her suggestion, at the least. Now, she left such things to Jorinda who, while younger, had proved the better leader. Few would be safe from Jorinda, but Deineike felt no fear, only comfort that Jorinda would take care of them. After all else, they had shaken off pursuit and would find somewhere to settle down soon enough where all the horrors of their pasts would fade into dim memories. Their life would be peaceful for the rest of their days.

Or would it? She turned again to Jorinda. "You swore a vow last night. Did you mean it?"

"That I did. I will not kill again."

"Would you kill to protect me?"

Jorinda sighed. "You are a contradiction at times. Would you have me kill to protect you?"

Deineike pondered the question. "That I would not."

"Good. Then I suggest you recommence the exercises you once spoke to me of, for it will fall to you to protect us."

Deineike laughed. "Cast it into the waves."

"Cast what into the waves? You?" Jorinda smiled.

Deineike gave her a gentle push and grimaced as the effort sent a spasm of pain up her right arm. "Ouch. A foolish thing to do." Jorinda looked concerned, and Deineike hoped to reassure her lover's worry. "I am fine." She paused. "I meant the fan. Cast it into the waves. Then you can no longer kill."

Jorinda did not speak for so long, Deineike wondered if the younger woman had been struck deaf a heartbeat prior to her suggestion to cast the fan over the rail until, without a word, Jorinda reached into her boot, took out the fan, and threw it far from her. It spiralled end-over-end until it fell into the water with a small splash and vanished beneath the blue surface of the Torr Sea.

Another silence fell over them. Jorinda broke it after some time. "I love you."

"As I love you." Deineike smiled, content to enjoy these days of peace together before they reached Alcmouth.

That night, Jorinda sat bolt upright in the small bed in the cabin. Deineike woke and reached out a hand to her. The younger woman's body dripped with sweat. "What is wrong, my love?"

"A nightmare. Styrrach entered the cabin and killed you. I could not save you for I had no weapon. I cannot protect us." She began to cry. "I can no longer protect us." Her sobs shook her entire body.

Deineike held her tight. "You did right, Jorinda. There is a phrase. I cannot quite recall it, but I think it went, '*Live near the blade…*' Curses, I cannot remember."

At that, Jorinda laughed and kissed her. "It is '*Live by the blade, die by the blade*', and you are right. We are safe for now, safer than if I still carried that wretched thing, for it drew attention to us as a flame draws a moth. I will deal no more death. If it comes for us, then we shall meet it together."

Deineike, nauseated again, managed a grim smile. "That we shall, but by the fates, I hope we face it on the land and not aboard this despicable contraption."

The ship ploughed through the water until they were no more than a day from Alcmouth. Deineike sat on a small crate, her legs out straight before her. The wind whipped her black hair about her face as the ship rode the waves. She had never sailed on a ship, but she now sat on the deck of one as Alcmouth drew near, and the sails billowed and cracked above her head. The nausea remained, but she fought the qualms in her stomach the best she could. Jorinda appeared unaffected by the movements of the vessel, and Deineike envied how easy it seemed for her lover to eat any meal she pleased with no need to fetch the greater part of it up into a pail.

Deineike struggled to her feet and hobbled to the rail, where she stood next to Jorinda at the rear of the ship. It still staggered her that the little ship bobbed along in the water, and she could see no sign of land wherever she looked. Her body had been battered outside Torric, and her heart had taken worse punishment in the southern city, but she felt both could heal, that when Jorinda threw the fan into the sea, the pain it carried sank with it. Deineike's mother's murderer had been killed, and Jorinda had lifted a burden from her heart she had thought might never leave her. It seemed unlikely Jorinda could understand what had been set free from Deineike that night. "*It matters not,*" she thought. "*We have the rest of our lives. I will find a way to explain it to her. And to thank her.*"

Deineike turned to look at Jorinda, who smiled back at her. She took Jorinda's hand, then gazed back over the vastness of the Torr Sea. With a contented sigh, Deineike said, "I love you." Then she fetched up.

THE END

ACKNOWLEDGMENTS

"Universe Of Total Strangers"
   Performed by Adventures With Alice feat. Catherine Porter
   Written by Debbie Rollason
   © Hand Elephant Records 2020
   Lyrics reprinted by permission

Cover by Jamie Flack - https://www.catandcrown.com

Cover models:
   Corelle/Jorinda - Erin https://www.instagram.com/afaerytalecos/
   Deineike - Katya https://www.instagram.com/katyafern/

Map and scene divider by André Barbeto

SPECIAL THANKS

Ailsa, without whom, none of this could have happened.

Solar, for her vital insights and editing skills, and her friendship.

Jo & Rob, for their unwavering support of every creative impulse I have ever had, and for the feedback about the last chapter.

Tam & Danae, for the fun nights, and the words of encouragement.

The Beta Bunnies: Ailsa, Danae, and Jon, for the test readings, and the feedback.

Andre, for the map and scene divider.

Jamie, Erin, and Katya, for the you-beaut cover.

Christopher Cross, for his music, which I listened to every day as I wrote.

Rosie, for not adding too many pawprints to my manuscript

LINKS

Here are some links I hope you will find useful.

My website: https://hayleyprice.net

Download Universe Of Total Strangers free: https://go.wetransfer.com/t-0zGDALnPAX

Pre-order The Vermilion Cross: https://geni.us/The_Vermilion_Cross

Please leave a review for this book at: https://geni.us/
TheVermilionRibbon